FLEISHMAN
IS IN
TROUBLE

FLEISHMAN
IS IN
TROUBLE

TAFFY BRODESSER-AKNER

WILDFIRE

First published in the UK in 2019 by WILDFIRE
an imprint of HEADLINE PUBLISHING GROUP

11

Cataloguing in Publication Data is available from the British Library

Hardback ISBN 978 1 4722 6705 4
Trade paperback ISBN 978 1 4722 6706 1

Title-page and part-title-page photograph: © iStockphoto / Dmitry Mitrofanov
Book design by Mary A. Wirth

Offset in 11.5/16 pt Sabon MT Std by Jouve (UK), Milton Keynes

Printed and bound in Great Britain by Clays Ltd, Elcograf S.p.A.

HEADLINE PUBLISHING GROUP
An Hachette UK Company
Carmelite House
50 Victoria Embankment
London EC4Y 0DZ

www.headline.co.uk
www.hachette.co.uk

For Claude

Summon your witnesses.

—AESCHYLUS

PART ONE

FLEISHMAN IS IN TROUBLE

Toby Fleishman awoke one morning inside the city he'd lived in all his adult life and which was suddenly somehow now crawling with women who wanted him. Not just any women, but women who were self-actualized and independent and knew what they wanted. Women who weren't needy or insecure or self-doubting, like the long-ago prospects of his long-gone youth—meaning the women he had thought of as prospects but who had never given him even a first glance. No, these were women who were motivated and available and interesting and interested and exciting and excited. These were women who would not so much wait for you to call them one or two or three socially acceptable days after you met them as much as send you pictures of their genitals the day before. Women who were open-minded and up for anything and vocal about their desires and needs and who used phrases like "put my cards on the table" and "no strings attached" and "I need to be done in ten because I have to pick up Bella from ballet." Women who would fuck you like they owed you money, was how our friend Seth put it.

Yes, who could have predicted that Toby Fleishman, at the age of forty-one, would find that his phone was aglow from sunup to sundown (in the night the glow was extra bright) with texts that contained G-string and ass cleavage and underboob and sideboob and just straight-up boob and all the parts of a woman he never dared dream he would encounter in a person who was three-dimensional—meaning literally three-dimensional, as in a person who wasn't on a page or a computer screen. All this, after a youth full of romantic rejection! All this, after putting a lifetime bet on one woman! Who could have predicted this? Who could have predicted that there was such life in him yet?

Still, he told me, it was jarring. Rachel was gone now, and her goneness was so incongruous to what had been his plan. It wasn't that he still wanted her—he absolutely did *not* want her. He absolutely did *not* wish she were still with him. It was that he had spent so long waiting out the fumes of the marriage and busying himself with the paperwork necessary to extricate himself from it—telling the kids, moving out, telling his colleagues—that he had not considered what life might be like on the other side of it. He understood divorce in a macro way, of course. But he had not yet adjusted to it in a micro way, in the other-side-of-the-bed-being-empty way, in the nobody-to-tell-you-were-running-late way, in the you-belong-to-no-one way. How long was it before he could look at the pictures of women on his phone—pictures the women had sent him *eagerly* and *of their own volition*—straight on, instead of out of the corner of his eye? Okay, sooner than he thought but not immediately. Certainly not immediately.

He hadn't looked at another woman once during his marriage, so in love with Rachel was he—so in love was he with any kind of institution or system. He made solemn, dutiful work of trying to save the relationship even after it would have been clear to any reasonable person that their misery was not a phase. There was nobility in the work, he believed. There was nobility in the *suffering*. And even after he realized that it was over, he still had to spend years, plural, trying to convince her that this wasn't right, that they were too unhappy, that they were still young and could have good lives without each other—even then he didn't let one millimeter of his eye wander. Mostly, he said, because he was too busy being sad. Mostly because he felt like garbage all the time, and a person shouldn't feel like garbage all the time. More than that, a person shouldn't be made horny when he felt like garbage. The intersection of horniness and low self-esteem seemed reserved squarely for porn consumption.

But now there was no one to be faithful to. Rachel wasn't there.

She was not in his bed. She was not in the bathroom, applying liquid eyeliner to the area where her eyelid met her eyelashes with the precision of an arthroscopy robot. She was not at the gym, or coming back from the gym in a less black mood than usual, not by much but a little. She was not up in the middle of the night, complaining about the infinite abyss of her endless insomnia. She was not at Curriculum Night at the kids' extremely private and yet somehow progressive school on the West Side, sitting in a small chair and listening to the new and greater demands that were being placed on their poor children compared to the prior year. (Though, then again she rarely was. Those nights, like the other nights, she was at work, or at dinner with a client, what she called "pulling her weight" when she was being kind, and what she called "being your cash cow" when she wasn't.) So no, she was not there. She was in a completely other home, the one that used to be his, too. Every single morning this thought overwhelmed him momentarily; it panicked him, so that the first thing he thought when he awoke was this: *Something is wrong. There is trouble. I am in trouble.* It had been he who asked for the divorce, and still: *Something is wrong. There is trouble. I am in trouble.* Each morning, he shook this off. He reminded himself that this was what was *healthy* and *appropriate* and the *natural order*. She wasn't *supposed* to be next to him anymore. She was *supposed* to be in her separate, nicer home.

But she wasn't there, either, not on this particular morning. He learned this when he leaned over to his new IKEA nightstand and picked up his phone, whose beating presence he felt even in those few minutes before his eyes officially opened. He had maybe seven or eight texts there, most of them from women who had reached out during the night via his dating app, but his eyes went straight to Rachel's text, somewhere in the middle. It seemed to give off a different light than the ones that contained body parts and lacy bands of panty; it somehow drew his eyes in a way the others didn't. At five A.M. she'd written, *I'm headed to Kripalu for the weekend; the kids are at your place FYI.*

It took two readings to realize what that meant, and Toby, ignoring the erection he'd allowed to flourish knowing that his phone was rife with new masturbation material, jumped out of bed. He ran into the hallway, and he saw that their two children were in their bedrooms, asleep. *FYI the kids were there? FYI?* FYI was an afterthought; FYI was supplementary. It wasn't essential. This information, that his children had been deposited into his home under the cover of darkness during an unscheduled time with the use of a key that had been supplied to Rachel in case of a true and dire emergency, seemed essential.

He returned to his bedroom and called her. "What were you thinking?" he whisper-hissed into the phone. Whisper-hissing still did not come easily to him, but he was getting better at it every day. "What if I'd gone out and not realized they were there?"

"That's why I *texted* you," she said. Her response to whisper-hissing was eye-rolling glibness.

"Did you bring them here after midnight? Because I went to sleep at midnight."

"I dropped them off at four. I was trying to get in for the weekend. There was a cancellation. The program starts at nine. Give me a break here, Toby. I'm having a hard time. I really need some me-time." As if all her time weren't completely and totally her-time.

"You can't pull this kind of shit, Rachel." He only said her name at the end of sentences now, Rachel.

"Why? You had them this weekend anyway."

"But not till tomorrow morning!" Toby put his fingers to the bridge of his nose. "The weekends begin *Saturday*. This was your rule, not mine."

"Did you have plans?"

"What does that even mean? What if there had been a fire, Rachel? What if there had been an emergency with one of my patients, and I ran out without knowing they were here?"

"But you didn't. I'm sorry, I should have woken you up and told you they were there?" He thought of her waking him up, how it could have been catastrophic to his progress in understanding that she was no longer part of his waking up.

"You shouldn't have done it at all," he said.

"Well, if what you were saying last night is true, then you could have predicted this would happen."

Toby searched his bleary brain for their last hateful interaction and remembered it with the force of a sudden, deep dread: Rachel had been sputtering some nonsense about opening up a West Coast office of her agency, because she was not busy enough and over-whelmed enough as it was. Honestly, it was a blur. She'd ended the conversation, he remembered now, by screaming at him through her sobbing so that he couldn't understand her until finally the line went dead and he knew she'd hung up on him. This was how con-versations ended now, rather than with the inertia of marital apol-ogy. Toby had been told all his life that being in love means never having to say you're sorry. But no, it was actually being divorced that meant never having to say you're sorry.

"This hasn't been easy on me, Toby," she said now. "I get that I'm early. But all you have to do is drop them at camp. If you have plans, ask Mona to come. Why are we even still talking about this?"

How could she not see that this wasn't a small deal? He actually did have a date that night. He didn't want to leave the kids with Mona—that was Rachel's solution to everything, not his. He couldn't seem to convey to her that he was a real person, that he was not a blinking cursor awaiting her instructions, that he still existed when she wasn't in a room with him. He couldn't under-stand what the goal of having all these agreements in place was if she wasn't going to even pretend to adhere to them, or apologize when she didn't. He'd given her a key to his new apartment not to pull shit like this, but so they could have something that was ami-cable. Amicable amicable amicable. Did you ever notice that you only use the word amicable in relation to divorce? Was it because it was so often used for divorce that you didn't want to poison anything else with it? The way you could say "malignant" for things other than cancer but you never did?

The kids were stirring and it was just as well because his boner was gone.

Solly, his nine-year-old, woke up, but Hannah, who was eleven, wanted to stay in bed. "Sorry, kid, no dice," Toby told her. "We have to be out the door in twenty." They stumbled into the kitchen with unfocused eyes, and Toby had to muck around in their bags to find the clothing they were supposed to wear for camp that day. Hannah snarled at him that he'd chosen the wrong outfit, that the leggings were for tomorrow, and so he held up her tiny red shorts and she swiped them out of his hands with the disgust of a person who was not committed to any consideration of scale when it came to emotional display. Then she flared her nostrils and stiffened her lips and told him somehow without opening her teeth that she had wanted him to buy Corn *Flakes,* not Corn *Chex,* the subtext being what kind of fucking idiot was she given for a father.

Solly, on the other hand, ate his Corn Chex cheerfully. He closed his eyes and shook his head with pleasure. "Hannah," he said. "You *have* to try these."

Toby was not above being grateful for Solly's sad show of solidarity. Solly understood. Solly knew. Solly was his in a way that made him never wonder if all of this had been worth it. He had Toby's same internal need for things to be okay. Solly wanted peace, just like his father. They even looked alike. They had the same black hair, the same brown eyes (though Solly's were slightly larger than Toby's and so gave the appearance of always being a little scared), the same comma-shaped nose, the same miniatureness—meaning not just that they were short, but they were short and regular-sized. They weren't slight or diminutive, so that if you were to see them without a height benchmark, you wouldn't understand just how short they were. This was good because it was hard enough to just be short. This was bad because it meant disappointing peo-ple who had seen you in just such a benchmark-deprived way and had expected you to be bigger.

Hannah was his, too, yes, except that she had Rachel's straight blond hair and narrow blue eyes and sharp nose—her whole face an accusation, just like her mother's. But she had a specific kind of sarcasm that was a characteristic of the Fleishman side. At least she once did. Her parents' separation seemed to ignite in her a humor-lessness and a fury that had already been coming either because her parents fought too often and too viciously, or because she was be-coming a teenager and her hormones created a rage in her. Or be-cause she didn't have a phone and Lexi Leffer had a phone. Or because she had a Facebook account she was only allowed to use on the computer in the living room and she didn't even want that Facebook account because Facebook was for old people. Or be-cause Toby suggested that the sneakers that looked just like Keds but were $12 less were preferable to the Keds since again they were exactly the same just without the blue tag on the back and what about being too-overt victims of consumerism? Or because there was a sad popular song on the radio about a long-gone romance that meant a lot to her and he had asked her to turn down her speakers while he was on the phone with the hospital. Or because later when she explained why that sad popular song was so mean-ingful by making him listen to it she seethed at him because he didn't appear to magically understand how a song could ignite in her a nostalgia that she couldn't possibly have had, never having had a boyfriend. Or because he wondered if her skirt was too short to sit down in. Or because he wondered if her shorts were too short if they showed the crease between her buttocks and thighs and were even so short that their full pocket linings couldn't be contained by them and so extended beyond the shorts' hem. Or because he asked where her hairbrush was, which clearly implied, to her, that he thought her hair looked terrible. Or because she. did. not. want. to. see. *The Princess Bride* or any of his old-man movies. Or because he ran his hand across her head one day in a display of tenderness, ruining her very perfect middle part that had taken ten minutes to get right. Or because no. she. did. not. want. to. read *The Princess Bride* either, or any of his old-man books. Yes, her contempt for her parents, which seemed manageable when it was aimed at both Rachel and Toby, was absolutely devastating in its current concentration when it was directed only at him. He had no idea if she saved any of it for Rachel. All Toby knew was that Hannah could barely look at him without her lake-water eyes narrowing even further into lasers and her nose becoming somehow pointier than it was and her lips turning white with purse.

They inched toward camp, irate and unfocused, because they were tired (See, Rachel? See?).

"I *hate* camp," Hannah said. "Can't I just stay *home*?" She'd wanted to go to sleepaway camp for the whole summer, but her bat mitzvah was in early October, and she had still needed June and July to learn her haftorah.

"You're leaving in like a week. One more lesson left."

"I want to leave *now*."

"Should I maybe rent you an apartment in the interim?" Toby asked. Solly laughed at least.

They arrived at the 92nd Street Y, along with all the mothers in their brightly patterned leggings and their exercise shirts that said YOGA AND VODKA or EAT SLEEP SPIN REPEAT. This place cost about as much as sleepaway camp, and Hannah kept asking if she could skip being a camper and instead become some kind of counselor assistant, which you weren't allowed to do until tenth grade anyway.

"Even then, it still costs money to go," Toby said when he looked at the Y's website. "Why do I have to pay for you to learn how to be a counselor while they use you as an actual counselor?" he'd asked her in the spring.

"Why did you have to pay to learn how to be a doctor while they used you as an actual doctor?" she'd answered. It was a good point.

Toby thought then how sharp she was, and how he wished she didn't deploy this sharpness exclusively against him. She was becoming, it seemed to him, the kind of girl that it was completely exhausting to be.

They had made it with maybe six minutes to spare. The Y took them to a campus in the Palisades every day, and if you dropped them off too late, they had to spend the entire day in the room with the very little children. Hannah declined her father's offer to escort her to her gathering classroom, so he took Solly to his. Toby watched him as he participated in the last minutes of the morning slime experiment, and was just about to exit the lobby when he heard his name being called.

"Toby," called a low, breathy woman's voice.

Toby turned around to see Cyndi Leffer, a good friend of Rachel's who had a daughter in Hannah's grade. She took a moment to survey him. Ah, this. He knew what was coming: the head tilted twenty degrees, the exaggerated pout, the eyebrows simultaneously raised and furrowed.

"*Toby*. I keep meaning to reach *out* to you," Cyndi said. "We haven't seen an inkling of you." She was wearing turquoise spandex leggings that had purple clawprints on the upper thighs, like a streak of purple tigers was climbing toward her crotch, trying to get to it. She wore a tank top that said SPIRITUAL GANGSTER. Toby remembered Rachel telling him that parents who sub out y's for i's in the middle of their girls' names, and vice versa at the end, are not giving their daughters much of a chance in the world. "How are you *doing*? How are the *kids* doing?"

"We're okay," he said. He tried to not adjust the angle of his head to match hers, but his mirror neurons were too well developed and he failed. "We're plugging along. It's a change, for sure."

Her hair was dyed in that new way where the top was purposefully dark and it progressively faded until the ends were blond. But the dark part of the roots was too dark—it was the darkness of a younger woman—and against the border of her forehead all it did was accentuate the relative raggedness of her skin. He thought about a physical therapist he'd slept with a few weeks ago, about how she had the same hairstyle but that the dark part had a warmer cast to it and wasn't so stark against her same-age-as-Cyndi skin.

"Had things been hard for long?" she asked. Jenny. The physical therapist's name was Jenny.

"It wasn't a spur-of-the-moment thing, if that's what you're asking."

Toby and Rachel had separated at the very beginning of June, just after school ended, the culmination of an almost yearlong process, or maybe a process that began shortly after their wedding fourteen years before; it depends whom you ask or how you look at a thing. Is a marriage that ends doomed from the start? Was the marriage over when the problems that would never get solved started or when they finally agreed that the problems couldn't be solved or when other people finally learned about it?

Of course Cyndi Leffer wanted information. Everyone did. The conversations were always artless, and they were always the same. The first thing people wanted to know was how long things in the marriage had been bad for: Were you unhappy that night at the school gala, when you were showing off your college swing dancing lessons? Were you unhappy at that bat mitzvah when you took her hand and kissed it absentmindedly during the speeches? Was I right that at parent-teacher conferences when you stood by the coffee and she stood by the office checking her phone you were actually fighting? How it shook people to see someone extricate themselves from a bad situation; how people so brazenly wondered aloud every private thing there was to wonder. Toby's cousin Cherry, who was prone to long, disappointed stares at her husband, Ron: "Had you tried therapy?" His boss, Donald Bartuck, whose second wife had been a nurse on the hepatology floor: "Were you unfaithful?" The camp director at the Y, when Toby was explaining that his kids might be a little shaky since when camp started, they'd just separated: "Did you guys have a regular date night?"

These questions weren't really about him; no, they were questions about how perceptive people were and what they missed and who else was about to announce their divorce and whether the undercurrent of tension in their own marriages would eventually lead to their demise. Did the fight I had with my wife on our actual anniversary that was particularly vicious mean we're going to get divorced? Do we argue too much? Do we have enough sex? Is everyone else having more sex? Can you get divorced within six months of an absentminded hand-kiss at a bat mitzvah? How miserable is too miserable?

How miserable is too miserable?

One day he would not be recently divorced, but he would never forget those questions, the way people pretended to care for him while they were really asking after themselves.

He had spent the early summer in a haze, trying to find footing in this strange world where every aspect of his life was just slightly different than it used to be and yet immensely so: He was sleeping, just alone and in a different bed. He was eating with the kids just like always—Rachel hadn't come home before eight or nine on weeknights in years—but after dinner he dropped them off at the old apartment and walked the nineteen blocks home to his new one. That slippery fuck Donald Bartuck told him he, Bartuck, was being promoted to head of internal medicine and that he was putting Toby up as his only candidate for subdivision head of hepatology in the gastroenterology division once the current one, Phillipa London, evacuated the post to take Bartuck's job. He didn't have the natural first person to tell. He thought about calling me or Seth, but it seemed too pathetic to not have an actual family member to tell. He almost called his parents in Los Angeles, but the time difference put them at five A.M. when he learned; then he debated if this was news that Rachel should hear or know. (He did tell her, later when he dropped the kids off, and she smiled with her mouth but not her eyes. She did not have to pretend to care about his career anymore.)

But now, in late July, as summer was rounding second base, he felt steady again, like at least he had a routine. He was coming along nicely. He was adjusting. He was cooking for one less person. He was learning to use the *I* instead of *we* to indicate availability for barbecues and cocktail parties, when he was invited, which wasn't often. He was taking long walks again and learning to bat away the feeling that he should let someone know where he was. Yes, he was coming along nicely, except for conversations like this one, with Cyndi. He had been wallpaper to the Cyndi Leffers of the world before this; he'd been a condition that came co-morbid with his family. Successful Rachel's husband, or social Hannah's father or cute Solly's father, or, hey, you're a doctor, right, will you just look at this bump I've had for a week? Now he was someone people wanted to talk to. His divorce had somehow given him a soul.

Cyndi was waiting for an answer. Her eyes were searching his face the way soap opera actors looked at each other in the seconds before commercial breaks. He knew what was expected of him. He was working on trying to not fill in this pause; he was working on letting the discomfort of the silence be the property of the person who was mining him for dirt. His therapist, Carla, was trying to get him to learn how to sit with uncomfortable feelings. He, in turn, was trying to get the people who were pumping him for information to learn to sit with uncomfortable feelings.

But also: There was no way to talk about a divorce without implying terrible things about the other person in the marriage, and he didn't want to do that. He felt a strange call for diplomacy now. School was a battleground state, and it would be so easy to get people over to his side, he knew that. He knew he could allude to Rachel's craziness, her anger, her tantrums, her unwillingness to immerse herself in her children's lives—he could say things like "I mean, I'm sure you noticed that she never came to STEM Night?"— but he didn't want to. He didn't want to undermine Rachel's status at school out of an old sense of protectiveness that he couldn't quite shake. She was a monster, yes, but she had always been a monster, and she was still his monster, for she had not yet been claimed by another, for he was still not legally done with her, for she still haunted him.

Cyndi took a step closer. He was only five-five, and she was a full head taller than him and skinnier than any woman needed to be. Her face was large-featured and pumped full of hyaluronic acid and botulinum toxin. Her concern, which was mostly transmitted via a slow back-and-forth shaking of the head and an exaggerated protrusion of her mouth, was mitigated by the fact that her brow-line was completely ossified, and had been since he'd known her. This was what she looked like when she was happy, too. "Todd and I were so sad to hear," she said. "If there's anything we can do. We're *your* friends, too."

Then she took *another* step closer, which was two too many steps close for a camp lobby encounter with a married woman who was friends with his wife. His phone buzzed. He looked down. It was Tess, a woman he had plans to meet for the first time later that night. He squinted at his phone to see a close-up photograph of the fertile crescent where her thighs and her black, netted panties formed a delta.

"That's work," Toby said to Cyndi. "I have a biopsy to get to."

"You still at the hospital?"

"Uh, yeah," he said. "As long as people still get sick. Supply and demand."

Cyndi gave a one-syllable laugh but looked at him with, what? Sympathy? All the school parents did. A doctor wasn't a thing to be anymore. Just last year Cyndi's husband, Todd, had looked at him earnestly at parent-teacher conference night, while they waited outside classrooms for their names to be called (no Rachel in sight, because she was at a client dinner and would not arrive in time) and said, "If your kids told you they wanted to be doctors, how would you advise them?" Toby hadn't quite understood the question until his walk home from school, at which point he'd realized it was a guy in finance feeling sorry for a guy in medicine. A doctor! He had been raised to think that a doctor was a respectable thing to be. It *was* a respectable thing to be! When Rachel got home that night, he told her what that douche Todd had asked him, and she said, "Well, what *would* you say?" They had all turned on him.

"You better get going, then," Cyndi said now. "We'll see Hannah tomorrow night, right?" She leaned over to give him a full frontal three-point hug with connection at the head, chest, and pelvis. The hug lingered for a millisecond longer than any previous physical contact he'd ever had with Cyndi Leffer, which was zero.

He walked away from the Y, wondering if the vibe he got off Cyndi—that she wanted to comfort him, yes, but, also, to fuck him as well—was real. It couldn't be. And yet. And yet. And yet and yet and yet and yet and yet she was clearly wondering what it might be like to fuck him.

No, it couldn't be. He thought about the way her nipples lined up so evenly and soldier-like under her stupid tank top. He was getting carried away, which is an easy thing to do when your phone is literally dripping with the lust of women who did definitely and assuredly claim to want to fuck you, fuck you bad, fuck you bad all night long.

Each little holler he got—each little [winky emoji] or [purple devil emoji] or bra selfie or actual photographed upper-region ass crack—made him revisit the essential questions of his youth: Could it be that he wasn't as repulsive as he'd been led to believe by the myriad rejections of just about every single girl he'd ever made eye contact with? Could it be that he was maybe *attractive*? Was it not his looks or his physique but the desperation inherent in his attempts at a rigorous sex life in those days, or any sex life really, that rendered him something less attractive than he actually was? Or maybe now there was something about his current situation, being newly divorced and a little wounded, that had somehow made him that way. Or maybe absent mirror neurons and pheromones and other things that could not penetrate phone screens, all you had was a reflection of the intersection of your own horniness and your own availability, and the minute someone else's horniness and availability matched up with yours, voilà and kaboom. He didn't like to think that, that sex was no longer about attraction, but he couldn't pretend it wasn't a possibility; he was a scientist, after all.

He'd met Rachel when he was a first-year in med school. He thought about that time nearly constantly now. He thought of the decisions he'd made and whether he could have seen the warning signs. Her at that library party, her eyes flashing sex, her hair the same blond Cleopatra shape it would continue to be forever. How his eyes filled at the sight of the gleam of her geometry hair. How the blue of her eyes was both cold and hot. How the Cupid's bow beneath her nose was a dewdrop mountain to be climbed; how it mirrored the cleft in her chin with the kind of symmetry that science said initiated male sexual imperative and created visual gratification and hormonal feelings of well-being. How the sharpness of her face seemed like a correction to the Semitic girls he was bred to want—her father hadn't been Jewish, and by the account of her grandmother and the few pictures that existed of him, she looked just like him, and that, too, felt dangerous—that someone raised as traditionally as Toby would love a woman who looked like her absent Gentile father. How he was made dizzy, how he utterly dissolved in lust, by the way she stuck a hip out when she was trying to decide something. How, after knowing him just four weeks, she came with him to California for his grandmother's funeral; how she sat in the back and looked sad for him and came to the house afterward and helped put all the catered food on trays. The way she undressed him—no, he shouldn't think about that now. Thinking about that would be detrimental to his healing.

The point was that she had *wanted* him. The point was that someone wanted Toby Fleishman. We'd watched him watch the world pass him by; we'd watched him bewilder at his inability to attract someone. He'd only had one real girlfriend before, and other than that, just some drunk girls he had rolled around on the floor with at parties; he'd had sex with just two women before Rachel. But then college was over and the girls in med school were almost all attached to some guy from before. And there had been Rachel, who didn't look at him like he was too short or too pathetic, even though he was, he was. He looked across the room to her at that party, and she looked back at him and smiled. So much time had passed since then, and yet that was Rachel for him. He had spent so many years in the service of trying to relocate that Rachel within the Rachel that she kept proving herself to be. But even now, it was that version of Rachel that was the first that ever came to mind when he thought of her. He felt he would be doing worlds better if it weren't.

It was true that Toby had a biopsy in forty-five minutes, but really he wanted to spend a little more time with his app, so as he walked out onto the street he opened it up and headed west. It was already too warm, just about at the forecasted ninety-four degrees with storm clouds, but nothing quite so dangerous or threatening yet.

In the park, the beautiful young people—they were all beautiful, even if they weren't—would be lying out on blankets even this early, their heads tilted up toward the sun. Some of them were sleeping. Back when Rachel consented to go on long walks with him, they would make fun of the sleeping people in the park. Not the homeless people, or the strung-out ones. Just the ones who'd made their way over to the park in their sweatpants, laid out their blankets, and pretended that the world was a safe place that only wanted you to be well rested. Neither of them could imagine having so little anxiety that you could fall asleep in the middle of a park in Manhattan; the anxiety was a thing they had in common to the end. "I can't even imagine wearing sweatpants in public," Rachel would say. She wore the leggings the other moms wore to exercise classes and the tank tops (BUT FIRST, COFFEE, read one of hers. Another: BRUNCH SO HARD), but those had their own professionalism to them. She felt that with all the alternatives to pants now—yoga pants, leggings, etc.—sweatpants had become an overt, if definitionally passive, statement on a woman's state of mind. "Sweatpants," she always said. "That's just giving up."

As he walked, he hit the search function on his screen, where he found a sampling of the women nearby who were available for digital insertion and nipple stimulation and hand job execution and other adult activity at eight-thirty A.M. on a Friday: an Indian woman in her late forties holding an infant; a droopy-eyed white woman with black nails in her mid-forties sucking on a lollipop; one with orange-tan skin and pastel purple hair and tortoiseshell glasses; a pale woman of indeterminate age (but adult) with a pacifier in her mouth; a freckled woman's cleavage (just her cleavage); a pale woman's ass crack (just her ass crack); a pockmarked woman with scared eyes who wore a heavy layer of wrongly matched foundation that had the effect of spackle and a button-down shirt, whose mouth was tightlipped and betrayed a nervousness at the act of being photographed; a brunette whose hair was in two Swiss Miss braids and who was holding one of them across her upper lip to make a mustache; a silver-haired woman who looked to be his mother's age holding a martini glass, a sliver of a man's shoulder not cropped out completely. There were also the usual numerous women holding nieces and nephews to signal a kind of casually incidental maternalism in case the reviewer of the photo was looking, consciously or not, for a permanent situation instead of just some of that digital insertion, etc. He swiped right on a woman who'd angled her photo so that she was literally hanging off her bed at about her T6 vertebrae (right in the middle of her thoracic spine), the camera poised up and over, the valley between her maybe-saline-filled breasts like a canyon road.

There was something in him that liked the world as his dating app presented it, something that liked to think of New York as a city covered with people just having sex constantly. People who walked around with only one imperative: to fuck, or to somehow otherwise touch/lick/suck/penetrate/apply hot breath to, the first warm body who agreed to it, people crazed with sex and fire, people who were still alive, maybe after a few years of death, like him, and who looked just like regular people but were deep down barely able to stop themselves from humping a stranger's legs as they walked down the street to the drugstore or a meeting or a yoga class. It was nice to know that energy was still out there, even at what felt like a very late date in his life. This gave him peace and hope, that anything he'd missed out on when he married Rachel so young was still there, waiting. That other people had screwed up and were starting over, too. That he was still young enough to participate in what he had assigned as a purely youthful endeavor, which was spending a lot of time finding someone to fuck. Yes, there was joy and peace and comfort to learn of this layer of New York that existed under the layer of New York he knew before, that he could now only see with his separation glasses, with his *freedom* glasses, and which amounted to a zombie apocalypse for pussy.

Hr, which was what his preferred dating app was called, was now his first-thing-in-the-morning check. It had replaced Facebook, since when he looked at Facebook, he became despondent and overwhelmed by the number of people he hadn't yet told about his divorce. But Facebook was also a landscape of roads not taken and moments of bliss, real or staged, that he couldn't bear. The marriages that seemed plain and the posts that seemed incidental and not pointed, because they telegraphed not an aggressively great status in life but a just-fine one, those were the ones that left him clutching his heart. Toby hadn't dreamed of great and transcendent things for his marriage. He had parents. He wasn't an idiot. He just wanted regular, silly things in life, like stability and emotional support and a low-grade contentedness. Why couldn't he just have regular, silly things? His former intern Sari posted a picture of herself bowling at a school fundraiser with her husband. She'd apparently gotten three strikes. "What a night," she'd written. Toby had stared at it with the overwhelming desire to write "Enjoy this for now" or "All desire is death." It was best to stay off Facebook.

Less Facebook left him more time for dating apps, of which he had four: Hr; Choose, which was supposed to be for Jews, though he found some Asian women and a few Catholics there, too; Forage, which was an old website that had been updated for smartphone use but was still used almost exclusively by Luddites, of which he was one, maybe; and Reach, through which only women could initiate contact, and that was just as well with him at first, since he was still trying to gauge exactly how appealing he was in his current state: still just five-five, still with his hair, some creases around the mouth, some bags beneath his eyes, but still thin, and don't forget, still with his hair.

It was Hr that emerged as his clear favorite. It greeted him with an inspirational quote while it loaded, something sunny like "Eye of the tiger!" or "Go get 'em, boss!" One of his hepatology fellows, Joanie, had downloaded it for him one day. Toby had been upset by a text that Rachel had sent about child support (she'd called it "alimony"—accidentally, she said, but who was she kidding?). It had put Toby in a bad mood and he had snapped when Logan, another fellow, had misread an MRI in a way that could happen to anyone—in a way that was a teaching opportunity for Toby, not a snapping one. Logan looked surprised, and Toby felt he had no recourse but to tell them: He and Rachel had separated and would be divorcing. He was sorry, but he was on edge. There were about ten seconds of silence before Logan said, "Are you doing okay?" Toby said, "Yes, I've had a lot of time to process this." And Joanie, with a let's-call-it-nontraditional nose and colorless hair that she arranged as much over her face as possible, smiled with half her mouth and said, "Well, then. This will be fun."

He tried not to smile while she spoke. He tried to squint seriously like he was consulting on a patient, but he couldn't help it. It hadn't occurred to him that his news could ever be received as anything but tragic. He thought he'd have to look at his shoes in sadness every time it came up, out of some kind of respect or decorum. But he had suffered enough. He had suffered for years in the limbo

of failure and self-immolation that was the end of his marriage—
that was the end of any marriage. Yes! This will be fun! He looked
out the window just then and saw that it was summer. It was summer!

He looked back at his phone where Joanie was pointing. She
showed him a number in the corner that allowed the woman to rate
her own "availability" at any particular moment.

"Like if she's free right now?" Toby asked, his face scrunched at
his phone.

"Like how ready to go she is!" Logan said.

"Ready to go?" he asked.

The fellows all laughed. "How horny they are!" Logan said.
Toby looked at Logan's handsome, large-jawed face. A guy saying
that back in Toby's day was a lascivious creep. He looked over at
Joanie to see if she was offended or uncomfortable, but she was
laughing. The sexual conversation was now out in the open, as ac-
cessible as this free app he was now somehow downloading. How
horny they are, Toby's mind repeated for him, and Toby, still aware
that he was a professional in a professional setting, treated this as
medical data and nodded and thought about autopsies in order to
forestall an erection.

Later, in the doctors' lounge, he pretended to be casually checking email but he was actually exploring his new app. It quickly
proved too much for him. He was immediately paralyzed by the
amount of information that needed to be input into his member
profile: The questions were inane, and the truth was either too
banal or too ugly to put out into the world, and so he sat and stared
at the questions, knowing the truth wouldn't quite work. What
would he be if he weren't what he was (a book critic is somewhat
true and a good choice, right?), what his spirit animal was (what?
What did that mean?), his favorite food (hummus? It was true, but
is there a food that's less sexy than hummus? There is not), his favorite movie (he wanted to put down *Annie Hall* but wasn't sure

that was still okay), how he liked to spend a rainy afternoon (reading and watching porn and masturbating).

He was stymied. It wasn't that he couldn't fill out the forms; it wasn't that he wasn't ready to date—truly, by the time a marriage is over and the leaving is done, a person is more than ready for something new. But the *paperwork*. As if the prospect of combing through New Yorkers looking for love weren't its own existential nightmare. He had done this when he was younger, hadn't he? Hadn't he resolved it? Hadn't he ended this bullshit by getting married?

Then one Saturday morning, two weeks after he moved out of Rachel's place, Toby woke up and realized he was alone. His new apartment seemed like a set in a depressing play, bare and filled so sparsely with objects that had been purchased not from need or desire but simply to fill the space. Nothing was strewn anywhere, like in his old apartment, which had been alive with a family rushing to the flute concert and the dance recital and the playdate and the birthday party. Now there was a brown microfiber couch and a gray chair that turned into a futon and a stupid swirly orange rug that was going mudwater brown at its edges already and a TV whose wires were unruly and unhidcable and a shitty particleboard bookshelf and everything stayed the same every day. Nothing moved. The kids came in and out but they were guests now, and nothing moved. The light coming in every morning was blue, then yellow, then white, then blue again, but nothing moved. The kids came after school and ate dinner and did homework, but he walked them home and came back and it was as if they hadn't just been there. It felt like a fake life.

And it was so, so quiet. He used to like the quiet, when it was intermittent. "Can you hear that?" he would ask Rachel when the kids were gone to school or camp or they both had playdates. The nothing was almost its own sound. Now the nothing wasn't the exception; it was the condition. Now the nothing was his roommate.

And so he sat down on the beanbag chair he had bought for Solly and pulled on his chest hair with his right hand as he filled out with his left hand the Hr form finally with scientifically titrated answers (job: book critic; spirit animal: schnauzer; food: chicken Caesar salad; movie: *Rocky II;* rainy afternoon: a crossword puzzle, a museum, a walk—"Why should rain keep you inside?"). It wasn't not true, except for the Caesar salad. Toby's dedication to never once using an added fat was held like a patriotic or religious principle.

He clicked Send Form and watched his profile do its loading action, and within what felt like a millisecond, women were pummeling him with messages:

> *Hey you.*
> *Hi there.*
> *Whazzup?*
> *[tongue emoji]*
> *[purple devil emoji]*
> *This is my ironic poke.*
> *[eyes looking emoji]*
> *[jokey face emoji]*
> *[eggplant emoji]*
> *[double purple devil emoji]*
> *[investigator emoji]*
> *[woman dancing possible samba in evening gown emoji]*
> *Let's fuck?*

Well, friends, he lost a full day of his life that weekend. Or maybe it was more? Maybe it was a day and a half? Two days? Our friend Seth called him twice during that time and it didn't go straight to voicemail, but it went after-seeing-Seth-was-calling straight to voicemail. The sun went up, the sun went down, he realized he'd had to pee for an hour, and at some point he thought to order Chinese food (steamed chicken and vegetables, no water chestnuts, please), but mostly he remained aloft on the wind of the messages he was getting—women who wanted to LOL at his every joke, and send winkies, and pictures, and set his weary heart afire with double entendre. Some sent emojis like [smiley face] or [winky face]. Some sent absolute operas with their emojis, like: [woman raising her hand emoji] plus [male construction worker emoji] plus [man and woman emoji] plus [bathtub emoji], which he cannot begin to describe how this turned him on. He swiped and swiped, gobsmacked at the sheer volume. Face, face, face, face, full body, face, face, just collarbone, face, face, face, just ass crack, face, tongue, just sideboob, oh man just lips, face. It was dark on the second day when it occurred to him that he had to take action on some of these conversations. He realized it because a woman he was messaging with wrote, *So will I see that cute face anytime soon or not?* He realized that what was happening on his phone, which was now streaked and hot to the touch, was also happening in real life. He looked up briefly and felt the strain of his eyes refocusing on the room around him. He hadn't stopped smiling for hours now, but he looked around and the room was dark, which made him panic a little, and suddenly he remembered that very little in the world stands still like this, that forward momentum will always pluck you out of your fugue-jelly state.

He'd initially been democratic in his search parameters on the subject of age. Anyone over twenty-five who wasn't yet dead was fair game, he'd figured, though he quickly began to tire of looking at the young ones. It wasn't how it ached to see their youth, how their skin still showed glow and bounce, how they delighted in the seam of their buttock folding over the top of their thigh like it was on springs—though it absolutely did ache to see those things. It wasn't how they so clearly believed it would always be like this, or perhaps how they knew it wouldn't and so decided to enjoy it; that would be worse, if they were enjoying their youth because they knew it wouldn't last, because who had the sense to do that? It was that he couldn't bear to be with anyone who didn't yet truly understand consequences, how the world would have its way with you despite all your careful life planning. There was no way to learn that until you lived it. There was no way for any of us to learn that until we lived it.

Toby knew about consequences. He was living them. Before and after his hookups, there was something like a conversation. He quickly learned that that conversation had the potential to make him feel like he wanted to die. People under forty had optimism. They had optimism for the future; they didn't accept that their future was going to resemble their present with alarming specificity. They had *velocity*. He couldn't bear velocity just at that moment.

And, practically, they mostly still wanted children—even the ones who pretended they didn't out of some silly imperative to seem cool or wild or other or invulnerable or more like a man, as if that's what men wanted. These young women could be easily led astray by kindness, and Toby didn't want to have to worry that treating a woman well would result in some sort of expectation of an upward, forward-pointing trajectory. He could not imagine himself on any trajectory right now, much less an upward, forward-pointing one. He knew that was an unpopular point of view for a man in his position—our friend Seth would barely believe him if he confessed this; his own Hr search parameters had begun at twenty and expired at twenty-seven despite the fact that he, like us, was forty-one.

"Why not nineteen?" Toby asked. "Or eighteen even? That's legal."

"I'm not a perv," Seth said, even though there were literally hundreds of women who would absolutely have classified Seth as a perv.

So Toby changed his search parameters to thirty-eight to forty-one, then forty to fifty, what the hell, and it was there that he found his gold mine: endlessly horny, sexually curious women who knew their value, who were feeling out something new, and whose faces didn't force him to have existential questions about youth and responsibility. There he found women, most of whom were divorced, and most of whom had been discharged of their marital duties with a great second wind of energy, with the wonder of new chance flowing through their lymph, which he could smell through his phone like a pheromone.

There were other benefits to dating women his age. They weren't porny in their avatar poses, the way the younger ones were. It was only this strange millennial generation that thought that a bitten lip or open mouth or half-closed eyes or totally leaned-back posture (where were her hands?) was alluring—that only giddy, half-dead submission could turn a man on. And maybe it was true for some—maybe it was true for the young men whose first primary sexual relationships were with porn—but not for him. The women who took a nice photo with a smile, who looked directly into the camera without artifice—those were the women who were interesting to him. They were the ones who were starting all over, like him, and waking up like newborn birds in a nest, eyes just opening, also just like him. Slowly, slowly, he began to see through their pictures and profiles a way to move on. "It's like they're showing me the way," he'd tell me. "It's like they're leading me to the next version of myself." He had begun, through these women and their confidence, to see a way to reenter the world.

The lesson? Fill out the form, even when it fills you with dread. The other lesson? Go with what you want instead of what you are supposed to want. All around him were instruction manuals on middle age: the car you should want to drive, the cocktail waitress you should want to fuck. More and more he found that he had to block these things out and ask himself what his particular condition required. It was never a sports car; it was rarely a cocktail waitress.

So as he was entering the park that morning, his need for confirmation of his fellow New Yorkers as a rabid bunch of writhing hornballs who could not make it to lunchtime without an orgasm validated, his phone began to ring and it disconcerted him for a minute. It was Joanie, her blushing ID photo picture coming up through the hospital's internal caller app. Her picture overtook the picture of a personal trainer in a bikini, confusing the superhighway in his brain that had been prepping itself for lust.

"We have a consult in the ER, nonresponsive woman," Joanie said.

"Okay, I'll be there in twenty," Toby told her. "I had the kids this morning unexpectedly."

He hung up and saw a text message. It was from Tess.

We still on for tonight?

He hated to leave the kids, particularly on a Friday night. But more than that, he hated Rachel. His weekend wasn't supposed to start till tomorrow. Fuck all of it, he thought.

Of course. Looking forward to it.

Truly, none of us could have predicted that this was how it would end up for Toby. We were twenty when we met on our junior years abroad in Israel. We didn't know yet that there were variations on insecurity; we thought we were all maximally insecure, and, sure, those insecurities took different shapes, but we were all suffering. We all had faith we'd eventually get over it, though. We didn't know that a happy future wasn't guaranteed to us, that it wasn't our right. But about Toby specifically, we didn't know that being short and fat as a child had made him unacceptable in his own eyes—first in his mother's eyes, and then in his own, and then, like a self-fulfilling prophecy, everyone else's. We didn't know yet that he wasn't going to grow anymore—he'd read somewhere that people sometimes sprout up a few inches in their early twenties. Most of all, we didn't know how severe the damage had been to him for being someone who had desires and wanted to be desired back and hadn't been.

The night we met, twenty years ago, he was sitting on the floor of a tourist trap called the Hous [sic] of Elixir, where they served warm wine with a sugared rim, which is disgusting to think about now but was exotic-seeming at the time. Bob Marley was playing—Bob Marley was the only CD the place owned, and so it was always playing, though we didn't know this yet. Toby was sitting against a wall, looking to his left, watching Seth move in on one of the waitresses. Seth was tall and athletic and had a floppy, prep school haircut. Toby's hair would never hang down if he grew it out; it would just grow upward and outward. He and Seth were new roommates. They'd met three days earlier and had been out together every night, and every night, Toby watched a scene like this. By the second night, he no longer wondered if having Seth as his roommate was a great twist of luck or the worst thing to happen to his already tattered self-image.

The waitress had spent the previous hour ignoring Seth, probably used to the hypnotic effect she had on recently arrived American students. But she had never encountered Seth before. He kept asking her how to say different words on the English menu in Hebrew, and these were just factual questions so why shouldn't she answer them? "C'mon, c'mon," he said, "just tell me. I'm new in this country. Please, we are compadres, we are comrades, we are countrymen." Toby watched as her tide rose toward him like he was the moon. She grew warmer and began leaning her body closer while she was reading what he was pointing at, and then watching his face as he repeated it back to her. It was amazing, the way people melted onto Seth—the way women melted onto the Seths of the world. Toby had been in college for two years by then, long enough to learn that high school had not been an anomaly. He had learned that he was permanently relegated to support staff status for guys like Seth. It was either his height, or his feelings about his height, or maybe he just truly lacked charm and good looks and charisma. Whatever it was, he watched those Seths of the world perform an animal mating dance in public in a way he would never dare to.

I had taken a bus down from Tel Aviv with my roommate, Lori, a bucktoothed redhead from a part of Missouri that wasn't St. Louis—this would be the first and maybe only night we ever spent together recreationally in Israel. We sat down next to Toby on the floor, and while Lori looked around, I watched him watch Seth watch the waitress, a National Geographic Channel circle jerk. The waitress was now sitting on the floor with Seth. I was sitting, too, but with my arms across my midsection. Toby turned to take a drink from his wine and saw me watching him.

"I thought Israelis learned defense skills in the military," he said.

He was from Los Angeles and a bio major at Princeton. He came from a family of doctors and had always wanted to do something in medicine. I was from Brooklyn, from a family full of girls who were expected to transfer from their childhood bedrooms to the bedrooms of their husband's homes with no pit stops along the way. I was commuting to NYU, and a junior abroad program in a country my mother approved of was the only way I could get out of the house. Toby and I kept talking, watching Seth seduce the waitress, commenting on it like we were sports broadcasters. Within five words of each other, I knew we understood each other. Our defenses were the same: sarcasm, pettiness, a protective well-readiness that we hoped conveyed that we were smarter than everyone. I liked him. I could have even *like*-liked him.

But: Two hours later, Lori announced that the last bus to Tel Aviv was leaving in fifteen minutes. He said he'd walk me to the bus stop, and I began to stand and then so did he, but when he stopped standing, I kept going, one inch, two inches, three inches. Toby was used to being short; I wasn't used to being very tall. I was only five-eight, which was tall but not giant—well, depending on who you're standing next to. My poor regard for my own body couldn't withstand the kind of hulking that a relationship with Toby would have required. I couldn't be larger than a man in bed, or at the movies or at a dinner table or, honestly, even on the phone. I didn't want to feel big and graceless and a thousand pounds of just lumbering; I didn't want to have to contend with that every time his hand reached under my shirt. I felt too bad about myself already. I immediately said to him, "I feel like you and this girl from my dorm might get along?" I said it to either deflect what I thought might have been his interest, or to make up for how bad I felt for counting him out immediately. He put his hands in his pockets and smiled with just his lips. We walked out the door to the bus, and we saw Seth in a shadow kissing the waitress, and we both ignored it and talked about our classes, lest sex show up between us. Toby wasn't heartbroken; he didn't want me, either, except that we both wanted somebody.

After that night, Toby and I met in Jerusalem on and off, first by going back to the Hous of Elixir the next week and being happy to see each other again, then by making intentional plans on our dorm telephones. Seth would come to town with Toby, where he would chase all the skinny girls who knew how to flirt. Toby and I stood and watched them, reducing them to caricatures, even as we shook our heads in bewilderment over how easy it all seemed to come to them. I found a guy that year eventually—Marc—who loved singing the *Les Mis* soundtrack on the Tel Aviv beach, spreading his arms wide as he sang, and going moisturizer shopping at Dizengoff Center with me and maybe you can see where this is going. He dumped me suddenly and unceremoniously because I never dumped anyone; I never had faith there would be anyone else. Toby told me he thought Marc was trying to let me down easy because I deserved better than a boyfriend who wasn't attracted to me, but then I saw Marc spooning with another girl in another dorm, and I came to Jerusalem to see Toby and cry.

"Why am I such an idiot?" I asked him.

Toby had never understood what I liked about Marc. "I don't

know," he said. "You're so special and Marc is so dumb and regular."

That was nice, but I still did two shots of Goldschläger, which was one and a half too many shots for me, even in my youth. We sat on a curb of the cobblestoned Ben Yehuda Street, where no cars were permitted. I leaned against his shoulder, which required a full coccyx-to-neck side curl, since his shoulder reached considerably below any part of my head, and so that I had to bend my torso-neck-head into the shape of a C. He patted the top of my head, wondering how ridiculous we looked to passersby.

Then, amid the too-drunk American students crowding Ben Yehuda came Seth, walking alone. He saw us and sat down on my other side.

"What's going on, guys?" he asked.

"Marc dumped me. He said he was never that into me."

"That's because you don't have a penis," Seth answered. "You are too pretty to be limiting your options this young." I smiled through the snot on my face and switched my lean toward Seth. Seth's shoulder was higher than mine when we sat and so my new lean had more dignity.

That was November, right before Thanksgiving, and it marked the time that we became a predictable threesome. We saw each other every Thursday night, then on Saturday night, too, and always on holidays. During Passover break, when half our fellow students went back to the States to visit their families, we instead went on a hiking trip to the Galilee with a group of randoms who organized it through expat bulletin boards. We hiked through waterfalls at sunrise and at sundown we ate pigeon that we were told was chicken. We sat one night on the banks of the sea and listened to a Christian pastor who was converting to Judaism tell the story of his life. It was on that trip that Seth introduced me to cigarettes, and then pot, and boy, it was like I discovered the cure for myself. We spent our last night in Israel together, high and crazy, and took separate flights out the next day. The three of us stayed close even after we returned home, straight through college, after Toby graduated from medical school, after my first published article in a cheerleader magazine, after Seth's first brush with the SEC. It was only after Toby got married that we all seemed to drift apart.

About twelve years ago, I married a lawyer and had kids and moved to the suburbs. I had long since faded from Toby's life—we'd barely spoken since I'd gotten married. I thought of him with sadness sometimes. Sometimes months would go by and I wouldn't think of him even once.

Then, this past June, my phone rang. I was in the kitchen, cleaning up after dinner. My husband, Adam, was putting the kids into bed. Toby's number was the same as it had been years ago. His name flashed across the screen like it was nothing, like it was a regular occurrence.

"Toby Fleishman." I turned the sink off, dried my hands, and turned around, leaning against the sink.

"Elizabeth Epstein," he said.

"I'm afraid you have the wrong number, sir," I said. "My name has been Elizabeth Slater for quite some time."

"Really? In your magazine, it always says Epstein."

"I'm afraid you have the wrong number, sir," I said. "I haven't been in a magazine in quite some time."

"Really?"

"*Toby,*" I said. "Toby, what is going *on?*"

He told me he was getting a divorce, and that his therapist had said to reconnect with friends that he missed as one of his steps toward "reclaiming his life." "That's her phrase, not mine, I swear." No, it wasn't a surprise. Yes, it was a long time coming. Yes, he had big gaping wounds in his stomach and his spleen and he was leaking fluids at an untenable rate. Yes, she got the apartment and the car and the house in the Hamptons.

"What *happened?*" I asked.

"It turned out she was crazy. I worked so hard to find someone who wasn't crazy and I ended up with someone crazy. We went to a couples therapist. He told her that she had too much contempt. He said contempt is one of the four horsemen of the marital apocalypse."

"What are the other three?" I asked.

"Maybe one is shutting down? Oh, defensiveness. There's a fourth. Honestly, I can't remember."

"Is one of them being a total bitch?" From my son's bedroom, Adam shushed me. What was the point of owning a big fucking house in the suburbs if you couldn't laugh in your kitchen at night? I whispered, "It has to be that one of them is being a total bitch."

The last time I'd seen him was years ago, when Adam and I went over to their place for dinner, and it was a nightmare. Sweet, affable Adam tried to make conversation with Rachel about the agency business, and she answered his questions like she was a Miss America pageant contestant, in full sentences, no room for follow-up, and kept rushing the courses. At the end of the dinner, Adam said goodbye and thank you and I didn't. I just looked at Toby and left.

Anyway, the night he called me, Toby had prepared an entire, tearful speech about what he'd been through, meant to dissolve any anger I had—any anger I *righteously* had—so that he could just have a friend again. "Be angry at me later," it went. "I deserve it. But I could use a friend." Maybe his voice would crack when he said "friend" and I would hear that he was for real.

But something else happened when I saw his name on my phone. I traveled back in time to the last place he left me. I heard the anxiety in his voice and I was filled with love and relief, and I filed my catalog of grievances for a later date.

I was going through something right then, too. I had left my job as a staff writer for a men's magazine about two years before. I was now what was called a stay-at-home mother, a temporary occupation with no prospect of promotion that worked so hard to differentiate itself from job-working that it confined me to semantic house arrest, though certainly I was allowed to carpool and go to the store. When I told people what I did, they'd say, "Being a mother is the hardest job there is." But it wasn't. The hardest job there was was being a mother and having an *actual* job, with pants and a commuter train pass and pens and lipstick. Back when I had a job, no one ever said to me, "Having an actual job and being a mother is the hardest job there is." We had to not say those things so that we could tiptoe around all the feelings of inadequacy that we projected onto the stay-at-home mothers; in fact, you couldn't even ask a woman you suspected of stay-at-homery what she did because there was no not-awkward way to ask it. ("Do you work?" I once asked a woman back when I had a job. "Of course I work," she said. "I'm a mom." But I was a mom, too, so what was what I did called?) But also: No one had to tell me it was harder to have a job and be a mother. It was *obvious*. It was two full-time *occupations*. It's just *math*. Because having a job made you no less of a mother; you still had to do all that shit, too. Keeping track of your kids from afar isn't easier. Entrusting them to a stranger who was available for babysitting by virtue of the fact that she was incapable of doing anything else is not something that fills a person with faith and relaxation. Now that I have worked and stayed at home, I can confirm all of this. Now that I stay at home, I can say it out loud. But now that I don't work, no one is listening. No one listens to stay-at-home mothers, which, I guess, is why we were so careful about their feelings in the first place.

Anyway.

It's not like I wasn't busy. I was an officer in good standing of my kids' PTA. I owned a car that put my comfort ahead of the health and future of the planet. I had an IRA and a 401(k) and I went on vacations and swam with dolphins and taught my kids to ski. I contributed to the school's annual fund. I flossed twice a day; I saw a dentist twice a year. I got Pap smears and had my moles checked. I read books about oppressed minorities with my book club. I did physical therapy for an old knee injury, forgoing the other things

I'd like to do to ensure I didn't end up with a repeat injury. I made breakfast. I went on endless moms' nights out, where I put on tight jeans and trendy blouses and high heels like it mattered and went to the restaurant that was right next to the restaurant we went to with our families. (There were no dads' nights out for my husband, because the supposition was that the men got to live life all the time, whereas we were caged animals who were sometimes allowed to prowl our local town bar and drink the blood of the free people.) I took polls on whether the Y or the JCC had better swimming lessons. I signed up for soccer leagues in time for the season cutoff, which was months before you'd even think of enrolling a child in soccer, and then organized their attendant carpools. I planned playdates and barbecues and pediatric dental checkups and adult dental checkups and plain old internists and plain old pediatricians and hair salon treatments and educational testing and cleats-buying and art class attendance and pediatric ophthalmologist and adult ophthalmologist and now, suddenly, mammograms. I made lunch. I made dinner. I made breakfast. I made lunch. I made dinner. I made breakfast. I made lunch. I made dinner.

"Why haven't you been in touch?" I asked Toby.

"We would fight in public," he said. "It was too embarrassing. She just didn't care who she started in front of."

"I thought it was me!" I told him. "That whole time, I thought maybe this is a perfectly normal, nice person and that she just couldn't bear me and turned you against me." Now, suddenly, I couldn't believe I ever thought that. "She was a horrible person, truly. I hated her the minute I met her."

That first night, on the phone, Toby was so grateful that I wasn't going to make him pay for his abandonment of me or treat him like an injured kitten that he became giddy, and he laughed more and so I laughed more. And in our laughter we heard our youth, and it is not not a dangerous thing to be at the doorstep to middle age and at an impasse in your life and to suddenly be hearing sounds from your youth.

———

We met for lunch in the Village after that first conversation, at a restaurant that had replaced a diner we used to eat at when Toby was in medical school. It was hard to look at his face and see the changes on it—in my mind, he'd frozen in time the way Han Solo did at the end of *The Empire Strikes Back:* the image of his face in a sad, panicked goodbye the last time I'd seen him.

"She was just angry all the time," he told me.

I asked him the questions he hated: So then what happened? It's so drastic and hard to end a marriage. Something had to have happened. Did she cheat on you? Did you cheat on her? Did you hate her friends? Did the kids kill her libido? But marriage is vast and mysterious and private. You could not scientifically compare two marriages for all of the variance of factors, most particularly what two specific people can tolerate. I made my face placid and curious, the way I did during my old magazine interviews, pretending the stakes were just regular when really everything hung on the answers.

"But you're not asking about *now,*" he said. He pulled out his phone, opened it up, and my God. "Look at all them." All these women, lined up—literally you could scroll through them—asking for the attention of Toby Fleishman. Toby Fleishman! I stared.

"This is what it's like now?" I asked.

"This is what it's like. You don't have to leave your house to be humiliated. You don't even have to be humiliated. It's totally opt-in. Everyone who is there is there to participate."

The scroll of women who wanted to interact with Toby sexually was nowhere near ending. The pictures, the texts. Toby Fleishman!

"It's just like 'Decoupling,' right?" he said. "Who knew back then that it was an actual instruction manual?"

A long time ago, in 1979, the men's magazine where I used to work had published a famous story about divorce called "Decoupling." The writer, Archer Sylvan, was our in-house legend, the man who stood for the magazine as much as any logo. I'd been reading Archer since I was young (probably too young), and in Israel, I'd had his books on my nightstand. Toby borrowed one of them, then the next, then the next. I'd grown up not allowed to read the same young-adult novels about babysitters and pretty blond twins that my friends read. My mother thought young-adult books were trash for degenerates and were certainly a red carpet to teen pregnancy and drug use. So I read the Archer Sylvan books my studious older sister brought home—*Decoupling and Other Stories, City Turned Upside Down,* and *Everybody into the Pool.* The covers of Archer's books had big Helvetica block letters and seemed important, like literature. Inside, they were the dirtiest, darkest books I could imagine, and maybe sixth grade is young for the commingling of dark and dirty. Stories about nudist colonies, sex parties, Zapatistas, communists, politicians in secret occult clubs, polyamorous scientists. You couldn't believe what he found. You couldn't believe what this world we lived in was made of. Once, he was in Chile and a chef who never repeated a dish out of some strange Buddhist philosophy that didn't track cut the head off a live goat and reached directly into its skull through its broken jaw and ate its brains *raw.* He offered some to Archer, and without hesitation, Archer ate them, too, right there with his bare hands.

When I became a professional writer, I tried to write like Archer: that way he had of releasing the valve of his anger slowly, tensely, beautifully so that his vortex of empathy, when sent through the prism of the anger, created a generalized disgust for the state of the world that seemed like the only conclusion a smart, thinking person could come to. I was disgusted, too. I was angry, too. But I never landed on anger—I never ended a story there—and I think maybe that was where I failed. My empathy only created more empathy, which sounds good, yes, but was born of inherent cowardice. I was too scared to finish with anger. I was too scared to be wholly disgusted with my subjects, who were, of course, real people who had given me their time and their trust and also had my phone number. I didn't care so much whether they hated me; I was never going to see them again. But I was afraid to stay angry, to leave it all hanging out there with no resolution. I was afraid of seeming too hateful, and so I settled on hating myself for caring too much. That's not to say I was a bad writer. I was good, and I was liked, and people said I was compassionate and that it was nice to read warm things, and only I knew that it was actually a failure of bravery and will to be as compassionate as I was.

But I wasn't like Archer Sylvan in other ways; I was never given the opportunity to try. Archer would sleep on tour buses with bands or camp in the desert with an actor or do ayahuasca with a politician and come to the realization that he had to divorce his wife and marry his research assistant, whom he now realized he knew twelve lives ago. He got lost for days waiting for a reclusive rock star. He spent $7,000 on stripper tips once, submitted the expense without a receipt (naturally), and was reimbursed *even though no stripper ended up in the story*. Once, I had to check a second bag on a flight from Europe where I was interviewing an actor and I got a pissed-off call from our managing editor and I never did it again.

Archer had written the article version of "Decoupling" in 1979, fourteen thousand words just following a man pseudonymed Mark —editorialization in even the names—through his divorce. Even before the Internet, the story made the rounds. It was a scandal, calling out women for changing the rules on men with no warning because of their vapid women's lib and their stupid sexual awakenings. Sexual awakenings were not supposed to extend beyond what was merely an upgrade in enjoyment for men.

It was also an undeniably great story. It was electric and incisive. It extended its observations into audacious extrapolation in a way no one in nonfiction had really done before. It became the kind of story that was dragged out every time someone wanted to make a comparison with a piece of new reporting. "This is basically 'Decoupling,'" or, "Well, it's no 'Decoupling.'" In the restaurant with Toby, my scrolling landed on a fifty-year-old woman riding a horse in a bikini who wanted Toby to know she was into nipple play, and a line from "Decoupling" occurred to me: "His misery was a fog that obscured slightly but not completely an entirely new land of opportunity. He did not realize that the land of opportunity was obscuring something even more potent."

I looked up from Toby's phone. "I never understood why you married her."

He leaned back and began to pull on his chest hair. "I got married because I fell in love."

After that, we saw each other every few days. I'd drive my big, dumb SUV to the Upper West Side and wait for him at the diner next to his hospital, or I'd take the train into Penn Station, and we'd meet for diner food and rehash it all.

Our second lunch:

"Or maybe when we get married we have no ability to know how long forever could possibly be," he said as he ate an egg-white omelet. "Think about all the times something feels like it lasts forever. Forever seems like the duration of high school, which is four years but that's only because we've only been alive for sixteen years and so four years of that is a huge chunk of our lifetime—a quarter of it. By the time we make this decision, to hook ourselves to a person for the rest of our lives, we're what? Twenty-five? Thirty? We're babies. We don't even know what we're dealing with. How could we fathom what it would be like to be on our best behavior for that long? Or know what is funny or charming to us now but intolerable in the future? How will we know what we need? Your tastes in TV haven't even changed yet. I loved *Friends* when I was young and then I loved *Friends* in reruns in my twenties and now if I hear the sound of the opening music I want to die."

"You only say that because your marriage didn't work out," I said, eating a blintz. "If you'd ended up happy, you'd think it was just fine."

"You only say that because your marriage *is* working out."

"You don't know anything about my marriage," I said.

"I know that it's continued. And even if continued marriages aren't happy, they are still categorized as happy."

Our third lunch:

"Marriage is like the board in that old Othello game," he said as he ate a chicken breast baked dry, no added oil, please. "The board is overwhelmingly full of white discs until someone places enough black discs in enough of the right places to flip all the discs to black. Marriage starts out full of white discs. Even when there are a few black ones on the board, it's still a white board. You get into a fight? Ultimately fine and something to laugh at in the end, because the Othello board is still white. But when it finally happens and the black discs take over—the affair, the financial impropriety, the boredom, the midlife crisis, whatever it is that ends the marriage—the board becomes black. Now you look at the marriage, even the things that were formerly characterized as good memories, as tainted and rotted from the start: That adorable argument on the honeymoon was actually foreshadowing; the battle over what to name Hannah was my way of denying her the little family she had. Even the purely good memories are now haunted by a sense that I was a fool to allow myself to think that life was good and that a kingdom of happiness was mine." (I told him I understood his metaphor, but also that's not how you play Othello.)

Our fourth lunch:

"It's like group therapy," he said, eating a scoop of cottage cheese, and talking about all these new people he'd dated, so many of whom had been through the same thing. "It's like group therapy, if at the end of group therapy the therapist put your penis in her mouth."

Our fifth lunch:

"It couldn't be me," he said as he ate four turkey slices with mustard and no bread. "There are too many of us who want the best for our children and our spouses. Sometimes you end up married to someone who didn't realize she didn't want to be married. I mean, look at this."

He swiped up a photo. A perfectly lovely woman with dimples, wearing a bathing suit and squinting in the sun. I liked to see the pictures on his phone, which included things I couldn't imagine myself, and I liked him to give me a play-by-play so that I could ask him questions about why he said what and how long before he went to bed with someone. (I also liked to see Rachel's text messages come in, if they happened to while I was looking at his pictures, and marvel at what a pterodactyl she could be because I could be bad but I was never quite that bad.)

"How can you look at this woman and say she's a failure?" he asked, pointing at the picture. "Sometimes it just doesn't work out for you. Don't think of it in such a binary way. Your marriage not working isn't always about you. Your life not working isn't always about you. It could just be about your life." Which, sure.

By then he was tan from all his walking around the city. He had been filled with the notion lately that there was so much life in him yet. He now felt young and somehow this made me feel even older. It was like I wasn't looking, and then suddenly I was gone. I looked up again at Toby straight in the face, but he had taken his phone back and was responding to a new text.

St. Thaddeus had once been a mental hospital that was owned by the City of New York, which then sold it to Columbia University, which tried to renovate it into just a regular hospital but did a half-assed job so that as of the mid-1980s, it still looked and felt and even smelled (they couldn't get the smell out no matter how much they tried) like an asylum. It wasn't a public hospital, but nobody wanted to go there for surgeries—not when you could go to Lenox Hill or Mount Sinai. In 1988, a finance group bought it from Columbia, which dumped $100 million into it and turned it into a modern marvel: glass and metal and stainless steel and state-of-the-art everything and the smell finally gone. Being at the hospital was like being inside the future, but as it was imagined by science fiction films in the last part of the twentieth century, not the actual future we ended up with, where everything just turned out being smaller and flimsier than it used to be.

An unconscious woman awaited Toby in the ER. "Karen Cooper, forty-four. Unresponsive since arrival, some delirium prior to arrival, reported by her husband. Elevated AST/ALT," Clay said. Clay was the runt of this round of fellows. He had a slightly lazy eye, which would stray only when he'd been staring at you for a long time, as if the eye were done with the conversation and was hinting at the rest of him that it was time to go. It was unclear if he knew about his blackhead situation.

The patient, a blonde with the kind of nose job done so early in her teens that the columella nasi was dripping out from beneath the tower of the septum so that you could see the two small tabs inside the nostrils, was completely out. She wore one of those satin dresses that is either a nightgown or a very slinky evening gown, and her hair was spread out across her pillow in a very Sleeping Beauty vibe. Toby briefly wondered who did the hair thing.

Beside her, in a chair, was a man, about Toby's age, his hands clasped on the top of his hair. He stood up when Toby walked in and extended his hand. His name was David Cooper; he was the husband. His head was power-shaved, and he was at least six feet tall. Maybe six-one. Did it matter after six feet, though? He was tall.

"I'm Dr. Fleishman," Toby said. "Can you tell me what happened?"

Karen Cooper had spent a weekend in Las Vegas with her best friend. They'd had a wild time, celebrating a friend's something-or-other, and when she came back, she seemed woozy. This was a week ago. "She was just much clumsier than usual," David said. She was falling over and tripping and even listing when she was just standing still. She had joked that she must still be drunk. Then, yesterday morning, she started slurring, "also more than usual," he said, "and she was saying crazy things."

"Like what crazy things?" Toby asked.

"Like out of nowhere, things that didn't make sense, like she was going to have a carpool pick me up from work, and to make sure I told the mom driving thank you. The kids don't even have a carpool. They have a driver. She talked about our bowling league, and I can tell you, we've never bowled together more than twice in twenty years."

"Is she on any other medications?"

"She's on Zoloft. She went to the doctor maybe a year ago saying she felt out of it a lot, and he said she was depressed and gave her Zoloft. Hey, does she look yellow to you?"

She was yellow like a highlighter. "That's jaundice," Toby said. "That's why I was called. I'm a liver specialist. Let's go back to this morning for a minute, though. When did she stop responding to you?"

"I woke up and she looked what I thought was pale but then yellowish and she was sort of dazed, so I put her in a car to take her to the ER, and the minute we got her into this bed she fell asleep, but now—" He looked over at his wife's body. "I don't know if she's asleep or if she's unconscious. They said she's unconscious, but it looked like she was just tired and fell asleep. She wasn't in the middle of a sentence or anything." Now he was panicked. "Which is it? Is she unconscious? Or is she just asleep?"

"Well, we're going to figure that out," Toby said. "She's in good hands now. If you wouldn't mind, Dr. Clifton here is going to show you our family lounge, and we're going to examine your wife and find out what the heck is going on."

"I can't stay?"

"It's best that we do our exam and get a handle on what might be going on, and you look like you could use a cup of coffee."

Clay guided him out.

"Can anyone tell me what's going on?" Toby asked.

Logan was first. "It's alcoholic cirrhosis, right? She went on a bender, and her liver is just too injured. She's probably been a secret drinker for years."

"You sure?" Toby asked.

Joanie said something but nobody could hear it.

"What's that?" Toby asked. Clay slipped back into the room and looked between their faces to see what he'd missed.

"It couldn't not be," Joanie said. She said it dreamily, almost to herself, her pen pressed softly to her lips. How Joanie loved this stuff. How her love for the diagnostic quest always superseded the usual worries in these moments—of appearances, of ego, of failure, of reputation. Clay wanted to get through the material and stop sweating so much. Logan wanted to show off and make his eight P.M. tennis game. Joanie wanted to understand and worship the miracle of this stuff. She wanted to be amazed.

Joanie stood against the wall. Her hair was a kind of sepia—straw tinged with red at a certain angle. She wore little-girl clothes: knee socks and parochial school–style skirts and cardigans, which, in its thrift store way, stopped just before it became appealing to Toby. She blinked slowly behind her glasses when she was trying to figure something out; she mouthed words silently, concernedly, when she was trying to remember something.

"What did he say *exactly*?" Toby asked them. He walked over to Karen Cooper and leaned down to listen to her heart. He opened her eyes.

"He said she was clumsy and she was slurring—both signs of neurological events," Clay said. "Her liver is failing."

Toby straightened up and looked at them. "What did our friend Sir William Osler say?"

" 'Listen to your patient. He is telling you his diagnosis,' " Logan said.

"So what is Mrs. Cooper telling us?"

Clay looked at Karen Cooper. "The patient is unresponsive, Dr. Fleishman."

Toby inhaled slowly, and spoke on the exhale. "Her *husband* said what? Her *behavior* prior to becoming unresponsive said what?"

"That she was clumsy and slurring, which all fits into—"

"Yes, Clay, no one is arguing that she's not having neurological symptoms. No one is suggesting she's responsive. What did he say *exactly*, though? He said she was clumsier than *usual*. What this means is that something's been going on longer than just the last week. Does she have kids?"

Clay checked her chart. "Twin ten-year-old boys."

"Okay," Toby said. "So that means her blood was clean at least when she delivered, which she probably did—" He lifted her blanket down a few inches from her waist, and pulled her nightgown up a little. "Yes, C-section. Okay, that means if she'd had a clotting problem back then, she would have known it."

"Right," Joanie said. "So it developed more recently than ten years ago."

"Let's find out from her internist if she has a history of elevated AST/ALT." He looked at her chart. "She's on Zoloft, as of a year ago. Guys, a woman comes in complaining about anything, she gets sent away with a script for antidepressants. He probably missed the signs of this while he could have helped, before neurological problems set in. Insurance won't pay you for more than fifteen minutes of your time, but you still have to listen. You have to fill in blanks. You have to ask questions. Now, open her eyes."

Joanie lifted Karen's eyelids. She looked up, surprised and thrilled. "Wilson's!" Clay and Logan followed her, each of them taking a moment to look into her eyes. Joanie looked at Toby like she'd just seen the stars for the first time.

Toby went over to look. Wilson's disease was the body's inability to process copper through the liver. The copper acted as a toxin in the brain. The easiest and most visible sign of it was a copper-colored ring surrounding the irises.

"Right," Toby said. "So, Logan, go get her internist on the phone." Toby took his exam gloves off. "See, guys? Listen to the patient. Always listen. Even if the patient can't talk, most of the time it's all right there in front of you."

He did his rounds. He touched base with a pediatric hepatologist whose teen patient had graduated to Toby's care. He consulted in the ER with a college kid who had gotten hepatitis C from a shitty tattoo parlor. He saw a woman his own age with liver cancer.

He gave a sonogram to an MTA worker whom he had diagnosed with hemochromatosis a year ago. Now the man's liver was a little scarred, but it was better. It was regenerating. It was almost new again. Toby pushed the wand over and around the man's liver. He loved this part; every sonogram, every biopsy, was always like the first time. You couldn't believe what the liver was capable of. This never got old for Toby, not since the first time he saw it in medical school, in a textbook of time-lapse pictures of a healing liver. Livers behaved in some erratic ways, sure, all the organs do. But the liver was unique in the way that it healed. It was full of forgiveness. It understood that you needed a few chances before you got your life right. And it wouldn't just forgive you; it would practically forget. It would allow you to start over in a way that he could not imagine was true in any other avenue of life. We should all be like the liver, he thought. We should all regenerate like this when we're injured. On the darkest days of his marriage, Toby attended to his hospital business, and out of the corner of his eyes was always the liver, whispering to him that one day, there would be not much sign of all of this damage. He would regenerate, too.

Toby felt a hand on his shoulder from behind. It was Joanie. Her hand was warm and thin and womanly through his lab coat. He turned. In his ear, she whispered that Karen Cooper had been moved to a private room. He stood up. The whispering was strange; it was too close. The hand on his shoulder, too. It all felt oddly post-coital. When she pulled her hand away, he still felt it there.

Later, they visited her room after rounds. Joanie went over to Karen and lifted her eyelids again. "I can't believe we got a Wilson's case," she said.

"I've only seen it once before," Toby said. "It's awfully rare."

"The ring makes her eyes so pretty," Joanie said.

"Yes," Toby said. He looked over her shoulder into Karen Cooper's unresponsive eyes. "As far as life-threatening diseases go, it's a pretty one."

That was also the day of our big reunion. I'd arranged for lunch with Toby and invited Seth via Facebook message. His phone number had changed, and my text had bounced. He had lost his original phone number when he moved to Singapore a few years ago, and he had to get a new one with a newbie area code, which embarrassed him. I was so disconnected from my youth that one of its most prominent figures had a new phone number and I didn't know it. I was so far apart from my life in New York that it was like I'd been sent to another planet to breed and colonize.

Seth and I arrived ten minutes before Toby did. He'd stayed thin and had a well-executed fake tan and fake ultra-white teeth that played well against his leonine hazel eyes that picked up every shade of light brown in what remained of his hair. On his face he had the kind of two-day stubble growth we used to suggest that cover stars at the magazine nurture before their photo shoot that looks like benign neglect but is actually so evenly shaded that it could only be the work of meticulous planning. Man, all of it, he was still so handsome I could barely look at him.

Which is not to say he looked the same. He'd lost a good part of his hair, but in the best way possible if you're going to lose your hair, with sharp-angled power alleys of baldness between his widow's peak and temple on each side. His eyes felt like lightning to me, and I wanted to look away, but he wouldn't let go. Finally, we hugged, and I felt the seratonic chemicals of reunion rush through my body as I leaned my cheek against his chest. He put his hands on my shoulders and pushed me away and looked at my face. "You are looking good, Ms. Epstein," he said. He was lying. I looked like

I did when he first met me in Israel, before I lost a bunch of weight. It was my second pregnancy, it just got away from me and never came back no matter how I chased.

We sat down. He told me he subscribed to the magazine, but that he hadn't seen any of my stories recently. "I had so much pride seeing your name in there. I showed everyone I knew. I said, 'Boom. That's my girl right there.'"

I told him I'd left the magazine two years before, that I was trying to work on a coming-of-age novel about my youth. What I didn't say was that it never held my attention long enough for there to be progress. I kept the document up on my computer, but minimized, and I only turned to it every few weeks before feeling overwhelmed about what it was that I was trying to do with it. A book should convey your suffering; a book should speak to what is roiling within you. I thought maybe I could do this through a good young-adult novel, but YA novels were all fantastical things these days, with werewolves and sea creatures and half-bloods and hybrids. My story was small and dumb. Nothing even really happened in it.

"I guess with kids, it's hard," he said. His shirt was so crisp and well ironed, like he'd just put it on. I no longer wore clothes that required ironing.

Toby pulled into the booth next to me just then. "What the hell is going on here?" he asked. Across the aisle from us sat two women wearing yoga pants. One was enthusiastically feeding a baby in a stroller, making big eyes and mouth and noises with every bite in a desperate bid to drown out the noises in her head about her life choices. The waitress came to our table. Toby ordered a chicken Caesar salad with no cheese and no dressing.

"So like a piece of chicken and lettuce?" she asked.

"I guess so, yes."

"Do you maybe have any diet lettuce for him?" Seth asked. The waitress looked confused and Seth laughed, which made her even more confused, so she gave up and walked away.

Seth looked at us both and the blood rose in his face. "God, it's so good to see you guys," he said. "I should have brought Vanessa. You guys would really like her."

"Is she the one?" Toby asked.

"She might be the one," Seth said. "They all might be the one."

"You thought Jennifer Alkon was the one," I said.

"Who is to say I wouldn't want to see Jennifer Alkon again?" He looked down at his nails as if he were grooming them and raised his eyebrows. "Who is to say I haven't?"

I'd introduced Seth to Jennifer Alkon. She'd lived in my dorm. Seth had spent February crazy about her, flooding her with invitations and flowers and notes. On their last date together, they'd been fooling around in the bathroom downstairs at the Israel Museum— the Israel Museum! With its religious artifacts and the Dead Sea Scrolls! Seth couldn't quite get to the promised land, though, so Jennifer Alkon had gotten down on her knees and done her best work but to no avail. Seth, in frantic lust—he'd been raised by Orthodox parents and only had one kind of lust, and it was frantic— finished himself off while she watched. Within hours everyone knew this story from Seth. Later that night she went back to the dorm and tried to call to break up with him but he wouldn't answer, and it seemed clear to the girls who knew the whole story that he wouldn't answer because he didn't want to be broken up with, whereas the boys knew that Seth had ejaculated in front of her and could not maintain his interest in territory he'd already conquered.

"Really?" Toby asked now.

"Yep. And it was amazing. Fifth base!" He held his hand up for a high five to Toby.

"What's fifth base?" I asked.

"Anal," Toby said.

But he was too confused to return the high five. "Wait, when did this happen?" Toby asked. "She's been married forever."

"Marriage is a societal construct, Tobin."

"Is that what you told her? Is that what you're going to tell Vanessa?"

Seth's eyes softened when he talked about Vanessa again. "You guys should meet her," Seth said. "What are you doing tonight?"

"Going home to my children," I said.

"I have a date *and* I have the kids," Toby said. "Rachel dropped them off in the middle of the night. An entire day early. Because that's how peaceful co-parenting works."

"That's fucked up," Seth said.

"Well, that's how she is," Toby said. "It's fine. I actually enjoy my kids."

The conversation was starting to get a little grim for Seth, whose great skill was at throwing parties and knowing when the vibe needed adjusting via, say, swapping out different music or bringing out dessert. "I know," he said. "We should think of a curse for Rachel."

Toby laughed. "A curse!"

A curse. We had met the Beggar Woman in November of our year in Israel, when I'd gone to their dorm to have an American Thanksgiving. After dinner, we took a long, drunk walk and ended up in the Old City. We zigzagged down the streets, and right before the Western Wall became visible, we saw an old woman sitting on a milk crate, her hands and face wrinkled and brown and scaled from the sun. As we walked by her, she bellowed at us in Hebrew for money. Toby felt around in his pocket and found a five-shekel piece; Seth had two agorot, which counted as less than an American penny. I had only a hundred-shekel bill that I'd just had changed from my weekly allowance.

Toby approached the woman and gave her the money. The woman nodded vigorously and began making a dramatic sobbing sound, lifting her hands to the heavens and beseeching God himself, "Blessed are you who keeps me vital and safe! Blessed are your true believers, who allow me to serve you! Blessed is this small man, who will heal the world with his kindness! May he stand taller than those around him, above his jealousy!"

Toby gave her a half bow and moved back toward us again. Seth wanted some of that action, too, so he moved in to give her the ago-rot. The woman stared with disgust at the nothing coin he placed in her hands. But Seth did not read her disgust, and so he waited to see if she would thank God for his existence, if she would bless him, but instead when she looked up at him, she hissed through a wrinkled nose and aggressively squinted eyes, "May you never marry. May your hair fall out before you find a woman able to tolerate your snoring and farting. May your true self always be a lie."

"Yikes," Seth said.

Toby and I stepped forward to pull Seth back and keep walking, and the woman, realizing I was never going to give her anything—I couldn't! I only had a large bill!—said, "May you never dance at your daughter's wedding, for her name will be so spoiled throughout the town from her promiscuity that when she dares to leave her home to go to the market to buy fresh food for the Sabbath, the spiritual leaders of her community will congregate to throw rotten fruit at her head. May you never know satisfaction. May the Lord who watches over you give you a long life with no contentment. May you drink and drink and always find yourself thirsty." We broke into a run then, tripping on the cobblestones and getting dirty looks from people who were out late on pilgrimage to pray at the Western Wall.

Later, we told this story to everyone, but no one else found it funny, so we just kept telling it to each other. Then we began to make up curses for each other. We made up curses for our teachers. We made up curses for our exes and our roommates. We made up curses about the people who didn't understand us or love us the way we felt we deserved to be loved.

At the diner, Seth cleared his throat. "Okay, me first," he said. "May she find in her next routine visit to a toilet that her pubic hair has turned to dust. May the next man to visit her undercarriage sneeze so hard from the dust that an air bubble fills her torso, forcing an embolism."

"That's not how embolisms work," Toby said.

"I didn't ask for fact-checking," Seth said. He looked at me. "Your turn."

"Oh God," I said. "Okay. May she finally make her way home from work on the subway after a long day only to discover that the pustule she'd dismissed as a simple zit had become infected when she collided with the turnstile she was walking through."

"Wait, where was the zit?" Toby asked.

"Like on her pelvis," I said.

"You get zits there?"

"You can get zits anywhere you have skin!"

"That's so gross," Seth said.

"Too much," Toby said. "Also, too convoluted. Were we on the subway or were we at home at the point of impact?" But he was laughing.

I walked back to the train alone. The last two actors I'd profiled before I left the magazine were in their early fifties. Two of them had had first marriages to actresses when they were younger and had had children with those women before they'd gotten divorced. The actresses' careers were ruined. Their bodies had changed and they were on the ground for the daily life of child-rearing, and they had to make hard choices about how much they worked, knowing that women in certain professions have expiration dates. The men went off and had wild lives, which resulted in their divorces, and a decade later married their much younger co-star and much younger makeup artist, respectively, and then had two more children. Now they'd be able to do it all over with two entirely new kids, knowing now what it meant to regret how much time you didn't devote to your children. Another chance. Another chance at life. Another chance at youth. A way to obliterate regret. And here was Seth, who would fuck every single person in every single orifice and only once he got tired of it (if he ever did) would he find someone young and take *her* life away by finally having children.

I was never wild. I never stayed out late or got way too extremely drunk more than five or six times in my whole life. I didn't sleep around. I had such conservative desires. I liked going to the movies late at night—all the movies, even the bad ones, even the ones I'd seen. I liked eating too much. I liked smoking pot and cigarettes alone in my apartment. That was maybe the worst insult of adulthood, that even your silly, non-life-threatening, nonbase desires got swallowed up by routine and maturity and edged out of your life for good. I got to Penn Station and I walked past it, till I found myself downtown at the Angelika, sending a text to my babysitter that I'd be home very late.

That night, Toby took the children to synagogue like he'd done every Friday night before the separation. The problem with Rachel taking any Friday nights was that she never took them to synagogue, and so it began to creep into their heads that maybe Friday night services and dinner and family time were optional, a whim of Toby's that was subject to debate. They had never liked synagogue (no one does), but they especially didn't like it after camp, where they had to change clothes and go stand with their father under and astride his tallis while he listened and prayed, more out of muscle memory than anything else but still. Hannah now sat reading a book, not in her lap but up against her face, belligerently. Solly just ran up and down the aisles with whatever other nine-year-old he could find.

When Toby brought Rachel to meet his parents for the first time, their plane landed in Los Angeles in the late afternoon and they arrived at Toby's house in Sherman Oaks right in time for Friday night dinner. Toby had grown up in a fairly traditional Jewish home, and Friday night, no matter what, everyone was home. Everyone gathered. Everyone sat. His exhausted sister sat down with her two children, her head wrapped in a scarf. His anemic brother-in-law stood and waited for silence while he blessed the wine and the challah that Toby no longer went near. ("Just have some challah," his mother said. "Everyone has *some*." But Toby wouldn't, in perpetual punishment to her for how often she told him to not eat the challah when he was a chubby kid.) Toby's aunt and uncle had come, along with the synagogue's cantor and his wife. Rachel sat in awe of it: The harmony with which they passed chicken to each other, the banter at each other's expense, the review of the week. How they all gathered, how they sat down, how there was a basic rhythm and ease to it. They had all been gathering like this for so long that they knew how to do it; it was, Rachel later said, almost arrogant the way they all flaunted their comfort and ease.

"They just knew how to sit there and *be*," she said. "Like it was their birthright to be there."

"But why does that annoy you?" Toby asked.

She couldn't explain it. Only later would he see that when something created annoyance in her as a result of envy, that was how she knew she wanted it. Rachel had grown up barely aware of her religion in a house where her parents were divorced and her father had fled before she could form a cohesive memory of him, and then her mother died when she was three. She was raised by her mother's mother, who treated her like a houseguest and encouraged her independence. Rachel's grandmother had no tradition or ceremony in her, just a combination of pity and annoyance that she was stuck with her daughter's orphan in something that resembled a Dickens novel.

"So this happens every *week*?" she asked Toby.

"Without fail," he said.

"What if you were away?"

"Where would we be?"

"What if your father was at work? What if he had a patient emergency?"

"He'd let someone else take care of it."

Rachel could barely get her head around this. "I want to do this."

"Me, too," he answered. They had been dating for eight months by then. He proposed to her formally four months later, but he always felt like on that night, she had proposed to him first.

When they first married, Rachel made sure that whenever she got home from work on Fridays, sometimes earlier and sometimes later, they would do the thing Toby had grown up doing: lighting the candles, blessing the wine and challah. By the time the kids were born, though, she was already on what she called her "trajectory," and Fridays became the nights that Toby played a game of chicken with Rachel. She'd miraculously become available when the Rothbergs or the Leffers or the Hertzes invited them over for a Friday night dinner. But otherwise, she'd call and say that she "needed" to stay at work because she "needed" to get things done, knowing (she had to know) that she was being outright dishonest in her use of this word—that it was actually her resistance to spending time with her children and to some notion of a traditional role as a mother that made her *want* to work that much. Rachel knew how to work. She liked working. It made sense to her. It bent to her will and her sense of logic. Motherhood was too hard. The kids were not deferential to her like her employees. They didn't brook her temper with the desperation and co-dependence that, say, Simone, her assistant, did. That was the big difference between them, Rachel. He didn't see their children as a burden, Rachel. He didn't see them as endless pits of need, Rachel. He *liked* them, Rachel.

In June, the first Friday night that Rachel had them alone, he'd called her at work to ask if they shouldn't maybe all have dinner together, just to show the kids how much of a family they still were. She'd told him that she'd had to get Mona, their nanny, to stay with them because her client, the playwright Alejandra Lopez, had some kind of negotiation problem and she had planned an emergency dinner to make sure she was happy. "Please," she'd said. "Before you persecute me for working again, I am trying to manage. I have more expenses than ever. Do you know how much mediation cost me?" Unspoken: You idiot. Can't you read? We're not a family anymore. What do you think all this paperwork is about if not a formal dismantling of our family?

Outside the synagogue that night it had begun to rain. Toby

didn't have an umbrella, which was fine because the rain wasn't so bad and certainly it wouldn't kill him, but then some dipshit with a golf umbrella that took up the sidewalk because what would happen if even a drop of rain got onto his asshole Tom Ford suit nearly knocked him into the street.

"Can I go to sleepaway camp the whole summer next year?" Hannah asked.

"Sure."

Solly was silent. He didn't like talking about sleepaway camp. Rachel had spent much of the early spring lobbying hard for him to go for the month, "like all your friends, Solly," but he kept saying that he enjoyed being with his parents—"You're my friends, too"— which made Toby want to weep.

"Next year," Solly said, "I want to come back to the Y but I also want to go to golf camp."

"We'll make it happen," Toby said, though he then wondered if he was raising a golf douche. His mother had always told him to look at his neighbors and ask himself if he wanted his children to turn out like them, because they would. Neighbors, she'd said, were a far more powerful force than parents. Neighbors were how you voted for a child's future. But Toby hadn't taken that seriously, because how could his children be like his neighbors when his neighbors, who were all WASPs of sparkling genetics and crystalline breeding, were wholly unfamiliar, and his children still spoke and sang in the echo of his voice?

They returned home and had dinner—Toby had ordered soup and chicken from the deli, which he hated doing; he knew how much takeout they had with their mother. They ate, and Toby listened to Solly's report of the day, and how many kids were not returning to day camp after next week but were leaving for sleepaway. Then he let them leave the table and flee to their rooms to do whatever they wanted to until Mona arrived. He cleaned up the dinner and took a shower and began to prepare his body and mind for this woman whose crotch he was now very familiar with. He sat on his bed, a towel around his waist, searching his phone to make sure he knew what her actual face would look like from her Hr avatar, so that he could return her, briefly, to personhood.

At first, he told the kids he was on "appointments" when he had a date that was coinciding with their night with him. But Hannah began asking questions about what kind of appointments kept happening on Saturday nights, and why he had to change his clothes for them.

"Are you going to get married again?"

"I don't think so," he said. "Once might have been enough for me."

He always told Solly and her the same thing: "I go on playdates sometimes, just like you do. I will tell you when there is someone you should know. That person will be someone you like. I am lonely and I am making new friends, and not all of them will be my girl-friends, but some may be girls who are friends."

"Your mom will eventually have playdates, too," he told them.

"Will they be with doctors?" Solly asked.

"No, they'll be with people who are different from me. They'll be with a man named Brad who has a Porsche and wears boat shoes and really wants to come to your soccer game." The kids laughed. "Now: Who am I going to date?"

And they responded in unison, as he'd trained them to over the course of the many times this question came up: "Someone we will like!"

"And who will Mom date?" he asked.

Again, in unison: "A man named Brad who has a Porsche and wears boat shoes and really wants to come to my soccer game." Solly could never finish that last part because he was always laugh-ing too hard by then. It even got a smile out of Hannah.

"You'll like him, too, when it happens," Toby said, though he didn't think that was true. If he was honest, he didn't even know that Rachel would ever date again, so disgusted was she by the con-fines of marriage, so ruined had she been by the compromises of another person trying to have an equal say or even just an opinion in her life.

Toby's usual dating outfit was a pair of gray twill flat-front pants and a tailored light blue button-down shirt. He was still wearing the clothing Rachel had insisted on dressing him in, materials finer than you could find at the Banana Republic he liked on Third Avenue. She liked for him to look like a rich person. ("You *are* a rich person," I'd say. "Yeah, but not for long," he'd say. I meant that he was richer than most people on this earth; he meant that he made $285,000 annually, and that was on the extremely low end for the neighborhood.) But he noticed that his shirts were starting to fray. It was time for new ones, but he kept punting the decision. How do you go back to Banana Republic now, after all that time spent being measured for a shirt by the Italian tailor on Sixty-fifth Street who made clothing just for you? He could afford it, that was the truth; maybe he'd continue to do it, but now it was a choice. If he wanted to take the kids on vacation for winter break, if he wanted to think about buying an apartment eventually. There were decisions to make. "I left a lot of money on the table," he liked to say to people who knew the situation, to show that peace was more important to him than money.

He was set to meet Tess at Dorrian's, a bar on Second Avenue he never went to and only thought of as the hangout for prep school kids in the eighties before one of them murdered another one of them. Dorrian's was Tess's idea. Something felt distinctly noir about this, a woman in a wrap dress and mega-cleavage at a bar, dyed blond hair in a twist, him walking in to find her there already with a drink—a martini with *six* olives—tonguing the cocktail straw, which was a new choice for a martini but he tried not to judge.

The moment stretched out for what seemed like a month as he waited to see if she found him acceptable. There was nothing glaring about him that would make a woman walk out on him; his only clear abnormality was his height ("and your rage," Rachel would say). He watched her eyes to see her immediate reaction to realizing just how short five-five actually is. Could he see a glimpse of surprise in her eyes? Concern? Revulsion? He couldn't, and he was relieved. He was getting good at knowing if this was a nonstarter—the way eyes lost brightness when they were reflecting disappointment; a politeness that was trying to clean up the disappointment; the same wall I put up that first night we met when I realized I couldn't bear how short he was. He didn't like to waste anyone's time, least of all his own, least of all his babysitter money.

He ordered a Scotch and she told him her story. She had three kids, they were at Dwight, her husband was a banker who, three years ago, went on a life-coaching survival skills weekend. She had sent him on the weekend for his birthday for $10,000. It was led by a renowned life coach/healer who had recently graduated to being a shaman and who could maybe help him figure out why he was so depressed all the time. He had been talking about being on his private jet and wanting to jump out of it. He talked about wanting to make things with his hands, like bread and birdhouses. "Good, good," Tess said. "Go off and come back to me whole and happy again." Well, he went off for the weekend and he came home and he had warmth in his eyes again. He was smiling and talkative. She asked what he'd learned about himself over the weekend, and he'd explained to her that he'd been feeling suffocated by their life recently, and that he wanted to engage in some threesomes to make him feel less encumbered. She considered this request with a straight face, like maybe you sometimes do what your marriage asks of you, even if you didn't expect it. That was the worst part of this story, she said. That she was about to say yes to it. But then the husband said, "But not with you."

"What do you mean?" she'd asked.

"I mean, I realize I want the sexual freedom that comes with multiple partners," he'd said. "I want to explore my creative expression with other women. I think a lot of what I'm going through comes from having been so sexually repressed in my youth." This was news to her. By her count, he was the opposite of sexually repressed. He wanted it five times a week at the minimum, and sometimes he wanted it kind of weird, and she had always complied. Maybe that was the problem? Maybe she should have made him want it more?

"The life coach told you this was a good idea?" Ten thousand dollars.

"She helped me realize it, yes."

"That threesomes would make you feel better?"

"Yes. It was a no-judgment zone."

She thought this was a phase at first, but he brought it up every fucking night and eventually she had to deal with the fact that her husband was asking not just to sleep with another woman, but to sleep with *two* other women, any woman but her, basically, and could she please occupy herself while he's doing it. She finally asked for a divorce, her last particle of dignity rising up somehow, but her prenup was a prison; she only got something if he suggested the divorce, and he didn't—no, he contested it! Can you imagine? He didn't want to cheat on her, he'd said. He wanted to *expand* the marriage, was the word he used. "Yeah, to include everyone but me," she'd said. She just couldn't, she'd said. Her barely-hanging-on sense of self couldn't allow her. He said it must mean that she didn't love him that much. Now she looked at Toby. "You couldn't possibly understand what it's like to be owned by someone." Toby took a long swallow of his Scotch.

He watched her as she spoke. She used an aggressive concealer to cover up some periorbital shade beneath her eyes she wasn't happy with, but she was tan, and the concealer was maybe purchased in a winter month; it had the effect of making her look as though she'd been on a tanning bed with large sunglasses. She had long black nails that ended in an actual point, like a spade. Her hands had large spots on them. He was pretty sure she was not forty-one.

She moved the tiny straw around in her martini, looking down and then looking up at him while her head was still angled down. She was being flirtatious, and it occurred to him for the millionth time, but the first time on this date, that it was strange that they were making introductory talk when he had already seen her crotch. It was not that he was advocating for an immediate rush to bed. It was just that he thought it would make more sense, now that he'd seen her in her see-through underwear, to start in the middle somehow. Though maybe this—the stories and the confessions and the could you believe what he did to me—*was* the middle.

Tess and her husband had gone to couples therapy. "Of course I was sure that when he heard himself talk about this, he'd realize how crazy he sounded. You would cause this much of a crisis in an eighteen-year marriage because of what? Because you wanted a threesome? With *other* people? I said to the therapist, 'You think that's *normal*? You think a man should just say he wants to cheat on his wife with not one woman, but with two other women? That his wife should be onboard with this?' But who was paying the therapist? He was. And the therapist knew it."

She kept the cocktail straw as the bartender took her glass away, and ordered a second drink. She stuck the straw into the second glass and picked the toothpick out of it, and tried to scrape the olives along the side of the glass. They wouldn't yield, so she had to take her knife-nails to them, using them to spear the olives and pull them off.

Toby nodded in sympathy. "People sometimes change."

Tess looked up. "No, he didn't really change. He was always into threesomes. That's how we met."

"You met having a threesome with him?"

"Yes. Graduate school. Late night. Me and my roommate. We all went out to breakfast the next morning. It was totally civilized. He had this other girlfriend at the time, and she came to the breakfast, too. My roommate and I could not get over that. But then he called me and told me he broke up with his girlfriend and wanted to see me again." Tess shrugged and went back to her straw. "Who could have predicted this?"

Was this how dating always was? Were there always this many stories? He didn't remember the telling of stories, but maybe that was because back when he was young, nobody had stories yet; everything interesting was happening right then, not in the past. The stories he heard from divorced women were all the same—not the details, but the themes: This thing I thought was just a whim was actually an important part of my spouse's identity, and still I'm surprised. This thing they had always been doing they kept doing and still I'm surprised. Here is how innocent I was and here is how cruel my spouse was.

He wondered if he sounded like this from his parallax view. He wondered if there was a version of this story in which he was the villain. He wondered if Rachel was sitting in some ashram somewhere telling anyone who would listen what a victim she was. A victim. Yes, of a husband who put his own career aside and raised the children and gave them consistency—the children they'd both wanted! A husband who rooted for her at her every milestone of success. What could she possibly say about him? That he was "unambitious"? He was as ambitious as he was allowed to be. There isn't room in one marriage for two people who are hogging all the oxygen. One of them has to answer the phone when the school calls. One of them has to know where the vaccine record is. One of them has to do the fucking dishes. It was entirely possible that the only version of a story like this you ever heard was from the aggrieved party, the one who made the sacrifices and thought that the sacrifice gave you one up on your spouse, but it didn't. It only made the spouse feel more entitled to take. Trust me, Tess's husband was somewhere right now, one woman sitting on his face while another sucked him off, and he was certainly not talking about the ways Tess let him down.

"So," she said. "What happened to you?"

Later, at her apartment, when she was sitting atop his penis, bouncing up and down, her hands in her own hair like she was in a shampoo commercial, her head rolling around in what had to be exaggerated ecstasy—the sex was fine, but come on—he had the feeling that came up a full eighty percent of the time he'd been having sex with a new woman these days, which was that it didn't quite matter to her that he was there. He was just a warm body. To imagine that the sex act was dependent on him was to miss what was going on here. The point was that the parade of women interested in intercourse with him was steady and strong. He was enjoying this. Did he even need to say that? *He was enjoying this.*

Here is a mostly complete inventory of the women that Toby had encountered romantically, both sexually and otherwise, since he first moved out of his marital home and into the Ninety-fourth Street apartment where he sat on a beanbag chair he'd bought for Solly and first understood his phone's new role in his life.

His first date was with a divorced mother of three from Long Island, a setup that came from his cousin Cherry in Queens. Laurette was pretty and nice, nodding rhythmically and frowning as he explained who he was and what he did and what his life was like. After dinner he walked her through a park to her car and he got every signal in the world that it would be okay to kiss her: She was standing close, she was waiting, she wasn't busying herself with keys or anything. And so he kissed her and for the first time since 1998, not even this century, not even this millennium, he put his lips on another woman and she kissed him back.

Kissing another mouth, wow. He and Rachel had stopped kissing long ago. Even in the best of their times, Rachel was all business when it came to sex; she didn't have time for extras. She barely had time for foreplay. This was different, and not just because it wasn't sex. It was the strange feeling of taking ice skates off after wearing them for hours and walking on plain ground—you know how to do it but it's different. Just wow. He and Laurette made out for five gooey minutes, Toby devouring her face, unaware of its corners and limits. Afterward, Toby skipped back to the train. Holy moly, he thought. You could opt out for fifteen years, and you could be beaten down to within an inch of personhood, but this was waiting on the other end, like a reward for all you had withstood.

He and Laurette went on another date, and then another. On the third date, when dessert arrived, she leaned across the table at the steakhouse they were eating in and said, "You know, I'm looking to get married again, and you just got out. We are in very different places." He wasn't heartbroken, just surprised. He was surprised by the totally new-to-him notion that relationships didn't all have to go anywhere; they didn't even have to be relationships. And here a revelation came to him, that he was under no real moral obligation to marry a woman he kissed. He felt like he might combust from the freedom he felt. All this new opportunity! There weren't enough hours in the day!

The first person he met on the app was Lisa, a thirty-six-year-old public school teacher in Harlem who led with how proud she was of her work—"Yes, it's important, of course," he kept saying—and defensive about the fact that she had never been married, which he hadn't asked about. They had had dinner at an Italian place in the Village, because in the beginning it felt strange and disrespectful to be seen with another woman in his neighborhood, where he regularly bumped into his and Rachel's friends and other parents from the school, and oh lord, Rachel and the children, too. Lisa asked Toby about his life, and he told her the truth, that he was confounded by his new situation, about how to manage all this with the kids, and she got angry and said, "I get it. You were married." Toby went home after dinner without ordering dessert and masturbated.

Keisha was a twenty-seven-year-old occupational therapist who strutted into the Murray Hill bar where they were meeting, ordered two Kamikazes, despite him saying, "Actually, no, I'm not really into—" and so drank both herself, then yelped a "Whoo!" and later, after four more drinks, wrapped her arm around his neck and a leg around his waist and told him to take her home. He couldn't. "Come on, what's wrong with *this*?" The *this,* she made clear, looking down, was her body on his, and he ached so badly for her but how could he? How could he take advantage of this young girl who was positively soaked in alcohol? He went home and masturbated, but he couldn't come.

Stacy was a thirty-eight-year-old dentist who wanted to make him dinner at her apartment. He said yes but then had to cancel because Rachel suddenly needed him to watch the kids. He texted a nice apology and went to pick up the kids and when next he saw his phone it was filled with eleven vicious texts back from Stacy, who apparently couldn't believe she'd let herself trust another one of these assholes. *You are human dirt,* she texted him. Then she texted him a picture of her body in the mirror, just the neck down, and she was wearing an apron and fishnets and fluffy slipper heels and nothing else, and he was kind of relieved because that felt like maybe too much pressure for a first meeting.

There was Haley, a PhD student, who put his hand on her upper leg and then, later, as they started to make out, she told him she liked some light pressure around her neck, maybe to make things cloudy. He declined and said he felt like maybe that was a violation of the Hippocratic oath, and she was either immediately embarrassed or immediately disgusted and sent him home, where he masturbated furiously in his self-loathing.

There was Constance, a personal shopper, who told him she'd always wanted to get fingered underneath a table in a restaurant. He declined and said he felt too nervous, like maybe he was a father and shouldn't risk a public indecency charge, but later, at home, regretted it and masturbated furiously in his self-loathing.

There was Shivonne, who cried from the minute they sat down. "It's my first date," she said. And Toby sat and held her hand and said he was only a few in himself and he felt as scared and ambivalent as she did. "Why don't we not drink tonight?" he asked her, and they ordered iced teas and ate pasta. He went home and felt too fat to masturbate but did it anyway.

There was Robyn, who was twenty-eight, and the last person in her twenties he went out with before sealing up the age-range matter on his search criteria. She was a nursing student at Columbia who liked older guys. They went for a drink in the Village and then to hear live jazz. ("Why live jazz?" Seth asked. "Because that's what you do," Toby said. "Nobody does that," Seth said. "People who say they like jazz are lying.") At the club, Toby felt like he was everyone's father, and the only older guys in the club were people who had a whiff of desperation. He had to keep reminding himself that he was not old enough to be the father of anyone here. Maybe technically, but not truly. Meaning something crazy and awful would have had to have happened in his life for him to have fathered a child that young. Anyway. Robyn didn't understand why they were there. She didn't understand the two-partness to the date: Why would you arrange a second part of a date? Didn't they know where this ended up? She started kissing him then, her hand immediately on his knee, then higher, and he hated his penis for jumping toward her hand, but it did. Before she could notice how aroused he was, he made an excuse, saying he wasn't feeling well, and went home and watched *Serpico* until he fell asleep, trying to imagine a universe in which he felt like jerking off.

There was Jenny, who was a lawyer. While he gelled his hair before heading out, he had made a solemn vow to heed Seth's advice and this time allow the date to go where she leads it. "Assume you will get the best and you will get the best," Seth told him. Then dinner was over, and he asked if he could walk her home, and two blocks in she took his hand and three blocks in she started caressing his wrist and by the time they made it to her elevator she was giving him long, tonguey kisses. He went inside and she pulled him into the bedroom and she made car-motor noises—vroom, vroom—during foreplay and meow noises when they fucked. His life had begun.

There was Sara from Oregon who wanted to be a painter and had a death grip when she gave hand jobs. There was Bette, who had once been in a porno, or maybe just a homemade video that an ex-boyfriend then distributed, and who said, "That's what she said" four times over the course of two Cape Cods. There was Emily, who was done with the ratfuck of dating women. There was another Rachel, and he couldn't say her name. There was Larissa, who had grown up in a cult that operated out of an apartment building in a Queens project and told him that she was totally open to anal, and he had to figure out a way to say that he was not accustomed to that item being on the sexual menu and he didn't have an automatic want to put it in there and could he please think about it? (He pretended the babysitter called and went home early.) There was Sharon, who had been raised ultra-Orthodox. There was Barbara, who he realized ten minutes into a story she was telling was actually related to him through her father's great-uncle. There was Samantha, who was tall and more than a little chubby but leaned into it, with a round butt and tight jeans and red lips. Her resting face communicated lust via half-lidded eyes and a slightly parted mouth. He brought her to her door after they ate chicken wings at the forties-themed bar she'd chosen, and she yanked him inward, and in the dark she took him—yes, it was she who took him—and he didn't have to make decisions. No, he only had to not say no, and so he didn't.

There were women who had no pubic hair but did have armpit hair. There were women who said unspeakably filthy things right to his face. There were women who cried after sex. There were women who wanted to be pinched or hit or spanked or slapped, *which made him very uncomfortable.* There were women who wanted him on the top, on the bottom, on all fours. They wanted him to go faster and slower with his mouth on their crotches. They wanted to know if *he* wanted to be spanked. ("No, thank you," he said.) They wanted to know if he was gonna come hard. ("I'm coming! I'm coming!" he yelled.) They wanted him to come to Mommy. They wanted to call him Daddy. Each of these nights, he fell further in love.

H e told this all to Seth the first time they got together after all these years. He'd called him the way he'd called me, to tell him he was getting divorced. Seth said he was with his girlfriend but that she had dinner plans with her friends and could Toby meet for a drink after five-thirty. At a sports bar near Toby's apartment, Toby told him the sad story of his marriage, but Seth didn't have any questions. Seth didn't give him a hard time. There was no penance to be made. Seth was just excited to see his friend again.

"Dude, the world is your *oyster* now," Seth said. "Lick it up." It's crazy that the friends you're fondest of from your youth sometimes resemble people you would cross the street to avoid as an adult. An idea came to Seth. "Go back to your apartment and put on shorts."

"Why?"

"Yoga."

"It's Saturday night."

"It's actually late afternoon. Just do it, Tobe."

"I just had a drink."

"Trust me, dude. I go to a place right near my apartment owned by a guy who trained under Bikram and started a splinter group that nearly brought the political system of India to its knees." When Seth was single, he said, this was where the majority of his dating life came from. You could be generous and like Seth and still think of what he called his "dating life" as a series of auditions, mostly successful, for sex partners. He explained to Toby that presence in a yoga class, no matter your ability, was a shortcut to showing a woman how evolved you were, how you were strong, how you were not set on maintaining the patriarchy that she so loathed and feared.

"Does Vanessa go to yoga with you?"

Seth shooed this away. "Yoga isn't for us. It's for me." Meaning he still liked to go to yoga and see if there were better prospects.

But Seth wasn't just a lecher. And he wasn't stupid. He had stayed out in the world long after all his friends got married for a reason. "Marriage is for young people who don't have a concept of time," he'd told Toby. "It's for people whose lives will be made measurably better by it." He told Toby that he was confused by the guys at work and their complaints: their haranguing wives, their underachieving kids, their vacations that were now just miserable trips, their looks dwindling and their schedules unrecognizable and their paunches becoming more and more pronounced. Seth told Toby how he'd go to their homes for Thanksgiving or setups or whatever, and he'd see their wedding photos on the dining room wall and wonder if it was tragic or fortunate that these guys thought that this was what they still looked like, that this was what they still felt like, that this was who they still were.

"This is the goal?" he asked Toby. "How could all these guys look at the history of the world and want this for themselves?"

Toby didn't know how to answer it. He didn't regret getting married. He didn't even regret marrying Rachel. His children were perfect. He'd been happy for a period. At least he thought he remembered being happy for a period. There may have actually been a time when he looked at the Seths of the world with pity for the happiness that he had that they didn't even seem to know to want.

Seth had been engaged once, in his early twenties. He'd asked a girl he'd met in college named Nicole to marry him about four months before Toby asked Rachel the same question, and she'd said yes, and then one day he'd been asked to dinner with Nicole's parents. He'd shown up, and Nicole hadn't come, and the father had said that he hadn't invited her, that they had something to talk over with Seth. They told Seth they would buy Nicole and him the house of their choice, but it had to be on Long Island, and they'd have to attend the same synagogue as the parents and their children would have to go to an Orthodox day school, which they assumed would be fine, right, because Seth had. They were also hoping Seth would go into the family business, which was real estate, and Seth would be set for life if he acquiesced to these simple requests. Who could not want these things?

Well, once Seth gathered his wits about him, meaning once he understood he had been invited to an ambush, he waited for the guy to finish talking, stared at him for a full ten seconds, then stood and walked out. He took a cab directly to Nicole's apartment, walked right past her when she opened the door, and asked for his ring back. Toby never understood this. At the time, in their young twenties, the whole dream was to end up on Long Island with your mortgage paid and a good private school for your kids and a stable job. "Yes," Seth had said. "Just let it be *my* idea."

But he never grew to want it; it never became his idea. Who really knew why Seth was perennially, diagnostically, terminally afraid to marry? It was just because his parents seemed miserable. Or because he hated organized religion but was too fearful and ambivalent to decide to marry someone who would not allow him to change his level of observance once he got old and sentimental. Or because he didn't want to have to answer to anyone when he got home at night and put on a headset to pretend he was a fighter pilot conscripted to kill aliens in a game box he kept in a closet when friends came over not because he was ashamed of it but because he couldn't concentrate on anything else when it was in the room. Or because it was still so fun to see where a night out with his Wall Street friends could take him. Or because he saw the looks on those very friends' faces the next morning—the shame, the bereavement— because those guys had definitely gotten hand jobs from women who weren't their wives and why should you ever feel guilty about a hand job? Or because his mother had whispered into his ear when he was very young that he was perfect and there would never be a woman good enough for him. Or because everyone expected him to get married, and if he did this one big expected thing his life would sink into all the other expected things, the very things that

Nicole's father had tried to fast-forward him into. Or because it was so rare to be able to fuck two women at once when you were married, and Seth could see giving up a lot of his vices in middle age but not that one. Or because he had not yet met a woman who was down with him watching porn on Sunday mornings the way other men watched football. Or because there was a point at which sending horny text messages to a woman became less dangerous and/or arousing the minute those text messages were also peppered with the logistical questions of life: *When will you be home? Did you pick up milk?* Or because he had found too often that a woman who was willing to let you lick her anus and vice versa when you were at the beginning of a relationship so quickly became someone who acted like she'd never even considered the idea once you moved in together. Or because sometimes, maybe every six months or so, he liked to order a pizza from Angelo's all for himself and eat it and afterward spend the entire night doing sit-ups and workout videos on YouTube that had the word SHRED in them, and also some eighties aerobics videos. Or because his biggest fear was to be known and rejected, and the only way he could face the rejection that comes along with being human was to never let himself be known—that way, what was rejected wasn't him at all, but a projection of him.

Toby joined him at yoga that night. He didn't meet any women—they were young and didn't make eye contact with him and their KALE and YOUR WORKOUT IS MY WARMUP tank tops reminded him too much of Rachel. They weren't interested in him anyway. (Maybe he didn't emit the pheromones that Seth did, or his theory that a woman needed to be prepared for his height via a dating app profile was correct, or his theory that the over-forty version of Seth was a star only in his own estimation was correct, or his theory that women weren't as simple as Seth made them out to be was correct.) But Toby kept returning to class after that day, because it made him feel good to move and not go anywhere, to rely on nothing but his own body weight for resistance, to learn that the ground beneath his feet was firmer than he had presumed. What he liked about yoga was that sometimes they spent a full minute on something called Mountain Pose, which was just standing. An entire pose just for standing! Yes, yoga really seemed to get his situation.

"How high is your closing rate?" Seth said that night, almost a month into Toby's new dating life.

"I think I'm at like sixty percent? Thirty percent? It's hard to know. I feel like in a month I have already become someone who considers every woman from eighteen to sixty-two a potential sex partner, so it's a failing if I take the kids to the doctor and the receptionist doesn't want to have sex with me."

"You should be at a hundred percent, dude. You should *only* be closing. You are prime time now. You are golden."

"It's not as easy as all that."

"You're too picky."

"Picky?" Toby asked. "I'd put my penis into a he-donkey right now is how picky I am."

"Then what's going on?"

"I'm coming out of a fifteen-year relationship with a woman who wouldn't let me pee standing up. I have some healing to do."

Seth shook his head, and then leaned across the table and put his hands on Toby's forearms and shook them so that Toby's whole body convulsed. He said, "I really missed you, man."

Rachel still wanted to fuck was the thing. This was Toby's secret. He'd had sex with nine women in the last month and a half, not including Rachel, which was a full six more than he previously had had sex with in his life. And yet on certain nights of the week, Rachel would text him after ten, wondering what he was doing, and this was his signal to say "Nothing," and for her to ask if maybe he wanted to stop by, and for him to find that any hatred and resolve he had against her melted away instantly and made room for enough self-loathing and neediness for him to grab his keys and walk over. Their sex was silent now, which it hadn't always been. There were sounds of friction and tossing, but there were no sighs anymore, nor any moans. There were certainly no words. The sex existed outside any interpersonal tension, the way it always had. They got the job done. He knew what she wanted—a little nipple action as she did some kind of deep intentional meditative thing with her breath, then flipped over so that she was flat on her stomach and he lay on top of her.

Throughout the years, he'd heard jokes and complaints from some of the other married doctors at the hospital about how little sex they were having. Allen Keller, one of the attendings, just thirty-six, told him that he and his wife had last had sex four months before. Poor Allen kept waiting for his wife to notice, but it didn't seem to bother her. When he brought it up, she said she was tired at night and why didn't he think he should accommodate her schedule instead of the other way around. "'Uh, because you don't *work*?'" Allen Keller said. His wife told him that if she had sex too close to bedtime it would make her anxious and keep her up all night. "What the fuck is that?" Allen asked Toby. "That's not a real thing, is it?"

Toby allowed himself a brief moment of smugness when he heard stories like this. Even during their worst times, he and Rachel fucked all the time, three times a week *at the very least*. It allowed him to think, Hey, maybe we're normal. Maybe we're better than normal. Three times a week! By this metric their relationship was good. By this metric, their relationship was *aspirational*. If you looked at it in that light, well, who doesn't have some tension in their lives from time to time? Of course, people who are trying to be good parents and also good at their jobs fight. Maybe even every day. Maybe even more than once a day. Maybe even just about every time they were together, and viciously and cruelly. Right?

During their marriage, Rachel was demanding about sex in a way that wasn't always kind or relenting. If he wasn't in the mood, it would move her to rage. He had been too tired the night they got

home from their vacation to Mexico, and she accused him of having an affair. He'd been too turned off by her the first time he saw
her yell at a subordinate at a company Christmas thing where she
got drunk and she told Toby he was a chickenshit. *He'd* been too
drunk after the annual hospital gala and she laughed at him cruelly
and called him an old man. Once, she woke him up in the middle
of the night after she came home from some event, and began poking around in the blanket for his boxers like she was looking for
batteries in the junk drawer, and when she saw nothing was going
on down there, she said, "I guess this is it, then." He had no idea
what she meant. She began crying and screaming at him, telling
him how miserable she was. "Whatever you're doing now, it's not
helping," Toby pleaded. "It's making it worse." He realized she
was drunk, and eventually was able to pat her down to sleep the
way he was able to get their kids to bed when they were hysterical
in the middle of the night. The next day, she didn't say a word about
it. No apology. Nothing.

The last night Toby lived at home, Solly cried himself to sleep,
wondering what would happen if he was in his apartment alone
and had a heart attack or a stroke and nobody was there to help
him. Toby reassured him, and only when Solly was finally asleep
was Toby left to realize that now that he'd finally gotten what he
wanted, he was going to have to actually do it: He was going to
have to be alone. He didn't want to talk about it. He didn't want to
think of how much he liked their sheets and their bed and their
apartment and being around the kids and making them breakfast
every morning. He didn't want to think about how he was not repulsed by her yet and wished he were. And so he leaned over and
reached for her, thinking that of course this would be the last time.

But it wasn't. It never stopped. He'd drop off the kids late and
she would get angry that they were late but once the kids were in
bed she'd ask if he wanted to see something in the bedroom, and in
the dark, she would shut the door and apply herself to him and
they would have their soundless, scrappy sex that felt both familiar

and strange and forbidden and wonderful. These nights were detrimental to his healing. On those nights, after they were done, they would lie side by side, not touching, staring at the ceiling. He would make a move to get up, and she would not react to the move, instead turning over and closing her eyes. He would dress and walk to the door. On those nights Rachel stayed in bed, pretending she had fallen asleep.

On Saturday morning, Hannah and Solly ate pancakes he made while they watched a cartoon in the living room about a banana and a leek that were friends.

He texted Rachel:

What time will you be picking them up tomorrow? I have plans.

He didn't have plans. He waited for an answer. Nothing. He felt the beginnings of an explosion build in him, and he hoped she wouldn't call just then and hear his voice. She loved when he sounded angry, because it allowed her to sound peaceful and say with pity, "Toby, Toby, you are so angry. When did you get this angry?"

But he wasn't angry. "I'm not angry," he would say. "I'm frustrated." He was just *frustrated*. She had screwed him yet again. He wasn't diabolical like she was. He didn't have the energy for an endurance race of wills. Her capacity for fighting was endless. She was a fucking talent agent. She went into the fighting arts as a *career*. She could do the back-and-forth of one of those conversations forever. Just because he kept expressing surprise that she kept screwing him didn't mean he was angry. It meant he was an idiot. Toby stared at his phone for another minute. Nothing. He walked into the living room and his children didn't look up. "This is not what we're doing all day," Toby announced, and turned off the TV. They left the building and went to the bagel place and then headed west to the park. Solly rolled along on his scooter. Hannah hadn't wanted to take hers because everything was too embarrassing.

"What if I hold it for you until we get to the park?"

"Let it go, Dad," Hannah said. If only she knew how her dismissals cut him. "Can we get my phone today at least?" She'd been promised a phone for her twelfth birthday, but her birthday wasn't for three weeks.

"No," Toby said for the fourth time that week. "You get to be my baby for another three weeks. I am taking up the option on that." Hannah rolled her eyes.

"Should we go to the movies?" he asked.

But Hannah didn't answer. He looked over at her but she had stopped cold and turned toward a building.

"What's going on?" Toby asked. He called to Solly. "Solly, hold up."

"Nothing," she whispered. "Don't say anything. Don't do anything."

He saw a boy around Hannah's age coming down the street dribbling a basketball. He looked over at Hannah to tell her that he thought she knew this kid, but she had already seen him and her face was flushed. He had the white-toothed glow of an athlete and a rich kid. He said to Toby's daughter, "Hey, Hannah."

Hannah smiled and said, "Hey."

And the boy dribbled on.

"Who was that?" Toby asked.

Hannah turned to him, angry. Her eyes were wet. "Why can't we take cabs like regular people?"

"What is it? What happened?"

"I just don't know why we have to do this walking to the park all the time like we're babies. I don't *want* to go to the park. I want to go home."

"What is the matter with you? We always go to the park."

She sounded a great big aspirated grunt of frustration and continued walking ahead of them, her arms stiff and fisted and her legs marching. Toby jogged and caught up with Solly, who had stayed obediently until Toby got to him. "Why's she so angry?" Solly asked as he remounted his scooter.

"I don't know, kid." More and more, Toby never knew.

Hannah was invited to a sleepover that night. Sleepovers, as far as Toby could tell, consisted of the girls in her class getting together and forming alliances and lobbing microaggressions at each other in an all-night cold war, and they did this voluntarily. It had begun when Hannah was in fourth grade, or maybe before that, wherein the alpha girls set to work on a reliable and unyielding establishment of a food chain system—jockeying for position, submitting to a higher position. Licking your wounds when you learn you are not the absolute top; rejoicing to know you are not the absolute bottom. In November, there had been a sleepover at the Fleishmans' apartment. Rachel sat in bed on her laptop, ignoring the girls, but Toby sat at the small desk area in the hallway, paying bills and listening to what was going on in Hannah's bedroom. They were playing a game called Drather, as in, Who would you rather, this guy or that guy? The object of the rather was nebulous—rather what, Toby wanted to know. Was it marriage or dating or, oh God, was it sex? Was it sex already?

Lexi Leffer, the lion king of the group, went first. Little Beckett Hayes, whom Toby had known since she was four, named two TV stars. Lexi chose the obvious one, the star of a teen sitcom with the swoop of hair that fell over his eyes. Toby was disappointed but not surprised. He could have told you that Lexi Leffer's soul was made of plastic.

It was Hannah's turn next. He knew he should walk away and give her privacy, but he couldn't move. Lexi had to ask her. It was between two boys whose names weren't familiar to Toby. When Lexi said them, Beckett said, "Ooooooh!" and Hannah screeched, "That's impossible!"

"You have to answer, upon penalty of . . ."

"Of what?" Hannah asked.

"On penalty of . . ." She thought. ". . . having to call each boy and ask him how his day was."

"That's so evil!" Beckett whispered with apparent awe.

Hannah took a long time answering. Toby sat frozen at his hallway desk, inside this living nightmare, unable to discern what the stakes were, not knowing how to root for her. Hannah picked the second boy, and Lexi said, "Great. Pick my boyfriend, why don't you." There was a pause, and he could feel Hannah not knowing what she'd done wrong. Toby stood up and tried to think of a reason to interrupt them, but it would only make Hannah angry. He left and went to find Solly and watch TV with him. Lexi Leffer was a killer.

Toby walked the kids through the hot night over to Seventy-ninth and Park, where Cyndi and Todd Leffer lived. On the way, with Hannah still ignoring him, he listened to Solly make a case for watching *Indiana Jones and the Temple of Doom* again, and they passed a building where he had a clear memory of getting blown by a woman in a stairwell just three weeks ago.

The Leffers' doorman, who wore epaulets and never took off his coat, had been told that a group of girls with sleeping bags would be coming, and so he waved the Fleishmans across the marble lobby floor to the mirrored elevator bank. They took the brass elevator up to the twenty-ninth floor, which was the top floor. They were in the elevator long enough for Toby to break out in a light, panicked sweat over being in a small box that was probably mechanically compromised from age and use. Elevators had never bothered him before, but lately, his faith in systems was wobbly. Why had he put so much trust in elevators in the first place? Why did everyone? This entire vertical city functioned because of its elevator systems—ten million suckers in this city, not even thinking of the likelihood (and it felt likely) that one of the cables would snap or that they'd get stuck in the elevator for hours and run out of oxygen before anyone noticed. By the time they got to twenty-nine, Solly said, "Dad, you're hurting my shoulder."

The elevator opened up to the apartment's lobby—the *apartment* had its own *lobby*—and Todd was there to meet him in a polo shirt and mid-thigh shorts. He was probably five-ten. Yes, Todd, Toby thought, but when was the last time you were blown in a stairwell?

"How is the good doctor?" he said, putting his hand out and grabbing Toby's and pumping it so that his body moved like a tide he was fighting against.

"I'm doing okay." This was the kind of soft, pampered bro that Rachel wished he were. This was what Rachel would have preferred. It never even began to make sense to him.

Solly stood beside him, holding his hand, and Lexi Leffer came out of the kitchen with her mom, who was wearing capri pants and a tight, ribbed tank top that said ANGEL across it in script rhinestones.

"Toby," she said, all concern once again.

"Hey, Cyndi." The confusing thing about how much Rachel aspired to be like them was that Rachel also agreed with him that Cyndi was cheap-looking and that Todd was a jerk. Despite this, they represented all that she aspired to in school culture, and everything that Toby, and therefore she, wasn't and could never be because of Toby's embarrassing disability, which was that he was a successful doctor at a top-ranked New York hospital. She'd say "The Leffers go to Maine for Christmas" and "The Leffers have two cars, just in case" and "The Leffers make sure to do two international trips a year." Each December, the Leffers' Christmas card would arrive, a collage of scenes from their year and the parties that the Fleishmans hadn't been invited to, and it would send Rachel to bed in despair. "Why don't we have dress-up parties?" she would moan. Once, the Leffers had told them, at a dinner, that they had a German tutor, and that both they and the kids were learning German and that they were going to spend all of Christmas vacation next year in Germany, celebrating their new knowledge until they sounded like soldiers in the Third fucking Reich. Cyndi had dropped her voice down low and said, "You cannot compete with that kind of *immersion*," and Rachel had nodded emphatically and said, "So true, I never thought of it like that," like no one had ever said that practice was important for reinforcing information, as if the entire education and athletic supercomplexes weren't built on that notion.

"We were thinking of inviting you over next week to lunch at the club," Cyndi said. "But then Todd reminded me that you don't play golf."

"I play basketball."

Todd put his hands behind his head and did an elaborate and luxurious twist to the right, then the left. "Basketball really put my back out in high school. You a point guard?" Fuck you, Todd.

"Todd is so *stressed* by his job," Cyndi said, putting her gigantic, black-painted claws on his shoulders. "His back goes out because he works too hard. It's too much *pressure* for one person." She smiled at him. "Anyway, we'd love for you to come. We're still *your* friend, too, Toby."

"I appreciate it," he said, giving a little nod toward Solly that maybe now wasn't the time to talk about his new social status.

He and Solly stopped at the bookstore afterward to get a book called *4000 Facts About the Universe*. Solly walked back home reading it, letting Toby stop him when he got to street crossings. At a light, while Solly read about kinetic energy, Toby texted Rachel:

I dropped Hannah off at her sleepover. She has her last lesson with Nathan tomorrow. Don't let her be late. Will you pick her up from Leffers' or here?

Two hours later, he texted her again:

???

———

Had he not stayed up late trading pornographic texts with a voice-over actress who lived in Brooklyn, had those texts not led to him wondering what her special, monetizable voice sounded like, had that question not led to her calling him up and whispering into his ear for a full hour of the most erotic phone sex he'd ever imagined, he probably would not have been in such a bad mood when he picked up Hannah from the Leffers' the next morning.

It did not help that the shades the apartment had come with were cheap and translucent and seemed to telescope the light instead of shielding him from it, and therefore deprived him of at least two hours of extra weekend sleep. How much did you invest in a rental, though? You wanted to feel at home, but it really wasn't your home. And yet you'd only feel at home if you made it your home. He shouldn't be cheap with himself. His therapist, Carla, would say that buying new shades was practicing self-care. He would respond by telling her that actually being solvent was self-care, saving up for a better place was self-care, not wasting his time measuring and buying and returning when he inevitably fucked it up was self-care. She would look at him patiently because therapists got to decide what self-care was.

"I need to get new shades for the apartment," Toby said as they crossed Lexington Avenue.

"But I'm so tiiiiiiired," Hannah moaned. "Can't we just go hoooooome?"

He didn't want to fight. They might as well go home. The rabbinic student from the synagogue was coming over to give Hannah her final haftorah lesson before she left for the Hamptons with Rachel on Monday. Toby, realizing that Rachel would probably run late on her way back and create even more chaos, texted him to come to his apartment instead of Rachel's. When he arrived—twenty-three, awkward, studious—Hannah came out of her bedroom in a new outfit, smiling and with her hair brushed. Jesus, Toby thought.

Solly watched *The Wizard of Oz* in Toby's bedroom while Toby sneaked looks at his phone. The voiceover actress had sent him a text that was just two butterfly emojis and a picture of her shoulder, which itself had two tattoos of the exact butterfly emojis—not butterflies, but butterfly emojis. The tattoos sat astride a bright blue lacy bra strap. And we're off, he thought.

Tess had texted, too. She wanted to know when they were going out again, and sent a picture of herself that was confusing because it was taken at very close range. Some of those pictures that women sent him reminded him of the back page of the *Current Science* magazines he used to get in fifth grade, the ones that featured pictures of everyday items taken so close up that it was disorienting to the eye: a Band-Aid, a tomato, the half moon of a fingernail, all familiar but inscrutable for a few seconds until the obviousness of the object overwhelmed him with a strange kind of relief and the neural restoration of order kicked in. You couldn't discern anything recognizable in them—you needed real tools of inference to figure it out, like: That is lace and that is bulging and so it must be a bra and a breast, or that is shadow and fabric and so must be a butt crack and the outer edge of a thong. He softened the focus of his eyes at Tess's picture, which had bumps and satin and was therefore her areola. His head sank farther into his pillow.

Hannah poked her head into his room after her lesson. "I'm going to pack now," she said. "I don't have my bathing suit. It's at Mom's."

Where the fuck are you? he texted her.

Then: *How does it feel to never be where you say you're going to be?*

He wrote to her again as Sunday dinner came and went. *They don't have camp this week. You have them. You're taking them to the Hamptons tomorrow. You promised them.*

She often allowed the weekends when he had the kids to extend to Monday mornings, and who was he to ask her to keep to the schedule they'd agreed to? Just the father! Just the only other person in this arrangement! Sometimes she'd send a last-minute text from a business trip: *I'm trying to get some stuff done, mind taking them to school tomorrow? Thx.* Hell, when they were married, she'd sometimes stay an entire day or two on a business trip "just to finish things up." Usually she at least *asked* him, or let him know under the guise of pretending to ask.

But nothing.

Then again, she was at a yoga retreat. Maybe they confiscated phones there? Maybe the whole point was to not use a phone. He would love that luxury, too, you know. He would love a weekend without his phone. Or rather, he would love a weekend with only his phone and its dirty messages and pictures.

When Hannah and Solly went to bed, he messaged Mona and asked her to come the next day. She texted back that she thought she had the week off, that her son was visiting from Ecuador. He told her he really needed the help. She told him she had confirmed with Rachel months ago that she really wanted to take off to be with her son, whom she hadn't seen in three years. Toby said he was very sorry and he understood that, but he had some sick patients and would it be possible for her to come for a few hours? He would make it up to her. He told her that Rachel had disappeared again, and if there was one person who would understand what he meant by the soft and gross negligence that Rachel was capable of, it was Mona. Finally, Mona acquiesced and said she could come until three but not after that. He sent her a thousand emojis of thanks.

The next morning, he was making toast with cream cheese for the kids. Hannah came out of her room and closed the door heavily, which startled him and made him burn his finger.

"Fuck!" he yelled.

Solly yelled back, "Bad word!"

"Aren't we supposed to be with Mom?" she asked.

"You are." He ran his finger under cold water. "She's delayed."

"By what?" Hannah's voice was panicked. "We're supposed to go to the Hamptons. *Everyone is going to the Hamptons this week.*"

"I don't know what to tell you. Call her and tell her that."

"I would, but I don't have a phone."

The tests were conclusive: It was Wilson's disease.

"It's the liver's inability to process copper," Toby told David Cooper while his fellows stood behind him. "Her liver doesn't work, that's why it can't process it. Have you noticed a change in eye color?"

Toby lifted her eyelid and showed David. He stared at it. "No. What?"

"See that ring around her iris?" She'd had symptoms for a while, Toby said. "But they're symptoms that are easy to dismiss." Her clumsiness and her daffiness might have seemed like something wacky coming on in middle age, or like she was acting out, but she was concerned about it and went to the doctor. Her internist had missed the signs. Then she went to Las Vegas, where she drank a lot, which exacerbated the situation. She would need a liver transplant.

"Will she wake up?"

"She will, right after her surgery, which we'll need to do very quickly."

"And whose liver will it be?"

"The first viable one we get as soon as she's put on the list."

He stood quietly with David, giving him a chance to think of other questions. I once asked him if the worst part of his job was telling people that their loved ones were dead. Yes, that was bad, of course, he told me. But it was nowhere near as awful as telling them that they or their family were sick. Dead was a diagnosis, and it was definitive. People knew about it. Its reputation preceded it. But illness—illness was a vast chasm of maybe. The patient and anyone who loved and needed the patient felt desperate, and there was a temptation to use your power as a doctor to make everything okay, or to allude to a future okayness of everything (in a malpractice-insurance-clad way) that would be totally acceptable and get you off the hook from a true confrontation of emotion until further down the line when things got too bad to ignore. That was ethically okay, to provide hope, but it was not the right thing to do. The right thing to do was to consider how much hope you allowed the people involved. You knew that having hope might help. It would help in their stress levels, it would help them function throughout treatment. But you had to titrate it right, because how much hope should a person have in a situation that was somewhat hopeless?

David began to hyperventilate. He searched the room with wild eyes and Toby put his hand on his shoulder and guided him back to his chair. He looked over at his fellows. All three were looking down at their clipboards, busying themselves with note-making.

Toby knew guys like David, with close shaves and nice suits and soft leather shoes and cars waiting for them downstairs the minute they were ready to leave. David Cooper was scared, like anyone would be, but he also had the particular surprise that belonged to those who had been insulated from bad things. He had been born under a lucky star—a wealthy star, a healthy star. There were so many layers of protection between him and the things that could hurt you in this world. But this was nothing he could have prevented. All those safeguards against the outside; this was coming from the inside.

"Is there someone we can call for you?"

David looked up. "No, I have to call work. This is a thing you take off for, right?"

"Right," Toby said. "You take off from work and make arrangements for the kids. Call your friends and your family and tell them what's going on. You're going to need some help, no matter how this goes. We'll get all the paperwork started and get her on that list."

"Can I spend the night here?"

"Anytime." David took Karen's hand and held his mouth on it for a minute, looking at her. He began to cry into her hand. Toby watched them, and a dagger of jealousy struck his weary heart. This was the spectrum: one man begging God for his wife to be healed; another wondering where the fuck his wife was and why she couldn't be bothered to return a text.

Toby left the room and found his fellows right outside the door, waiting for him. "What is wrong with you all?" he asked. They looked surprised.

"Dr. Fleishman?" Logan asked. Joanie and Clay looked at each other.

"You were making notes while that man was *crying*." Toby began walking and they followed, but then he stopped and turned to face them. "You have to look these people in the eye. This isn't organs. This is *people*." He kept walking and arrived at his office. "The people who come to you—they're not here for checkups. By the time they get to you, they know something is wrong. They're sick. They're *afraid*. Do you know how scary it is for a body you've had your whole life to suddenly turn on you? For the system you relied on to just break down like that? Can you just close your eyes and try to think what that might feel like?" He was filled with disgust for the three of them and the way they looked bewildered. "Maybe you should all go into surgery if you hate people who are awake so much." He walked into his office and before he closed his glass door, he said, "I'm very disappointed."

Guilt wasn't enough. He wanted self-flagellation. He wanted chest beating. You can't shut down this early. God, these idiot children. What did they know about life? What did they know about suffering?

———

Toby sat in his office, with his back to the glass wall, staring out the window. His fellows were milling about in the hall, waiting for instructions. He looked at his phone. Still nothing from Rachel. He dialed her cellphone. It rang and rang and finally went to voice-mail. He decided to call Kripalu.

The hippie who answered the phone gave a full two-sentence greeting about what a beautiful day it was here at Kripalu and how the divine in her was inspired and "in-graciousness" to hear the divine in the voice of the caller and her name was Sage and how could she help facilitate—

Toby took the phone from his ear and stared at it and put it back to his ear to find that she was still talking. "My wife is there and I need to speak with her. Or she *was* there. She was supposed to be home by now and she isn't. I've tried texting her but I imagine you don't get a great signal up there."

"May I have your wife's name?"

"Rachel Fleishman."

Silence.

"So can I speak with her? Can I speak with my wife?"

"Would you mind holding?"

"No," but he was already on hold with chanting monk music.

Seven whole minutes passed and Sage was back at the phone with her full-sentences greeting.

Toby cut her off at "divine." "That was a really long wait," he said.

"I was . . ." But Sage was flustered.

"Well, is she there?"

"I'm so sorry, but I am not at liberty to discuss our guests' check-in status. It's a privacy issue."

"I'm not asking because I'm *curious*," he said. "I'm asking because I'm her husband and I haven't heard from her since Friday. I'm worried about her." Twice he said he was her husband. Both times he hated himself for it, but it was also true; he was still her husband.

"I'm so sorry," she said. "I'm just not at liberty to give out that information." He noticed the quiet surety in her voice. She had gotten calls like this. Her job was to tell them nothing.

He closed his eyes and joined the two ends of his stethoscope around his neck with one hand, pulling it down like a reverse noose. He changed his approach. "Look, it's okay. She wouldn't be cheating on me. We're separated. All but the paperwork, you know? If she's there with someone, it's okay."

"I'm sorry, but I can't—"

"Fine, it's fine." He hung up.

He paced in his office for another minute. The walls were glass and they faced right out onto the nurses' station. One of the surgical nurses was looking at him. He took a deep breath and looked down at his phone again. He sent another text to Rachel:

Hey, I'm worried now. Can you just tell me you're alive and when you'll be home?

He waited for the three dots that showed something—receipt, engagement, proof of life, something. But they never came and his fellows were waiting.

Deep down, he'd believed that Rachel would show up while he was at work. He would never have kept poor Mona there for so long if he hadn't. It would have been just like her to pick them up during the day to avoid a confrontation. She would have loved the fuck you of him having sent all those texts, only to come home and find that she'd picked the kids up hours before. But no, here they were.

He unpacked the groceries he'd picked up on the way home. He went to the computer in the living room to look up a meatloaf recipe that Solly had liked, but the Internet was running slow. He restarted the router and still it was slow. He went to check the history—sometimes Solly went on some of the kids' sites to play games that loaded the computer with viruses. He checked the cache. He unchecked the cookies box. He checked the history and—whoa boy, he stopped there.

The last ten sites visited in the last three hours were hardcore porn sites: circle jerks, MILFs, cougars, barely legals. "Sweet Jesus," Toby whispered. The Google search that set this off was "girl bagina," and when Toby saw that, he practically fell over in his chair. He went to the last site visited. It was a kaleidoscope of gifs and pulsating figures, a penis squirting ejaculate into a gleeful woman's face over and over and over and over and over and over and over and over and over, a woman taking it brutally from behind with delight. Before he himself could get aroused, he forced himself to remember exactly what he was supposed to be doing here, and he ran a virus check and erased the day's search history. He was sad to realize that his first reaction was to hope that Mona had done it, that she'd sent the kids to his bedroom to watch TV and then sat down at the computer and treated herself to a big old afternoon full of porn—Mona, the meek Ecuadoran woman who had helped raise their children from the time they were born; Mona, the pious Christian who was the most consistent presence in their day sometimes.

Of course, his theory fell apart when he realized that probably she knew how to spell vagina. There had to be an explanation.

He phoned her. She answered flatly on the third ring: "Yes."

"Hey, Mona, I was just looking at the computer and it looks like someone has been looking at some really inappropriate websites for the last few hours."

"No, I was there."

"Okay . . ."

"Hannah was on the phone with her friends before she watched TV. Solly was playing games."

Maybe it was a virus after all. Please, God, let it have been a virus.

"I'm not so crazy about the fact that they were just in front of screens for hours," he told her.

Mona was quiet.

"What kind of games was Solly playing?" he asked.

"Computer games."

"You really need to be taking them outside."

"He was outside all day."

"Well, you need to be watching him, Mona. Are you really arguing with me that you should be watching him? I'm telling you he
watched pornography in the middle of the living room for *hours*."

Mona hung up, maybe thinking that the fact that Toby had
stopped talking was the end of the rebuke, and that this was an appropriate sign-off, the acknowledged receipt of the request, acquiescence with a soldier's silence.

"Hannah, Solly, would you come out here?"

They came eventually.

"Who was using the computer today?"

"I was just on the iPad," Hannah said. Toby looked over at Solly
and saw his eyes wide and his jaw gripped in a terrified trembling.

"Hannah, you can go back to watching TV."

Solly closed his eyes. Toby sat on the couch and said, "Come
here. It's okay."

"I didn't do it," Solly said.

"Solly."

He began to cry and wheeze. "I didn't do it. I don't know how
those things came up. They just came up."

"Is it because—here, Solly, sit, there's nothing to be afraid of—is
it because you were curious about girls?"

"I just wanted to know what it looked like underneath."

Toby nodded. "I understand. Should I get you a book with
drawings that's made for kids your age?"

Solly's eyes opened wide. "No," he said. "No, I don't want to see
it again."

Toby pulled Solly by his shoulders so that his head was in Toby's
lap and let him cry while he patted his hair. Solly was nine. Toby
supposed he was nine when he started wondering, but there was no

Internet yet, so he had to go to libraries to see the art books. Other kids he knew went for the biology books, but those were so clinical. He knew from his museum visits with his parents that art was far dirtier than science. One day, he sneaked his first volume of Picasso, which was probably the wrong move there in terms of establishing a uniform understanding of anatomy. He went from there on to the Courbets and then the O'Keeffes and was very, very confused for a long time until ultimately he looked at one of the anatomy books just to rejigger it all back to reality.

Finally, at ten, he found porn. His parents had taken him to his older cousin Matthew's house in the San Fernando Valley one night. After dinner, he followed Matthew to his bedroom, where Matthew, who was fifteen, had dirty magazines and a VHS tape of a young man who wakes up from his sleep in a big suburban house and comes downstairs to find his mother participating in an orgy that she was hosting. It seemed he had awakened because orgies are not silent events, all that gasping and moaning. He came down the stairs groggy-eyed. The mother saw him. She was wearing a halter dress, not naked yet, probably because of hosting duties, and she guided him back upstairs—nothing to see here, sonny—and she got him to bed but he'd seen enough to be turned on as hell and so he kept reaching underneath her halter for her breast. Well, now she was turned on, too, but she knew this was wrong, and so she kept pulling his hand away and then putting her breast back inside the dress. This went on three or four times before she relented and they started really going for it and suddenly Matthew's mother busted in screaming, "AGAIN? AGAIN?" and little Toby, who was only ten, scurried out and pretended nothing had happened and that the weird new stirring in his pants wasn't there. He was terrified for months that his aunt would tell his mother and that his mother would hate him. As it was, he couldn't look his aunt again in the eye for years. And for years he worried that he was incomprehensibly fucked up from his first exposure to porn being about incest. There was a large sliver of revulsion in him, but it sat alongside a small sliver of priapic excitement, and he worried about this smaller sliver. He worried he conflated these things; he worried he'd be a sexual misfit or that if he ever once had a sexual thought in the same *week* as a thought about his mother (his dreidel-shaped mother), he was a pervert. This manifested itself by the fact that the first few times he had sex he immediately thought of his mother upon ejaculation, so anxious was he that he actually would think of his mother upon ejaculation.

This was what he thought about as he patted Solly's hair. He thought of how the kid was probably traumatized and almost mortally revolted by an encounter with adulthood that came too early for his little brain to synthesize. He thought that for a long time Solly would wonder if it was normal to ejaculate onto a woman's face, and if she would cry out with pleasure and delight if he did. He thought about how hard growing up was. There was no way to avoid youth. His father used to say these were the best years of life. He'd think, Are you fucking kidding me? Then kill me now. Yes, he thought of how *disgusting* growing up was—like literally, the disgust response that comes with so much of it, the horrible revulsion at another small acre of your innocence being incinerated.

His phone buzzed. It was Rachel, he was sure of it. Some beam of nuclear energy had radiated from the apartment to her mountaintop and activated the remaining shreds of her maternal instincts. She was besieged with wanting to know how her family was. She had probably gotten the message at the desk from Sage and was rushing to reassure him. She had been in a meditative trance for three days and had just woken up and was sorry. She was rushing to tell him that a couple of days of enlightenment had done her good, that she had been wrong to behave as she had and she would like for Toby to come home. "I'm the Rachel you met at the library party," she'd say. "I'm her again." He would give her a hard time; she'd hurt him so much over the years. But he would say yes. Of course he would say yes. Not because he missed her, but because he would have given anything for all that had happened—all of it—to have been a great big misunderstanding. He wriggled around trying not to disturb Solly while he retrieved his phone from his pocket, saying, "Sorry, buddy, it might be the hospital."

He looked at the screen and saw the lace-sheathed nipple of Nahid, the Parisian woman he had been texting back and forth with on his walk home from work. The nipple was erect.

He put his phone down and resumed patting Solly's hair, which he did without stopping for the next two hours.

"I have some bad news," Toby said when Hannah came out of her room on Tuesday with her bag packed. She thought she was going to the Hamptons, even a day late, and that absent her mother picking her up, she could will herself there by packing for the trip.

Hannah's face tightened. "No." She said it like she was chiding a dog.

"Your mom called. She had to take a sudden trip for work. She's really sorry."

Hannah started shaking her limbs out about how unfair it was. "You don't *understand*," she bellowed as she folded into a position that his yoga teacher called a Standing Forward Bend, clutching her stomach like it hurt. "I'm meeting up with *everyone* there. They're *waiting* for me. They're all *already there*."

He tried to approach her, but she was vicious and snarling and her nostrils were flaring. She was beautiful like her mother and she was ridiculous like her mother.

Late the night before, he made three unanswered calls to Rachel, plus a series of texts:

Come on, Rachel. This isn't cool.

You know I have a life, too.

Then, in the morning, pleading:

I'm getting worried. Please call me.

Then, one rabid-feeling hour after that, he sent another. It made him sick to send this one:

I won't ask you any questions. Please just call.

Then he'd messaged Nahid, who kept texting him body parts and who now wanted to schedule a date. This one hurt. He said that his ex-wife was tied up and he needed to watch the kids and could they maybe do later this week? Nahid texted him back a [purple devil emoji] and then an [angel emoji]—maybe meaning she was angry but ultimately a trouper? Or he was in hell and she was the heaven? He didn't know. That stupid [purple devil emoji] was everywhere. What did it mean? What was being communicated? Was it the digital manifestation of women's pent-up lust from their suffrage days? There was a woman he was sending dirty messages to a few days back who would make an allusion to oral sex and then when he responded with [panting tongue emoji], she wrote back with [mouthless emoji]. What did that mean? Was she offended? Was she literally withholding the thing she'd just offered? Was she shocked? He always took that one to mean speechless, or shocked. But he didn't know. *He didn't know.* Anyway, he thanked Nahid for understanding, and then a wave of nausea came over him and he wondered if he would still be in the same position on Thursday as he was today, on Tuesday. It couldn't be. Rachel owned a successful business. People relied on her. People relied on her, she always said. Yeah, well, people relied on him, too, Rachel. For their *lives*, Rachel.

He had looked at his phone as the hour struck midnight. What could he take away from her? How could he hurt her? He didn't know. How could he inconvenience her? He didn't know. He swore what he did next wasn't related to these thoughts, but, well. Crazed, vicious, he texted Mona:

*My 9-year-old watched porn on the computer for hours in
front of you today. We will no longer be requiring your
services. Good luck to you.*

Rachel would have feelings about that, but, well, if Rachel wants
input, Rachel has to be there to give it, right? Toby was never allowed to give instruction to Mona. Rachel said it was bad manage-
ment to have two bosses. Mona would ask, "Should I take Hannah
for new shoes for the first day of school?" and Toby wouldn't know
the answer—he wouldn't know if Rachel had already ordered some
or planned to take her herself and he didn't dare risk the dressing-
down that would come with him showing any initiative. "Mona is
the only person who accepts me on my own terms," Rachel once
told him. "All I have to do is pay her. I never have to explain myself.
I never have to put up with any bullshit."

Now, he deposited the kids in the conference room at the hospital, and Hannah seethed. Solly was fine. He couldn't believe how
much screen time he was getting as a result of this windfall, but
Hannah. Hannah was angry at *him* somehow. How could he tell
her that her mother had ditched them all without a thought? How
could he tell her that her mother seemed to be in the midst of doing
something he couldn't begin to put words to?

He headed to the chief's office.

"Can I see him?" Toby asked the secretary, and the secretary
gestured that he could.

He entered the chief's chambers, which was wood paneled like a
law library and had shelves filled with Plexiglas awards dating back
to the 1980s—awards for research and community contributions
and bedside manner. Donald Bartuck was the chief of hepatology,
MD, FACP, etc., etc. He was a good doctor, but he came out of the
womb destined for an administration job, all handshakes and

winks and remembering wives' names. Back when he was Toby's attending, he had taught Toby and his fellow fellows the same kind of care Toby taught his fellows, which was why his move toward admin upset Toby so much. If you get it, if you love the work so much, why would you want to do this thing that was the opposite of the work? If you like fundraising and paperwork so much, why not just go into finance like Seth, and make a ton of money doing what you do instead of just extremely good money that's tied to high-stakes medical decisions?

Bartuck was looking over his thick black glasses at something in a manila folder when Toby walked in. He looked like a stretched-out Ted Kennedy: six-seven, muscular and lean with a big gray wave of too much hair and walrus jowls on a hangdog face. When Toby walked down the halls alongside him, he could only think about what different species they were—Gulliver and a Lilliputian. On his desk was a picture of him with his second wife, Maggie, and their three children, all in tennis whites. On the other side of the desk was a picture of Bartuck with a former president. Toby sat down in a leather chair that emitted air at impact.

"Toby."

"Do you have a minute?"

Bartuck put down the paper he was looking at.

Toby sat down and took a second before he said it out loud. "I need to take a day or two off. Personal days."

Bartuck folded his hands and leaned into the desk. "It's not ideal. Karen Cooper's husband works for the hedge fund that hosts our bone marrow drive every year." Hedge funds hosting bone marrow drives reminded Toby of fraternity houses doing bake sales. Anything to clean up the conscience.

"I know. I wouldn't ask if I didn't need to."

Bartuck was silent as he waited for an explanation. Everyone wanted a show.

"Rachel got stuck on a business trip," Toby said. "She was supposed to be back and take the kids for the week but she can't, and the babysitter is off."

Holy shit. *He'd fired Mona.* He thought he might have diarrhea. Bartuck was silent: Keep going. "She let my son watch porn yesterday." *Mona.* He'd fired *Mona.*

"Hooboy. So you'll just stay home with them?" Bartuck asked.

"It's better than the conference room. I'll be around for any phone calls. Phillipa is here, and so are my fellows." He didn't mention the Hamptons because a guy as self-conscious as Toby couldn't fathom saying "the Hamptons" in front of a guy who knew what he made—which, yes, was a very decent amount of money by American standards but it wasn't Hamptons money. Bartuck had a house in the Hamptons. Bartuck had parties and donors to entertain. He had people to emphatically agree with no matter what the fuck came out of their mouths. He had to parade his degrees to people who were impressed with them while bragging about how he oversaw the people who were still actually being doctors.

"Hoo," Bartuck said. "Okay, then. Take two days, but make sure your people are on top of Karen Cooper. I'll check in on her, too. I told David Cooper that you were the best we had."

"Thank you, sir."

Toby left his office and went into the conference room. Hannah and Solly looked up from their iPads.

"Who wants to go to Long Island?" Toby asked. Solly cheered and the misery on Hannah's face evacuated itself as if it had never been there.

I had just gotten through Penn Station when Toby texted me that he couldn't meet for lunch. *Rachel unilaterally decided to stay at her stupid fucking yoga retreat for a few extra days,* he wrote.

Still? I asked.

She does this. Don't ask.

A man with half of one leg missing limped by on crutches. A fourteen-year-old dressed like a clown cried into her phone. A woman from Long Island with five nine-year-old girls dressed the same in dance recital costumes screamed at one of them, "I didn't say that to her!" Penn Station is the fucking worst. I looked up at the *War Games* tracking board. The next train back to New Jersey was leaving in fourteen minutes, but I couldn't bear to get on. I didn't want to—I couldn't—sit next to some dipshit drinking a sixteen-ounce Bud Light Lime twice in one hour.

I decided to walk downtown instead, just for a little while. Rachel was where? At a yoga retreat? Somewhere punishing Toby? Somewhere just not considering Toby? My mother always used to tell me that you can steal hours, not days. But Rachel was stealing days, just like I used to. The magazine used to send me on trips to nice hotels in foreign cities that I was probably never going to visit on my own, and once, in London, I stayed two extra days just because I couldn't bear to get back on a plane after my two-hour interview. I changed my ticket (never once did I book the trip for longer, I merely extended the stay) so that I could stay two days extra. My daughter was eight months old at the time. But it wasn't just that I was tired, and it wasn't just that it was unreasonable to ask me to go to Europe from New York for two days. It was because I felt like the hotel, the city, the aloneness, these were times where I could feel my skin again; I could feel my body again. I existed again without context—without a stroller, without a man holding my hand. I wouldn't wear my ring on these trips. It wasn't because I wanted to fuck around. It was because when I was on airplanes my fingers got cold and skinny and so my ring would drop off and I couldn't take the panic of worrying that I'd lost it. But also maybe it was the other thing, the context thing, I don't know. Put it this way: You can feel your body for the first time in a long time, you can feel your skin, then suddenly you can also feel this ring around your finger and the weight of it is suddenly unbearable.

Adam would have been okay with it; that's the truth. Instead I told him the interview was delayed. I walked around the castles and museums and along the Thames. I suddenly liked Impressionism, like the feline idiot that I had become. I suddenly liked sitting at a bar instead of a table for dinner. I suddenly liked espresso but without milk! Who drinks coffee without milk! Once, I sat next to a businessman on a plane to Lisbon who paid me close attention, even though I was wearing dirty clothes and glasses and talking about my kids. He wanted to know if we could have dinner when we got there. We did, at a café at night in the heat down an alley, and inside my body I felt something tapping on the window of consciousness—not hard, just a muffled knock. It made no sense. The guy was just like Adam—responsible, kind, a little oblivious. And all I wanted was for him to try to kiss me. Adam wanted to kiss me. Why wasn't that good enough? I left the café abruptly. I don't want to talk about it. Just to say these tiny rebellions were so laughable. I was such a joke. I don't want to talk about it.

I was in the Village before I knew it, on the little stretch of Sixth that leads to Carmine Street. I passed the basketball playground and the old movie theater, which was now the new movie theater. My parents had gone to NYU, like I had, and when my father visited me at school he'd talk about what stores used to be what stores and I thought it was the most tedious thing in the world, except that it was nuts to me that the student union was now a center for religious studies.

I walked up and down Carmine for a little bit, just that tiny street, trying to feel the jolt of something nostalgic or beautiful. I lived there after college, in my first own apartment. It was everything my mother was afraid of, a *Looking for Mr. Goodbar* fuck den of iniquity (which meant having sex with like one person I wasn't married to) filled with takeout containers. Once, I met a man at the Angelika during a screening of *Laurel Canyon,* which led to actual intercourse in my apartment—I just took him home. I only did that once.

I was still living on Carmine Street when I fell in love with my first editor, Glenn, back at the first magazine I worked at out of college, *TV Tonight*. Glenn was married, with three children. He wasn't the most handsome guy in our office, but he was the one who telegraphed a kind of stability that I was boring enough to find sexy. On the nights he came back to the apartment with me after work we would have sex and he would get up to leave and go back to Westchester and I would cry every time. I smoked then. I had started smoking in Israel. My mother smoked my whole life; I was never going to do it. But when I was twenty, I figured it was okay to finally try one, since I was clearly out of the danger zone of addiction. Well, who could have predicted that they would be so delicious and gratifying? (Yes, I know.) Who would have seen so clearly that my fidgeting all these years was just me waiting to discover cigarettes? Cigarettes really got me. Cigarettes were the thing my fingers and mouth had been looking for since maybe birth.

Glenn was not really a predator. It was more like he was powerless against the attention I, a young person, was giving him. The first time I met him, he was standing in a doorway, backlit, holding a magazine proof that I had to read for an edit test. Something happened in that innocent exchange—the simple placing down of a piece of paper on my desk with a kind word. Something electric, something addicting. I sought him out at every turn. I asked for help where I didn't need it. I swiveled around his desk, obvious to everyone around me, unable to stop myself. He walked past me and my breath caught. He was not that handsome or interesting. I'm telling you, it made no sense.

But then, too, I could feel my body. I could feel it opening to him, and I saw just how it all worked: evolution, attraction, procreative imperatives. I saw for the first time that I was powerless to these forces. I'd had crushes—I'd even been in love. But nothing as, I don't know, full-body as this. This was why people wrote poetry. This was why all the songs were about love. I get it now, I thought. I get it. One night, in an elevator, he told me he found me distracting. I told him we should talk about it over dinner. He called his wife in front of me from a pay phone to say he was stuck in the city for a few hours. And that was that.

I thought about that time now, about how eager I was to please him in bed. I can't think of that without thinking about poor Adam, about how the gift he gave me was a lack of volatility, and as a result he gets a less volatile me—a less eager me, a less humid me.

Anyway.

When Glenn was in my bed, I would light up a cigarette and blow it toward him so that he would smell like cigarettes when he got home, hoping it would tip off his wife and move some sort of needle. I'd spend my days imagining that something happened to her or them—usually it was a tragedy, not just a divorce—that would necessitate me moving into his house and taking care of his kids. I thought of that time now, how I imagined wanting someone else's life instead of doing the work of imagining my own. God, what a fucking idiot I was. My dreams were so small. My desires were so basic and showed such a lack of imagination. In my life, I'd go to weddings where the bride wore a red dress. I'd meet people in open relationships. I'd wonder why I was so unoriginal. I had been so creative in every other aspect of my life; how I'd turned out so conventional and so very *establishment* was bewildering.

It occurred to me walking on Carmine Street that I'd gotten the kind of life I wanted. I'd become like Glenn's wife—married, suburban, tame, waiting for a man to come home. I'd met Adam through work, too. I'd been on a story about a lawsuit against a Christian-only dating service and he was the young associate assigned to be my minder at the litigation firm. He was tall, with kind eyes and thick black glasses. He wore undershirts and Weejuns; he had knit ties and regular ones. He occupied a world where you knew how to dress for what, and it was always with a Brooks Brothers blazer. He came from a wealthy family who expected him to be wealthy, too, and because the perpetuation of wealth among the wealthy was expected, it came naturally to him.

While I was on the story—I was at the men's magazine by now—we'd have lunch, and I'd try to squeeze information out of him, and he wouldn't give me any, but he remained steady and cheerful, never annoyed. What a strange thing, a lack of darkness. What a strange thing, for your job to not stress you out, for good things to make you happy and bad things to make you sad. Simplicity is a cool shower after a hot bath. My emotions never tracked quite so logically. Maybe that was what I was drawn to in the first place with him, that his peacefulness was a necessary correction for me. It did not occur to me how I would have to spend my life explaining my darkness and dissatisfaction to someone who didn't even understand the concept of it.

We had a great sex life, and then we had a regular one, and then (as in now) we were in the wilderness. We had sex once a week, then not once a week, then every other week, but then twice in that next week so it must be okay, right? Here is the problem: You can only desire something you don't have—that's how desire works. And we had each other. Resolutely. Neither of us with a stray glance at another. After Adam and I were married, when I'd go out into the world, I'd see that the men I found myself drawn to were almost replicas of Adam, just like that guy in Lisbon. I wanted nothing different. I just missed the longing. We are not supposed to want the longing, but there it is. So what do you do with that? Forget it, there's no use talking about this. Talking about this doesn't make it better.

My phone rang and I sat down on the bench in front of the church on the corner. It was my babysitter, wanting to know what she was supposed to feed the kids for dinner. I looked at the time. It was five already. I'd been wandering for six hours.

When I got off the phone, my earbuds were still in from the call and my phone started playing a song, which it sometimes does, without my explicit instruction. The song it played was a U2 song from an album that was released when I was finishing high school, an album I played on a CD boom box, lying on my bed, staring up

at the ceiling, thinking about how I was at the end of some beginning, which made what came next the beginning of the end. I
walked over to the bodega on a corner at Sixth and bought a pack
of cigarettes. The man who sold them to me didn't look at me
funny; he didn't tell me I was too old to be playing games like this.
I went back to the bench and lit a cigarette and inhaled, the smoke
entering my body and filling it with poison, with something.

The house in East Hampton was no longer Toby's, as if it ever was,
but that wasn't official yet. Same with the car, though of course
when he went to his old garage he was sweating and terrified that
the car was either not there and he'd have to play dumb, or that the
garage attendant knew about his divorce and he'd have to skulk out
like a known criminal. But all he said was "Going somewhere fun?"
and Toby loaded the car and pulled out. The evening was clear and
the sky was turning dark and the children looked out their windows. Toby's hands gripped the steering wheel. For a long time
there was silence, and his interactions with the garage attendant
festered.

Suddenly, from the backseat: "Where's Mom?" Solly asked. It
had taken four days for him to ask.

"I told you, she had a work thing," Toby said.

"Can we FaceTime her?"

Toby looked at him in the rearview. "Probably not with the time
difference, bud. She's probably asleep." His sentence created an
image in his mind—her in a hotel somewhere in Europe, asleep,
was the thing he conjured—and for a minute he felt panicked.

He put on the radio because casually putting on the radio felt
like the best way to convince them that this was all normal, which
it was not. His eyes settled back on the road and the bottom of his
stomach began to burn and he imagined for a moment that the
rock inside his gut was Rachel and that he could perform surgery
on himself right there in the car without even pulling over and sur-

gically extract the rock, find her in it—that's where she went!—and throw the whole thing out the window, where the acid of her toxicity would burrow a sinkhole into the highway pavement and then farther down into the Earth's core and out the other side to China and then, with renewed velocity, propel out into the space over Asia and through all kinds of dark matter and parallel universes that didn't get cellphone reception and made it so that he never had to hear her fucking voice ever again.

He pulled off at exit 70, bracing himself for the Hamptonian excess that was the stuff of Rachel's dreams and of his waking dread. Slowly, slowly, the houses took on a more polished, regal quality, integrated with special lighting and a thing that could be called a lawn but could also, the farther away from the highway he drove, be called a field.

It was all such an insult, the Hamptons. It was an insult to economic disparity. It was an insult to leading a good life and asking hard questions about what one should sacrifice in the name of decency. It was an insult to having enough—to knowing that there was such a thing as enough. Inside those houses weren't altruistic, good people whom fortune had smiled down on in exchange for their kind acts and good works. No, inside those columned, great-lawned homes were pirates for whom there was never enough. There was never enough money, goods, clothing, safety, security, club memberships, bottles of old wine. There was not a number at which anyone said, "I have a good life. I'd like to see if I can help someone else have a good life." These were criminals—yes, most of them were real, live criminals. Not always with jailable offenses, but certainly morally abhorrent ones: They had offshore accounts or they underpaid their assistants or they didn't pay taxes on their housekeepers or they were NRA members.

And the worst of it all, the biggest insult there was, was where this all was situated. It was at the tip of Long Island, which itself was a bunion on Manhattan. This luxury tip was so precariously placed and so prone to terrible weather, surrounded on most sides by water as the Hamptons was, that the most offensive part of it all was that such wealth was planted in such tenuousness. One bad storm and all of these houses were blown away. And you know how these pirates felt about that? They didn't give a shit. Go ahead, let God blow the wrath of shame and destruction down on us. Not to worry, we'll make a killing on the insurance, and also we have a place in Aspen!

Toby pulled into the driveway of their home. Rachel had convinced him that she had earned a house in the Hamptons, and he had convinced Rachel that it should be a more humble one than they could afford. She acquiesced somewhat. It was still enormous. Five bedrooms and a three-car garage and a living room and a den and a sitting room and a solarium and a deck that overlooked the ocean. It had belonged to an old *Vanity Fair* editor, back when magazine editors could be rich. He was a dinosaur, and he died and was now extinct, and now the only time journalists went to the Hamptons was when we were invited because of the noble oddities we were sometimes perceived to be or because of how interesting and powerful we used to be or because a publicist rented a beach house on behalf of a luxury watch company and wanted to full-court pummel us with information about an exciting new opportunity for our December gift guide. The *Vanity Fair* editor's son took over the house when his father died, but then the son was sent away on an insider trading charge, and so there was a fire sale and Rachel bid and bought the house. She didn't like to tell people the fire-sale part.

He parked in the driveway and the kids ran into the house. A seagull flew over the car. He hadn't been there since the night she'd agreed to the divorce, in January. They'd gone out for a weekend, even though it was off-season, because they were touring camps for Hannah, who was considering a theater day camp in Dix Hills that was having an open house, and then there was a snowstorm and they decided to just stay through Monday. They'd fucked that night—one of the joyless, mechanical fucks of their last years together. It had been a year since Toby had first asked for a divorce.

His request had come not from anger but from the irritation of the hole it bored in you when you were lying to yourself. Each time he brought the topic up he had only been met with hysterical threats. She screamed at him that he would never see the children again if he tried to leave her, and that he would be left penniless.

"But why?" he asked. "You can't be happy like this."

She didn't have an answer. She just kept threatening. He relented, terrified and even sadder. But somehow, as it snowed onto the skylight into their bedroom, and it was quiet in a way that it was never quiet there during the summer, a peace seemed to settle on her. They lay in silence, the air cold but the bed full of heat, and she said to the ceiling, "I think we should get divorced." He turned over on his side to face her and he was filled with an aching love for the thing they had destroyed and tears were coming down her face and he wiped them away with his thumbs. "It's going to be okay," he said.

The weeks and months that followed that night were some of the happiest of their marriage. They laughed. They were light together. They rewatched an episode of a sitcom that had made them laugh years before. They shared raised eyebrows and deep inhales over Hannah's tantrums. They found each other's eyes again when Solly spent a day trying to say the word sarcophagus, both of them trying not to laugh. It had been a long time since they'd had intimacy in love. In recent years, only their hatred had true intimacy, meaning that when they fought, they were able to say the most specifically cruel things they'd mined from years of experience with each other. He trod hard on her extraordinary maternal inconsistency; she went for his masculinity like it was an artery. But when they weren't fighting, the intimacy was gone. Their conversations were so cold and distant that if you'd overheard them in a restaurant on one of their forced date nights, you would have wondered if they'd known each other for more than a few weeks. Now the intimacy was back again. Rachel picked up dinner on the way home when she knew he'd been running late to relieve the babysitter, even though dinner was his responsibility. He ran downstairs to get her Chinese food when she mentioned that she hadn't had a good chicken dumpling in years. They held hands sometimes, which they hadn't done in years, and which he realized was a completely counterproductive, backward thing for them to do. There was calm, and with the calm came relief, and the relief felt in his body the way endorphins did, and he became worried that he would mistake that for love. He couldn't understand why, if they could be happy in each other's presence while they were in the last days of their marriage, why couldn't they have been happy for real?

They decided to wait out the school year for him to move out, but he began looking for an apartment in April, and eventually found one five blocks north, on Ninety-fourth Street and Lex. He bought furniture online. With every lease-related document he signed and every Confirm Order button he clicked, he felt like he was falling into a terrible hole. And every confirmation email he received found him at the bottom of that hole, panicked and unsure, until eventually he ordered a set of bright blue enamel pots from Sur La Table and he clicked Confirm Order and it wasn't so bad, and then the shipping confirmation email came and suddenly he was so excited about these pots. Rachel had only wanted stainless steel pots, as if she had ever even once prepared a meal herself, saying that the bright blue enamel ones he liked were too flamboyant and made the place look like a circus. "We're not farmhouse chic, Toby," she'd said. "We're going for mid-cench here." He remembered that specific day, when she'd hired a decorator ("I'm actually called an interior designer"), a thick-ankled penguin of a woman named Luc, to come in and assess their design situation in the apartment in the city. She went through binders with Toby and Rachel and soon determined that (a) Toby had no interest or authority and was only there to prevent the kids from interrupting; and (b) after a series of flash card questions, Rachel's preferred style was midcentury modern. "You're mid-cench!" the designer had said, and Rachel had clapped her hands together at the revelation, as if she had just learned where her ancestors came from, like maybe she'd been wondering this since she had become sentient and it was the mystery of her life and now she finally knew. Now everything else in her life could fall into place.

"And yet she wants everything to be new," Toby had said at the time, thinking this was funny. Rachel and Luc blinked at him.

All this to say he never thought he'd darken this particular doorstep again. All this to say he thought he'd never again have to lay eyes on an Eames chair that looked like it could crack your coccyx after an hour of polite conversation. All this to say that when he got the email that his new Le Creusets were shipping, he nearly evaporated from the joy he felt. He would feel this feeling every day when he left Rachel's apartment for good, he thought. This was what it was going to be like all the time—life on *his* terms, a home and a day erected out of *his* choices. As he walked toward the door of the Hamptons place now, down the gravel driveway, he put his hands on his children's heads, which were immediately sticky from the proximity of the salt water. He realized that some part of him had been at least somewhat attached to the idea that she'd be there—that he would open the door and they would find her, waiting. He didn't know why she'd be there: Maybe she'd be on a bender, maybe fucking some guy, maybe fucking some girl, maybe crying in the bathtub, maybe dead on the patio. Just there.

But he turned on the lights and he felt the humanlessness in the house and knew she wasn't there. He hadn't *really* thought she'd be there, he guessed. So why did he feel empty and betrayed all over again?

That night, he lay in that bed alone for the first time and he felt his waking-up feeling: *Something is wrong. You are in trouble. Fleishman is in trouble.* The bed, which had cost $26,000, and the mattress, which had cost $7,500, cradled his body like it was his mother. He lay on his right side, looking at the vast empty space where another person is supposed to be. A California king was excessive. They hadn't needed this much space. He looked up through the skylight at the stars and he thought about what was beyond the atmosphere and beyond the stars in the vast and infinite space which made him even smaller than he was on Earth.

His phone made a choo-choo train noise from incoming text messages, and he reached over to see who it was. It was Nahid, whose body parts he was becoming so intimate with through his phone that he couldn't reconcile that they hadn't yet fucked, or even met for that matter. He felt his dick begin to get hard. He could think of no better idea than to jerk off on Rachel's bed to photos of another woman—women who *wanted* to please him, women who *wanted* to delight him. He fell asleep with his phone in his left hand.

In the morning, he made the kids pancakes with mix left over from last summer, but Hannah didn't want to eat. She just wanted to see her friends.

"But none of your friends are even up yet," he said.

She walked off to her room.

Toby went into the library room, or what was sold to them as the library room, though Rachel had never put a book inside it, just an ugly green leather couch and a TV, and he sat down to call Rachel's assistant, Simone, on her cell. The phone rang once, then went to voicemail. He stared at the phone for a minute. He was nervous. God, what was he scared of? Fuck you, you fucking pussy, he said to himself. He called again. Again it rang and went to voicemail. He decided to text.

It's an emergency, pick up.

He stared at the phone. Nothing. He was about to walk out of the library room when the phone rang.

"Hi, Toby," Simone said. She sounded defeated.

"Where is she?" he asked.

"You said there was an emergency?"

"Is she there?" He began to consider the possibilities. "Can you have her call me back? She's *days* late and I have a hard case at the hospital and—and it's her turn. It's her agreed-upon turn. She can fuck with me, but she can't fuck with the kids."

"If there's no emergency, then—"

"Simone. My kids are waiting for her. Where is she?"

"I'll leave word."

Simone hung up. How Rachel abused her. She'd been on Rachel's desk for four years. Usually it was just two, but Rachel told him Simone was a good assistant but too timid and nice to be set loose and made into a junior agent.

"So you're just going to let her believe she's going to get promoted someday?" Toby had asked.

"It's not like I've *lied* to her," Rachel had answered.

Hannah had arranged to meet up with Lexi Leffer, mousy little Beckett Hayes, and Skylar something or other, whose mother used to audition her for commercials. They pulled up in front of the café. Hannah informed him that he would. not. be. walking. her. in. and she would need sixty dollars (not his sad twenty dollars) and that other kids got a hundred dollars and sure she would let him know when it was time to pick her up but how could she do that when she was the only person on the planet with no phone. Hannah had not yet opened the door to the café when a group of boys the same age as Hannah called her name. Hannah turned around, and her face became pretty and light. Rachel could do that, too.

"I didn't know there were gonna be boys there," Toby said to no one.

"Maybe it's just a coincidence," Solly said. He was reading his facts about the universe book.

Toby sat in the car for a minute, just staring ahead.

"Dad, Dad, are you okay?"

Toby looked in the rearview mirror at Solly for a few long seconds before hearing the question. He put the car into gear and began driving. "Yes, no, sure I am. Just figuring out dinner."

"Dad, what's the block universe?"

"Block universe theory? Where did you hear about the block universe theory?"

"It's in my book."

"Gosh, it's pretty complicated. Okay, you ready? It's a physics theory. It's the theory that there are infinite universes in infinite dimensions, all going on at once. Like no matter what's going on, that moment still exists forever. Time isn't forward. It's all happening at the same time. Does that make sense? I mean, it doesn't, but does it?"

"So that means that right now whatever happened on this spot in the past is still happening?"

"Yes. And in the future. Or what we think of as the future."

"Then how come we can't see it?"

"Well, we can only see our own dimensions. Our brain can barely even grasp it."

"How do we know which dimension we're in?"

"We're in all of them, according to the theory."

Solly leaned back and closed his eyes, his bottom teeth biting his upper lip.

"You okay, buddy?"

"It's stressing me out."

"Why?"

"I don't know. It's all happening all the time. It's so *busy*."

"I know. But you're only responsible for right now."

"But it's all right now!"

"But you can't control it except for right now."

"But all the me's need to control their right now."

"But they can all handle it." He turned around. "It's just a theory. It's probably not true."

Toby couldn't bear to talk about the block universe anymore. He didn't want to talk about any theory of life in which the thing you were dealing with wasn't absolute reality. He couldn't bear the scope of regret and other chances and other choices that might verily crush him if he considered them. He'd chosen to live without regret. He'd chosen to believe he had nothing to regret. He'd had opportunities, but he also had values. His whole marriage, he was repeatedly punished for honoring his values, for not getting sucked into the vortex of want with the people around him. He didn't want to think about possibility anymore. Possibility was a trap.

Four years earlier, the Fleishmans had been invited to a New Year's party at the second home of Miriam and Sam Rothberg (though how do you decide which is your second home when you have four homes?). Solly was friendly with Jack Rothberg, and Rachel went to Pilates with Miriam, who was the object of all of Rachel's social-climbing ambitions. Miriam was a Rothberg, which made her rich and influential, but she was born a Sachsen, which made her someone with access to the wealth of two or three small European countries. Sachsen was the family that donated the most money to the school's building fund, which was why their name appeared on it in at least five places and also on the school stationery, and also on the new annex at MoMA, which would be named for them.

The house was upstate, in Saratoga Springs, near the racetrack. How could Toby describe this house? It looked like Monticello—sprawling and colonial with two redundant staircases in the entry hall. Outside it was endless; inside it was endless. There were nine bedrooms, Rachel told him. Each invited family got their own bedroom, which turned out to be a suite of bedrooms—one for the parents, one smaller inset of a bedroom for the kids to share, one bathroom per family. There were more than twenty families invited, though, and the ones that didn't fit in the house Sam Rothberg himself put up at a charming historic hotel down the road.

"Why are we at the house and not at the hotel?" Toby wanted to know while they were driving up.

Rachel, at the wheel, shrugged. "Who knows?"

"I feel like it's strange that we merited house status."

"Probably so the kids could play? And, uh, some people like me, Toby."

Toby stared straight ahead. At least at a hotel he would get a break from these people. He could take Solly on a nature walk, or skip a meal with the crowd. Instead, they were put in a room with a canopy bed and cloth walls, all done up in a bland Queen Anne style. Toby put their bags down and thought how this weekend was going to be unrelenting.

The next morning, at breakfast, Sam asked Toby if he wanted to take the kids bowling in town. Toby briefly searched his mind for a way to say no, but he looked over at Rachel, whose eyebrows were pleading.

"Sure," he said.

At the bowling alley, Sam's giant hands selected a marbled red ball and flung it through the air so that it could land on the oiled alley like a swan and score him, yes, his third strike. Sam was tall even by regular standards and it looked like he had all his hair, but with blond guys you can't ever know for sure. He had what looked like a strong chin but he also had an underbite, which meant that his chin wasn't so strong and maybe even was weak. When he laughed, it was just his jaw making a parallel clapping motion, like a marionette. He sat down next to Toby while Jack got up to bowl his second strike. He said, "You still at the hospital? We're looking for someone to head up our marijuana program."

"Fendant is going into marijuana?"

Sam laughed loud. "Lord, no. We're looking for someone who could help lead up a new, important division. It would be dedicated to debunking myths about alternative therapies, reminding the world that medicine is best. There's a lot of misinformation out there. As I'm sure you know."

"I don't know," Toby said. "I see a lot of cancer patients benefit from pot and acupuncture—"

"Don't get me started on acupuncture," Sam said.

"—I mean, not cured. But relief, yes."

"Be that as it may. Isn't the best relief a cure?" Toby thought of Bartuck, whose face was [dollar sign eye emoji] and who was aggressive about grants and fundraising. It disgusted Toby, but what was he going to do? That kind of greed was essential to allowing Toby to do his job—there was no job without it. So there was something for everyone in medicine. He understood that. But this was new. Bartuck at least had to pretend he was interested in healing patients; Bartuck at least at one time had actually done the healing work! What was new was to be in a room with someone who was so nakedly disinterested in healing people, and so nakedly interested in thwarting progress.

"I'm a doctor," Toby said. "I do best with patients." He hoped this would end the conversation before Sam mentioned a number, but hope is for idiots. Toby got up to bowl. He took one pin off the edge in a glorified gutter ball.

"It's the head of a big division, Toby. You'd be bringing in a mil before bonuses. You'd manage an entire team. Great hours. The works."

Toby tried to imagine what it would be like to be on such intimate terms with money that you could abbreviate it into nicknames. "That's really nice, but it's just not what I do."

"Rachel said you would resist this. Did I mention the bonuses? The hours? We have a chalet in Zermatt you could use for skiing. Every director-level gets a key. I'm serious."

"When did you and Rachel talk about this?"

It was Sam's turn to bowl. He banged out another strike, and when he came back, Toby wanted to ask the question again but couldn't think of a way of repeating himself without sounding panicked and paranoid.

Toby vowed to not address this with Rachel until they returned to the city. There was no private place to argue, and he knew he'd have a hard time pretending things were fine at dinner once she began saying awful things to him about his career.

But Rachel had other plans. That night was New Year's, and waiters in black and white passed hors d'oeuvres and champagne and Toby sat on a couch alone until about eleven, when Solly came to sit with him for a minute and fell asleep on his lap. He carried Solly up to bed, wondering if he could get away with falling asleep in bed with him, but Rachel followed them upstairs.

"Well?" she whispered. "I've been waiting to hear."

"Hear what?"

"What did you and Sam talk about?"

"You know what we talked about. You colluded and orchestrated it behind my back."

"Collusion! That's a big word for this. He mentioned it a few weeks ago. I thought you might like the opportunity!"

"It's actually the opposite of an opportunity. It is the antithesis of what I do. He wants me to head up a division that encourages the deprivation of legitimate avenues of healing to sick patients."

She sat on the bed, looking up at him. "I know. But you're so good at your job. You should be rewarded. You should have a break from the grind."

"I don't need a break from my job. My job is not a grind."

"You are screaming," she said through her teeth. "Do not embarrass me."

"How about you embarrassing *me*? By implying that I have so little integrity—"

"Integrity? You think insisting on keeping your job when you have an opportunity to literally what—quadruple your salary and make our lives better is integrity? Me working myself into an early grave so that you can do what you want to do instead of what you have to do is integrity?"

"What is the problem here? I'm perfectly—"

"You're still an attending."

"I'm an attending because I like working with patients."

"You totally pissed away that grant—"

"Jesus Christ. The grant again."

Her lipstick, her always-red lipstick, had somehow gotten onto her teeth. It made her look like a lunatic on the subway. "You are so wedded to this narrative that you are good and everyone else is bad. It's not *bad* to want money. It's not *bad* to have a teaspoon of ambition. It's not *bad* to work hard to make your family happy."

Solly appeared in the doorway, rubbing his eyes.

"Why are you fighting?"

Rachel stood up. "Go back to bed, baby, it's okay."

"What are you fighting about?"

"Go to sleep."

Toby stood up and without a word took Solly by the hand and led him back to his bed, where he lay down next to him, facing him. He put his hand on Solly's cheek, and Solly responded by putting his hand on Toby's cheek.

"I want to be a doctor when I grow up, Dad."

"You do?"

"I want to have patients and make them better."

"You will be great at doing that. Go to sleep."

Some time later, the door opened, and Toby could feel Rachel seething at the threshold. He kept his eyes closed and pretended he was asleep.

A week later, out of nowhere, or maybe not, Rachel decided she could no longer live on Seventy-second Street in their perfectly good three-bedroom with a doorman and what Solly thought was the fanciest elevator in all of New York City. She began looking, on her own, for a new apartment. She would take Hannah with her, and Hannah would report back over dinner that there was no anteroom or the kitchen door opened straight into the living room or there was no additional storage or there was no parking or there was just a living room and no den.

There was a new building being built on Seventy-fifth Street at the time, at the corner of Third. There were new buildings being built on Eighty-sixth and Seventy-ninth, too—all glass and metal with advertisements over their scaffoldings about the amenities and tennis courts and Jacuzzis and community rooms and how easy and glamorous life could be. They were exactly what Rachel wanted, but she didn't want them. Rachel was more interested in the building on Seventy-fifth Street that would not have amenities. It was being built new to look like one of the old art deco buildings—one of the old-money buildings their richer friends lived in. It had bronze arches and high ceilings and metal doors, and it was to be called the Golden. The Fleishmans went to see it one night after dinner.

"They're not even officially showing it yet, but Sam Rothberg knows the developer and got us in early," Rachel said.

"I don't know why we need something so big," he said.

"This isn't big. This is a regular size for a family of four."

"Those modern buildings are so much nicer. They have swimming pools."

"We have the club for that. And I don't want to live in all that glass. It's so old-school and romantic here."

"Maybe there's a gym here," Hannah said.

"There isn't," Rachel answered, looking at the crown molding in the apartment.

"How do you know?" Toby asked. The agent hadn't yet met them in the model apartment.

Rachel stopped for a minute. "I asked Sam."

"Have you looked at this before?"

"Of course not. How would I?" He was pretty sure she was lying.

They closed on the apartment three weeks later. He wasn't asked. He was told. It was his punishment for not taking the Fendant job. Fine, he thought, as he helped label boxes for moving. As long as this means we're even.

Now Toby found himself back at their house, Rachel's house, with the car running in the driveway.

"Dad?" Solly asked.

Toby blinked. He had no recollection as to how he'd gotten here. He had thought they were even, but they weren't. They never would be. When he was seventeen, he got into a car accident with his parents' Volvo. The next three days, all he could think was: What if I'd left exactly one minute earlier? What if I hadn't stopped for gas? It drove him crazy, and more than that, it didn't matter. It didn't matter because it wasn't the reality he was living. What if he had taken that job? Or what if he'd even been open to talking about it? What if his lab had flourished and his grant had been renewed? What if he'd never gone to the party where he met Rachel? What was the point in even asking? Do you see why he didn't want to talk about the block universe anymore? Because somewhere, in one of them, he was still a hopeless idiot who didn't see this all coming.

The next day they spent in the Hamptons breaststroked by in excruciating slowness, with Hannah rushing him to different places for a drop-off, then bargaining via the text message function of a friend's phone that she be allowed to stay longer and do more. He drove Hannah to playdates. He took Solly down to the beach to collect rocks. He called the hospital. He took calls from the hospital.

Toby and Solly sat by the pool on too-expensive chaise lounges while Solly played Minecraft on his iPad. Toby stared out at the sunshine water until he realized he'd had it. He took out his laptop and looked up the name of the lawyer he'd seen two years before, when he realized he wanted a divorce and knew that everything they owned was supported by Rachel's income. The lawyer, a woman in her late fifties who had handled the divorce of another doctor at the hospital, told him that he could file, but she said that at the point where Toby's money ran out, he would have no choice but to acquiesce to everything she demanded, if the stress of knowing that his "resources" were more finite than hers didn't force him to acquiesce much sooner.

"Even people we see as awful tend to be reasonable," she said.

"Yeah, I'm not so sure about that," Toby answered.

She charged him $750 for the forty-five-minute conversation. "Mediation is much more humane on all of you. If she's offering it, I'd take it. You'll need your money for your new house, unless you can get some alimony out of her."

If the months of a peaceful marriage-like existence made Toby worried that the inertia of these nearly fifteen years would make him want to try again, their twice-weekly mediation meetings cured him. In those meetings Rachel would make stone-hearted demands. She wanted the houses and she wanted the BMW and she wanted the stock and the Knicks tickets—why on earth would she want the Knicks tickets?—and the club membership, which, fine, he hated that place but still. She had so much and wanted to keep it all. She wanted to leave the father of her children without any relic of the last fifteen years. But that wasn't the worst part about this. The worst part about this, other than all the other worst parts about this, was that it put Toby into a position where he had to actually think about what he wanted.

The only way he had survived in his marriage, with a wife who not only made about fifteen times his really quite good doctor salary but who, the moment she surpassed him on the earn-o-meter, found herself completely disgusted by his earning ability, was that he made a big show of only barely tolerating the perks of the money. He *allowed* Rachel to buy the Hamptons house, he *allowed* her to buy the monstrous new-money/fake-old-money apartment at the Golden, he *allowed* her to buy the convertible. He never allowed himself to realize that Rachel's things had become *his* things, even as he partook in their thingness. He didn't buy them, but they were also his. And now he hated mediation because it felt like wanting any of it, claiming any right to it, would have been admitting that he derived pleasure from it, too. Fine, he said with every tiny acquiescence. Take it all, take it all.

When he became overwhelmed like that, Frank, the mediator,

who only had hair above his ears and wore shawl collars, would say, "Let's take a breath, Toby."

He could grapple with the loss of stuff. The car and the Hamptons house and the club would disappear from his life overnight and he would adjust since he was never really meant to be a rich person in the first place. But now he was being treated like a housewife who had taken care of the children, and Frank was telling him to fight for what was his, the way he probably had to tell the housewives to fight for what was theirs. And Frank was right. He *was* owed something. He was owed something for allowing her to kneecap his career with her insistence that she be allowed to work late, that she had one more phone call to make. He was owed something for being diminished and counted out. He was owed something for having to shiver in her shadow all these years, for being made miserable, for being forced to fight to the death every night. Did he sound angry? He wasn't angry. He was just explaining things.

What Frank was trying to say was that there was no way to get what he had wanted in the first place, which was a happy marriage. He was certainly never going to receive any apology or understanding for the way their relationship had gone awry. In cases like this, material compensation was the only hope. Frank knew this. He'd seen this so many times. You have to take the stuff because it's the only thing that will comfort you when you realize that everything else is gone. But Toby couldn't bring himself to fight. It was all too humiliating to beg for things he never wanted in the first place. Getting used to things and enjoying things wasn't the same as wanting things. Was it?

Mediation ended, and then the lawyers were involved again, but not the divorce lawyers. This time it was document pushers and notaries, signing name-removals from deeds, as if he'd come back with a claim, which was only even further degrading, that after all this they couldn't part as people who trusted each other—that he might be someone so desperate for money that he'd squat in her apartment or sue her for her car. He was just a poor doctor, after all. A poor doctor who, by the way, made more than a quarter of a million dollars, thank you very much.

He pushed air out of his mouth like a motorboat. He couldn't bring himself to contact any of Rachel's friends and ask if they'd heard from her. There was something about this that was so deeply embarrassing that he couldn't handle anyone knowing it. Yes, divorce was ugly and people understood that, but getting abandoned by the wife you're already separated from seemed even too humiliating for him, even after the public fighting and the tense entrances to parties and the times she mocked him openly for his lack of sophistication. *His lack of sophistication*. Him. Not sophisticated. Him. He who read Pulitzer finalists and had four-count-them-four museum memberships; he who checked the *Time Out* every week for new cultural events, who donated to the Central Park Conservancy and suggested opera and cello concerts and Mummenschanz?

He opened a new window on his computer and logged in to the bank account he had shared with Rachel. They'd separated their accounts after Frank told them to, with Toby transferring his direct deposit to the new account at the bank on the corner of his new apartment building. His computer still autologged in to the old account, though, and he thought maybe he could see where Rachel was and what she was doing if he could see where she was spending her money. He pulled up the page and clicked on the account login, and he was presented with a screen that said that his password or username was incorrect. He tried again. He got the same screen that said he had two more tries before the account was locked. He tried one more time, and now the screen said he had one more try. He tried one of the credit cards; same thing.

He closed his computer and indulged in a single "Fuck you, Rachel" in his head. His therapist, Carla, had been adamant that an inner monologue could be poisonous, and how an internal "Fuck you, Rachel" wouldn't solve as many problems as it would create—problems that were all his, not hers, by the way. But fuck you anyway, Rachel, he thought. Like a cool drink of water.

———

At night, he continued to receive messages from Nahid, and with every nipple/lip/abdomen picture and double entendre, he thought what a crazy world this was, that he was in a deep torture-spiral of anxiety about where the hell his wife was—a spiral that he smiled through so as not to tip off his children—and he was sexting with a woman he'd never met as if everything were a-fucking-okay. He marveled for the millionth time that summer about how a person could be this miserable and bewildered, and this horny and excited, all at the same time. What a piece of work is man.

And during the days he would stare out at the beach and consider the block universe of the little stretch of land in front of the house, too. In the block universe, he is there, six summers before, the day they decided to buy this house and he took the kids to the sand while Rachel spoke to the real estate agent and then came outside and they hugged and kissed and he thought of those Syd Hoff books he used to read to the kids, the one about Sammy the Seal. Sammy the Seal leaves the zoo to go explore the world, and he goes to school and he goes to restaurants and it's all fine, nothing great, until finally he happens upon a bathtub and he says, "Ah, here is a place!" And that was the thought Toby had that day on the beach: Ah, here is a place! She maybe felt this too in that moment, and they kissed. And then in the next frame of the block universe he's playing Frisbee on that same beach with Hannah and he is once again thinking, Ah, here is a place! And Rachel comes out and screams at them for getting sandy after their showers and before they are supposed to go out to dinner.

Hannah was invited to a friend's house Friday and Toby took Solly to drop her off. The girl's mother, Roxanne Hertz, with her small mouth and her platinum hair and her indie rock seventies bangs, tried to pry from Toby how it was that Toby was in the Hamptons when according to the information they'd culled throughout the summer, Rachel had been the one to keep the house.

"I thought Rachel was supposed to be with them this week," said Roxanne.

"She was, but she had to leave town for a bit," Toby said.

Roxanne stood in the silence. She swayed her head, back and forth, ear to ear, like a metronome, and there was something hypnotic about the gesture that made him mirror it, too. No, he had to be strong. He lifted his head upright.

"So," he said. "How's the summer been for you guys?"

She smiled with half her face in wretched pity. "It just must be so hard for you all right now. Change is hard. I always say that."

"It is." He pursed his lips to keep them from talking. Roxanne was going to lose this particular game of chicken.

Roxanne seemed to understand that she had lost and sighed. "Well, you know how new relationships are. I'm sure you'll get back into a routine."

God, why wouldn't this end? From out of the hallway, Roxanne's third-grader, Max, emerged.

"Oh, hey, Max," Toby said. "Solly's in the car. Want to come say hi?"

Max looked at Roxanne. Roxanne's eyes flashed at her son in anger. "Go say hi." Then, to Toby, "Why don't you bring Solly in and keep him here for a while? He and Hannah could stay for dinner. She and Brielle have a lot to catch up on!" She smiled benevolently, which pissed him off a little, for its implication that it was hard for him to have his children with him (false) or that he was suffering visibly (fine, true). Toby said he'd ask Solly, and he went outside and waited a full minute before pulling Solly out of the car and telling him that it was time for a playdate with Max.

"You can text me when you're ready for them to come home," Toby told her.

"She still doesn't have a phone?" Roxanne asked. "Toby, the girl needs a phone!" She said that last thing in some kind of mockery or imitation of something, like a Groucho Marx voice. He remembered that Rachel had once said about Roxanne that she could only confront people or ask for something if she was doing a weird voice.

"She's getting one for her birthday." He thanked Roxanne and smiled and told her he'd return the favor next time.

"It's no favor!" she called as he walked away. "We love having them over!"

He got into the car and stared straight ahead. Roxanne had said "new relationships." "New relationships are hard," something like that. He had nodded and smiled through it, since it felt like an expression of concern, and he had just wanted to get the hell out of there. But now the phrase itched in his head. New relationship? Was he receiving new information? The car was suddenly unbearably hot and he realized he hadn't started it yet.

As he drove the twenty-five miles per hour one was allotted down Dune Road, he thought how Roxanne, who was not particularly close with Rachel, had known she'd be here this week. They had made plans for the girls to spend time together. Maybe the new relationship between Rachel, a now-single mother, and her daughter was hard? Or Rachel and Toby? Or Toby and Hannah? He twisted this scenario into a hundred poses before he allowed himself to turn and look Roxanne's most obvious implication in the eye: that her seething cauldron of rage and ice and heartlessness had been penetrated to its molten core layer by another. That not only was Rachel gone, but she was gone with a man. That poor fucker, Toby thought.

But his arm hair stood up: Something real was happening here. That perhaps the always thin, unraveling tether she had to them had finally broken and she was adrift in space somewhere—somewhere, but where? She was no longer answering to him. She was no longer answering him at all. Panic washed through him. She was now an inner ear problem, something affecting his balance. His proprioception was off. He didn't know how to feel about her because he didn't know where to direct his aim anymore. He didn't know where she was, and he no longer knew what she was capable of.

He pulled into the driveway. The house looked deadly. Inside, it was empty and quiet, and he stood still for a minute at the doorway. When he was young, he would become terrifically scared in the dark when his parents and sister were asleep. If he had to get up to get water or go to the bathroom, he moved as quickly as he could, humming to himself the whole time, so that he could never really hear the quiet. He was afraid if it was too quiet, he would hear what was beneath the quiet—ghosts moaning or whatever. He didn't want to know. But now, standing in his ex-wife's home, he was brave. He made himself as still as possible, thinking if it was quiet enough, she would somehow appear. He stayed that way for a good five minutes, just standing there in the quiet. Then he took his clothing off right there in the living room, and went outside and jumped naked into the sparkling water of the pool of the house into which he was technically breaking and entering.

Sunday morning came and Toby knew that the traffic would get worse and worse on a weekend like this (that must have been at least part of the source of his mounting dread, right?), so he packed them all up, hating himself for how meticulously he left the kitchen and made the beds, and drove them home.

"Where are we going now?" Solly asked as they drove through the Queens Midtown Tunnel. "Can we have dinner at Tony's?"

"Let's go to EJ's," Toby said. EJ's was a diner-style not-diner on Third Avenue that served twenty-dollar pancakes.

"Breakfast for dinnerrrrrrrr!" Solly hollered.

He looked at Solly in the rearview mirror and saw again how easy it was to make him happy. Hannah was scowling out the window with her arms crossed. Toby said, "But first we're going to get your sister a phone." He looked in the rearview once more and saw Hannah come alive with something that looked like love once again. It was cheap love, purchased with blood money, but he didn't care. He'd take it.

Afterward, Toby thought he'd spend the night showing Hannah how to use the phone, but of course she already knew. She already had an Instagram account, and Toby would have liked to talk to somebody about whether it was a good thing for an eleven-year-old to have those things, but Rachel was never someone to ask, even when you knew where she was. Toby followed Hannah on Instagram, and her posts always screamed a deficit in confidence. They fished for compliments. They bragged in ways that were false. All this made him want to put her on his lap and rock her and sing her to sleep.

He got a new text from Nahid, asking if they were finally getting together. She was wearing a gold beaded necklace in the picture that accompanied the question. She'd never sent a picture of her face, but this one at least included her neck and a scrap of chin. The necklace hung off her neck, and was strewn down her breasts and around the lace embellishment on a white bra. Fuuuuuuck.

I still have my kids, he texted.

She texted back with a gif of Alejandra Lopez crying, a scene from *Presidentrix,* Alejandra's Pulitzer Prize–winning musical about Edith Wilson, who secretly ran the country after her husband, Woodrow Wilson, had a stroke. This gif had her literally, defiantly, miserably ripping up the Treaty of Versailles as she sobs over her husband's bed.

Alejandra was a client of Rachel's. Trigger warning, Toby wanted to write back.

He was going to cancel on Nahid again. It didn't feel right to leave the kids just now. *He was going to cancel on her.* But he looked at that picture again and fuuuuuuck. The part of him that could think clearly could also think angrily and hornily. And that gif— sent almost as a reminder of how tangled Rachel still was in every move he made. No. He wasn't having it. No matter where Rachel was, no matter what she was doing, she was no longer going to mess with his life.

He wrote back that yes, they were finally going to meet. Could she do tomorrow? She could.

HIM: *Can I take you to the new French place on Third? Can*
       I take you to the old French place on Lex?
HER: *[Purple devil emoji]*
HIM: *Does purple devil emoji mean Third? Or Lex?*
HER: *How about just at your place?*

And in his head, in rapid fire:

Holy shit oh my God yes
Is she going to rob me
Fuck you, Rachel
There is no such thing as sex that is this easy

That was the thought that stayed with him. There just isn't.
He'd had sex with women immediately on dates. He'd talked dirty
to women and ended up having phone or FaceTime sex. But he'd
never been literally and plainly invited over for sex. Maybe she was
a prostitute? Maybe this was a scam? He hadn't seen her face, he
realized. What if this was a joke? What if this was one of his colleagues? It wasn't. He calmed himself: *It wasn't.* He was spiraling.

HIM: *Ah, my kids will be home. I wish I could. Badly.*

There was brief silence and his heart was in his throat, but then
she wrote: *You can come here. 9 pm. Don't be late.*
She gave him an address on Seventy-seventh Street on the West
Side and he gave her a [purple devil emoji] back. You know, someone could rob you even inside *their* home.

HER: *You're not going to rob me, are you?*

Right, okay, but that was exactly the kind of text he'd send if he
planned to rob someone: He'd get in front of it. He scrolled back
up to look at her pictures, then closed out of her message. He

thought about texting Joanie. She'd babysat for him before; it wasn't unreasonable for a doctor to hire a resident or a fellow to babysit (or do research, or do personal-assistant work). But Joanie seemed too familiar with him lately, the way she addressed him, whatever it was in their relationship that made her at least think of him as his first name, and he worried about that. So he texted the yoga teacher/performance artist who had babysat for the kids a couple of times.

He finally turned to face the nagging in his chest. He had no permanent babysitter. Now that they were back, he realized that he could return them to day camp, which ended at three, but honestly, this was untenable. He wanted to call Mona; he wanted to show up wherever she was right now (Queens? Staten Island?) and tell her what came over him, how sorry he was, how she was the glue hold-ing this family together or some such. She would understand. She knew what it was like to be brought to madness by Rachel—she had to. She'd been working for them for almost twelve years.

But he couldn't. This was Rachel's mess to clean up. She was the reason he was so hair-trigger. And firing Mona was the right thing to do. It was, right? Hours of porn! He had an idea. He went into his bedroom and called the camp director at the sleepaway camp to see if there was room in the fourth-grade bunk, too. The director said yes, but it was too late to enroll.

"I'm having some extenuating circumstances here," Toby said.

The director was quiet.

"My wife and I, we just had a separation, and I feel like it would really be good for the kids to have some distance from home right now."

"I met your son on the tour. He seemed pretty adamant that he didn't want to go to camp. We don't want to create a situation—we have so many kids here who think they are ready for camp and aren't. The ones who don't even think they're ready, well . . ."

"The tour was in April. Things change."

"So he wants to come now?"

"I'd really like to give him the option."

"Let me discuss with the division director. I'll call you back as soon as we connect."

He put down his phone and stared out his bedroom window for a minute before he stood up and went into the living room, which was dark, except for the glow illuminating Hannah's face from her new phone. He entered Solly's room to read him a chapter book they'd been reading every night about a boy who is abducted by his teachers, all of whom were secretly aliens all along.

"I bet that could happen," Solly said.

"You never know."

Toby shut off Solly's lamp and started scratching his back. He took a breath and dared himself before saying, slowly, "I think you would love camp." Solly stopped breathing in the dark. Caution, Fleishman. "It's a shame you don't want to go."

"I don't want to be away from you and Mom."

·"That's okay. You can stay home. I'd never force you to go." Toby began scratching Solly's arm like he liked. "But it's just really cool. They have movie nights. Max is going. Jonah is going. It's just for a month. But you have to do what you feel like when you're ready. Don't let anyone force you into anything."

"Right."

"Do you know they have an archery program there?"

"Yeah," he said wistfully. "I saw when we visited."

"Yeah, it's usually for the older grades, but this year they're letting fourth-graders try it."

"Really? Well, it's too late anyway."

It was wrong. It was terrible. He shouldn't do this. But if he could just get Solly to go away for a bit, Rachel would come home and the kids would never have to know what was happening. And if she wasn't home in a month, he'd deal with it. But he needed to buy some time. This was for Solly's own good.

"Of course, the decision is yours. It just might be that everyone comes back from camp and they're talking about stuff and you feel left out."

Solly considered this. He looked up at Toby in the dark. "Maybe I should. Do you think I should?"

"I think you'd love it. I don't want to make any decisions for you, but I think you'd love it."

"And if I call you and I hate it?"

"I'll pick you up. You don't have to stay somewhere you don't like. But Hannah will be there, and if you're scared or homesick, you can always go talk to her."

"Maybe I should," Solly said.

Solly fell asleep but Toby kept scratching his arm.

B y Monday morning, Karen Cooper was number twelve on the transplant list, and still unresponsive. Toby met his fellows at the nurses' station outside her room. They looked him hard in the face to see what today would be like for him and them, and he realized this and instantly felt bad about how angry he'd gotten at them. That was no way to teach, to scream at your students like that.

"How's our patient?" Toby asked. They relaxed.

"No change," Logan said. "Continued acute liver failure, normal signs of activity in the brain, but nothing upward."

"How was your vacation, Dr. Fleishman?" Clay asked.

"It wasn't really a vacation. More of a childcare issue." Silence. They wanted blood, too. Well, they couldn't have it. "It was fine."

They entered Mrs. Cooper's room. She was even yellower than she'd been. In the corner were two boys around Hannah's age. Joanie introduced them as Jasper and Jacob Cooper, the patient's twin sons, looking miserable as they played on iPads. David Cooper made them stand and shake Toby's hand. David had spent the weekend reading WebMD and watching YouTube videos of people with Wilson's disease and having his assistants compile dossiers about it. But he still didn't understand that Wilson's disease was tricky and rare, and that it was hard to diagnose, which was why so many people who had it found out about it late, and mostly when it got to this point, it was irreversible. They never heard that part, that there was damage already done. That a miracle would be her staying alive; restoring her back to who she had been was no longer on the menu of possible outcomes.

"We are going to do our best to get her back to her old self," Toby said. "But depending on how far along the disease is, and it was probably exacerbated by her Vegas weekend, we don't know if she'll still have neurological symptoms. They might still be there. They might even be worse. But we could stop them from progressing."

His phone pinged. It was the director from Hannah's sleepaway camp.

We have one space for Solomon's age

He looked back at David Cooper and tried to focus. "We'll get through this," he said.

He went back to the conference room to tell Solly the good news.

Just a few months ago, Rachel had wanted Solly to go to sleepaway camp for the summer, and Toby had fought hard to keep him home.

"No fucking way," she said one night. "He has to learn. He's eight. That's when Hannah went. That's when he's going."

"But he doesn't want to go."

"Well, we don't always get to do what we want. We're supposed to lead them into adulthood, Toby."

"Oh, is that what we're supposed to do?"

Rachel's annoyance at all this was compounded by the fact that

Solly had also recently watched a Disney Channel show about tween figure skaters, two of whom were boys, and he had asked if there were figure skating classes he could take. "I'll look into it," Toby had said, and Rachel was silent, and yes, the phrase "this is too easy" did flash across Toby's internal Chyron, because later that night, when Solly was in bed, Rachel said, "I'm sure we agree that he's doing basketball this year." This was how she spoke with her employees. She began all her demands and notions that weren't up for debate with "I'm sure we agree."

"He wants to ice-skate. Why is that bad?"

Rachel stared at him like don't make me say it.

"Come on, Rach."

"He wants to figure skate," she said. "It's not a great sport. He needs a great sport he can play his whole life. It's our job to create a diversity of experience for him."

"Is 'diversity of experience' an agent thing? Because it's not a real-life thing."

"You don't get to decide everything, Toby. I'm his mother."

"And you don't get to decide just because you're paying for it! I'm not your assistant."

It was only in the last year that they both had begun to acknowledge that the money that Rachel brought in was money she somehow controlled. Back when she was an assistant at Alfooz, Toby had outearned her even with his starting salary as a resident, but the money was considered both of theirs. It went into a joint account that they both had access to. It did all these years later, too, but there had been a shift. The more she worked, the more money came through the door, and it was only six months into her new agency, and they had a savings account, one that could support them for two months if something bad happened. Then it was a year, and Toby's med school loans were dwindling to almost half of what they had been. Then it was four years later and they were going to Europe and South America on vacations and putting money away for college. Their choices became easier. Their desperation left them. She wanted to go on a vacation (and so it was happening), she wanted a summer rental (and so it was happening), she wanted to redecorate (and so it was happening). He convinced himself that that was just the strong-willed woman he married. He bet Bartuck's wife made domestic decisions like that. But then, recently, it became more overt: This is this money and here is how we're spending it and if you want to be able to make those kinds of decisions, you should make this kind of money. It was never said. It was just beyond what was said, and he knew (and she had to know) that he wouldn't be able to bear to hear it actually voiced, and so he tiptoed to the edge but never plunged into the abyss of it.

"I just think that this approach to parenting, where we're not supposed to know what's best for our children, is ridiculous," she was saying.

"The kid should be able to do what he wants to do." Overwhelm shook Toby before adrenaline did; the result was light-headedness.

"I don't want him to be made fun of," she said, her hands in fists and talking through upper and lower teeth that were still clenched together. "Do you know what the kids will do to him if they find out he's in figure skating camp?"

"He likes it, though. And the gym teacher had said we should enroll him in some kind of full-body flexibility sport. Remember? At the last parent-teacher conference? Oh, wait, you weren't there."

"Oh, yes, please persecute me for actually doing my job and giving us this life. We can't all clock out at five, like you. I'd think I was married to a banker, except if that were true, well."

"How long have you been waiting to use that one?" he asked.

"I would just hate for him to not even understand the implications of what he was getting into. That's not me. That's the world. And the world doesn't really get him. Does he have as many friends as he should? I don't think so."

But that was bullshit. Solly didn't not have friends. He just preferred to be with his family, or reading one of his *Star Trek* books.
"He has friends. How about Max?"

"Max is only friends with him because I'm friends with Roxanne."

"Max is friends with him because he's a delightful boy."

"Of course he is. But that's not how this works. They're friends
because I put in the time with Roxanne. The parent encourages the
friendship between her child and the friend whose parents aren't
nightmares. I put in time with Roxanne, therefore she suggests Max
for a playdate since it might mean we can spend time together."

"You put in the time with Roxanne because you're a social
climber and you want to be invited to rich people's houses."

Rachel stared at him for a cold two seconds. "He needs to go to
sleepaway camp so that he can grow and become independent."

"Why are you so eager to get rid of them, Rachel? We wanted
them, remember?"

"That's not what this is about. It's about interrogating exactly
why, when other children are finding independence, ours seem to
want to crawl back into the womb. God, you make me into such a
monster."

Later that night, as they found themselves in the usual chilly
détente that followed their fights, he wondered who was going to
restore things to the normal state of tensions. Rachel was sitting at
the kitchen table, on her laptop, and Toby wondered if she wondered the same thing. Hannah came into the kitchen while Toby
was making dinner. "I'm glad you're both here," she announced,
standing stiffly. "I would like an Instagram account like literally
every single person I know has. I am being left out of everything
and everyone comes to school every day in the middle of all this
stuff that happened on Instagram and I am clueless."

"You don't need Instagram," Toby said. He set the oven to pre-
heat. "It's stressful and you'll have that stuff in your life forever.

We're just trying to preserve a little sanity for you before we can't anymore." He rinsed off a few drumsticks and washed his hands. "You are going to thank us for this one day."

Hannah started screaming. "I am such a loser and this is so unfair."

Rachel finally looked up from her computer. "Maybe we should reconsider."

Toby whipped around to her. "Rachel!"

"She's making a good point!" Rachel said. "I don't like it either, but she shouldn't be made to feel different from the world we've pushed her into."

Toby stared at Rachel. "She will be twelve in less than a year. We have always said she can get an Instagram account when she's twelve." Then, to Hannah, "There are good reasons for this."

"Yeah, so that I'll have no friends, which is what you want."

"No," he said. "There are studies that talk about kids your age and anxiety and social media—that this will not be a good thing for you. It will make you feel bad, even though it's something you think you want."

"Don't tell her what she thinks she wants," Rachel said. "She knows what she wants. She's not an infant."

"Don't undermine the thing we already agreed to."

Hannah broke in. "Has anyone considered the amount of anxiety I have knowing that everyone is hanging out without me? Have you considered that?"

Rachel considered this. "It might be true. You know, Miriam Rothberg told me that she wasn't going to let the kids do it, either, and then she read that the anxiety of everyone else having it was worse than the anxiety that the thing actually gives you."

"We're not the Rothbergs," Toby said, holding a raw drumstick in his hand.

Rachel let out a one-note laugh with her nose. "I'll say." She looked over at Hannah. "Let me talk to Dad about it privately," Rachel said, a wink in her voice, and before Toby could really think, he turned around and threw the raw chicken leg at Rachel's computer. It hit the screen and slid down onto the keyboard, leaving a trail of God knows what.

Rachel and Hannah recoiled in disgust, their top lips curled up against the tips of their noses. He saw then that Hannah was being poised to grow into his enemy. He wouldn't have it.

"You're an animal," Rachel said, and went to the cabinet under the sink and took out a Clorox wipe to get the raw chicken juice off her computer but left the leg on the floor. Rachel turned and walked out, and Hannah did the same in an identical goose step.

It was unavoidable. They had to pick up their clothing from Rachel's place in order to pack. Even if he could rationalize to them the need for new clothing, he didn't want to waste money on new suitcases.

Hannah pouted the whole way.

"He *can't* come to camp with me." She had a vile look on her face. "He will *humiliate* me."

"Hannah. He's your brother."

They arrived at the Golden. The doorman, shiny and navy with badges and braids like a war hero, was on the phone while a deliveryman waited. Toby didn't recognize him. He must have been new. These were the gray areas. Did the doorman now have to call up? Let's not figure this out right now. He began a confident walk toward the elevator and the doorman didn't notice.

He sent the kids upstairs with the key while he went to the basement storage to get the suitcases.

He took his time. He didn't want to go into her apartment. He didn't want to see it. He didn't want to sit on the furniture chosen by Luc the penguin decorator in shades of white and beige, and he didn't want to stare at the large-scale modern paintings chosen by Rene the art consultant in peaches and taupes. But he lingered and they would be wondering where he was, so he finally went upstairs to the ninth floor and walked a dead-man-walking march to the front door.

Now the door made a noise and Toby jumped. Hannah said, "Took you long enough," and grabbed the suitcases from him. Toby told her she should pack them both up, and that he had to take a call from the hospital but would be waiting downstairs.

His conversations with Nahid had started the same way all the others had. She had reached out to him on Hr. He had used Seth's rules of sexting entry, which were as follows:

> 1. Resolved: Women are in absolute control of themselves one hundred percent of the time.
> 2. If, therefore, a woman says anything that a seventh-grade boy could interpret as sexual or respond to with "That's what she said," that is the woman's outstretched invitation to sex talk.

Toby and Nahid's second day of texting went like this:

HER: *How's your day been?*
HIM: *Went to moma.*
HER: *There's an exhibit there of movie costumes.*
HIM: *I've heard good things about it.*
HER: *You have to come sometime.*
HIM: *Sure*
HER: *No, really, I want you to come*

Was this it? Was this his chance? It seemed a little on the nose, and he didn't want to come off as a complete perv, but a lot of this shit was on the nose, right? He considered his next move for an entire thirty seconds. Then:

HIM: *[embarrassed face emoji]*

He waited while she considered her response, and in that maybe twenty-five seconds (or three minutes or two seconds, he couldn't say, he only experienced that time as a fever), he experienced regret, shame, revulsion, self-loathing, and then:

HER: *Nothing wrong with coming [purple devil emoji]*

In his experience, which, yes, was brief, okay, but still, the sexier and steamier it got via text message and app, the less likely an actual in-person encounter would be. And it was something of a relief that embarrassment and shame still existed on this level; it was what kept all the single, available people in New York from grabbing each other and dry-humping on the streets. His animal brain preferred the sexier interactions, even if they didn't lead to dates. Yes, real-life encounters are good, and yes, one should probably always opt for a real-life encounter, lest one wear his wrist ligaments down to nubs from chronic and alarming amounts of masturbation. But the phone stuff, man. He loved it.

All that to say that it did not seem, from Nahid's immediate and aggressive sexual relationship with Toby over their smartphones, that they would ever actually see each other. How could the human parameters of shame ever permit it? She was so . . . verbal in her wants. She was so . . . articulate in her texts. She wanted him to bend her over the bathroom sink so they could both watch her come in the medicine cabinet mirror. She wanted to pretend their kids were on a playdate together, and that she just needed him to change a lightbulb for her in the bathroom, and that while he was on the ladder, she would unzip his fly while the children knocked at the door begging for a snack—"Just one minute, honey, I have some screwing to do here." She proposed that she was a fighter pilot who was so horny she couldn't complete her mission unless she was riding his dick while flying her plane to save her country, him seated beneath her like he was her booster seat. There was something alluring about her strange creativity, about the bizarreness of her requests, and the lack of self-consciousness. But also, there were evolutionary biological factors outside his logic and reason working at this. They were the factors that made him call the yoga-teacher-performance-artist-babysitter. They were the factors that made him change his shirt twice, and toy with a blazer, but it was hot out, and in the mirror, he felt he'd looked clownish, like a boy pretending to be a man, and open the shirt one more button (then close it, then open it again).

"Where are you going?" asked Hannah, who had settled in for a romantic evening on the couch with her phone.

"I'm going on a playdate," Toby answered. He was fixing his hair in the mirror. He heard the doorbell ring and Solly open it and greet the babysitter.

"With a girl?" Hannah asked.

"Yes."

"That's gross."

"I know. Someday you'll understand."

"It's not because it's kissing a girl. It's because you're my father."

"Who said anything about kissing?" Toby put his hand to her forehead and left.

He practically jogged to the West Side. He practically skipped. He practically flew. Look at me, he said to all the lazy couples in the park. Look at me going to get laid. He told her doorman who he was. The doorman said she was expecting him. He arrived on the fourteenth floor. He was trying to think of a good opener, like maybe telling her she really lived on the thirteenth floor and who was she kidding anyway, which was his best fourteenth-floor joke. But the door opened before he knocked, and he was barely through the front door before his pants were around his ankles, his hands inside her, her hands on him and inside him, his mouth on her nipple, her finger in his rectum, which was not something he loved but it felt too new in the relationship to really nitpick. He pulled back to look at her face for the first time, since it was her one body part she wouldn't show him in texting, and she had lips that were plump and pink and hair that grew in every direction and dark eyes and skin one shade darker than olive. She was lovely, and most of all, she was not a gang of men conspiring to rob him and she was not a teenage boy playing a joke on him. He had no more questions. He closed his eyes and submitted to her.

He didn't take a cab home, even though he knew he risked annoying the babysitter by running late. No, instead, he stomped through the park, feeling big and tall and virile, like he owned this city and that it was all for him and that, once again, he was at the beginning of something profound and new and that smelled like sunshine.

He thought of Nahid in her bed, lying atop the top sheet. She was tracing his shoulder with her finger.

"So what do you do all day?" he had asked her.

She laughed. "That's your pillow talk?"

"Sorry," he said. He was embarrassed.

"Oh, don't be. Who knows what to say in these situations? I don't work."

He made his voice into a weird foreign accent. "Are you a kept woman?" He felt like an idiot the minute he said it.

She stopped her tracing motion. "This isn't a job interview, is it?"

He walked through his door at one, hoping he didn't smell too much like sex when he paid the babysitter. He took a shower and checked his phone to see if Nahid had been in touch already. When he entered the bedroom with a towel around his waist and looked up from his phone, he noticed that Hannah had woken up and was sitting in his bed.

"You have camp in the morning."

She was clutching her phone; it already had an appendage feel about it. He looked more closely at her. "Are you crying?"

"I texted Mom."

He sat down on the edge of his bed. "And?"

"She didn't respond."

On the day Hannah was born, as the surgeons sewed Rachel back up, Toby held her. He couldn't look away from her. "You are mine forever," he whispered. "I will always take care of you." Rachel was crying, her arms splayed out like she was on a crucifix, and still he couldn't look away from his new baby.

The next day, Rachel said that in the dysphoria and near-mania that followed that hellscape of a thirty-five-hour labor that failed in every possible way except the most important one, she watched Toby and their baby and felt like she'd been tricked. She said she suddenly realized that the whole goal all along had been to get her to have a baby so that they two could be together, Toby and Hannah, and she could be discarded. She raved about this in her hospital bed, and in the coming weeks and months, even as she slowly got better physically and emotionally, she still talked about this first instance of motherhood, about having felt she'd been tricked. People would come to the house to see the new baby, and she would answer their innocent question about how labor had gone, but she couldn't do it politely. She had to go into the details of how scary it was and how alone she'd felt, and she'd always end with the story about Toby holding Baby Hannah in his arms, and her conspiracy theory that her marriage had been a ruse for Toby to get his baby and leave her behind. It was unlike her. She usually kept things so light with strangers; she was usually so concerned about appearances. He didn't know why he thought about that now, except that Hannah looked so much like her mother when she was angry or scared or hurt or neutral. She only looked like Toby when she smiled.

"She doesn't know you got a phone," he said. "She doesn't know your number."

"But I wrote, 'It's Hannah.' And then I called her."

"And?"

"And it went straight to voicemail."

The last time he'd called her it went straight to voicemail, too.

"She could be in meetings. She could be asleep. She could just not be looking at her phone."

"Maybe she's angry at me for getting a phone before my birthday."

"No, that's silly. She could be sleeping, we don't know. It's late."

He reached for her hand but she pulled it away.

"Dad. Is she dead?"

"Oh God, no, Hannah. What? No, she's not dead. She's totally fine. She's working. You know how she gets. There are some places where there are literally no hours that we're both awake."

"You've spoken to her?"

"Yes, of course. She sends her love."

Hannah looked down at his comforter, where she kept tracing the same indistinct design.

"You should go to bed," he said. "You have to be up early and you haven't even packed your bus bag."

Hannah finished her tracing loop and then stood up and went back to her room.

Toby woke up to Solly standing over him and shaking his shoulders. "Dad," he said.

Toby jumped out of bed, bleary and panicked. "What is it?" It was still dark out.

"We have to go to the bus for camp. We're gonna miss the bus."

Toby looked around for a minute, then sat down on his bed. "Okay, let me get some coffee." Solly was jumping in place.

"It's okay if you're nervous." Toby looked at his phone for the time and saw that Nahid had sent a text. The night came rushing back to him. It was only four-thirty. "Bud, we have two hours before the bus leaves. Should we go back to sleep for a while?"

But Solly wasn't having it. He was dragging Toby by the hand to the coffee maker and talking like he'd just done ten lines of cocaine. "I'm bringing all of my *Green Lantern* comics on the bus because they're light but also because when people see me reading one they'll want to read one and then I'll have one for everyone."

"You think you should take all of them? They're special to you."

"I think it's a good idea. Also, I'm bringing Stealth Bunny." Stealth Bunny was a square of Solly's baby blanket that used to just be called Bunny. Rachel had told him on his sixth birthday that it was time to give up his baby blanket, that he'd never be invited to sleepovers, or that kids would make fun of him if they ever came over and found it. Solly went to his room and hid the blanket so that Rachel couldn't find it. Later, when Rachel was working on her laptop in the living room, Toby sneaked into Solly's room with scissors. He told Solly they could cut a piece of Bunny Blanket. It would have all the power of the rest of the blanket, since he'd put all his love into it over all these years. And best of all, it would be even easier to carry around. "We'll call it Stealth Bunny," Toby said, as he carefully cut the center square. "What's stealth?" Solly asked, watching. "It means that you're the only one that knows about it."

"Where are you going to keep Stealth Bunny?" Toby asked now.

"Just on me. In my pocket. At all times."

"You think that's a good idea? What if you lose it?"

"I would never lose Stealth Bunny."

They played chess for the next half hour. Toby got a whiff of Nahid and took another shower. Solly woke Hannah up, which Toby knew because even in the shower he heard her screeching at him. Toby fed them breakfast, letting Solly fill the room with his anxiety, answering all his questions and praying that Hannah's sullenness was the usual sullenness and that she was no longer thinking about her mother.

Toby read the text message from Nahid, who was wondering if perhaps after his kids were asleep tonight, he might want her to drop by *to do me in your elevator—no one will know [purple devil emoji, two eyeballs looking to the left emoji]*. Last night felt like a long time ago.

He asked Hannah to see her phone.

"Why?"

"Because I'm your father."

"No."

"I'm not really asking. This is part of the deal."

She handed it over, furious, and Toby scrolled through her Instagram, spot-checking like he'd read in a *Consumer Reports* special issue on kids and technology. It all seemed fine and innocent, if a little boring. Her avatar was a selfie where she was putting up two fingers like a reverse peace sign, like kids had begun to do in all their pictures—it was maybe something a member of a boy band did, or an athlete? He didn't know. He looked through her updates. She had twenty-two friends, and her only two updates said "Going to camp, so psyched" and "Check this out LOL," accompanying a picture of a cat in sunglasses with puffy text overlaid that read, "I think I'm allergic to mornings." What was she doing poring over this thing all day when she was basically posting once a day about what she ate, and waiting for likes, and then liking other kids' almost identical posts? It made him so sad for her and her friends for how self-conscious they were, how they had to grow up in a time when the world conspired to make them even more self-conscious.

"You'rc like the Gestapo," she shouted at him.

"I think you haven't learned enough about World War Two if you think that's the case."

"No, you are. You're the Gestapo."

"Stasi is more accurate, but even that."

Toby turned his attention to Solly.

"You sure you're feeling good about this, Sol?" Toby asked.

"I'm really excited. But will you be lonely without us?"

Toby stood up to clear the dishes. "I'm going to miss you very much, but I'll get a lot of work and stuff done, and maybe I'll even have a surprise for you when you get back."

Solly jumped. "What is it, Dad?"

"What does the word 'surprise' mean?"

"Tell me!"

"My lips are sealed. You'll have to wait."

At the bus stop, Toby could feel Solly's jittery hum in his hug. He crouched down and looked him straight in the eye. "You are going to do so well there. And I am going to miss you so much."

Solly pushed his face against Toby. "Will you be there on visiting day?" he asked into his neck.

"I will."

"And Mom will come, right? And she'll email."

"She'll do her best."

"And if I want to come home . . ."

"I'll come get you. I'll always answer my phone. It's not very far away."

Next, Hannah dropped her arms and turned her head and let Toby hug her like he was poison. He took her face in his hands and said, "I love you and I know you love me. You can act however you want to, but you're my girl and I am your dad." She wrestled her head out of his hands and boarded the bus without looking at him. Solly followed her.

He stood looking at the bus for a long time, waving though he couldn't see behind the bus's tinted windows, trying not to think about what he'd done. The bus left, and he waved until they couldn't possibly see him anymore. He walked away and sent a text to Nahid:

My kids just boarded the camp bus.

The answer came quickly:

Get here

So he did. He was only ninety minutes late for work.

———

That night, he had a dream that he was in space and Rachel was there, but he couldn't tell if she was a planet or a star, and he couldn't ascertain her orbit, and yes it was a little on the nose but what are you going to do. He woke up three times. The first time, it was panic: *You are in trouble. Fleishman is in trouble.*

The second time he woke up he was angry. It was more than a week now, which was long, yes, but that was just like her. Or it was thematically like her. She'd never pulled this kind of thing quite this long. He knew her too well, though. She was doing something he wouldn't approve of, and had decided to apologize later. Or maybe not! Her apologizing days were probably over as far as he was concerned.

The third time he awoke, he was back to panicking. He got out of bed before a dead image of his ex-wife could turn to him and say, "Why didn't you save me, Toby?" He thought that maybe the one upside to Rachel having vanished and the kids being at camp would be the tiniest shot that he'd feel something akin to freedom, but he didn't; he just felt untethered and lost. He thought of the kids now. When Hannah was a baby, there was a grocery store nearby that gave out balloons (this was before they realized the balloons were strangling the seagulls and discontinued the practice). Before they walked into the apartment, they'd say goodbye to the balloon by letting it go. They'd watch as it floated up and away, and Toby would feel disoriented and hug her tighter, like she was filled with helium, too.

It was four-thirty. He went to the gym in his building, which only had an old StairMaster and dumbbells and two treadmills, though one was broken seemingly forever. He took a shower, and when he got out, he checked his phone to see what new misery the weather would bring him today and he saw that there was a missed call from Simone.

It was six forty-five by now. Why would Simone be calling him? His stomach bottomed out and he sat, naked, on his bed, staring at the missed call. He called it back, but after a ring it got pushed to voicemail. He began to sweat through his shower-dampness.

Fuck this, he thought. It was Rachel, pulling her regular shit—having Simone call to arrange a pickup so she wouldn't have to deal with Toby. He got some pleasure thinking of Rachel arriving to pick up the kids to find out they weren't even here. He participated in an extended fantasy about moving to another city with the children and letting her figure it out.

At last, it was an acceptable time to show up at work. Early, yes, but acceptably early and he had some face time to make up for. Phillipa London arrived every day at seven A.M. He made sure to pass her office, since it was Phillipa whose promotion would create the vacancy that Bartuck said was basically (absolutely) Toby's. He'd always thought of her as one of the good ones, a doctor who was dedicated to healing, with no tolerance for bullshit. But now that she was gunning for Bartuck's job he thought that maybe she was like the rest of them. People thought the crisis in medicine had to do with insurance, but it also had to do with doctors who had checked out and now were just in it for a cash grab. He stopped in to talk to her.

"Hey, Phillipa."

She was sitting at her desk, her straight beige hair pulled into a cyclonic cone on the back of her head. She looked up from a case file she was reading. She wore silky blouses and pencil skirts and pearls and big glasses.

"Toby, hi." Her nose had an upturned quality to it, so that when she was sitting, she looked like she was too good for you and when she was standing, well, who knew because she must have been at least five-ten or maybe even five-eleven.

"I have a Wilson's case, so I thought I'd check in, but"—he was flailing—"I'm waiting on lab results."

Her four fellows appeared at the door. "Dr. London, there's a consult in the ICU."

She smiled at Toby. "I'm being paged."

Toby left her office and didn't quite know where to go. Phillipa's fellows called her Dr. London, and that was all you needed to know about her. Maybe it wasn't ideal for Toby's fellows to be so familiar with him, to download dirty apps for him and whatnot, but also he was breeding an environment where they felt comfortable enough to ask questions. He stood outside Phillipa's office, checking his phone. Absent his parental responsibilities, absent the forward motion of knowing that he'd eventually have to get home and cook dinner, he was now drifting. He missed his kids.

He told David Cooper that Karen was third on the transplant list. But Toby's reserves were depleted, of both rest and fluids. In his weakened state, he was susceptible and primed for the acute jealousy of the thing he saw before him, which was an utterly normal marriage, a thing he had tried so hard at and had wanted so badly. It was an enormous privilege to take your spouse for granted until something bad happened; that was life, and that was beautiful, this idea that you'd just be trudging along and remember each other's birthdays once a year and fall into bed exhausted and wonder if you had enough sex and then one day BAM! you become awakened to just how much you needed that person—some crisis like this, and that was all you'd need to remember how much you loved your spouse. That was all Toby had ever wanted. Sometimes you saw couples who seemed wild about each other, always holding hands, sitting on the same side of the table when they ate out, even when they were together alone. Rachel would say that those people were putting on a show, that they were covering up a real poison in their relationship, and that was the only time Toby ever felt like she was on his side: when she was working as hard as he was to make their misery seem normal.

He walked into his office and pretended to look at his phone because he needed a second to think. You couldn't be alone in this hospital. There was nowhere to just sit and be. Even when you just wanted to zone out in the middle of your own office, everyone could see. Nobody told you how important it would be to constantly appear stable while you were getting a divorce, because everything you said and did would be more meaningful and poignant than you'd intended. Standing alone in the middle of your office, staring into the middle distance, was not a sign of stability.

He looked up and saw Joanie, who'd been on call overnight. "You look tired, Toby." She put her hand on his upper arm, a move that could be taken for friendship but could also be taken for something else. She was looking hard into his eyes, trying to get behind them. He thought back to a month ago—was that just over a month ago?—when he felt young and new and like his whole life was ahead of him, and he sat in his lecture hall after class and Joanie had taken his phone from him and downloaded dating apps while he tried not to giggle. The summer had just begun then; it felt like it was never going to end. It felt like he would never feel pain again. Now, the heat was suffocating.

"Is everything okay, Toby?" she asked. Why was she calling him by his first name? He had a pit in his stomach from the intimacy— a regret that he'd allowed himself to be unseated as a giant to his students. They had seen too much of his personal life; they'd seen him too sad lately, and too worried. He'd stopped instructing them. He was awful.

He thought about telling her to call him Dr. Fleishman, but he couldn't quite figure out a tone that would allow him to pull that off—Joking? Chiding? Authoritative?

"Everything's fine," he said.

She took another step toward him, and it wasn't that she was close, it was more that she was advancing, and his only recourse was to let her or to step backward. He stepped backward.

"I'm worried about you," she said. "I know you're going through something."

"What do you know?" He tried to laugh. "What do you think you know?"

What was she doing? He didn't think she had this kind of boldness in her. After this round of fellows had completed their first year, he'd taken them to Chelsea Piers to celebrate with a trapeze lesson—it was the conclusion of an extensive in-joke they'd all developed over the year about offsite corporate events that included team-building exercises. She'd been too afraid to try, but she'd watched, and when he was done with his turn, he'd sat on the side with her and talked to her and learned she was in a club consisting of mostly old men who went to Marx Brothers screenings and that she did improv and was learning how to play bridge. She'd said, "I've been in training for old age my whole life," and he'd laughed, having not realized that she was funny; he'd thought she was just this mousy, studious type with alternative affectations, a wacky-neighbor character with no real footprint. He'd felt so bad for her, like how was she going to function in life if she couldn't even hang (literally, figuratively) with her co-workers. Then, finally, a year into her fellowship, he learned that despite her quiet, despite her apparent wish to fade into the background, she *was* a real person. It was just that she hid herself in plain sight. He began to see everything she did as deliberate. He didn't feel bad for her anymore. Instead, he just felt foolish, the way quiet, smart people can make you feel dumb just for existing.

Now she took one more step. She was wearing a plaid skirt that reached her knee and a flimsy, short-sleeve oxford shirt and saddle shoes. She reached to touch his hand, just really a finger brushing his hand, but in the glass wall behind her, the head nurse on the floor, Gilda, passed by with her lips pursed together in disapproval —not curiosity, not surprise, just lightning disappointment, as if this were something she'd always expected of Toby.

Let's just say, for a second, that he took one step toward her instead of one back. Let's say he and Joanie met eyes soulfully and what could he say, it was love? He would not have invented this.

Maggie Bartuck had been a nurse when Donald Bartuck was still with his first wife. Everyone had known what was going on at the time. His first wife would occasionally come to the floor with her dour face and hair dyed one shade too black for her age. And Maggie wore scrubs that weren't just like a pillowcase. She had sewn a waist into them so that they showed off her figure. Marco Lintz, back when they were both fellows, told Toby that he'd heard that Bartuck's secretary had seen Bartuck at the X-ray screen one day, looking at an actual film, and Maggie was in front of him, also looking, and Bartuck was sticking his pantsed erection into Nurse Maggie's scrub'ed rear end. A month later, Bartuck announced his divorce, and just two weeks after that his engagement to Maggie, who never wore scrubs again.

"What a cliché," Toby had said to Rachel at the wedding, which was at the Waldorf. They were eating chocolate-covered strawberries. Bartuck's fraternity brothers sang a Greek song to him. Someone told Toby they'd done the same thing at his first wedding.

"I don't know," Rachel said. "People should be with who makes them happy. There has to be someone for everyone, right?"

"Yeah, but not two someones for everyone."

"How do you know?" she said. "Do I have anything in my teeth?"

Joanie was young, but she wasn't a child. Twenty-five is—Wait. No. He stopped himself from completing his next thought. No, Fleishman, no, he thought. This was how you became frog soup: You go in the same moment from thinking of Joanie as a student, then not really a child, and before you know it you're meeting her for drinks, then fucking her in her dirty, shared apartment in Queens. Or no: They'd start with a real date, like an old-fashioned one. They'd do it privately, then wait a few months after she'd completed her fellowship to get engaged, then married. If they announced their relationship via an engagement, versus just maintaining a nebulous, quasi-legitimate state of boyfriend-girlfriend-dom, nobody would dare to impugn—

His phone made a sound. Purpose! He looked down. A message from Bartuck's secretary, asking him to stop by the office as soon as he can. More purpose!

"I have a meeting with Dr. Bartuck," he said.

"It's okay. We can catch up later. I . . . Logan and I broke up."

He stopped. "I'm sorry to hear that," he said. "I hope you have people you can talk to about that."

"I thought, I don't know. I know you just got divorced and I know it's not the same thing, but I'm sad and you're sad and I don't know."

"Human relationships aren't easy."

She leaned forward. "Love isn't easy."

Her voice and half smile were teasing. Women astounded him. They thought they weren't the ruling sex, but he was sitting there, watching her face in the light coming through the window behind him. Her skin was so flush and thick. Her youth was so staggering it was offensive.

"I have to see Dr. Bartuck," Toby said.

Donald Bartuck squinted and jutted his lips out and did a small nod that made his mighty jowl quiver.

"Toby, come in," Bartuck said. "I hope everything worked its way out at home?"

"Yes, thank you, it was a rough few days. The kids went off to sleepaway camp this morning."

"I wanted you to know that we're meeting about you tomorrow. I expect Phillipa to accept my recommendation."

"Well, what news," Toby said, and stood to shake his hand.

"I know it's been a hard time for you. I'm hoping this one washes off soon. Phillipa's job is not a small deal. Don't make me look bad here."

Bartuck had started at the hospital as an intern in the seventies, slick and bombastic and secure. His own father was the legendary head of the department at the time. Bartuck's career was handed to him—not just because of his lineage, but because of his confidence, the way you just wanted to hand responsibility over to Bartuck—and all he had to do was not screw it up. He hadn't.

He was a good doctor; he was even great. That was the worst part of Bartuck. He had been such a good mentor to Toby that it had been impossible to foresee that he'd become the oily money guy that he had become. Or maybe what was hard was accepting that you could be both a good doctor and a money guy and still choose to be the money guy? Either way it was sad. When Toby was one of his fellows, Bartuck told him war stories and gave him whiskey in his office at the end of their hard days. Toby remembered when Martin Loo, a subdivision head in gastroenterology, died from pancreatic cancer in a fast, sad sequence of hospital poetry that reaffirmed to Toby that what he did was good and worthy. Toby and Bartuck sat in Martin Loo's room for hours during his final weeks, and Toby listened to them talk about their good old days at the hospital, and stories from before medical records were digital and nobody knew anything. They laughed together until Dr. Loo was too exhausted and needed to rest.

Toby and Bartuck were in the room with Dr. Loo when he died. As his breaths began coming further and further apart, they'd stood up to leave him with his wife and children. But Martin's wife had stopped them and said she believed that Martin, three days unconscious by then, would have wanted them to stay. "You were as big a part of his life as we were." When finally his last breath was drawn, his wife put her forehead to his and said, "Goodbye, my love," and Toby had felt then that despite his early death, Martin Loo was a lucky man. So was Toby. Right then, he couldn't help but think what a privilege all of this was: to know these people, to try with them.

Afterward, Bartuck took Toby into his office and poured him a Scotch. Toby was still so dreamy from Martin Loo, and he would for so long associate the beauty of that terrible moment with Bartuck. It would only be much later that Toby realized what a too-slick fuck Bartuck was—how his compassion and camaraderie had been a display designed to advance him to the next level.

Bartuck had taken an interest in Toby. Not in Phillipa London—in him. Toby would go home and share news of the day with Rachel. "You have to ride this mentorship to the sky," she would say, which was the kind of imbecile power-talk they used in the mailroom at Alfooz & Lichtenstein. Until Bartuck had shown interest in Toby, Rachel had thought he should go into dermatology because of the money those doctors made, and how they took August off and made their own hours and never had emergencies. But Toby wanted to be a doctor to cure illness, and he didn't know any dermatologist who made his money on true illness and not plastics.

"But you could go to Africa or Asia or wherever over the summer and fix cleft palates," she said.

"I don't want to live a month of my life in apology for the thing I do the rest of the year," he said. "I want to live a good life every day."

"We all do," she said, exasperated. "Who has that luxury? I'd like to eventually own an apartment, you know?"

Toby's father was a doctor, and his uncle was a doctor, and his sister at the time was considering becoming a psychologist before she hung it up and decided to just marry and pray and breed. The Fleishmans had raised their children on the model of a person in a white coat giving solace and peace and healing to someone who needed it. On weekends, the kids of the neighborhood would hurt their knees or come down with high fevers, and the parents of the neighborhood would knock on the Fleishmans' door, even if Sid Lapis, another internist, might have lived closer to them. This was a good life, according to Toby. There was worth and valor in it. There used to be money in it. There was still money in it. There just wasn't money in it.

Fine, Rachel said. Be a hepatologist. But then do it at the highest possible level. "I know you're going to be the most successful hepatologist in New York. *In the world.*" She had no way of talking about a life's work without a quantifiable, athletic competition about it.

And now he was up for it. He was *up for it,* Rachel. You didn't have to be some slick motherfucker to get promoted. You could just be good at your job. He would advance to subdivision head, and then when Phillipa got another offer, which she would, he'd be offered department head. He'd turn it down because he knew that there were diminishing returns when it came to this stuff. He wasn't like them. He didn't want to join the right club and golf with the right people (or golf at all) and be on the right boards and committees. Donald Bartuck had Maggie Bartuck, his champion wife, inviting people to dinners and socializing and running fundraisers. That wasn't who Toby had married. That wasn't the kind of person he even *wanted* to marry.

Toby's mother had always told him, "There's only room for one star in every relationship." And even though Toby made jokes about having hooked his wagon to the right star, and Rachel would look at him out of the side of her eyes and say, "Damn straight," it never occurred to Toby that if what his mother said was true, it was Rachel who was the star of their relationship. Meaning that he was so in love with what he did that it didn't occur to him that the person on track to become someone with a big impact in the world (versus his smallish impact) was the star. By the time Bartuck was promoted, Rachel had left Alfooz & Lichtenstein, raiding the agency that made her a success and taking her clients with her to start her own shop. The clients followed her without a question; they knew relentless when they saw it.

Within weeks she had an income. Within months, she had solvency. It made Toby so proud—it would have made any husband proud. But her hours were long, and they both knew it would be years before she had a reasonable schedule if the agency was really going to work. Hannah had just been born, and neither of them wanted the kids raised entirely by nannies, so Toby began to schedule his work at the hospital so that he could be home at five-thirty every night no matter what. Same twelve-hour shifts, but starting earlier, never lingering, never staying for drinks in Bartuck's office anymore.

He complained that he missed her. He complained that money wasn't as important as what she should be providing to Hannah and, yes, fine, he admitted it: him. He watched old episodes of sitcoms at night alone. He took Hannah to the playground at Seventy-second Street and pushed her in the swing, saying "Go away" when he pushed, and "Come back here" when she pendulum-returned. He watched her love pears, then hate them, then love them, then become specifically human by loving pears only sometimes. He read the new Archer Sylvan collection and took walks and listened to the Rolling Stones and the White Stripes on his new iPod, then on his new iPhone, and he loved spending time with Hannah, but he was lonely for conversation and the company of someone who had chosen him. The sun rose and the sun set and the calendar pages flew off the wall. Hannah rolled over. Hannah sat up. Hannah crawled. Hannah walked. Hannah laughed. Hannah cried. Hannah wanted to do "this little piggy." Hannah fed herself. Hannah sat cross-legged in her stroller like a little woman. Hannah imitated her mother by taking Toby's phone and walking around with it and gabbing gibberish into it. Hannah hated "this little piggy." Hannah spoke. Hannah learned to count. Hannah started school. Toby loved her so much his heart was permanently on its knees.

His income was the expendable one, but Toby was not going to not work. That was ridiculous. And to Rachel's credit, she never dared to suggest it. But he continued to be the main parent. He was the one who got the first call when Hannah was running a fever at school, or when Solly had a diaper rash that defied traditional recourse. He was the one who researched music classes and sometimes sneaked out of work to attend them, even though they were called Mommy and Me (truthfully they should have been called

Nanny and Me). He signed Hannah up for enrichment programs, and eventually sports programs and after-school classes, and nurseries and schools and camps and Mandarin lessons and tennis lessons and orthodontists. He was the book fair volunteer and the brownie-baker for the Hebrew school fundraiser. He went on search engines and typed "bored of making dinner" and found websites that gave him recipe schedules to "mix things up" and "keep it fresh." The other women would say, "Look at Mr. Mom!" when he asked a question, and he'd find that offensive and feel the need to say, no, he was not the mom, he was the dad and these were his duties, but soon he realized that those women's impetus for making those comments was their own husbands' disinterest in their children or in contributing to the home, and so he just made a [smiley face emoji]. He'd have to stay home when the babysitter was sick, and ask his colleagues to sub a class or attend to a patient. He was no match for the upwardly mobile attendings like Marco who were all, yes, riding their mentorships to the sky.

What choice did he have? Rachel had to be somewhere, and then she had to take a yoga class because of the stress and a Pilates class with Miriam Rothberg for the social currency and then she had to do a quick email and "follow up" and "circle back" and talk sweetly to people who weren't owed it and lash out at Toby and the kids when she was overwhelmed by things that had nothing to do with them.

But he liked it all, that was his secret. He saw how fleeting it would all be, how quickly the kids went through the different phases, and how once those small things were gone, they never returned. A walking child never crawled again. So secretly, it was okay with him. Rachel loved her children, he was sure of that, but she was never natural around them. She was afraid to be alone with them most of the time. She grew impatient if they hung on her or talked too long, always feeling the pull of being elsewhere. Toby could have either or both of them on his lap for hours before even realizing it. At work, he was able to sit with his patients, knowing that this was not a stepping-stone for his life but life itself. Can you imagine what it's like to have arrived where you want to be at such a young age? That was what she never understood: that ambition didn't always run uphill. Sometimes, when you were happy, it jogged in place.

"We'll have good news next week," said Bartuck. "Go. See your patients."

But Toby didn't go to his patients.

He couldn't. There was no place in there to hide and put his head in his hands, or take a nap. His anguish at Rachel, which was now a roiling tornado that was picking up both winds of hatred and winds of concern, wouldn't allow him to concentrate on anything else. He'd done his rounds. It was four o'clock anyway. He'd been there since early. It was fine.

He walked through the park, and halfway through he began to meander on the pathways until he realized how tired and hot he was and took a seat on a park bench. He looked at his phone, pulling at his chest hair. He wanted—he *needed*—to check his apps. He needed a spike of that hot oxytocin-testosterone cocktail that would wash away these terrible feelings.

There hadn't been much action on Hr for him that day. He scrolled through old dirty messages, feeling nothing. He would never marry again. Marriage was for idiots. It was a bygone solution to a property problem he didn't have. It was a social construct invented by religious people (whose other values he mostly rejected) whose participants lived not past age thirty at the time it was implemented. So, no. He was not going to be falling into that particular trap again. He would have relationships and excitement and he would never put his emotional health into somebody's hands like that ever again.

In the second half of "Decoupling," Archer Sylvan finally meets with the woman that Mark was divorcing. She had heard there was a big magazine story being written about her divorce and she felt like she wanted to have her say, as well. "If you're going to write about this," she said to Archer in a letter, "you should have both sides of the story." She didn't have a name in the story. She was alternately referred to as "Mark's woman" (in flashbacks to better days) and "the woman" (after things went bad). In the story, she and Archer meet at one of the fancy tea places on Madison Avenue, where men dressed as butlers stand silently to the side. She tells him about Mark's affair with his secretary, which he had apologized for but then didn't fire the secretary. She tells him how she felt crazy all those months he was denying it but had ultimately decided to believe him until he actually went to a work event that she didn't know about with the secretary, for everyone to see. Archer sits with her for an hour and listens to what was a reasonable call to consider nuance—that all marriages are complicated and private, and by the time a marriage is over, maybe everyone can claim a totally justified grievance. When the Othello board turns to black (if you are playing the way Toby plays the game, which, again, is not actually how you play the game), it turns to black for both participants, after all.

But Archer left that conversation, and what he wrote next would be subject in journalism classes to hours-long conversations whose tenor would vary throughout the years: In the eighties, people praising him over what an honest reporter he truly was and how he said what was on his mind instead of what was politic to say. In the nineties, talking about whether there was ever a way to write without bias. In the new millennium, it became the subject of cris de coeur about misogyny, and one of the reasons that a person like me—a woman—would ever be hired by a men's magazine in the first place: to prevent it from happening again. By the time Toby sat in the park that day, "Decoupling" was no longer considered appropriate classroom reading. Even as a counterexample, it became the cause of too many strongly worded letters to deans published publicly on feminist websites about trigger warnings and safe spaces. When I went to guest speak at journalism classes after, say, 2007, I was warned not to bring it up in class, lest the conversation turn only to what an outrage it was to even talk about that story.

What he wrote—and this was the line that came to Toby right then—was this: "I left the restaurant, my hanky wet with her tears, and I thought about how the bitch will try to get you every time."

A tan man in a slim suit sat down next to Toby on the park bench. The sun was torturous and it was so hot and the park was filled with people who were enjoying it, and he hated them all. No-body had problems except for him. The man on the bench lit up a cigarette. Next to them was a large sign that said NO SMOKING. The sign was right there. Green, necrotic rage coursed through Toby, gliding through his lymphatic system, leaking into the musculature beneath it, invading his bones. Toby turned to the man and said, "Hey. You can't smoke here."

The man looked at him, and Toby's eyes went to the sign to in-dicate. The man looked past him. He put out his cigarette, and for a moment Toby wondered why he'd been so bothered.

He was prepared to be contemplative about this when 120 sec-onds later the fucker took out another cigarette and lit it right there in front of him.

"Look, man, you can't smoke here." The guy barely registered Toby except for a tiny eye roll, which he followed with another deep drag.

Toby stood up. His voice came out as a vicious holler. "I will call the police, you asshole."

The man took a long look at him, both surprised and . . . amused? Was that fucker *amused*? "You are a crazy motherfucker," the man said. Toby began to dial 911 on his phone. The man took one more drag, then flicked his cigarette into the grass and walked away.

Toby sat on the bench for another minute, pretending to look at his phone but beating with fury instead. When the man was out of sight, he got up and began to walk again vaguely toward the East

Side, though why? There was no one waiting for him. It was only five. His heart yearned for Solly, and broke for how he had manipulated him, for how he'd punted the problem of Rachel's disappearance down the road and didn't know if it would ever get resolved, how he badly wanted to watch *The Goonies* with his son and listen to his smart, adorable observations and answer his questions. He headed home because there was nowhere else to go.

What if. What if he wasn't taking Rachel's disappearance as seriously as he should?

Things did happen to women. They died. They got kidnapped. They were raped. They were held in compounds as sex slaves. They drowned with no one noticing. He almost reached for his phone to call the police but it seemed too crazy and he thought of all the cop shows he watched, and how he'd be the first suspect because he was the ex-husband and there was a trail of hateful text messages to find cause from.

The sun was still so high. The streets began to crowd with the freneticism of after-work youth in summer. No, not youth. Happiness. No, not happiness. Regularness. People with plans and goals and friends. He thought about going to a yoga class. He thought about calling Seth. He thought about getting back onto his apps and changing one detail about his profile, which would trigger his profile to reflood the system and be seen by an entirely new group of people. Mostly he felt weak. He needed to feel strong again.

Fruit. He decided that he wanted fruit. He'd eaten his last apple the night before. He was starting to feel the beginnings of scurvy, he was sure of it. He wanted shiny vitamin C. He wanted magnesium, because in the past three days his eyes had started twitching intermittently, and earlier in the day he'd gone to the men's room to see if the twitch was noticeable to the naked eye and it was. He wanted the optimism of a Whole Foods. Now with direction, he walked to the one on Eighty-seventh Street and through the aisles, letting the artisanal brown packaging fuel some kind of hope for renewal in him. He walked through the moisturizer aisle. Maybe he needed to shake up his skin care routine. Maybe he needed wild-flower aromatherapy. Maybe he needed hemp oil. Maybe he needed coconut water. No, but really, what if he started an aromatherapy routine? What if he got a diffuser that let the oils waft around him at night? He would wake up and be filled with renewed cells and hormone rushes and then he would start meditating and his life would—

"Toby."

He turned around. It was Cyndi Leffer and Miriam Rothberg. They were sweaty and frizzy so that their hair was only curly at the roots. Miriam wore a tank top that said RIDE OR DIE. Cyndi's said LIPSTICK & LUNGES.

"Two Fleishman sightings in a day," Miriam said.

"Oh, hi," said Toby. "Hello. I'm just buying some fruit."

"I thought you might still be in the Hamptons," Cyndi said.

"Yeah," Toby said. "There's been a lot going on. At the hospital. With my patients. But no, I'm not going to the Hamptons. Rachel got the house in the divorce. I don't really go there anymore."

"That's not what Roxanne told me." Cyndi said this in a suggestive singsong vocal fry, like it was sexual, but she was too old and so it came out as a kind of croak.

"Yes, I brought the kids because Rachel got derailed. Hannah missed Lexi."

"Well, last week of July is always Europe for us. Hey, have you gotten any of my texts? Hannah left her pillow at our house."

Toby faintly recalled being inundated with unimportant texts from Cyndi.

"You know," Miriam said. "You should come over for dinner with the kids. We don't choose sides, you know. Sam's parents are divorced, and we're very sensitive to that. Hey, are you still doing yoga? I thought I saw you with a mat a few weeks ago."

Toby couldn't focus. "What? I am. Sometimes."

"You should take Sam with you. He just went on a yoga retreat and he is wild about it."

"A yoga retreat?" Toby asked.

"Yes, the one in Massachusetts. The famous one. Wait. I always forget the name of it."

"Kripalu," Toby said. He realized saying it out loud that "Kripalu" sounded like "cripple you." How had he never noticed that?

"Yes! Kripalu! He just spent a weekend there and since then, it's every morning for him. We're hiring someone to come to the house. Finally! I couldn't get that guy off the treadmill for years. I would say, 'There's so much else out there,' and he just wanted to run. He did cross-country in high school."

Later, Toby would wonder why it was so important for him to play it cool in front of these people he gave not one fuck about. He would go over and over it in his head, that in this moment, his goal had been to protect Rachel's social-climbing interests instead of telling them exactly what kind of person she was, and what she'd done.

His brain tapped on his shoulder. He realized he had totally missed the first thing she said, so solidified in his mind was Rachel's utter goneness. "Sorry, did you say two Fleishman sightings? You saw Rachel?"

"It was so weird," Miriam said. "We saw her. In the park, lying on a blanket, asleep. In the middle of the day. I said, 'Ah, working hard, are we?'" Miriam laughed.

"Honestly, that girl works so hard it was nice to see her take a minute," Cyndi said. "I haven't seen her in what? Two weeks? And that haircut."

Miriam said something and then Cyndi talked for either an hour more or a minute more, but Toby didn't hear anything after that because his blood froze and his inner ear began to bleed and his brain turned to putty and began to leak out his nose and his face melted off his skull and his life would never be the same and he knew right then he'd never understand another thing ever again.

PART TWO

GOD, WHAT AN IDIOT HE WAS

The night Toby met Rachel, he had been enduring with wary fortitude and stoic martyrdom the longest dry spell of his post-finally-having-sex adult life. There was his first time, during our year in Israel, a drunken push-and-pull with my bucktoothed roommate, Lori, that he wished never happened except for the fact that it did happen, which at least meant he wouldn't die a virgin. He had turned twenty that year and the shame that accompanied leaving his teens with "your hymen intact," as Seth called it, was unbearable. He returned home to his dorm that night the way a soldier returns home from war: proud and a little haunted. His dorm mates crowded the lobby to lift him on their shoulders. It was embarrassing and also the best, just like the sex itself.

Then there was the first time (which was his second time) inside the confines of an actual relationship, six months into his senior year with a bland, anxious sociology major named Jeanine. Jeanine was the kind of student who took down every word a teacher said, and studied by reading that entire dictation back, memorizing it and never asking a question or applying a critical thought to it. She wasn't trying to learn anything; she was trying to survive the material she'd been given, squawking about how she was going to fail and then getting high B averages. She called herself "book smart." Toby thought to himself that "book smart" meant just not very smart at all, and he wanted to reassure her that intelligence was not the most important aspect of a person, and that it was also out of her control, plus she should just be happy with how hardworking she was and how she conducted herself on this planet. But there's no way to say that to a Princeton student who worked as hard as she did, and who really just said the whole "book smart" thing so all you could say was, "No, no, I am blown away by your natural intelligence."

"I am blown away by your natural intelligence," he said, and sometimes that would net him a hand job.

He spent nights waiting for her innumerable study groups to disband so that she would arrive home and consider having sex with him. More often than not, though, she would politely beg off because sex kept her up, which destroyed her chances of succeeding at the thing (the test, the paper) that was her priority. In this desert of opportunity, getting laid at least a little became his primary directive in the relationship, never asking himself if this was all there was to companionship, or if he even liked her. That was a dangerous question, and besides, he was in no position to ask it; he had to direct all his energy toward interpretation of whether a sloppily slung arm over the shoulder or a kiss directly on the mouth was a green light.

Their relationship ended unceremoniously after four months. One morning, after she had allowed him to have sex with her—or on her, or at her, which was probably more accurate—she said her parents weren't really okay with her dating someone who wasn't Catholic or Italian, and she'd rather not lose this much sleep if the relationship wasn't going to go anywhere. He objected to this loudly, not considering whether he actually liked her and wanted the relationship to continue. Out of pity, she offered to fuck him one more time, "goodbye sex," and he took her up on the option. He had felt humiliation pursuing sex in his life, but he had never felt humiliation during the act of it, watching her wait for it to be over, until now.

He moved to New York that June. He'd been accepted into NYU for medical school. He'd been accepted to Columbia, too, but he needed a change. He didn't want to be on a campus. He wanted to be surrounded by more than just jerkoff students like himself. He had a fantasy about meeting a girl, but not a medical student. He would be studying somewhere, and she would be reading a book—maybe a Roth or Bellow book, maybe Virginia Woolf—and he would walk over to her and make a joke and she would laugh and that would be that.

He wasn't supposed to attend the party at Columbia where he met Rachel. Seth was a year behind him, having stayed a second year in Israel when, just as they'd been about to leave, he'd met a twenty-one-year-old girl finishing her duty in the Israeli army, gone down to Dahab with her for a pot holiday, and decided to spend the next semester traveling with her to the places that Israelis just out of the army traveled to after they lived through their service: India, Thailand, Greece. He left her in Greece. Four months in, when she started talking too much about wanting to get married. "Women only exist on a trajectory," he wrote Toby on a postcard from Athens. "They can't just be. I hope you are getting laid, but I now know that there's no orgasm that doesn't come with a price." Toby wished Seth had sent that in a sealed envelope, but oh well. Seth was now finishing his senior year at Columbia. He and Toby had dinner one night and Seth told him they should go to the annual literary society party at the library afterward. But Toby hated Columbia parties and Columbia people. "You might get laid," Seth said.

Toby knew it probably wasn't true. But his parents were visiting the day after tomorrow from Los Angeles, so he figured that even if he had like a three percent chance at getting laid, it would at least fortify him for Sunday's work, which was cleansing his shithole apartment of porn and stink by the time they arrived and steeling himself for his mother's machine-gun fire to his ego and sense of self. At the party, he saw a girl named Mary that he'd had a crush on from Seth's dorm, and he briefly wondered if this was his shot. He went over to talk to her, and they spoke for a good five minutes. She laughed at everything he said, and yes, this was beginning to look like his shot, but then some chucklehead who apparently was her date came out of the bathroom. His name was Steve, and he was visiting Mary from Wharton, and would Toby even venture to guess the size of the deuce he had just dropped into the toilet. "Man, I hope the plumbing is good here," Steve said. Mary laughed, and it felt like a betrayal of everything he knew or hoped about her for her to laugh at that. In that moment, Toby was never further away from understanding why he was alone.

He was about to leave, having reached his nightly quota of humiliation and bewilderment, when he took one last look around the room. Standing next to a window was a girl talking to another girl who was drunk and hanging off a guy. He hadn't seen her before, which was strange because her looks were so severe: blunt bangs, blond hair that ignited a dangerous, dormant longing for Gentile women, pale skin, red lips. It was Rachel, who was looking down and nodding while she politely allowed the girl to rant, but then looking up, feeling his eyes on her, returning his look right back to him, and then looking away with that smile that girls made when they didn't want to smile—an aversion of the eyes, but not the face, then a closing of the mouth into something upturned. She was wearing a tight ribbed shirt and leggings like all the girls were wearing lately, with a flannel shirt tied around her waist. Always she had the look of someone who was too sophisticated to be wearing the same clothing that other college students wore—too formal, too pretty in a grown-up way.

Toby decided to wait this out. She was now speaking to one of Seth's old roommates, Otto, and the guy that Otto was flirting with. Toby got some punch. He held it, then looked at it and realized that even if he was going to drink the calories of alcohol, he would never drink the added fruit punch, so he poured it down the drain. But then he thought that maybe the punch was his in with the girl? He poured some more and brought it to Otto, and turned to her. Her smile went from coy to self-conscious to real.

"I notice you are standing here without the fruit punch," Toby said. "I highly recommend it."

She smiled at him. She was too pretty to be smiling at him. "Are you sure? Because you just poured some down the drain."

"It's a little sugary, actually," he said. "And I'm concerned about this girl trying to roofie me." (People made jokes like this back in the 1990s.) "And I'm not so sure about the ingredient in it that makes it that particular shade of purple."

"Really? To me that's the only reason to drink the stuff."

"I've always wanted children who smelled like purple."

She was an English major at Hunter, she said, but she wanted to go into some kind of business. She wanted a career that she could pause while she was raising her children without falling behind. She was practical, she said. She thought maybe she would go into marketing or advertising. But last summer she went to a symposium at Columbia's business school about negotiating, and she realized that if she could, she'd just negotiate for the rest of her life.

"All right," he said. Her eyes were a fishhook. "Negotiate with me."

"Okay," she said. "I'd like four for the price of two."

"I'm sorry, you have to pay for all four."

"I'll only be paying for two."

He made his body into a stubborn stance, crossing his arms over his chest and turning his head so that he could see her through side-eye. "No deal. What kind of Middle Eastern open-air market do you think this is?"

She smiled and shrugged, and she began to walk away, first one step, then two, and then it was clear she was really walking away. She moved to a couch across the room and sat down, her back still to him, and she struck up a conversation with the dude on the couch. Toby was amazed; he was *excited*. When was the last time he was excited and not just scared? He walked across the room and crouched down behind her and whispered into her ear. "I'll give you six," he said. "You don't have to pay for any of them."

They stayed up most of the night talking in his apartment. Rachel had been raised in Baltimore and didn't remember her parents, though she had a memory of a black-haired woman lying on a couch and she associated this memory with her mother because who else could it have been. She didn't have siblings. Her father had left her mother when she was a baby, and then her mother had gotten cancer and died, all by the time she was three. Her mother's mother raised her instead, but it was out of duty rather than love, and she only went back to Baltimore on Thanksgiving sometimes. She was a junior, and she was sad that she'd missed the opportunity to go away for a semester, but she was thinking she might go to Brazil or Budapest that summer on a work-study program. When she said that, he felt a sad reflux sloshing around in his stomach, that he would have to someday let her out of his bed.

They had sex that night, which was for the best, since he didn't think his ego could handle an extended period of time in which he wondered if she thought of him as a friend or an actual romantic contender. He kept thinking, "She's a real girl." Not in a sexist way. No, in a *Pinocchio* way. She was everything he thought a girl should be, even if he'd never known to pray quite so specifically: She wore red lipstick all the time, she listened to Neil Diamond and didn't give a fuck how weird that was, she could do a handstand for like ten minutes, she knew *The Karate Kid* by heart, every single piece of dialogue; she couldn't wait for the twelfth in a mystery series to come out to see if the heroine had really died (of course she hadn't); she wanted to learn how to play tennis but couldn't figure out how to find a partner who wouldn't mind how bad she was. Her septum was a little crooked, though you could only see it if you were peering from underneath, and she corrected it in her sleep by pushing her nose a little to the left so that she could breathe out of both nostrils. She was lonely and she didn't have so many friends because she had grown up with an impatient grandmother who was just trying to get her upbringing over with. Or because she was sensitive and took every bit of noninclusion as rejection. Or because she always wondered what was a little better than the thing she had, which was valuable in business but not really in any other part of your life. Or because she felt like she was always catching up to others because she hadn't been born wealthy or even into an actual family. Or because people didn't like it when women were so nakedly ambitious. Or because she couldn't keep her opinion to herself when she saw someone not meeting a goal or living like she thought they claimed they wanted to because she believed people wanted to know the truth. Or because she was always strangely out of step with pop culture, and would continue to be even after she became one of the top agents in the city. Or because friendship is elusive and being liked works best when you don't think about it constantly, and she absolutely did think about it constantly.

When he woke up in the morning after the three hours of post-dawn sleep they'd decided to allow each other, he watched her for a few minutes. She was still so pretty in the daylight, even with smudged mascara and caked saliva in the corner of her mouth. He went out to get breakfast. He stood in line for bagels and coffee, and he had never felt so normal and American in his life. He had a girl waiting for him back at his apartment, and it was Saturday morning, and so he was going to bring her a bagel and some coffee. He was overwhelmed by the simplicity of his emotions: gratitude for whatever moments had worked to make this moment happen for him; happiness, yes, just pure plain happiness. He loved his country! He was going to eat a bagel!

They ate their bagels, so normal, so normal, and they walked around the Village, then up Fifth Avenue, then west. They walked up through Hell's Kitchen, then diagonally through Midtown, then diagonally back west through the park, where it began to snow a soft and quiet early-March dust. They held hands and walked even more slowly. Toby loved taking walks. It was his greatest revelation of New York, that it was the largest city in America and you could scale it on your own two legs. Now he had someone to walk with. The white flakes came down on her white hair and she was talking talking talking and she wasn't prissy about the snow or the weather, and Toby thought how in love he was right then. They walked through the park to the Upper East Side, when the snow stopped, and then he walked her over to her apartment, which was right near Hunter. They were wet and exhausted and their feet hurt, so they ordered dinner, Indian food, and Toby stayed, while her roommate made some kind of annoyed noise about going somewhere else for the night. They slept in her twin bed, and as they arranged themselves, he knew that he had never been happier—that maybe this was a relationship or maybe it was *the* relationship, but it was finally happening for him and, yes, it had only been twenty-four hours, but it was as good on the inside as it had ever looked from the outside.

The next morning, he raced home to clean his apartment and remove from it all evidence of sexual congress, and sexual individualism for that matter, and then went out to buy even more bagels for when his parents arrived. He had toyed with asking Rachel if she'd want to come and meet them, but he couldn't risk scaring her off. He had to play it cool.

His parents came and inspected his apartment, once again airing their disappointment that he'd chosen NYU instead of UCLA ("And if you're going to stay in New York, why NYU over Columbia? *Who does that?*" his mother had asked).

His mother looked Toby over carefully and said, "You've managed to maintain your weight, but your face looks old."

"That's the mark of an eating disorder," he answered her.

His mother wailed plaintively at his father. "He's still punishing me!" Then, at Toby: "You were happier fat? *You were happier fat?*"

He didn't answer, and they went out for lunch in the West Village, where he ordered a chicken breast and a beet salad with no goat cheese or dressing or candied walnuts. ("So just beets on a plate?" the waitress asked. "Yes, with the chicken," he'd said, his mother's eyes boring into the side of his face.)

Later, he took a taxi with his parents to their hotel in Midtown and he dropped them off and took the cab farther uptown, right back to Rachel, who opened the door with a big smile. "I missed you," she said. He kissed her hard. She was just half an inch taller than he was, though she'd been wearing a short heel the night before and he now saw that they were aligned in a great way, her lower lip to his upper lip and that was really something.

Nine months later, he was on a plane to Budapest, where she had gone for the fall semester of her senior year, having not gotten it together to go in the summer, which Toby believed and hoped was because she was as delighted as he in the paradise of their new relationship. Over the months, he had taken her to movies at Film Forum and to exhibits at MoMA and the Frick because she told him she never went to museums or movies growing up. They went to Woodstock for the weekend and bought tie-dyed T-shirts. They sat in cafés and restaurants and locked eyes and each pressed the balls of their feet against the other's under the table.

He was learning from Rachel, too. They went skiing—he had never been skiing before, but she'd learned because her school had a ski trip every year and finally, when she was a senior, her grandmother handed over the $250 and let her go. She was helping him negotiate the strange, surprising, suddenly political machinations of medical school that were beyond good grades. His residency advisor didn't like how sarcastic he was; Aaron Schwartz, a sallow-skinned pigeon of a guy he knew not just from Princeton, but who had gone to his high school in Los Angeles, was also in his med school class and kept getting favored for surgeries. Rachel talked to him about how to talk to people. She taught him how the fact that he was naturally funny also meant that he had a side that favored a quick burn, which wasn't so good. She taught him to slow down and consider people's faces, that this was the most crucial exercise in all of negotiation, and eventually he did it—he learned to listen to people and to look them in the eyes. And wouldn't you know, when he finally was able to enact these skills, he became a better doctor, one who could understand his patients' suffering more specifically, who could listen more closely for clues. He shot ahead of

Aaron Schwartz, earning praise from the doctors in charge and his teachers for his sensitivity and intuition. He would always commend her for teaching him a skill that no one had taught him throughout all his years of med school, and she would respond, "That's because they don't want you to get ahead." When she said that, he'd realize she wasn't trying to make him a better person; she was trying to get him to advance. That was all she'd ever tried to do for him. But, he reasoned, that was because she thought he was a good enough person as it was.

He arrived in Budapest for Thanksgiving break, surprising Rachel on her birthday, and in her dorm, which had been converted from a castle, in front of her roommates, he got down on one knee and presented her with his grandmother's engagement ring.

They celebrated by all going to a park and ice-skating to an Ace of Base CD on repeat outside another abandoned castle. Rachel didn't know how to ice-skate and hung on to him. She wore no coat; she kept saying she was too happy to be cold. After ice-skating, they went out and danced all night in the Jewish Quarter, where the storefronts mysteriously turned into clubs at sunset, and it felt exhilarating and dangerous, not just to be a grown-up with a fiancée, but also to be dancing in the Jewish Quarter of a largely anti-Semitic city. That weekend, he took her to Lake Balaton, the closest thing Budapest had to the Hamptons, and with the outstanding strength of the dollar rented a full house and hired caterers for every meal. All his life, he had worried when he should have just trusted that there was a plan for everyone. But the not trusting is part of the plan, too. Praise God! Praise the Lord! Praise him in his infinite wisdom! He felt then the peace of systems. He felt the solidity of a middle-class path. The world finally felt solid beneath him.

They married in Los Angeles. Toby's mother was a longtime board member at their synagogue, and Toby's wedding was a real opportunity for her to show their community the kind of people she hoped they knew they were, especially after Toby's sister's Orthodox wedding, which was a social disappointment ("a fiasco") to say the least, with the separate seating and the pareve dessert and the shitty kosher wine.

"Her grandmother doesn't even seem to care that she's getting married," Toby's mother whispered to Toby as they put dishes away from the luncheon they hosted for visitors the day before the wedding. Rachel's grandmother had sat with her purse on her lap, polite but not at all curious about the family her granddaughter was marrying into.

"Or maybe she's being polite about what an idiotic big deal you're making over this," Toby told his mother. "Honestly, we should have just eloped."

But he only said that to wound her. He couldn't wait to show Rachel off to everyone. He couldn't wait for everyone to see what he'd accomplished in his life. Toby Fleishman! Introducing, for the first time as husband and wife, Mr. and Mrs. Toby and Rachel Fleishman!

They returned home after their wedding and brief pre-honeymoon in Santa Cruz to Toby's empty apartment on Ninth Street. They found a coffee table on the street during one of their long walks and they carried it above their heads, twelve blocks back to the apartment. They had sex all the time—they did it when it was raining and they did it when it was sunny. They did it before they went out to dinner, and they did it when they came home from dinner. They did it in the morning before they showered. They did it when they got home from work. They did it after dinner while they were watching TV, sometimes even angling themselves so they wouldn't miss the thing they were watching. Good! Normal!

Toby had had his pick of specialties in the end, and he went with hepatology. He heard that Aaron Schwartz became an upper GI guy and he thought what a sucker that guy was, doing endoscopies all day, and what a sucker Toby was to have ever been intimidated by him. He felt big, bigger, biggest of all. He no longer wished for anything to be different or to have been different. He now saw that even that accident with the Volvo created a set of circumstances, even all those years later, that allowed him to be exactly where he was when he met Rachel, and when Rachel, against all odds, fell back in love with him.

Meanwhile, Rachel had left the mailroom at the agency and was riding the desk of a young guy named Matt Klein, who had Michael Douglas in *Wall Street* hair and an overbite that made his upper teeth extend over his lower lip and therefore always look like he was sexually harassing you. Matt took her out to lunch almost every day and seemed determined to teach her all he knew. "My protégé," he'd call her. Toby secretly wondered if Matt was this hands-on with his previous assistants, or with asst2, the young man on his desk.

But Rachel didn't mind changing her plans or running late to dinner. She liked the midnight calls; she liked screaming obscenities into the phone when a deal fell through. She liked the performative assholery of it; she called it "my cardio." She liked waiting for good news, and answering her cellphone "Rachel Fleishman here." (Toby still felt erectile stirrings hearing his name on the back of hers, which she had taken because she had no allegiance to her maiden name, which came from a man who couldn't be bothered.) She took Toby to the premiere of a show that Matt had done the director deal on, and then just three years later, *she* was the one who was doing the deal, with a playwright and actress named Alejandra Lopez, whom she had discovered herself back when she was going to off-off-off-off-off-Broadway shows to scout for talent, and now she had her own desk, with her own asst1 and asst2.

She had met Alejandra for the first time at the community center of a low-income housing project in a part of Brooklyn that would never gentrify. She had heard that there was a woman performing a one-person show about Woodrow Wilson's wife, Edith Wilson. Rachel brought Toby that night, making for a grand total of six people in the audience—and four of them were extremely old and maybe had just been looking for a place to sit. Alejandra had been performing her play, which was then called *Big Wilson* (and then would be called *Half-Wilson* and then *Presidentress* and ultimately would become the cultural firestone it became as *Presidentrix*), for free for a few weeks now. She had been working at a gas station on Pennsylvania Avenue outside Starrett City during the day, and when it was slow, she would work on this play, which was part opera. She had taught herself to sing classically with tapes she'd borrowed from the library literally called *Teach Yourself to Sing Opera in Hours a Day*. Rachel knew her own success lay in finding a good client to cultivate, one big star to discover and to shine a spotlight on so that it could become clear that you had the eye, the nose, the ear—that you were the real deal. She had been reading community notices and going to obscure plays in faraway, off-the-radar venues. She'd found this listing next to a job-wanted section in the *Canarsie Courier*.

The play was about the way a woman could only really have her own story if she did it through a man—in this case, Edith Wilson's half-dead husband, Woodrow Wilson. Edith ran the country after his stroke and only got credit for it much later. During the big number, Edith Wilson lets a reporter into her husband's bedroom and he emerges with an interview, ascribing all of Edith's words to Woodrow. She is so happy her plan worked and everyone was fooled, but she's left with a hole in her because she's never seen for what she actually is, which is a genius who could run a country; she is also never even seen as the other thing she is, which is an excellent wife. Toby looked over at Rachel during the song, and her mouth was open and she was shaking her head slowly, tears in her eyes.

Toby and Rachel sat in the audience behind a man who was asleep across a bench in the front row and spooning with his cane. Afterward, he watched Rachel make her approach. Alejandra had noticed the strange yuppies in the audience. She looked over at Toby for a second while Rachel was talking. Rachel put her hands to her heart, punctuating what she was saying, not wiping away the tears that fell. He watched Alejandra go from confused to moved to happy to oh my God my chance is here.

Big Wilson played in a theater down on the Bowery to sold-out crowds, but no one wanted to invest in it because the magic appeared to lie with Alejandra herself and there was skepticism that any other one person could bring to the show what she did—when she moved on, or if she came down with the flu one night. The show was such a singular act, straight from her soul, that it felt like anyone else playing it would be imitating, so there went the touring potential. But the play did well enough to propel Rachel to official agent status. Alejandra then wrote an HBO show about a Latina lesbian in the 1970s trying to get ahead in her homophobic, racist office. It ran two seasons with a small, dedicated audience but only found real numbers after it was canceled. By then, Rachel had left Alfooz.

(Then it was five years ago when she encouraged Alejandra, who had been in a creative rut after marrying and having children, to revisit *Big Wilson* and extend it some way. What she came up with was *Presidentrix,* an extension of the musical, with other actors and dancers, too, and which became the talk of the city while it was still in workshops. *Presidentrix* won every Tony the year it debuted on Broadway. Its soundtrack became the soundtrack for the political roiling and feminist uprising around them. Tickets were sold out for seven years. Rachel was on the cover of *The Hollywood Reporter* and *Variety.*)

Toby and Rachel fought sometimes. What couple didn't fight? Yes, maybe Rachel was a little more vicious than necessary when he'd forgotten that they'd had dinner plans with her boss and he'd already cooked ("It's *okay,*" he'd say. "I'll put it in the fridge. This is not a big deal"), though technically, in that situation, the aggrieved status should have accrued to him. She filed all the ways she was put off under an enormous label called Weren't You Listening? When she was annoyed and she spoke with him, her face reminded him of the faces of people he'd seen die: The animating force taken away from them, they looked like completely different people. It terrified him.

But also, this was who she was. She was an animal in her work, and the hormones that she had to summon to hang with the boys upstairs couldn't just be shut off. He understood that.

At their three-year anniversary, they decided it was time to have a baby, and she became pregnant the first time they tried, which delighted Toby and sent Rachel into a kind of shock. "I thought it would take longer," she kept saying. But he knew that they were blessed and golden still, despite her moods and despite the fact that she was more prone to outbursts these days. It was the pressure she was under at work, he told himself. He still believed it was golden and good. All the bad things seemed like such an aberration, even when the tantrums began to outnumber the calm, sane interactions.

One night, Toby waited for her to come home, staring outside at a summer rainstorm. Rachel was five months pregnant, and running one hour, then two hours, later than when she said she'd be home. He'd made soup for her. She usually let him know when she was running late. He called her, but she didn't answer. He began to worry.

She arrived at eight. When she finally got home, her shirt wet and transparent, she stomped into the apartment, where he was waiting with his soup.

"Where have you been?" he asked. "I tried you a few times. What happened to you?"

"Can't I just walk somewhere? Are you the Gestapo?"

He left the kitchen. This was on Seventy-second Street, in a building called the Wellesley that Toby thought would be the fanciest place he ever lived, in their first apartment after his med school apartment, and it was small by exactly no one's measure; the place was so nice that when they had Solly, they moved upstairs to the eighteenth floor to a bigger version of it. He got her a towel and a robe. She seemed dazed. He sat her down, right on the brown velvet couch that one of the attendings had given him, practically un-marred. He tried to help her off with her blazer but she shooed him away.

"What happened?"

She didn't look at him. "I was passed over. I didn't get partner."

Toby took a second and leaned back. "What? Who?"

"Harry, of course." She stood up and went to the bedroom, where she sat down on the bed and began to take off one of her shoes but just stopped.

He followed her. "Not of course," he said. "You deserved it. Did they even say anything to you?" He gently pushed her down until she was on her back, rolled her a little to the side, and took off her wet pants. She was a rag doll by then, and so he continued with her blazer and shirt. He took her robe off the hook on the door. "Here, put this on."

Suddenly, she looked down and saw that she was mostly naked. She looked up at him, and in her eyes he saw something that he'd only seen in her when she was angry at others. "What are you doing? I'm not a fucking baby, Toby. I can dress myself."

She stood up and stomped off to the bathroom, grabbing her robe out of his hands and slamming the bedroom door.

He brought her the soup on the tray ten minutes later when she was sitting back on the bed. She ignored it but told him the whole story:

She hadn't yet told the partners or Matt that she was pregnant because there was an opening for a junior partnership and she didn't want to handicap herself. She'd gone through great pains to hide her pregnancy while candidates for the partnership were being evaluated. But she wasn't worried. There was no partner who had the kind of eye for discovery that she did—all the other candidates' finds didn't add up to one Alejandra, and it wasn't like Alejandra was her only discovery. She had resolved to tell them at the dinner that accompanied the celebration of her promotion. She was being strategic. That was what was so ironic, she would say later: She was being as strategic as she was taught to be by *these very people*.

She was in her office and staring through the glass wall (what was the point of an office if it had glass walls?) and saw Harry Sacks getting high fives, and heard the pop of champagne, and her stomach began to sink. A voice inside her head told her to pretend she had to go home early, but that voice didn't stand a chance, so she went into Matt Klein's office and confronted him.

"Rachel!" he said. "Hello!"

"It's because I'm pregnant, right?"

Matt's face went blank. "What? What do you mean?"

"Tell me the truth. I won't sue you. I just want to know."

"Are you talking about Harry's promotion?"

In their bedroom, she looked at Toby like she was deciding something, then said, "Two years ago, Matt hit on me. Of course, I said no."

Toby received this news like a boulder to the testicles. *Matt Klein?* Her *boss?*

"Yes," she said.

"He made a pass at you?"

"Two years ago."

"When? How?"

"We were in L.A. for the Golden Globes."

It was when she was still his assistant, after she'd been married for a year (and he'd been married for five). It wasn't just disgust that stopped her from falling into Matt Klein's arms, though. She liked being this thing that Matt couldn't have. She liked to imagine that he was longing for her. This was what Matt himself would call "data" in a negotiation. Your data was the thing you knew that no one else knew. She knew Matt wanted her. She knew that a man's desire for a particular woman never truly disappeared if the man didn't get to have the woman; it became a point of contention for the man's ego in addition to the desire itself.

("Uh," Toby said, in the bedroom.)

But standing in front of Matt, who was watching her with satisfied, cold eyes, she also knew that he might have played a long game. The truth of her quick advancement had to do less with her skill and with Alejandra and more with his humiliation over having made a pass at her that she rejected, and concern that if he just fired her she'd sue. She'd suspected this, but like the agent she was she also knew that opportunity was opportunity. But now she was being punished.

"Harry is a hard worker," Matt told her. "It was his time."

"Don't tell me about hard workers," she said. She was wearing a white shirt a size too big that, had she not been pregnant, she certainly would have tucked into her pants. She couldn't bring herself to pull the trigger on maternity clothes, at least not yet. Maternity clothes lacked plausible deniability. "Is this because of what happened in L.A.? Because I thought we were over that?"

He leaned back in his chair and looked her over as she stood at his desk. He was too smart to say a word.

"It's my pregnancy," she said.

"Noooo," he purred. "It's not your pregnancy. Well, not exactly."

"What do you mean?"

"Listen, I'm telling you this as a friend and not as your boss. Don't try to pull any HR shit on me because it won't work. I'm telling you this for your own edification. It's that you didn't *tell* us you were pregnant. You just walked around pregnant, visibly and obviously pregnant, and you never said a word to us. When you treat us like idiots—"

"I'm sorry, is there a mandatory time by which I have to tell you that I'm pregnant? Is a thing happening inside my body company property?"

"No, no. It's not that at all. Calm down, Rachel." Matt's thin gray eyes sparkled when he was being cruel.

Like every other woman in the world who has ever been told to calm down, Rachel had no idea how to behave.

"You didn't hold us in the same regard as we held you. It goes both ways, Rachel. You're a great worker. You are *valued* here. But a partner is not just a worker. A partner is a member of the family."

"You didn't tell me when Virginia was pregnant." He'd divorced his first wife and married an actress who had previously divorced her husband when things went bad after forgetting to thank him in her Oscar speech.

"I think you know why this is different." Same smile. "Listen, there's always going to be another opening. We *value* you. But why are we talking about this? More than anything, we're so *happy* for you. We can't wait to *meet* your baby. Your baby is a member of *our* family, too."

Toby now began to pace the bedroom. "He's *met* me. He knew you were married. We'd been out to dinner with him and his wife."

"Yeah, well that's how scumbags operate, Toby."

"Did you remind him that he knew me?"

"I'm sorry, Toby, no, I didn't, I really didn't realize this was about you at the time."

But it was a little about him, wasn't it? This was his wife! It's one thing to hit on someone whose spouse you don't know. But he was real. Toby was real. And Matt Klein didn't even see him as threat enough to stop himself from hitting on her. Matt barely registered Toby's existence. Matt was not afraid of Toby's wrath.

Toby had never liked that guy. At premieres and events that Toby was invited to, Matt would come over to him and lean over to give Toby a strong handshake, mention something about "our girl," and then ask if he could "just steal Rachel for a minute," not really asking, and guide her away, touching her waist as he led her. She didn't recoil or even jump a little—she even seemed like she might be used to it. Toby knew plenty of Matt Kleins, and the Matt Kleins of the world did not see anything like a husband as a reason to not do whatever they wanted. Or maybe, because he did know Toby, he didn't see him as an obstacle. Maybe if Rachel had married a tall, strapping finance bro, he'd have stood down. The Matt Kleins of the world stand down in the name of finance bros, Toby knew that for sure. He knew this type of guy from growing up in Los Angeles, where there was a certain tier of male whose Matt Klein–ness was sown and watered and given room to grow. There were people out there who thought Matt Klein–ness was the *goal*.

"Why didn't you tell me about this when it happened?"

There were several possible acceptable answers to this for Toby: that she didn't take it seriously, that she didn't want to hurt Toby, that she barely registered it the minute it happened, so in love was she with her husband—all these would have been fine. Instead she went with: "I didn't think to. It was just something that happened at work. Do you tell me everything that happens at your work? Actually, don't answer that, maybe you do."

He didn't like how not a part of this story he was. He didn't like that he was only hearing about this because it was mitigating information against something else that had happened that day. He didn't like that she didn't seem to think her marriage was relevant to all of this.

"I just think you should maybe think about the fact that you work for someone who has no respect for your marriage."

"But this isn't about our *marriage*, Toby. This is about *me*. They didn't promote me, because I didn't tell them I was pregnant."

"That's bullshit. They didn't make you partner, because you didn't sleep with Matt Klein and because they don't fundamentally respect you."

Her response came like a boomerang. "Fuck you, Toby."

It was hard for Toby to pinpoint exactly when he'd noticed the change in her. Yes, she spoke to her subordinates like they were pieces of shit, but that was the culture at Alfooz & Lichtenstein—that was how they taught their employees to survive, or something. Toby would express surprise when he heard her on the phone talking to an intern or an assistant—it particularly seemed that asst2 couldn't find his ass from his ass these days. He would hear her on the phone saying, "You forget who you are talking to," and "I'm sorry, but do you think I'm an idiot?" and "Honestly, I am listening to you and cannot believe what is coming out of your mouth," and "No offense, but when I hire at a Yale job fair, I expect someone with a little light behind the eyes," and "I saw those press kits and it looks like a homeless person off the street did them." He assumed the stress of her work was sending her into overdrive. But then she said things to her clients like "Oh my God, were we the same person in another life?" and "You are too much," and "That is amazing," and "You are amazing." See? She was also capable of that, which made the fact that she didn't do it at home harder to stomach.

When he put it all together and applied himself to the situation, he realized that he was being spoken to like the employee, not like the client. And he'd ask, "Do you ever notice that you speak to me like one of your employees that you hate? And that you're really nice to your clients?" And she would say, "God, Toby, do you really need me to put on a show for you, too?" And then she would do a sickly sweet impression of he wasn't quite sure what—a 1950s housewife? A version of herself she thought Toby wanted her to be? "I'm so glad my hubby is home! Should I get you a martini?" Her voice would be bouncy and bright and he would think for the first time that maybe he should murder her.

"I don't want this soup," she said now. "I want linguini and clam sauce. I want to go to Tony's."

"Okay, okay." It was good soup.

They stood outside their building. It had stopped raining, and Toby suggested they walk to Tony's.

"I'm not walking," Rachel said as she raised her arm in the air. "I've walked enough." It was only nine blocks, but Toby didn't say that. She was pregnant. It was fine. She turned to him. "I'm saying I'm tired of taking long walks. I don't like them. I never liked them. It's a waste of time."

He didn't say anything. She was upset and prone to tantrums when she was upset, and he didn't want her screaming at him on the sidewalk in front of their doorman. She hailed a cab. They never went on another long walk again. They never went out of their way to move through the city together except as means to getting somewhere if there were no cabs to be found and the train was out of the way. From then on, they would never find themselves side by side, just either facing each other, or back to back.

That night felt like a quaint memory when, four months later, Rachel was sent to the hospital with high blood pressure, and her obstetrician began an induction. At first it was fine. They played backgammon, and she watched reruns of a teen drama about orphans on a portable DVD player she bought just for this occasion. Toby felt this was a morbid choice, but he had also suspected that there was no real way for her to have children without confronting the fact of her own parentslessness.

The delivery progressed from boredom into a horror show. They couldn't locate her obstetrician. She screamed at Toby, "Do you have absolutely no pull here? You *work* here!" But her complications were vast and unforeseeable: She failed to progress, and her blood pressure climbed, and it was hard to get a consistent read on the baby monitor. Their normal obstetrician was in Hawaii, it turned out.

Finally, finally, another obstetrician came in, but neither Rachel nor Toby had ever met him; he was a new partner in Rachel's OB's practice. He had white hair and a tan and white teeth and glasses and an Italian accent, and he looked at Toby and Rachel through a cold squint. In the delivery room, as she screamed and writhed in the pain of the kind of contractions that Pitocin brings, he said, "Come on, now. Are you planning on being a baby, or delivering a baby?"

"Hold on a minute," Toby said. "You don't talk to a patient that way."

Rachel looked at Toby incredulously. "That's what you're going to say? You're going to *lecture* him?"

Toby's fellow residents came downstairs to obstetrics when they heard he and Rachel were there. They walked in, with balloons and flowers, when Rachel was saying, "Are you here to do anything but watch? What is your actual value here?" and she was talking to *Toby*. Toby walked them out of the room and tried to indicate that she'd actually been talking about the obstetrician, and they nodded sympathetically, but they also looked uncomfortable. He should have gone with a woman-in-labor joke.

A full day later, with her blood pressure stabilized, she was given a narcotic. She began to drift off—or at least she looked like she did. Instead she was plunged into a nightmare hellscape of hallucinations: She was on a swing in her old elementary school, back and forth and back and forth, but every time she swung forward, the school would get even bigger. But Toby didn't know this yet. Instead, he thought she was finally getting rest, so he kissed her on her pale, cold forehead and whispered, "I'll be right back."

He went to find Donald Bartuck to ask him what to do about this obstetrician. Bartuck, in his office, said, "Is it Romalino?" When Toby said yes, Bartuck said, "I know him. Good surgeon, total asshole. Loves sections." Toby went downstairs to speak with the chief resident and see how they could get another doctor in there—there had to be someone else, even though it was Thanksgiving. But there wasn't, and he noticed that while he was talking, the nurse's call button from Rachel's room was being rung incessantly and he ran back to the room and found Rachel in there screaming like an animal while Romalino, his hands up like it was a stickup, said, "I think we might need to get psych in here."

When Toby could finally understand what Rachel was saying, it was "GET HIM OUT GET HIM OUT," but no one else was in there and he noticed then that there was blood on Rachel's sheets and Toby said, "What the hell happened?" Rachel was still screaming and crying and shaking until finally, through her hiccups, she told him.

While Toby was talking to Bartuck, a nice-seeming nurse had examined Rachel and said that she hadn't progressed, but that her blood pressure, though still high, seemed stable now. She said, "You didn't hear it from me, but if I were you, I'd say that it's clear this induction isn't working. If you want to avoid a C-section, you should ask Dr. Romalino if you should pull the plug. You can offer to stay on bed rest or in the hospital, whatever he wants, but you don't want to continue this induction." Romalino came in a few minutes later, and Rachel asked him to come back when her husband was there, and he said he didn't know when he'd be able to come back since he had his own patients to deal with as well and he had to examine her. She said what the nurse had told her to say, and Romalino had made it seem like that was a reasonable idea. He said, "Tell you what. I'll examine you, and if you're still not progressing, we'll have a talk about not having this baby today." Romalino called for a nurse, and the same one who'd given her the advice came back in. "We can't wait for my husband?" Rachel asked. "He'll be back soon." Romalino said, again, "It's just an exam." He put on gloves and reached up between her legs into her vagina, and then, instead of just measuring her dilation, he reached past the usual area and began doing—something.

"What are you doing?" she screamed. "What is he doing?" The nurse held her hand and patted her hair and couldn't look at her. "WHAT IS HE DOING? HE'S NOT EXAMINING ME. HE'S DOING SOMETHING!!" She screamed as a lightning pain tore into her body, and still his hand was up inside her, needling at something and manipulating, until finally he pulled his hand out. Rachel realized the nurse was still holding her hand and it made no sense to her that she was screaming as if being attacked and this woman just wouldn't do anything to help her.

Toby understood immediately what had happened. Romalino had ruptured the membrane inside her uterus, the one thing keeping her water from breaking. Hospital policy dictated that women with ruptured membranes couldn't leave, nor could their inductions be halted once the water was broken.

The rest of the delivery went as Bartuck predicted: She was given a few hours to progress, and the stress of having to progress in a certain amount of time made her clench even harder, as if any of this were up to her, as if her entire world and sense of control in life hadn't just fallen apart in a fifteen-minute span.

At midnight, a baby girl was removed from her body. The baby was offered to Rachel behind the blue curtain that kept her from seeing her own organs splayed across her chest, but she said she felt too unsteady holding her in her supine position, paralyzed from the chest down. Even a half hour later, though, out of surgery, she wouldn't hold the baby. She kept saying she wanted to wait till she could feel her feet again. The nurse said it would be good for her to hold her baby, and Rachel started crying, saying, "Did you see what just happened? You want me to hold a *baby*?" So the nurse held the baby while Toby stood between his wife and child, unsure what to do. They had budded. They had turned into three. He was responsible for the third. She could handle herself. This new baby girl could not handle herself. The nurse stood, rocking the baby, until Toby came over and took her.

"It's time for you to hold her now," the nurse said to Rachel.

"It's only been a minute since you said that! I still can't feel my legs! How can I hold my baby if I can't feel my legs?" But then she looked from Toby to the nurse and back again and saw something alarming. She saw in their eyes that she wasn't acting normal and something bad would happen if she didn't start, so she held her arms out.

"Give her to me."

Hannah was ninety minutes old by the time her mother held her, and over the years, Rachel would tell Toby that she thought that everything that went wrong with Hannah—which was what? Tantrums sometimes? A refusal to eat pizza with a vegetable on it? Not liking ballet as much as Rachel had wanted her to?—was a result of the fact that she hadn't immediately bonded with her. Her own mother, refusing to hold her. What kind of person does that? That first night, Rachel lay awake, afraid to go to sleep, staring at the baby in the plastic bassinet beside her, Toby asleep in the cot at the end of her bed. When he woke up in the middle of the night, unaware of where he was for a moment, he just heard her whispering into the bassinet, "I'm sorry, I'm sorry."

Later Rachel would retell the story of her delivery—she would tell it over and over, both to process what had happened to her and to punish her husband for leaving her when she was most vulnerable—but she would add a detail. She'd say that as the doctor was removing his hand, she'd kicked him in the chest, causing him to fly against the back wall. This wasn't true; it couldn't have been true. And yet she seemed to really believe it, enough so that she'd say it in front of him, even though he knew the truth—that she had turned not into a warrior after he did what he did, but into ash. This detail would always remind him that what happened to her that day had loosened something in her, maybe permanently broken it. It would make him worry that she was beyond repair.

Toby filed a complaint within the hospital. He took an extended paternity leave to see to his wife. They went to psychiatrists and psychologists. She went to a postpartum depression group, which, she said, was filled with sad, flat women with no affect whom she couldn't relate to, whom nothing happened to except their mysterious new sadness. They went to a fifth psychiatrist, one who worked in the hospital, who told her that she had PTSD, and this made her very ashamed. All she'd done was have a baby. She hadn't gone to war. *Everyone* has babies. *Everyone* has been born. Why was *she* a person to get traumatized by it? She wasn't the traumatized type. She was the trauma! Then they passed a sign in the lobby of the hospital after her six-week checkup with her actual doctor (whom she was very mad at) that said RAPE TRAUMA COUNSELING HAS BEEN MOVED TO FIFTH FLOOR. She told Toby to go home and she brought Hannah inside and sat in the group.

"But you weren't raped," Toby said when she got home. "It was bad, but it wasn't *rape*."

"I don't think I've been raped," she said. "This man did something awful to me. They get it. They understand me. No one else does."

They interviewed approximately ninety-two women and one man (Toby's suggestion) to be their nanny. None were good enough, and Rachel was convinced that a man who wanted to be a nanny was a pervert. Finally, in came Mona, a forty-year-old Ecuadoran woman with hair that was long and uneven with a severe middle part and who had just been discharged of her duties when the Alexander Schmidts moved to Switzerland to run a new bank. Rachel had at first gone through an agency, but she felt like she wasn't getting the best candidates because she didn't have the higher-tier offerings of an Upper East Side family: a car just for the nanny's use, a separate suite, credit cards, gifts.

Mona had a son of her own who was twelve, back in Ecuador, and all she needed was two weeks a year to go back and see him. Rachel knew Lala Schmidt from barre class and thought she really had her shit together. Mona was slow and spoke like a crocheted blanket. She was the only person they interviewed who asked if she could hold Hannah. She took her into her squat, dense, velvet body, and Hannah, who could not yet see clearly, seemed to make eye contact with her. Maybe it was seeing her baby in someone else's arms, calm. Maybe it was seeing the confidence and authority Mona had. Rachel began to cry in a way that Toby had never seen, sobs that overtook her. He put his hand on her back. Rachel nodded.

"I think you have the job," Toby said.

Mona began work immediately, though Rachel wasn't set to go back to the office anytime soon. She spent days at the apartment, cleaning bottles and getting to know Rachel and Hannah. She sent Rachel to a postnatal yoga class for women who'd had C-sections—Mona had heard about it from someone inside her network of nannies, a shadow group that knew all the secrets of these apparently poised women of the Upper East Side. Rachel went, and when she came back, she told Toby that she cried the entire time and felt unbound to the earth, like she was not subject to the rules of gravity if her baby wasn't with her. But it got better little by little, this feeling, and she went back until finally she wasn't crying all the time.

One Wednesday, he came home and asked her about her day. She said she'd decided to stop going to the rape group.

"I'm fine now," she said.

He noticed a spiral notebook at the end of the table, filled with notes in her small, tight handwriting. She seemed placid and undisturbed for the first time in weeks. He decided to ask no questions.

At the end of the first day of his second week back at work, Toby raced home late to see Rachel and Hannah. He had an emergency consult on a hemochromatosis case. It was eight when he walked through the door. There he found Hannah, but no Rachel. Just Mona.

"Where's Rachel?" he asked as he washed his hands and took Hannah from Mona's arms. Mona had been feeding her with a bottle of thick, white liquid—thicker than any breast milk.

"She's out for the evening. She said she'd be home by midnight."

"Is that formula?" He hadn't realized she'd stopped breast-feeding.

Toby sent Mona home and sat in Rachel's glider, rocking Hannah and watching a *Cops* marathon on TV.

It turned out that earlier that morning, when Toby left for work, Rachel had called Alejandra Lopez and asked if she could stop by her apartment to ask her something. Rachel had called her two assistants and four of the associates who worked under her and asked them to dinner at the Green Kitchen Diner on First Avenue, where no one would see them. She told them she was going out on her own, that she was taking her clients with her—that Alejandra Lopez was one of them—and who would like to get in on the ground floor of Super Duper Creative? She stayed out that night, drinking and celebrating, until four A.M., when she tiptoed into their apartment, where she found Toby waiting up for her.

Now Toby stood in the middle of his apartment, clutching a jar of peanut butter like it was a baby. He had picked up the peanut butter as soon as he walked away from Miriam and Cyndi so that he wouldn't look like some psychopath who just window-shopped at Whole Foods. He held it in both hands against his chest, like someone was trying to take it away from him. He wanted to tear the flesh from his face. He wanted to rend his garments. He wanted to smash this peanut butter jar with his bare hands but actually it was just hard plastic.

Focus, Fleishman. He turned to the kitchen, and his computer. He looked up Sam Rothberg's name on Facebook. His last post was the Funny or Die video that everyone had passed around ten years before. He scrolled down through more: a Tawny Kitaen meme, some craft beer blog posts, a picture of him and Jack at STEM Night at the school, a picture of him and Miriam at the fundraiser for scleroderma that Miriam's mother had bought a table at (said the caption). Then, most recently, two weeks ago, a picture of a pizza restaurant called Baba Louie's with the caption "More like Baba booey, am I right? [crying-but-laughing emoji] [crying-but-laughing emoji] [crying-but-laughing emoji]." He typed the name of the restaurant into his search bar. It was in Great Barrington, Massachusetts. He then searched Kripalu. Twelve miles away. What a dumb fucking joke. Rachel was fucking a Howard Stern listener. He sat back in his chair, staring at the screen. Cripple you.

Last year, Toby and Rachel had invited the Hertzes and the Leffers for Friday night dinner. Toby had cooked the entire night before, and then he served dinner, and the women were oohing and making pointed jokes toward their husbands over how nice it was to be waited on by a man, and to have a man who *participates*. The understanding at the table appeared to be that Rachel had cooked, and Toby, in thanks, had let her sit throughout the meal. But it wasn't true. He'd made chicken Milanese, one of his favorite recipes, and when Cyndi commented on it—"Mmm. Is that oregano?"—he'd said, "No, it's tarragon." He'd seen Rachel's face darken at this, and he wondered what crime he had committed. How was it possible that he could work so hard so that she could impress her stupid friends and still disappoint her so deeply?

Later he was in the kitchen plating the dessert the Hertzes had brought, and Rachel came in and snarled into his ear that he could, ostensibly, have more self-respect than making sure everyone knew that he'd made the meal. "I could make a meal if I didn't have to work day and night."

There were so many ways to respond, Toby thought. Should he tell her that he hadn't even thought about it when Cyndi asked? That he was sure it hadn't registered with her because she was only making polite small talk? That she was making a fool of herself leaving her guests at the table while she stage-whispered a tantrum that everyone could hear?

"Do you need some help in there?" Roxanne called from the dining room.

"You know what?" Rachel said. "I'm sick of this."

Toby looked at her and put the plate down with a slam. "*You* do this. *You* contribute to this."

He walked into the dining room and sat down, trying to keep his face neutral. He didn't give a shit about these people. But Rachel did. This was how he could punish her. He could punish her by reminding her that none of this mattered to him, that he was doing this absolutely, devotedly, for her. But that one day he could cut that cord and see where she drifted to. Yes, he should punish her by walking out. He should punish her so that she would never ever do this again.

"We're just talking about free passes," Roxanne said, as he sat down. "Rich and I are allowed five in our marriage each." Rox-

anne's husband was a hedge fund manager and his name was literally Rich.

"Oh, we only have one between us," Cyndi said. "Mine is George
Stephanopoulos. His is Naomi Campbell."

"Whoa," Todd said. "Still? She must be in her sixties."

"Late forties," Rich said. "Nothing wrong with experience."
They all laughed.

"Mine is Mark Wahlberg," Cyndi volunteered.

"Gross," Roxanne said.

"See what I'm dealing with here?" Todd said.

"There's just something about him that makes me think I could
save him."

"Mine is Ariana Grande," Rich said. "I like a sexy, glammy
type."

Toby laughed. "What's a sexy, glammy type?"

"I don't know. Someone who looks like she's a little too good for
me? Like my beautiful wife here, of course."

Roxanne made a pretend angry face. "You're just saying that so
that I forget your free pass is with an actual child."

"She's in her twenties! At least!"

Rachel walked in with the plate of desserts arranged in a fan.

"Who's your free pass, Rachel?" Roxanne said.

Rachel sat down. "What do you mean?"

"It's who would you sleep with if Toby gave you a free pass."

"This is what we're talking about?" Rachel asked.

"Come on, we've all answered," Rich said.

She thought for a half second. "Sam Rothberg."

"Sam Rothberg?" Roxanne almost fell over. Todd nose-burped
his drink. Cyndi's eyes opened so wide Toby could see into her
skull. Toby closed his eyes.

Silence fell on the table. Rich and Todd looked over at Toby, who
might have been sad to see his wife so humiliated had the implication of what she'd just said not faulted to him being the world's
biggest loser.

"What?" Rachel asked. "What did I say that's wrong?"

"You're not supposed to pick a person who you *know,* Rachel," Cyndi said. "God. You're supposed to pick a *celebrity.*"

The room became so uncomfortable that Rich tried to get a round of Drather going on the school's teachers, but Roxanne shut that down immediately. Toby opened his eyes. Rachel narrowed hers in a way that would have been imperceptible if everyone at the table hadn't known they had just been arguing in the kitchen. They sat on opposite ends of the table, staring at each other while their guests grasped desperately for a neutral subject.

Sam Rothberg was everything Rachel wished Toby were: ambitious, successful, tall, at home among the wealthy. But he was also vain, vapid, superficial, ostentatious, an idiot bro who played in fantasy leagues. Sam Rothberg was all that Toby felt he needed to protect his family from. Sam Rothberg was who he pictured when Solly said he wanted to go to golf camp and Toby's blood ran cold from the implications of this place where he lived inside but felt he existed outside—this place he was in but not of. His children were of it, though. He realized that now. They never stood a chance. What had he been thinking?

But while Toby was fighting the pull of this soft, stupid life, Rachel was opting into it on every level. He realized suddenly, looking at this dipshit's Facebook page, that it wasn't just more money and more success Rachel had wanted out of Toby. She wanted him to be a different person. She had outgrown him. She was ready to level up. She didn't want to renovate Seventy-second Street. She wanted to move on up. She wanted Seventy-fifth Street. She wanted the Golden.

She'd been gunning for him the whole time, he thought now. Did she orchestrate the entire misery of their lives just to get a divorce? Or wait. *Unless.* Unless unless unless unless unless unless. What if this had started before? It couldn't have, right? The job at

Fendant—but why? Why would a man try to get his lover's husband a job at his own company? Why would she want him to work for her boyfriend? What kind of masochistic mindfuck was that? Or did they fall in love over the plotting of it? Or did they fall in love when he was finding her an apartment to live in? Or did he find her an apartment because they were in love? He closed his laptop as if that could make the questions stop.

So they, Toby and Rachel, they never stood a chance, either. Rachel—his beautiful, smart, successful wife—had dabbled in this world too much to be able to resist it. She had jumped into the pool and was wondering why she was so wet. Or no! She was not wondering! There was no more wondering. There hadn't been any wondering for *years*. You couldn't go to the private school without wishing you were one of them. You couldn't go to buy a house in the Hamptons and then wonder who you were. You *were* one of them. How had he missed all of this? God, what an idiot he was.

But Sam was married. That's right. Sam was married. Miriam was not talking about her ex-husband at the Whole Foods. Miriam was setting up a fucking yoga playdate with Toby for her very current husband. What kind of idiot monster fucks a married man? The apps work for women, too, Rachel. You can find someone who is available and not wreck a marriage over this, Rachel. There were finance bros carpeting this city like Astroturf on a college football field and she was still pretty and thin and could have any single one of them.

"Listen to the patient, you fucking asshole," he said to himself, right there, aloud, in the living room, the twilight descending through the unshaded windows. She is giving you the fucking diagnosis. His brain had always tried to make her behavior excusable. It didn't have to do that anymore. They were over. And also, there were no excuses, no possible reasons for this behavior. Christ, why couldn't he just face it? What had he done? What had he done aligning his life with this kind of person? Shut up, shut up, he told his brain.

It was now almost two weeks since Rachel had dropped off the kids. She was ten days late to pick them up. Rachel was gone. Toby had been replaced. She'd upgraded. Now she was *free and relaxed*. Now she was *sleeping in the fucking park,* finally calm and at ease enough to become one of those people she'd stared at with derision and longing back when the princess was still willing to grace the park with a walk-through. Now she was free.

The peanut butter he bought was *useless*. It had *sugar* added to it. He would never *eat* that. He would never feed it to his *children*. He was his children's only chance in the *world* now. Everything and everyone was fucked *forever*.

He put the peanut butter down and left the apartment. He didn't know what time it was, but it had been light when he went in and now the sky was a violet dusk. Outside, he broke into a run. He headed toward Seventy-fifth Street. At a stoplight, he paused and saw a familiar woman crossing Third Avenue. She was pretty and young, and he looked hard at her face, breathless, and she, feeling she was being looked at, looked back at him. They remembered each other at the exact same moment. She was from Hr, he realized—a crazy night early on where they'd gotten on the FaceTime functions of their phones and watched each other's faces as they'd masturbated—her suggestion. Nothing else, no body parts, no talking, just watching each other's faces. She hung up the minute they both came, as if she couldn't bear being connected any longer with a person who would do these things. Yes, now he remembered. She was staring at him, but he kept going. Lauren. Her name was Lauren. He took off into a run again. He could not bear the Internet. He could not bear that it was treated like it was not real and yet it was filled with real people who could just walk the same streets as he did. He hated himself so much right then he wanted to die. Well, Lauren, this is what you can expect from the mutual masturbation community on your online dating app. You can expect your former jerk-off partner to be found running wild-eyed through the streets looking for his ex-wife; that's the caliber of person you are dealing with when you are someone who stares into a phone while whacking off.

He arrived at the Golden—Rachel's home. His former home. His children's home. His children's former home. Toby slowed his jog as he passed George, who had been his favorite doorman, and raised his hand in his rushed greeting. Toby ran into an open elevator and frantically pushed the close-door button. He arrived at the ninth floor, overcome with fear combined with rage combined with anxiety. He felt his heart beating in his face. Maybe he would die and it would seem like a terrible tragedy and only he would know that he was saved from whatever it was that lay behind her front door.

Maybe he was weak. Maybe he was weak like she said. He put the key in the door. It still worked. He walked in. He knew on an animal level the sounds and feelings of that place, both when it was occupied and when it wasn't. He felt the emptiness of it. No one was home. He was relieved. Why are you such a pussy? he asked himself.

He'd been inside less than a month ago, picking up Hannah's haftorah worksheet, since her lesson was being moved to Toby's house at the last minute. That day, the place still felt like where he'd once lived. He'd stopped and had a moment, like Emily in the last scene of *Our Town:* Had he ever realized what a nice apartment it was, when he was so busy registering his scorn for the materialism of all of it? Now he saw it compared to his new apartment, the outstanding feature of which was no longer his Le Creusets but the metal shades and the wobbly air-conditioning and the popcorn ceiling. He'd left that day angry at himself for allowing his brain to do the thing that his brain always did, which was to assume that things weren't as bad as they were when they definitely had been.

And yet, beneath the veneer of order was their history. This was where his life took place for the last four years. This was where his marriage fell apart, yes, but this was also where he did homework with his kids and showed them the *Star Wars* movies and fucked his wife. This was where they fought, yes, but this was also where they made up and laughed and listened to Hannah practice her flute or watched Solly rehearse lines for scenes during his brief foray into acting lessons—he was to play the oldest Von Trapp son in the Y's all-kid version of *The Sound of Music* and it was a disaster. This was where he built a fingerprint crime scene set for Hannah's third-grade science fair and where he built a solar system model that actually had a motorized rotator with Solly for his. He couldn't hate it here. Ascribing blackness to this place felt like a betrayal of his children, who had been through enough.

He walked through the silence. The small things that appeared changed since he'd lived here—the definitively mid-cench easy chair on the other side of the room, a new lamp to replace one that Hannah had knocked over a year ago—it all had a discombobulating effect on him. The chandelier was down two lights, even though he'd bought a dozen replacements before he left. In the kitchen, there was an almost soundless leak coming from the sink faucet, still there after he'd warned her about it a month ago. Why had Toby assumed that when he was gone, she would become a person who knew how to take care of things?

He opened the refrigerator. There were six Chinese food containers all lined up. He opened one. Beef lo mein. She didn't eat lo mein. She ate shrimp in lobster sauce. Solly ate lo mein, but Solly didn't like beef. He smelled inside the box, but it didn't smell especially pungent. Maybe it was someone else's lo mein, or maybe Rachel had just bought the wrong lo mein, not remembering her children's particularities. Or. Or Rachel could be either eating lo mein or fucking a guy who liked lo mein. Both options seemed fairly impossible and extremely likely.

He opened the second box. It was also beef lo mein, though half of it was eaten. He opened the next two boxes, dread and eeriness mounting like in a horror movie: They were all beef lo mein. It didn't make any fucking sense.

For a moment, in his mind's eye, he could see it. Rachel and Sam on the couch. Her lying down since now she was a relaxed type, now she was someone who slept in Central Park, her legs carelessly draped over Sam's sitting-up legs. Both of them with beef lo mein containers, eating out of the carton like fucking pigs. She was typing on her phone because her phone was actually the love of her life—don't kid yourself, Rothberg—while Sam read one of a pile of *National Reviews*. She looked up and said, "I'm so happy to be trying new things again. Toby would never think to order me beef lo mein, and it's delicious."

What was he doing there? What was he imagining? It wasn't helpful. He knew that. He walked into the bedroom. The bed was unmade. He tried to discern if both pillows had head indentations. They did, but who knows? Maybe she was spreading out on the bed now that he was gone. He stood very still and tried to feel the energy of the place. Had sex been had here? He missed that bed; it was so comfortable. He looked at it longingly. What the fuck, he decided. He lay down like Goldilocks on his side of the bed and turned, staring at what had been hers. Toby moved his body to the middle, still with his shoes on, and made himself into a starfish shape, an elegy for this amazing fucking bed that he loved and maybe also to spread his scent and remind any new visitor to this bed that he was not the first—no, Toby was. He leaned his head into a pillow. It still smelled like her. Or maybe not her. Maybe it smelled like her and Sam Rothberg.

Maybe this was where they ate their lo mein and plotted their affair. Now he could see them, post-coital, propped up on their elbows on their sides, facing each other, still sweaty and panting while they voraciously housed the lo mein.

"God, all this time I was eating shrimp and lobster sauce like a complete asshole," she said to Sam.

"You just didn't know better, baby," he said back.

"I have so much to learn from you."

This was a bad experiment. Toby stood up.

The master bathroom door was open. Maybe he could discern a male pubic hair, or any pubic hair; she sure as hell hadn't had pubic hair in years. Her toothbrush was dry. There was another toothbrush next to it. It could have been one of the kids'. It could have been his old one. He didn't remember. He opened the medicine cabinet. There was a bottle of Ambien. There was a bottle of Ambien prescribed to Sam Fucking Rothberg.

"Ah!" Toby said out loud. He was momentarily triumphant for putting all of this together; then he remembered that the loser points in this scenario actually accrued to him. But now he was remembering Tiger Woods, how he'd eat like twelve Ambien and go on a twilight sleep-sex binge. People did crazy shit on Ambien: killing people and making five-course dinners they couldn't remember making and jumping out of windows. The mother of his children, high and crazy.

Oh Jesus, now he could see that, too, Rachel on all fours on top of the dining room table, totally naked, supporting herself with one hand while stuffing beef lo mein into her face with her other hand, Sam banging her from behind—on his knees on a Swedish modern table Toby had been allowed to help pick out but had never had sex on himself—while also holding a carton of beef lo mein and eating it with his hands.

He went back into the kitchen. Now he saw, lined up on the counter, six different boxes of specialty teas that were brands he didn't recognize: Dr. Albert's Lemon Balm Fizz tea. Heavenscape Lavender tea. Serenity Valerian tea. Serenity Passionflower tea. Rachel hated tea. She drank coffee. Tea, she said, was a too-complicated way of drinking water. It was useless and she had no patience for it. So Sam was an insomniac. It was nice that even sociopaths could be haunted by their decisions.

He looked down on the floor. It was her workout tank top, his least favorite one: ANY YOGA I DO IS HOT YOGA, it said in hot-pink letters against a blue background. Beneath it were her leggings, which were patterned in multicolor lightning bolts. He picked up the tank top. He smelled it. It was her. It was Rachel, right there. He wanted to eat the tank top, to consume it and make it go away. Was it warm? Was he imagining that it was warm?

A voice came into his head that put an end to all the questioning: She's been here recently. She's been here because she lives here. She's been here recently with someone else. Someone who drinks tea. Someone who eats lo mein. She'd been exercising while he'd worked hard to allow their children to imagine for a few more weeks that their mother loved them. She'd had sex on his bed with a married dickfuck. She's been here. You're the last person to know, Toby. Fuck you, Toby.

If he wanted to bring the kids here at night and drop them off when they got back from camp, he could. He could just leave them here and let her deal with it. But the kids didn't deserve a mother who was at the very least ambivalent about them. And she certainly didn't deserve the kids. It didn't even matter that she didn't want them; she didn't deserve them, either.

He picked up the phone. This was how to do it. He called her cell. It went right to voicemail. He called her office.

"Rachel Fleishman's office." Simone picked up on the first ring, but her voice was tentative. "Rachel?!"

"It's Toby. Is she not there?"

"Oh! Hi, Toby!" She sounded sweaty and terrified. "You're calling from Rachel's house. Are you there with her?"

"She's not here. I'm here to pick up some stuff for the kids."

"Did you see her? Was she there when you got there?"

"Tell her I said that I know everything and she can just go fuck herself and she will never see these children again if I have anything to do with it. We do not need her. We don't need any of it."

On his way out of the apartment, he noticed that the rug was now gone, replaced probably by the penguin with the kind of

million-dollar custom Turkish rug he'd read about in the Style section. He left without locking the door. Let her wonder, he thought.
He got into the elevator, which still smelled like home to him. It
was about all he could take. Could a place have a soul? Could a
woman who was alive be a ghost?

"Goodbye, Dr. Fleishman," George said cheerfully. Toby gave
him a salute, nothing wrong here, and walked right out.

He couldn't remember when last he'd eaten and some force of self-
preservation allowed him to find himself, soon after leaving the
Golden, standing on gelatinous legs at the salad place on Eighty-
fifth Street in an interminable line of young women who had just
worked out. He looked at his phone, the way they all looked at
their phones, but he didn't know where to start. He was barely a
man anymore. Within minutes he received a text that Karen Cooper's liver was ready before his salad was.

At the hospital, David Cooper was being informed over his
wife's now-empty bed by Marco Lintz, the surgeon, while Toby's
fellows and Marco's surgical fellows were there. And one person
extra: Phillipa London. Now, what the fuck was Phillipa doing
there? Reporting on him and his not having been there to Bartuck,
he bet. Well, he was here now.

"Dr. Fleishman," Phillipa said. "I was just attending until you
got here." Was that an accusation? Was he supposed to just be
waiting around for a liver to come in? Phillipa was too serious and
too punishing. She lived the doctor's version of a monk's life: racquetball three days a week, swimming two, work by seven, no aberration. There was no universe in which she could understand a
crisis like the one Toby was enduring. Toby admired that, and he
resented it, and he was snide about it: Look at this person in total
control of her life, look at how much she gets to control her life,
look at that control freak and her sad life.

They all took notes while that pretty boy Lintz lectured David

Cooper. He once heard Joanie describe Lintz's eyes to Clay as being "like melted coffee beans." He didn't know why this stuck with him or why she didn't just say chocolate. And by the way, he wasn't that handsome. He just wasn't.

"Does she even know what's going on?" This question came from the corner, from a woman Toby hadn't seen before. She was about Karen's age and had the same processed uptownness to her: stripy blond hair that was ironed straight, a fraying at the ends.

"She doesn't," Marco said. This made the woman's face ball up into a crying fist.

Toby walked David to the family lounge with the woman, whose name was Amy. In the lounge, the Cooper twins were on the Xbox, Jasper still crying while he played. David went to talk to them about ordering dinner.

"I was in Vegas with her the weekend before she came here," Amy was saying.

"Really?" Toby asked. "What was she like? I mean, how was she?"

Amy thought for a second, then smiled. "Free." Then, "Oh my God, did we drink."

"Yeah," he said. "Usually a disease like this is in the works in the background, and then after a bout of drinking, it comes to the fore."

Amy looked stricken. "Do you mean that the drinking did this? It was just a weekend. It was a *Vegas* weekend. What are you *supposed* to do?"

"Nah, it was coming anyway."

Amy took out her phone and pulled up some pictures. It was Karen Cooper. Karen Cooper with Amy at Madame Tussauds, her leg wrapped around a waxen leg attached to a member of Mötley Crüe. Karen Cooper pretending to lick the face of waxen Prince Harry, of all people.

Having an unconscious patient was like talking to someone on the phone for hours before ever seeing them: It was hard to reconcile that they hadn't been what you pictured, and your brain, having never seen the person, corrected for them to be more of what you wished they were. Toby had pictured someone smart and complicated, though he didn't know why. He had not pictured someone who posed for pictures lasciviously, with her tongue hanging out. But there she was, on Amy's screen: alive, with thoughts and opinions and preferences and animating forces, like a breath was blown into her and she was made sentient. The exact opposite of what actually had happened, which was that a breath was blown out of her and she was made into just the sum of her biological parts. He looked at a picture of her holding up a shot of something at a bar. She looked into the camera with defiance. It was awfully sexy. The picture could easily be one of the supplementary pics from a Hr profile, not the main one but a third or fourth. He had to look away from the phone in order to restore her to personhood and patienthood, and only briefly did he think to wonder if he was doing a bad job of thinking of the women he dated as people.

The next morning, Toby found himself too awake at five A.M., and so he went for a meandering walk. By six, he had made a decision. He called the law office of Barbara Hiller, telling her he had a custodial emergency. Her secretary called back at eight to tell him she could squeeze him in before a morning deposition. Toby was waiting in front of Barbara's locked office by the time she showed up in a tennis skirt and a weathered navy polo shirt that was turned up at the sleeve hems and at the collar.

Barbara Hiller looked like she'd been crushed in the trash compactor in *Star Wars*—a perfectly normal-looking person who had been condensed so that everything about her seemed flattened sideways and stretched upward: She had a face so narrow it was hard to believe it could accommodate both eyes. Her nose protruded so much that she had the countenance of a toucan.

Her office was decorated in soft blushes and taupes, what Rachel's decorator might have called "eighties-era mortuary," the whole room designed to calm and soothe. Above her desk was an abstract painting that Toby immediately Rorschached into a portrait of the actress Kristy McNichol sitting at his parents' dining room table.

"Tell me," Barbara said, calm behind her desk, holding a pencil over a clean sheet of paper in a leather notebook. So he did. He told her that he had no idea where Rachel was, that he had some inkling that she was okay from her assistant, but that she was literally nowhere and seemed to have opted out of his and the children's lives. Toby told her about their divorce arrangement and their custody agreement—him every other weekend, but also still every day after school/camp until she got home.

"Wow, she's got you on a leash," Barbara said.

"That's one way to put it, I guess."

"I'd be angry, too," Barbara said.

"I'm not angry. I just have to figure this out. It's been two weeks since she's answered my calls. She's sleeping with one of the dads from school."

"Whoa."

"She's home. I went to her apartment . . ."

"You really shouldn't do that."

". . . and there is evidence of her, like, shacking up with a guy which makes no sense because his wife clearly doesn't know anything's going on."

"Slow down," Barbara said, writing on a legal pad. "Okay, are you prepared to assume full custody of the children?"

"I already do. That's what I'm saying. I already do everything. She is like a non-issue in our lives. Like a special guest star."

"Remind me of your work again?" She narrowed her eyes. "You work, right?"

"I'm a hepatologist at St. Thaddeus."

"That's lungs?"

"Livers."

"My father was a patient there a few years back, but in the cardiology department."

Toby nodded, unsure of what he should say or if this discussion applied to her hourly rate. "They're very good doctors in that department."

"Yes, he's home now. He's fine. Just a scare."

Toby waited.

"Sorry. So the arrangement?"

"I have them most of the time. She has them when she says she can. I'm the—I'm the main person. But again, she's just gone. I sent the kids to camp. She doesn't know it."

"And that's going to be finalized as part of the agreement."

"We have general outlines of who gets them when. I have them for half the vacations, and every other weekend."

"And has she been keeping up to this agreement?"

"Not really. It's only been about two months. There's only been Memorial Day and July Fourth for a holiday. I had them Memorial Day. She was supposed to take them for July Fourth, but she took them for just the Sunday and Monday of it because she wanted to go to Fire Island."

Barbara Hiller looked up. "But she still took them?"

"Only for half of what was agreed to."

"You should get more formal times in writing. Some people, it's usually the dads, they end up being more slippery than you think they'll be. Especially when everyone puts on such a good show for the mediator. Why did you go to a mediator?"

Toby blinked. "Because you told me to when I came in for advice?"

"Right. Yes. The problem with a mediator is that it's like bringing a knife to a gunfight, you know?" She looked off, considering. "She has all the money, right? She's a . . . lawyer?"

"Agent."

"*Agent*. She works at one of the big firms."

"She owns her own firm."

"Right, right. Now I remember. She reps Alejandra Lopez, right?"

"Right."

"Right, right. My wife and I and the kids sing the *Presidentrix* soundtrack, like, day and night. It's really something spectacular. I couldn't believe it when I saw it. I was in tears. I never cry." She looked out the window, absurdly lost in a wonderful memory while he sat right the fuck in front of her.

"So what can I do?"

Barbara Hiller leaned back in her chair, luxuriously expelling air from her solar plexus. "You know, this is a hard one. You could decide not to sign the final paperwork and ask for full custody, but she might withdraw financial support. She pays for everything, if I remember?"

"Just for the kids."

"But private school, camp, lessons, tutors, that sort of thing."

"Yes, she pays."

"And how do you propose to keep all this stuff up on your salary?"

"Well, I can put them in public school. . . ."

"So you'll take them out of the school that they've been in for years right after their parents get divorced."

Toby didn't say anything. He thought of Hannah not being able to attend school with her friends anymore.

Barbara looked down at her paper. Then she looked back up at him. She leaned forward and clasped her hands together and she said the next thing like it was a secret.

"You know what I tell the wives?" she asked.

Toby waited.

"I tell them that there is only so much in your control, and that the system is freighted toward the husbands."

"I don't feel like the system is freighted toward me right now."

Barbara narrowed her eyes and shook her head. "No, you're the wife."

———

Toby sat staring out his bedroom window into the humidity, everyone and everything wavy in the heat. It was too hot. Why was it so
hot in his room? He leaned over to the air-conditioning to turn it
on, but he saw it already was. He'd have to call the super in the
morning. Then he'd have to wait for the super. Or miss work. Or
miss something.

How could it be? he wondered. How could it be that you take
extremely difficult, extremely healthy steps to get your life in order
only to have the person you extracted yourself from more in charge
of your happiness and well-being than she ever was?

He lay back on his bed, staring at the ceiling. There was a brown
stain on it. How does a ceiling get a stain?

God himself must have sent the three pings to his phone in response. He looked at his phone. Karen Cooper had made it through
surgery. She was in the ICU on a ventilator. Toby called Clay, who
had stayed overnight.

"I think we're fine," Clay said. "Patient will be awake tomorrow."

"Mrs. Cooper."

"Mrs. Cooper will be awake tomorrow."

"You sure you don't need me?"

"I think we're fine? ICU has her."

"Okay. If you think I should come in, just ping me. I'm around."

He hung up. This was a new low for him, basically begging his
fellow to ask him to come in. He called Seth, but Seth didn't answer, which was for the best. What could Seth do right now except
show him how much easier a life he could have had if he'd married
the right person or if he'd never gotten married at all? It was an
exercise in stupidity to wonder those things. He missed his kids.
Hannah had gone to sleepaway camp for two summers by now, but
Solly—how could he leave him alone like that? The camp forbade
contact for the first week, and all he could wonder was if Solly was

begging an apathetic teenager to let him call his dad. The apartment was too empty; it was too quiet. Toby was too alone.

His phone buzzed next to him. He couldn't bear it. He wanted to throw the thing out the window, just be done with all of it. Just be done with everything. But he turned his head and he saw her name.

Nahid.

Sweet holy Moses in a wicker basket, it was Nahid.

Within minutes, he was sitting in the back of a cab, willing it to beat the lights, but it didn't. His heart beat in time with the opposing street's DON'T WALK blinker. What a turn this was. Today! Of all days! Sex! Toby! A sex partner! A beautiful woman with an accent and a glorious body. A woman who was reaching out to *him*. On the TV in the cab, a late-night talk show host did a lip sync challenge with an elderly British actress. The Chyron beneath announced that the heat wave would continue for some time. "Is it hot enough for ya?" the weatherman asked him. Weathermen! Did he ever consider what a hard job that was? How awful it was to have to evaluate the weather based on other people's values: a nice day, bad weather, etc.? Here in his cab, the driver was having a screaming fight with someone on the phone. The weatherman, the driver—those guys were prisoners. He, Toby, was free.

At her building, he announced that he was there to see Nahid. The doorman waved him along. He shared a brief look with the doorman, which Toby tried to interpret: Was he one of many who showed up? Did the doorman just know to let panting, horny guys up there? Did it even matter?

When he arrived on her floor, she was waiting for him. Silently, they entered her apartment. She took his hand and pushed it under her skirt and made thrusting motions until he took up her cue. Suddenly he wished for nothing to be different. Rachel, camp, the kids—if they were different he wouldn't be here, and he wanted to be right where he was right then, alive and with his hand up this woman's skirt.

They fucked on the floor. Afterward, she rested her head on his chest and he put his cheek into her palace of rough, wild hair. She had a gap in her teeth. It was one of the first physical traits that ever reliably made him weak, dating back to a girl named Alyssa in fourth grade who put her tongue through hers while she was writing. How she broke his heart when she got braces in sixth grade.

They lay on the carpet in her living room, under a top sheet, staring at the ceiling and talking. Her parents had emigrated to Paris from Iran right before she was born. Her family had moved to the U.S. when she was twelve. Then, when she was nineteen, her family moved to Queens. Her father sold vertical blinds in Kew Gardens Hills. She said she felt like she was the only Iranian whose family didn't escape the shah with a treasure chest of jewels. Just down the road in Forest Hills, there were Persian women laden with riches whose homes were filled with sculptures. Nahid? She had blinds in every room.

She went to Baruch, where she met her now ex-husband in an accounting class. She wanted to go into costume design and run her own business, and so she took a few business classes, and there he was—smart, handsome, ambitious. He was a Christian. It was the one thing he couldn't get around, marrying someone who wasn't. Her parents were Jewish, but she didn't care about religion so she converted. She thought it was romantic, that he cared about her so much that his worries extended beyond her death. She had a baptism. She took communion. Her parents stopped speaking to her, but what was she supposed to do? She was in love. This was a nice thing to do for someone you loved.

They didn't have children, even though they tried, but she felt like maybe a decision had been made for her. She wasn't born wanting children. She always thought that the moment would come when she did, but time went on and she attended her friends' baby showers, and she felt no urge. Then, every month, she'd get her period and she'd feel something awfully similar to relief.

Her husband was different. He thought this was a tragedy. He'd had such a clear picture of himself in his life: a wife, children, public service to the conservative values that he believed would save the world. She tried to explain to him the advantages of not having children: that they could travel, that he could run for office without being an absentee parent. He could think of his constituents as his children—his flock. They could have a good life, absent all the tension in the marriages of their friends, which seemed to be crumbling beneath the weight of their kids.

But he was so sad, and she loved him. So they tried, and then they tried hard, and then they tried harder, pumping poisons into her body and prying her and implanting her and injecting her and stimulating her parts. She thought with some relief that obviously this wasn't meant to be. She had been told from too young an age about God and how in charge he was. She couldn't help thinking that this was divine intervention, that God wouldn't give her children she didn't absolutely want.

He was bereaved. She would reach for him and try to comfort him, but he didn't want that. She said she wanted comfort. He said, "Don't you think it's weird how much sex you want?" She was taken aback. She'd never thought about it. All she knew was that her friends were constantly complaining about all the sex their husbands still wanted and all the sex they themselves *didn't* want. "It's not nice," her husband said. "It's not ladylike." She kept trying to tell him that wanting to have sex with her husband was normal. He would change the subject. She would leave to go to the bathroom and stare into the mirror at her lovely face and try to figure out what was wrong with it.

At some point, they stopped having sex completely. He wanted to adopt. That was the last thing she wanted. He wanted to hire a surrogate. That was the second-to-last thing she wanted. There was no way to talk about anything without it being about this. An unrelenting sadness crept into their home's foundation. He began to stay out later and later. He began to come home smelling like musky perfumes. And then, one sad night, she came home from a walk across the High Line and found him on his knees, with his personal assistant's penis in his mouth, which now replaced adoption as the last thing she ever wanted.

"I guess that explains him not wanting to have sex," Toby said. "Because I can't imagine."

"Tell me about you," she said.

He looked up at her ceiling. No stains. Did he want to tell her? Did he want her to know that there was an emergency going on? That his story was actually slightly different from the story he'd told her a week ago?

"My wife was an unfit mother," he said. "But she wanted children. She just couldn't manage to figure out how to love them, or to love us."

She waited. He didn't want to tell her anything else, mostly because he still didn't understand what he could say that wouldn't make him seem like all the women who had told him their stories. They'd always seemed like such victims. The way they would talk about the betrayals that led to hurt and the intensity that became apathy—it made him wonder what the men's side of the story was. Here he thought of Rachel and Sam one more time, lo mein cartons in hand. What could she be telling him about Toby? Surely not: "I changed the terms of who I was and what I wanted with just about no warning." Instead it was: "He was lazy and punished me for having ambition."

"Do you think maybe you want to go to dinner sometime?" he asked.

She smiled dirty. "I'd rather order in."

"No, seriously. I'd like to get to know you. I'd like to take you out."

"I can't. I'm still figuring things out with my husband and I don't want to go out with another man just now."

"Because it would hurt him too much?" She was quiet. "But you're not married anymore."

She laughed at him. "Divorce doesn't make you any less married."

It must have been that his dreams were too real, or else that he was never really asleep, because when he woke up that Saturday, it was like he'd been waiting to open his eyes. The whole night he had been stuck in the gloaming where sleep kept threatening, but all he got were hallucinations. He'd forgotten to pull the shades, so the room was too bright. The air-conditioning was working now but making a weird sound. He was still sleeping on one side of the bed, and every morning this made him feel pathetic. He closed his eyes and searched his brain for the thing that was bothering him but couldn't locate it. The apartment was so quiet that it was hard to think.

Why was all his life about white-knuckling his anxiety? Disgust rose in him and he knew he couldn't withstand the day like this, talking himself down. He texted Seth, who didn't answer. He was probably strung out in a post-Ecstasy, post-cocaine stupor from the night before. With a little dread, he texted me.

What are you doing today?

I told him that we were going to our pool club. *Come with! We'll bbq.* He looked outside. The trees were not moving. It was seven A.M., and the people below on the street were fanning themselves. The taxi television had been right. It was hot. He wrote back.

Tell me what train to take, I'll be there.

On the train out of Penn Station, his phone beeped. Seth was returning his text. *We're around.*

I'm going to see Libby in NJ. Pool. You should come.

Yeah, gonna skip NJ

She's bbqing

There is no bbq or body of water that will make me want to go to the suburbs

Fair

Dinner tonight? V wants to meet you.

Sure

He looked out the window of the train into the dark Penn Station tunnel. It was ten A.M. by now and the man across the aisle from him was shirtless and drunk. Toby would make it through the day.

At my house, I watched Toby watch me fight with my eight-year-old daughter, Sasha, who wanted to wear a bikini.

"What's the point of this argument?" I said to her. "We're not at a clothing store. You don't own a bikini. There is literally nothing that will get you into a bikini right now."

"I hate you," Sasha said.

Adam, tall and focused, stood in the kitchen packing the large boat bag. "Bet this is a familiar song to you," he said to Toby.

"Yeah," Toby answered.

I watched Toby watch me shoot Adam a look. He looked back, like wha? I shook my head and sprayed sunscreen onto our six-year-old, Miles. Then I watched Toby watch me at my pool club. Every family was just like mine: chubby, domineering mother; clueless, servile dad; disgusted child; happy-go-lucky child who just wants to know if the slide is open; sometimes there was a third child if the chubby, domineering mother and the clueless, servile dad had started early enough.

Through Toby's eyes, it was unsettling just how much all the other women really did look like me. It was what I resented about where I lived, that after a lifetime of feeling lesser than the skinny blondes with straight hair and noses in Manhattan, I most hated that everyone here looked exactly like me. Or did I hate looking exactly like everyone else? Or did seeing them en masse like this allow me to finally see myself clearly and the view was no bueno? Our navy tankinis were reinforced with steel paneling so that our bodies were all mashed and wrung into hourglass figures, while our limbs told the true stories of our discipline and metabolic limitations.

I wasn't self-conscious in front of the dads. This was how they knew me. But in front of Toby? Look at the withered thing I'd become. I'd seen his phone. Bodies were like produce to him now. He only looked at them for the ways they tempted and the ways they were blemished or unblemished. Legs, uncanny breast valleys, butts butts butts butts. I know what I looked like to him. Trust me, I had no sexual or romantic wish for Toby. I just didn't like the record he was holding. I didn't like being this way now with someone who still remembered me back at the beginning, back when I was all potential and kinetic energy. Everyone else here knew me as a carpool partner and a walking playdate calendar. By those metrics, I was a star. By Toby's, I was nothing.

I took Miles over for his lesson. Miles was scared of the water, so I stayed sitting on the side of the pool with my legs in the water, thinking of how my stomach folded over on itself. I crossed my arms in front of my chest. Bathing suits for women are unfair. Toby and Adam sat on chaises next to each other. They looked ridiculous together, Toby so short and Adam so long. Adam with his soft brown eyes and gray streaks in the hair that had the decency to thin evenly all around. They were having some kind of conversation that looked involved.

I caught Adam staring at me. He stared at me a lot lately, but he never asked questions. I had begun to go outside at night and lie on our hammock. Adam resented it. He's linear and infers rules from onetime behaviors, which drives me crazy. "But you hate going outside," he'd say. And yet, there I was, outside, busting open the contract he held on me. He'd go back in and put the kids to bed and I would look up at the sky. You could see some stars where I lived. You could never see them in Manhattan. That was one advantage of this place, I guess.

I'd been spending time on the phone with Toby like I was a teenager, leaving the room to talk even when the kids were asleep like Adam was my father, which sometimes he was. When he talked, I pressed the mute button on my phone so that he wouldn't hear the long drag I was taking from the pot vape that Seth had had delivered to my home, via his company messenger service. Seth had sent it over after that lunch we had, when I had told him that I'd all but stopped smoking. He was sad to hear it. "It was your *thing*," he'd said. "You were a *champion* at it." A few hours later my doorbell rang. With the vape was a note that said, "This stuff comes from Humboldt County and contains a new, genetically engineered strain that literally has a three-thousand-person waitlist but my guy gets me stuff."

I hadn't smoked pot in years, with one exception. About a year ago, Adam and I had gone to the backyard fortieth birthday party of one of the dads from our kids' school and someone had passed around a joint. I settled into my high, listening to the dad's brother's Tom Petty karaoke (it was always Tom Petty karaoke in New Jersey, even more than Springsteen), and I listened to a conversation among some of the other moms. In general, we only ever spoke about our children with each other. I didn't know if they were having better conversations and I was just excluded, or if this was all there was to talk about. At the party, I watched them take hits off a vape that someone had brought and then listened as their stoned conversations turned into every other conversation they had, but louder and more intense: Hunter was not outgoing enough for drama but he still wanted to do it and Raleigh is really just a sensory kid, you know? and I did not think the school handled that well but Oscar really doesn't have a sense of maturity beyond his years, which . . . and no it's called a specific learning disability in math but the math part is the specific part it's not specific within math—

The conversation got louder and the women began talking over each other as they grew more and more stoned, but the subject matter never changed. Even high, that was all they talked about. There was no other layer. There was no yearning. There was nothing beyond it. "It's not New Jersey," Adam said. "It's life. It's being in your forties. We're parents now. We've said all we needed to say." I began to cry. He patted my head and said, "It's okay, it's okay. It's the order of things. Now we focus on the kids. We mellow with age. It's how it goes. It's not our turn anymore." I tried to respond but instead sob-hiccuped. He said, "Why don't we get you home?"

Adam and I left the party, and we got into bed and tried to get through another episode of the drug cartel show we were watching that everyone said got really good at the end of the third season, but we were only up to the second, and we had existential angst about whether we should be watching something that only promised to be good but wasn't yet. We agreed the answer was yes, that hope was good, and in those moments—the ones when we endured, the ones where we agreed, the ones where we disagreed and found the other person's point dumb enough to laugh out loud, the ones where he still agreed to do our fully choreographed wedding dance in the kitchen for no reason at all and to no music, the ones where he showed me a window into how much smarter he was than I was and how even though he was that smart he never needed to flaunt it, the ones where we rolled our eyes at how dumb everyone else was, the ones where he evacuated me from my misery and made me a cheese omelet because I was stoned and wanted something warm and milky, that was when I remembered the most essential thing about Adam and me, which was that I never once doubted if I should be with him.

So then why did I need my secrets? In the last few days, I'd been smoking the vape in the morning. I'd hide it in time for Adam to arrive home. I didn't want to know what he'd think of my stoned parenting while I was stoned, but also, I liked the secret. (Mostly. At one point, he had to open up his computer because someone at work needed him to read over a document, and he was so annoyed and grumbling. My reaction was to keep saying, "Are you mad at me? Did I do something?" until he finally said, "What is your problem?" I left the room to give the kids their baths.)

After the kids were in bed, I'd call Toby. Adam would come outside while I was on the phone. "What are you doing out here?" he would ask. I'd put my vape under my leg and close my eyes. I'd stopped doing that when we got married. But when we turned forty he stopped eating red meat and yet, there he was, out in the open, eating it maybe twice a week with no apology.

"I'm on the phone with Toby," I'd say.

He'd wait a long second and turn around and go inside.

"I have to go," I'd whisper into the phone.

I'd go inside and sit at the top of my stairs and look at him on the couch in the living room, still so sharp at the end of the day, reconciling papers and laws. Saying, "Aha! I knew it!" like a cartoon character and then shimmying from side to side as he sent a triumphant email assuring everyone that as usual, he had the answers—that as usual, he had come through.

Back at my house that Saturday, Adam grilled lamb. At three, Toby began to say his goodbyes. I asked him what his plans were for the rest of the weekend.

"I'm going to see Seth tonight. For dinner. I'm meeting Vanessa. I'm hoping they don't take me to a club. They seem to go to a lot of clubs."

"Well, young people have a lot of energy," I said.

"Be nice. You guys are invited, if you want."

"We don't have a babysitter," Adam said. "Can I drive you to the train?"

"If you don't mind." Toby went to use the bathroom.

"Do you mind if I go?" I asked Adam. "He's having a hard time." Weekends were endless. If you needed to know the most disparate thing about Adam and me, it was that he loved them and I did not. I liked order and routine. Weekends were an abyss that was exactly long enough to stare back at me.

"I thought we were all going to watch *Ratatouille*." Adam looked at me hard. I looked at him, too, but I made my eyes unseeing.

"We can. I'll be back in a few hours."

"The kids will be asleep in a few hours."

"Then we'll watch it tomorrow. I mean, we watched it yesterday."

Adam looked down at the grill plate, then up again at me. "Sure. Have fun."

"You don't mind?" I kissed Adam on the cheek and ran out the door like a teenager who had just gotten permission to use the car.

Toby and I sat on the train across from each other in a four-seat pod. A minute passed by and Toby said, "I hope you're treating Adam well. He's one of the good ones."

I told him I knew that.

"I'm serious. You should treat him well. He's a good man."

"Why? Because he hasn't left me? How do you know I'm not the advantage in the relationship?" I reached into my pocket for my vaping pen. I offered it to Toby.

"Uh, no thanks," he said.

"Why not?" I asked.

"Because we're on New Jersey Transit?"

But no one was watching. People didn't look at me anymore. I'm allowed to go into bathrooms that are only for customers now anywhere in the city. I could shoplift if I wanted to, is how ignored I am. The week I turned forty I'd been sent to profile one of the New York Giants. I wasn't given access to the locker room, and my lanyard said RESTRICTED PRESS: NO LOCKER ACCESS in bright yellow and it covered half my torso. I walked into the locker room anyway and stood right there among all their penises, and the very people who had issued me the lanyard walked by me as if I were there to set up for the bake sale.

Toby didn't pay any attention to me on the train. He was texting with the new woman he was fucking, and so steeped in his own crisis and couldn't bear a conversation that didn't revolve around him. He didn't want to talk about Rachel anymore. He didn't want to think about her. But he didn't want to talk about me, either.

"Do you realize that you never react to anything I say unless it's about you?" I asked him.

"What do you mean?"

"I mean, I'm a real person with a soul and I could use a friend, too?"

"What possible need could you have?"

Was Toby always like this? I sat there, watching him look at his phone and stifle his erection, and I couldn't remember a time when he'd sat and listened to me. Even back then, our conversations were only ever about him and his insecurities. I always felt privileged for being told them, and I felt the role I played was someone who he recognized was equally lost. But now I was considering that maybe I was just a warm body.

We got off the train and Toby said we should take the E downtown to meet Seth, but I was suddenly seized with a full-body annoyance for him. Why wasn't I home, watching *Ratatouille*? What was I doing here?

"You know what?" I said. "I'm going to the movies." And I left Penn Station without waiting for a word from him.

———

Toby sat on the train headed downtown and saw a family with three children—two girls Hannah and Solly's age, then the third one, a toddler boy. The toddler slept against the mother's chest. Just three years ago, Toby thought he and Rachel might have another child. Solly was six and Toby had not begun to consider that the marriage, not the stressors to the marriage, might be the problem.

They had both wanted three kids. Every story Rachel told from her lonely childhood had such emptiness to it. "I really liked watching *Three's Company* while I did homework." Stuff like that. "Yes," she told Toby after they were engaged. "I want three children. Or four. I want them to never have to be alone in the house, no matter what happens to us." But Solly turned five and then six and then seven. They couldn't talk about anything without fighting. The discussion of a third child could only come up under the most prime conditions: when they were both briefly bathing in sentiment or satisfaction, when something happened that inspired them to want to keep this part of their lives going. Meaning: rarely.

This past Passover, they'd gone to Los Angeles to see Toby's family. They hadn't yet told anyone they were getting divorced, and they were in the honeymoon period of their separation. Before the first seder, Toby's mother, who was short and round with a puffy hairdo, and his sister, Ilana, who had started taking on the shape of their mother, were setting up the dinner table on the patio at his sister's house, since her house was pristinely kosher and they could only have holiday meals there. The kids were playing with their too-many cousins, and Toby and Rachel had a moment on the couch, united in their disgust for the self-righteous traditionalism of his sister, and the way his parents yielded to it. His sister kept casting brief glances over at them on the couch, then whispering to her mother, probably something about how they should be helping. His sister thought of Rachel as lazy. Rachel—lazy! She didn't understand that there were a lot of words for Rachel, but lazy was not one of them, and the thing that kept her from helping was far worse than sheer sloth.

Rachel said to Toby, "So this is the last time we're doing this, isn't it?" Off Toby's nod, her face flooded with sentiment. "Oh, Toby, who could have seen this coming?"

He wasn't used to this emotion on her. He couldn't imagine why it was appearing now, as opposed to at any other moment in the last ten years, when a display of acknowledgment of their past and their once-real passion for each other would have been most welcome. This means nothing, he told himself. You do not have to react to this, he told himself.

"We were meant to be best friends, I think," she continued. "I think that's what went wrong."

He nodded in what could be perceived as thoughtful agreement, but he truly didn't understand. Wasn't friendship the thing they never had? Wouldn't friendship have made all the fighting bearable? She was not his friend. If there was one thing he knew, it was that. He had to proceed with caution here, lest this become a scene, so he kept silent, hoping that the conversation would end before he could no longer bear this new delusion.

But she didn't stop. She turned to face him. "I think what's nice is that we're young enough to still have another full life, you know? This entire thing"—she spread her hands in the air toward the entirety of their lives—"doesn't have to define us."

"Like, our marriage and children? It doesn't have to define us?"

"Okay. I know you're being snide right now, because anger is, like, your only mode ever, but just think about it. We could have another chance to do it right."

He hadn't gotten as far as future plans yet. His only thoughts about the future were how he was going to make it up to these children that they'd had to live among such grueling animosity and unhappiness, all the fighting they'd heard, the times he yelled at them when he was angry at her, the times they saw him throw things or punch walls. He was trying to figure out a way to redefine himself as a good parent to them, and as a role model of what a man should be like and what a household should be like. That was what he'd been thinking about lately, how much he'd taken out on the kids, how much bile they now knew their parents were capable of.

"I keep thinking," she continued. "What if you have more kids? What if I have more kids?"

His response to this was so visceral and fast it even surprised him. What came out of his mouth was a sound, a yawp, a growl, a great guttural thing.

"What?" she asked. "What did I say?"

"Are you fucking kidding me with this?" he asked. "You want more children?"

Her face returned to fighting stance like it never left. "Why can't I want more children?"

Was she kidding? He raised his arms and yelled at the ceiling, "Because you totally neglect the children you have!"

He saw his mother turn on the patio to see what was going on. He lowered his voice. "Your *current* children need you. Your real, already born children need you. If you are interested in children, I have two perfectly good ones for you to parent."

On the E train, the parents of the three children stood up to leave at the next stop. He watched their faces as they negotiated who would carry the baby and who would get the stroller and arranged themselves thus. He wanted to see a hint of the hatred between them that their marriage and children bred in them. He wanted to see animosity and regret the way he wanted a glass of water. He couldn't find any. They got off the train peaceably and Toby stared at the Hr ad that they'd been hiding, which was just a picture of the bottom part of a twenty-five-year-old woman's face, lip bitten in either excitement or indecision or sexual anticipation, until his stop.

Seth and his co-workers were born imperialists, and so would pillage the city for tiny, cash-only ramen places or Thai restaurants that had a secret, ultra-authentic room behind the kitchen where the staff also ate and where they would insist on eating, too. They were the best and the only and the highest and the chef was trained in Beirut as a prisoner of war and the waitstaff had to get scuba training so that they could understand what it meant to touch pleasure and the restaurant itself used to be a church or a secret meeting place for the Illuminati or a Tibetan monastery that only the hottest, most favored Tibetans were invited to. It was not just about owning the city. It was about owning everything beneath and above and behind the city, too. Finance guys were the fucking worst.

Seth told Toby to meet him at a rooftop bar that was located through an attic door whose ladder you had to climb inside a shitty Korean bodega. It was only six P.M. Seth and Vanessa were the only people at a table. Vanessa stood to meet Toby, rising above him four or five inches. She opened her arms to give him a soft, blond hug. "I am so glad to finally *meet* you," she said. She held on. Her warmth made Toby a little dizzy. "I've only met Seth's co-workers. I was beginning to wonder why there weren't more old friends!"

"I've heard great things about you," Toby told her. "This is the first time in many years Seth's dated someone long enough for us to make plans."

"That's not true," Seth said. To Vanessa, "We've been out of touch for a while."

Her face suddenly melted into concern. "Because of your divorce," Vanessa said.

"Well, because of my marriage," Toby said. She was nice. She was engaging. She was hot. She was golden and tan, like an Oscar with hair. She was really fucking hot.

She was a publicist for a restaurant group. Her work required her to be out nearly every night.

"That's how I met Seth," she said.

"How? He was eating?"

She laughed too hard. "Seth said you were so funny! No, we were having a tasting at one of my restaurants, LuPont down on

West Third." She turned to Seth with a look on her face like she'd discovered gravity. "I know! We should all go there sometime!"

"Vanessa can get us in everywhere," Seth said. "Even places she doesn't rep. She has like a dog whistle with hostesses. It's amazing. Her shop was on a *Forbes* list."

Vanessa's dress was mostly opaque but not completely. She was wearing one of those bras that a lot of the women who sent him pictures wore that only hit midbreast, above the nipple but with plenty left out in the open air. It was called a demicup, he thought he remembered from his hours masturbating to his sister's Victoria's Secret catalogs when he was a teenager. Rachel didn't wear bras like that. She wore utilitarian bras with a three-inch strap that used four hooks to clasp. Nursing, she'd said, had ruined her breasts. Stop thinking about breasts, Toby.

"Do you like your work?" Toby asked.

"I do," she said. "Chefs are definitely the artists of our moment."

"Huh." Toby didn't know what to say to that. Tweens were tedious. He knew this from all his time with Hannah. But something he'd learned from his relatively recent introduction to dating apps and his brief, initial foray into a younger age range was that women in their twenties were tedious, too. They weren't tedious to other people in their twenties. They were fine. Maybe people in their fifties thought people in their forties were tedious? He'd find out in ten years. Toby's fellows were always in their twenties, and there were more than a few times that he realized that the cluelessness and cockiness of their age was the only thing that allowed them to believe they could take a person's life into their hands and become a doctor. That was why you heard about people in their thirties and forties going to law school but never medical school. It wasn't just the time it would take to get licensed. It was the realization as you got older about how fallible you were in every aspect of your life.

Now Toby looked at Seth and Vanessa. They were revolting. Her hotness was revolting.

Vanessa's phone pinged. She picked it up and began to answer a text. She put her phone down and stood up. "I'll be right back." She headed toward the ladies' room.

"She's nice," Toby said.

Seth looked off for a minute, then closed his eyes. "I got fired."

"What? Oh, man, I'm sorry."

"I haven't told Vanessa yet. My boss, Mitch, went on this fucking coke binge at work in the middle of the day—it was totally epic—but then was fired by his boss when the guy's secretary complained to HR because he wouldn't stop calling her 'sweet tits,' and then all of us who were hired by him were fired. We're all going out tonight, late, like eleven. Please pray to your God that I don't meet a hooker that I temporarily fall in love with. Mitch does that. He gets hotel rooms and hookers."

"Yeah, well, Rachel has been fucking a guy from school."

"Jesus, what grade?"

"No, no. A dad."

"He's divorced?"

"No! He's married to like her best friend there!"

"Are you kidding? Is that who she's with? Is that guy leaving his wife?"

"He hasn't yet! I'm telling you, dude. You did the right thing. Not getting married."

Vanessa appeared out of nowhere. "Everything okay here?"

"Yeah," Seth said, sitting up straight. "I was just giving Toby here a hard time."

Vanessa was talking about their future—a weekend in Aspen they were expected at next month, her old roommate's destination wedding in Rio. Seth draped his arm around Vanessa like she was a banister. But Toby couldn't hear it anymore. Instead, he heard his phone: The hospital called, and his entire body felt relieved for it. He did not want to be around to watch Seth pretend that he wasn't unemployed. He did not want to keep staring at this poor, beautiful girl making plans with Seth, who was hoping that he wouldn't fuck a prostitute that night but wasn't a thousand percent sure.

"A patient needs me, guys. I have to go uptown. I'm really sorry."

Vanessa looked at Seth, alarmed. Toby looked between them.

"We had someone we wanted you to meet," Seth said.

"Tamara, my friend from work," Vanessa said. "She is *so* smart and funny. Seth thought you would hit it off."

Toby stood up and put his phone into his pocket.

"Your money is no good here," Seth said.

"I wasn't going to give you any. I didn't order anything."

Vanessa stood up and pressed her breasts against his body. "You sure you can't stay just a sec—"

Just then, Vanessa began waving at the door. "She's here! Just stay and meet her for a second!" The object of her greeting, a tiny teacup of a woman in a summer dress and sandals, walked in. She wasn't just short, though. She looked like a child: maybe four-eleven, skinny, with no shape to her body. She had a face that could be either fourteen or twenty-five, but not more than that.

Toby shook her hand. "I'm really sorry about this." He was annoyed that he had to apologize when he hadn't done anything wrong. He wasn't married anymore. He didn't have to constantly apologize when he didn't mean it. If he'd known this was a date, well, he wouldn't have allowed it. He didn't want to be set up with people. He didn't want to know what his friends thought he was worthy of. All of this was still so new that the only thing he could tolerate was the ice-cold democracy of a dating app. Look at this Tamara. Was that not confirmation enough? She was a tiny child-woman. His friends didn't think he deserved a full-grown woman. They didn't think he deserved the full swimming pool of breasts that Vanessa had. Seth, his friend, didn't think Toby had the right to all he had.

Toby walked out without saying real goodbyes. The text from Logan said it was time to wake Karen Cooper up. Toby liked to be there for that. He wanted to go meet his patient. He wanted to be there for the good part.

It was time to take Karen Cooper off the ventilator.

Joanie, Logan, and Clay headed down the hall toward him. Joanie looked different somehow—older, or more relaxed. Confident, maybe? But why so suddenly? He couldn't explain it. Something about how familiar she seemed right then was jarring, how she was wearing her hair in a braid and he knew that if she turned to the side just a little, the braid would have thinned at the bottom because of all the layering of her hair.

He wondered for a minute what meeting Seth and Vanessa would have been like if Joanie had been with him. They would have had lunch and then the two of them would have left and spent the rest of the night maybe in Chelsea, or walking around the Meatpacking District, making fun of Vanessa. Joanie was at least Vanessa's age. But she had self-awareness and intelligence. And she was person-sized, not like Tamara. Plus, she was smart and not ostentatious about it. She had eccentricities that were her own, that she'd earned. He would be proud to have someone like Joanie by his side. She would show Seth who Toby really was in the world.

"Come on," Toby said. "Let's do it."

Toby and Marco and their collected fellows watched the anesthesiologist extubate Karen Cooper. Toby involuntarily held his breath along with his patient, and only exhaled when he saw that she could.

Karen's eyes opened and she blinked. Toby put himself over her in her line of vision. "Mrs. Cooper," he said. "I'm Dr. Fleishman. You're in the hospital. You've just had surgery." She searched his eyes, trying to focus. The copper rings were luminous, her blue irises rising up and out of copper earth—it really was a beautiful disease. "There are a lot of people who will be happy to see you."

An hour later, Joanie brought David up to see his wife. David scrubbed his hands and put on a surgical gown and cap and face mask. Toby stood at the foot of her bed, making notes in her chart while his fellows stood near the monitors. Karen Cooper shook her head in muted delirium, her eyes opening and shutting. Her husband dropped to the chair next to her bed and cried into her hand. Yes, this was the good part. Toby felt eyes on him and looked up to see Joanie looking directly at him, her face overcome.

That day, when I left Toby, I checked out the movie times, but nothing was playing that I even registered as a movie, just midsummer comic books come to life, so I ambled over to Central Park. I had my wallet and my vape and that was all I needed. I found a green space in the Sheep Meadow and lay on my back, untethered and light. The green in the trees against the blue of the sky. The smells of the season. A wireless speaker playing the Beastie Boys somewhere nearby. When is the last time I did this, I thought. I had a sudden longing for Adam, or at least for a theory of Adam: a man who knew me and loved me and wanted me and wanted to hear from me. I was no longer capable of conversations with him.

I took out a cigarette and smoked it all the way to the edge. In Israel, I smoked an Israeli brand called Time. Seth told me one night that it was an acronym. It stood for This Is My Enjoyment. That came back to me now. I inhaled and exhaled and thought: Yes, this is my enjoyment.

Two years ago, I was visiting my editor at the magazine when word that Archer Sylvan died came in. We had been talking about a story I was assigned about an actor who people thought was gay and how I was going to "handle" the controversy. It was one of those stories they sent me on because they knew that you needed one oppressed minority to handle another. The editor in chief's assistant came into my editor's office and told him they'd just heard from Archer's first wife. He was found dead earlier that morning. He died as he lived: in a hotel room in Las Vegas, practicing autoerotic asphyxiation. There were two young women with him at the time, both sex workers.

Anyway, the day he died, our editor announced we were ending the day early. We all went to the Grill, where Archer was known to have a Manhattan on Friday night at five each week he was in town, a hangover from the magazine's previous editor's era. He and his old writer friends who also hunted bears and lived gigantically would meet that editor in chief for rounds of Scotch until they all blacked out. Our editor in chief, who took over after Archer's original editor, ordered a round of Manhattans in his honor. I drank three, even though vermouth makes me sick. We toasted him and talked about what a lion he was, how he hung in the background of all of our stories as a specter of what was wanted and expected of us.

The editor talked about a few of our stories, saying he could really see Archer's influence in them. None of mine made it into his speech. I smiled and pretended not to notice. I nodded thoughtfully and squinted in understanding. But all the while, all I could think was: What was I doing there, drinking Manhattans and trying to fit in with people I no longer had anything in common with? I had children now. I lived in New Jersey. Maybe I never had anything in common with them, but I was still trying and then suddenly, quite suddenly, I wasn't.

To be a woman at a men's magazine is to have a very specific task: It's either to be compliant or noisy, to be the category: other person asking the questions that a man wasn't allowed to ask in a time of burgeoning political correctness, or to be the wide-eyed kitten that maybe had sex with her subject. After I had Sasha, I wasn't sure which one I was anymore, though I had been both at a certain time. Whatever kind of woman you are, even when you're a lot of kinds of women, you're still always just a woman, which is to say you're always a little bit less than a man.

All the papers wrote big stories about Archer and his legacy after his death. I read every single one. A day later, there was an

Internet backlash, a small battalion of young twenty-something women asking why everyone worshipped this man who was so clearly a misogynist. Archer's very young third ex-wife had written a memoir about the physical and emotional abuse she endured, though she was largely dismissed for her claims because she had then alleged the same things about her second husband. He hated women, they said, even as I could count a hundred examples in his writing of the way he worshipped them. Yes, the young women said, it looked like worship but it was actually something uglier. It was an obsession with sex and a wholesale contempt for what he saw as the condition of the sex, or its barrier, or its delivery device: the actual women. The actual women weren't really people. They were just a theory. He wrote about them the way he'd written about Vietnam—ugly, romantic, poignant, unwinnable.

I thought about that. I wrote mostly about men. I hadn't interviewed a lot of women. Whenever I did, the stories were always about the struggle to be the kind of woman who got interviewed— the writers who were counted out, the politicians who were mistaken for secretaries, the actresses who were told they were too fat and tall and short and skinny and ugly and pretty. It was all the same story, which is not to say it wasn't important. But it was boring. The first time I interviewed a man, I understood we were talking about something more like the soul.

The men hadn't had any external troubles. They didn't have a fear that they didn't belong. They hadn't had any obstacles. They were born knowing they belonged, and they were reassured at every turn just in case they'd forgotten. But they were still creative and still people, and so they reached for problems out of an artistic sense of yearning. Their problems weren't real. They had no identity struggle, no illness, no money fears. Instead, they had found the true stuff of their souls—of all our souls—the wound lying beneath all the survivalism and circumstance.

I could listen to them for hours. If you don't ask too many questions and just let people talk, they'll tell you what's on their mind.

In those monologues, I found my own gripes. They felt counted out, the way I felt counted out. They felt ignored, the way I felt ignored. They felt like they'd failed. They had regret. They were insecure. They worried about their legacies. They said all the things I wasn't allowed to say aloud without fear of appearing grandiose or self-centered or conceited or narcissistic. I imposed my narrative onto theirs, like in one of those biology textbooks where you can place the musculature picture over the bone picture of the human body. I wrote about my problems through them.

That was what I knew for sure, that this was the only way to get someone to listen to a woman—to tell her story through a man; Trojan horse yourself into a man, and people would give a shit about you. So I wrote heartfelt stories about their lives, extrapolating from what they gave me and running with what I already knew from being human. They sent me texts and flowers that told me I really understood them in a way that no one had before, and I realized that all humans are essentially the same, but only some of us, the men, were truly allowed to be that without apology. The mens' humanity was sexy and complicated; ours (mine) was to be kept in the dark at the bottom of the story and was only interesting in the service of the man's humanity.

But sitting there, I realized my problems were now different. They could no longer be grafted onto a man because they were so unique to the problem of being a woman. It was time for me to leave the magazine.

I reread a few of Archer's pieces that night. I cried a little because it hurt to be ending my career there before I was ever sent to Chile to eat the brain of a goat with my bare hands, but right then, maybe for the first time, I also realized I was never going to be sent to Chile to eat the brain of a goat with my bare hands. People could love my stories, they could go far and wide, I could do everything, but I could never be a man. But also, given the chance, I don't think I would have taken the goat's head and broken its jaw and done what needed to be done. Who could do that to even a dead goat? Maybe, in that way, the system worked.

I told Adam that I thought I should stop working. I said it was because I wanted to be with Sasha more, which was sort of true, but really I was humiliated and just wanted out and couldn't figure out where else to go. I went back into the office and gave my editor notice. My agent said I should have been smarter. I should have asked for a contract that allowed me to do one story a year, so I could "stay in the game." He didn't understand that actually I had never been in the game. I told him I wanted to write novels. I tried one, a YA novel about sisters who found out their parents were spies. Another, an adult novel about three sons who lose their inheritance. Another, a woman who moves to the suburbs and starts a violent gang among the other moms at school. I'd send two or ten or forty pages to my agent, and he'd say the same thing, that none of my characters were likable. I thought of Archer. His characters weren't likable. He wasn't likable. I thought of how hard I worked in my stories to be likable to the reader. I remembered a creative writing class I took in college, where the professor, a cynical screenwriter who'd written exactly one movie that got made, told us that when our characters weren't likable, you could fix it by giving them a clubfoot or a dog. I gave one of the gang members a clubfoot, and my agent wrote in the margin: "WTF?" He told me I had to write something closer to the truth. So I began writing this YA novel a few months ago, the one about my youth, the one that was going nowhere, and I sent him the first ten pages about four months ago but I never heard back. I read the pages again and I saw the problem. My voice only came alive when I was talking about someone else; my ability to see the truth and to extrapolate human emotion based on what I saw and was told didn't extend to myself.

I'd fallen asleep in the park and spent either minutes or hours in the delusionscape between asleep and awake. When I sat up, my vaping pen was nowhere to be found.

———

How was it still August? How many more days until the winter? How many more days till Toby's kids came back? How many more nights would he be alone? Still no word from Rachel, who did not know her children were at sleepaway camp—whose children could have been dead and she wouldn't know it.

It was intolerable to be at home. The heat hadn't dissipated with the afternoon. There were women in his phone and they just annoyed him. He thought about calling Joanie, but under what guise? What did he want from her? He watched a few videos of soldiers being reunited with their children. Nothing made him feel better. This fucking day wouldn't end.

He looked up the schedule at the yoga studio. There were no yoga classes, just something called YogaD the Method, which was strength training that combined yoga and dancing and "spiritual inner work." What the hell, he decided, and changed into shorts and a T-shirt.

He walked in, the only man there, and tried to figure out if he'd missed something on the description. Nobody seemed shocked to see him, though, so he pulled out a bolster, like they were all sitting on, and walked across the room.

"Toby."

He turned around. There, on the floor, in a one-piece purple spandex jumpsuit, was Nahid.

"Is this where you come to pick up women?" she asked.

He laughed. "No, it's where I come to see the women I'm intent on picking up." Maybe not as smooth as it could have been, but consider his week. "Is this seat taken?"

"Are you stalking me?"

"This is where I take yoga."

"You're very evolved. You might be the first man I've ever seen in this class."

"What are you doing here? You're a long way from home."

"I was meeting a friend who comes here but she canceled."

"Only someone very secure in his masculinity could come here. You know that, right?"

The class began. The teacher sounded a gong and began her speech. She wanted to talk about a new word she'd learned in Sanskrit: spanda. "It's the inhalation and exhalation of the world, the world's expansion and contraction. If you look around, there's a rhythm of it everywhere. You don't see it till you do, and then poof, you realize that your breath is just in harmony: in, out, in, out."

Toby leaned toward Nahid. "Actually the universe only expands. It's physics."

Nahid looked at two women looking at her and put her finger to her mouth sternly to shush him.

Toby got a hint of Nahid's smell just then—a plumeria shampoo, and was that a cucumber deodorant? He had a Pavlovian sense of longing, not just for those scents but for the ones underneath them, and he sought out a virtual slideshow of infected surgical wounds in order to stave off the erection that was bubbling in him like lava.

It turned out that YogaD the Method was a high-energy movement done quietly and mindfully with the eyes closed, a class that, mercifully, didn't include any dancing that required hip action or corkscrewing or swiveling. It was more of a calisthenics class with extended stretching at the end. He watched out of his peripheral vision: Nahid's beautiful, round body stretching like a cat in Downward Dog, her lovely ass pointed skyward.

When he was fourteen, he told his mother that he was ashamed of being fat and short and so she took him with her to a Weight Watchers meeting, where he listened to a room full of sad women talk about how unlovable they were and how temporary they felt in their bodies.

"Your life is now," said Sandy, the leader. She wore denim skirts and brightly colored shirts with matching tights and big, costumey earrings. "You have to live as if your life is already in progress."

Young Toby didn't understand what this was about. Of course life was now—at least it was for the grown-ups. He didn't understand why they had emotional barriers to the diet beyond the major one, which was that food was comforting and delicious and good. It all made perfect sense to him now: Food is comforting and delicious, but it is not good, and one shouldn't be seduced into thinking it might be.

Fine. He followed the plan, and he lost five pounds the first week. Then more, then more. The women would grumble at his weight loss: He was a boy and he was a teenager—his metabolism was ideal. His mother would drive him home and say, "See? They're jealous because you're successful." She loved that. She loved him, more than she had before. He never went off the plan until he was twenty-four and stopped eating carbohydrates completely. He was never going to end up like one of those women.

He told his mother he wanted to exercise, and this thrilled her, too. She did some research and took him to a step aerobics class in a loft space in West Hollywood. He was the only boy in that class, too, but he was so dazzled by all the long-legged blond girls in the class—girls designed to be superior, with straight, skinny legs and casual boredom about their beauty—that he was able to distract himself from the exertion. They were much nicer to be around than the sad sacks at Weight Watchers. Those girls never complained. Those girls knew that the world was better for them being in it. He watched them in the mirror during the class and imagined he wasn't with them but watching them from the other side of the TV. Yes, if they were in an aerobics video, and he was watching it, he could ignore how he looked beside them: fat, Jewish, clumsy, short, so short, when the hell would the growth spurt come, he was promised there would be a growth spurt.

At the end of class, the teacher would dim the lights and they would lie, belly down, on their elevated platforms and stretch to a slow song as twilight settled over the Hollywood Hills and came through the studio's long windows. Facedown on his step platform, he'd do as instructed: Reach one arm out, then the second. If one of the girls was on her step platform, belly down, but turned in his direction instead of away from it, meaning head to head with Toby and not foot to head, the result would be that it looked like she and Toby were on rafts, reaching for each other in a beautiful ballet of survival. A slow song played from the CD player: *Sometimes the snow comes down in June, sometimes the sun goes 'round the moon.* "Stretch left," the teacher would say. *Just when I thought our chance had passed, you go and save the best for last.* "Now stretch right."

And that was how he felt as he exercised silently, strangely, next to Nahid, this woman he didn't know and whose spandex-covered body was exactly as tempting as her naked one. Now they lay down on mats that had appeared out of nowhere and he stretched toward her and she stretched toward him, and on the iPod now there was a song that was the slowed-down version of a song that Hannah liked from the radio—*I'm in the corner watching you kiss her, oh oh*—how he loved a pop song made into a ballad.

Rachel was gone from his life. He had been looking at this like it was a bad thing. It was—it would destroy his children when they finally found out. But also, absent any choice he made that created the situation, which was not any choice, it was still true that he was young and could have a new life. Rachel had been right about that.

The yoga studio was in the eighteenth-floor penthouse of a residential building, a perk to its residents and an à la carte offering to anyone else. The windows were big and high up enough so that on a clear day, you could see the park. The sun was going down. He loved the dusk—the blue twilight, especially in summer, when the streets crowded with people who had knowledge of winter, who had seen endless days where the streets were inhospitable. The sky was a glowing purple-blue. Had he ever really taken a moment to appreciate the dusk? He loved it. He loved everything right then. He looked out onto the world and was so excited about the number of dusks that lay ahead of him. He wanted to use every single one of them well. He wanted to spend each one of them with only people he loved. He wanted to run to the camp upstate right this instant and take his children outside their bunks and apologize for all the wasted twilights. He wanted to pick each child up and spin them around. He wanted to tell them that if they miss a twilight, not to worry, it will always come again. He wanted to show them that this was how he was naturally, not the mopey jerk they'd seen lately, not the person who stopped believing in potential and excitement and surprise. He would remember this moment and he would become himself again. Poor Toby in all those other block universes. Poor Toby who was still just figuring it out. *This* Toby knew. *This* Toby couldn't believe his incredible fortune, to have this many twilights lying in front of him, and all the bad ones behind him.

He awoke with a panic in his stomach the next morning. Part of it was the strangeness of waking up in Nahid's bed, which he'd never slept in or on before last night—their sex had so far been confined to the floor and part of the living room coffee table. Part of it was that this was the first time he'd ever slept at a woman's house overnight. But his panic was also parental, the haunted realization that happened over and over that he was now his children's only parent and they were nowhere near him. He smelled coffee.

The night came back to him.

"I have a surprise for you," she'd said.

She had straddled his body and gone to work pouring different scented oils on his back and making circular motions and ticklish motions and spelling out words and making him guess them, leaning over, kissing his neck when he got them right, biting his ear when he got them wrong. This went on for an hour, and when it was over, he realized that he had never truly relaxed into it. He never stopped wondering what she was getting out of it. He did not know if there had ever been a time when someone had done something just to make him feel good, so when it happened, when it was finally happening, he could barely understand what was going on.

Now, Toby came out to see Nahid reading the *Daily News* at her table while she drank coffee out of a china cup. In the morning light, without makeup, he could see Nahid's face for the first time.

"How old are you?" he asked her.

"That's a rude question."

"I'm sorry," he said. "Okay, how much do you weigh?"

She laughed.

"Let's go out for breakfast," he said.

"I can make you breakfast here."

"I want to take you out."

She turned her face and raised her left eyebrow and looked at him from the side, as if she were trying to decide something. "I can't go out with you," she said. "I'll explain."

Her husband didn't want to get divorced. He loved her; they had been through so much together. He said he wanted to keep their arrangement as it was. She told him she didn't realize their marriage was an "arrangement." He was so handsome and kind-looking and soft-spoken that she still didn't feel hatred for him. She just still felt rejected. It didn't matter that she now knew why he'd rejected her; the feeling that something was off-putting about her to him didn't go away.

But it wasn't that he still wanted her because part of him still loved her. No, it was that he was a lawyer for a conservative news network, and his contract was under review, and his boss had sent out a memo about the company's employees respecting the "positive, godly values" of the organization. His divorce would be a problem. He asked her if she could stay married to him until his contract negotiation was up; if so, he would make sure she was financially taken care of for life. Then he would tell them that she was converting back to Judaism, and he couldn't stay married to her. She couldn't understand how he could erase their life together like that, but he didn't care that she didn't understand. He was always controlling and persuasive. Remember, he had been the one pushing her to shove hormones through her system so that he could have babies that he never asked if she wanted, too.

She became angry. She said no. She said they would just go their separate ways. He said he wouldn't pay any alimony unless she obeyed. She said her lawyer would get it out of him anyway, but it wasn't true. Her lawyer pointed out that she had a profession, an accounting degree, and that just because she had never worked didn't mean she couldn't. It wasn't like there were kids to take care of. She'd have to move. She'd have to start her life over somewhere in a city that wasn't this expensive. She was forty-five, and she'd have to live like a recent college graduate, and hope for a job in a gig economy.

He had her. He agreed to pay rent if she remained in the apartment, if she didn't tell anyone they were separated, if she forestalled the divorce until January, if she promised not to be seen out with men or doing anything that a company executive might see and deem unchristian. There was the "liberal media," always looking to delight in something like this. Worst of all—yes, worst of all— she still had to attend functions and dinners with him. She had to hold his hand. She had to be told where to go by the very same personal assistant she'd walked in on that day getting fellated by her husband.

Toby listened. He liked how she looked down at her hands when she talked. He liked how her mouth opened slightly and her eyebrows knitted together when she was listening. Someone else might think this was ideal, a beautiful woman you could just come over and fuck and who didn't even want to have breakfast. But him? He wanted a person. He didn't want to just hook up and leave. He wasn't Seth.

"I don't know," Toby said. "This is very fun, but I like you. I want to get to know you."

"I like you, too. But if I were seen around—" She stood up and took her coffee cup to the kitchen. She was wearing a satin robe. "Honestly, it's humiliating enough just telling you this. I haven't told this to anyone."

She'd slept with a few men by now, she explained. She'd never been with another man, before all this. Her parents hadn't talked to her about sex. Now they didn't talk to her at all. Her sister thought she was a heathen for converting. She was embarrassed to talk about sex with their friends, and besides, she wasn't allowed to tell anyone what was going on, and as a result, her friendships had all dwindled. So she went to men's apartments and had sex with them once, and then blocked them on the app and in her phone. She couldn't bear their touch. It was too intimate; it was too tender. Men who desired you touched you all over your body, not just in your erogenous zones, by number, hoping to pass for someone who actually wanted you. They touched your waist and your face. They touched your knees and the arches of your feet. They felt for the downy small of your back. The touches lingered. They took your breath away. Your softness was no longer a liability. The softness was now the point. The intimacy overwhelmed her.

But she was getting used to it now with Toby. They were in her space, and her body didn't recoil in spasms when it was touched anymore. She was going through the necessary phases of learning how to exist in her body with a man who desired her. She was catching up.

"Something happened and now I'm stuck," she said, "I accept it. I am no longer trying to change things. I go to yoga. I come home and I sleep with you. That will have to be enough for me. It's hard for men to understand."

After a while, Toby left and showered at his own house. It must have been a thousand degrees, and his air-conditioning had the equivalent cooling power of a cat yawning. He listened to a podcast about neuroscience on his way to work but couldn't concentrate on it. His inbox contained coerced emails from each of his children, which popped up simultaneously as he entered his office. Solly's was fairly substantial. It said he liked his counselor and that he hadn't lost S.B. (Stealth Bunny, abbreviated just in case anyone was reading over his shoulder) and that Max had found new friends but he guessed he understood, and there was a guy named Akiva he liked hanging out with and Hannah ignored him when she saw him. Hannah's email simply read, "C-YA on visitor's day." He stared at that email as if it might grow under his watch until his phone switched to its locked-screen time/date function.

That was when it hit him. Today was the day that child support was supposed to be directly deposited into his bank account. He had been so focused on managing the children, then so focused on figuring out where Rachel was, that he'd allowed himself to not turn directly toward a major question that had hovered over all of this: Was the money gone, too? Holy Christ, what if the money was gone?

He sat down in his desk chair. He wanted to be sitting up for this. He wanted to greet whatever information he found there like a man. It took him two times to log in to his bank account. When he finally didn't mistype his password, he watched the wheel spin interminably while his account information was being gathered, thank you for your patience. You can do this, he tried to get his brain to inform him. You can do this no matter what. But his brain had told him a lot of things over the years. His brain wasn't very reliable. He needed that money. He knew that he pretended to hate the money but that he needed the money and he wanted the money.

Or, fuck it, maybe he didn't. Maybe he should pick up and move. He would leave no forwarding address. He would buy a house in, what, Illinois, Kentucky, South Carolina, maybe somewhere more hospitable to Jews, like Philadelphia. He heard Nashville needed specialists, but he didn't want to live in the South. Maybe he'd move to New Jersey. No, that was too close. That was close enough so that if she decided to return to the kids' lives, she could have regular visitation. Nope, not for you, bitch. You made your decision.

And if you ever repent for this, you will have to give up this place that you love and decide that you love your children more. Exile will be your lifelong penance.

A message box popped up on the screen: *Your request has been timed out. Please try again later.* "FUCK YOU!" he screamed. Outside his office, a nurse's aide looked up from her cart.

He typed again. The wheel turned again and again and again. His body hurt. He missed his children so much that his body hurt. All of this was agony. This is what you wanted, Rachel? You wanted no one to wake up to?

Finally, the pinwheel stopped turning and the number came in: $7,500 more than there had been the day before. He couldn't even feel relief. He hated himself so much he couldn't bear it. He took a breath and sat down and stared at the number, then looked out the window. There was something about how the light came into his office in the morning, the way he could not evade the sharp assault of the sun, that made him depressed. He'd grown up in Los Angeles, where everyone bragged about the sun like they invented it, and all he could ever think about was how the lack of tall buildings meant the sun was forever rising and setting into his eyes. Now, in his office, it hit the stainless steel of his desk and of the mullions in the glass wall, making him surly.

He had to get out of here. He would take lunch. It was ten-thirty, but who says what time lunch is. He left the hospital and walked, and when he stopped walking, he found himself in front of the Museum of Natural History, almost as if his longing for Solly pulled him there. There was a new exhibit about colors centered on something called Vantablack, which was a lab-created material that was said to be the darkest black that existed. It absorbed 99.6 percent of the light. The article he read in the *Times* said that people who looked at it felt like they were freaking out. He walked in through the membership line and went right to the exhibit. The sample of the black was surrounded by tin foil so that you could understand what you were looking at. Toby stood in front of the exhibit and stared into the black until he felt like he was falling. He stood there for a full hour.

It wasn't that he had given up on thinking about Rachel. It was that he could no longer locate himself in this story and the fact of that made him panic. He used to understand the rules, that he was the direct object of her apathy and inconsideration. Now what was he? What were the kids? She was no longer in opposition to them. She was just gone. What do you do with that? How do you think about that?

The panic rose in him regularly. He wasn't eating (as if he ever had been). He wondered if the children would ever bump into her on the street. He wondered if the children would become pariahs when it became clear to the school moms that Rachel had drifted further away from the port than could ever be forgivable.

The next day, Tuesday, he did a sonogram on a young law student. Her liver showed no signs of scarring, so she could schedule a follow-up in October. Then he realized how soon October was, and that Hannah's bat mitzvah was coming. The invitations should have gone out last week, but he wasn't in charge of invitations, Rachel was. She had Simone on all of it: the caterers, the DJ, the motivators, the party favors, the venue. Toby was only in charge of making sure Hannah knew her lines. Should he cancel it now? How could you hold a bat mitzvah for a girl when her mother had just abandoned her? But also: How could you cancel a girl's bat mitzvah?

When he was out on the street after work, the rest of the day stretched before him. He didn't want to check his Hr app. He wanted a text from Nahid saying that she'd come around and would have dinner with him. He couldn't bear another evening alone. He couldn't explain it and he couldn't not talk about it. He looked at his phone to see what was playing at the movies but it wouldn't load. He began walking toward downtown anyway. He'd go to a movie. Normal people go to the movies when their children are away.

He was in the Sixties when he saw a pet superstore that was having adoptions that evening. He walked in, tried to adjust to the smell, and immediately locked eyes with a short-haired miniature dachshund with one eye.

"Can I pet him?" he asked the handler.

The handler gave him the dog, who was trembling. He placed him in Toby's arms. The dog was the size of an infant, and Toby held him that way, scratching his belly. All the hardness that had calcified over Toby in the last week began to soften. A dog! He should get a dog! The kids had wanted a dog for a long time, but the Golden wouldn't allow it. He'd forgotten that he'd chosen his new building based on the fact that it would allow small animals. A dog would turn things around. Someone loyal, someone to bring the family together and replace what they'd lost. He looked up at the handler.

"Can I have him?"

He walked out ninety unnecessary minutes later with five pounds of dog food, two leashes, a water bowl, a food bowl, seven chew toys, and the eight-pound dachshund, whom he named on his adoption papers "Bubbles." Hannah used to say when she was in first grade that she wanted a Chihuahua named Bubbles. Rachel would never allow it. Who had time to walk a dog, she'd ask. And who will clean up? Who will replace the furniture?

He was walking Bubbles home, wondering if the tininess of the dog made Toby look bigger or smaller than he actually was. He walked the dog into his building, where two teenage girls yelped, "Awwwww!" He found himself wondering if he should call Joanie and ask her for dog advice; he remembered her saying that her sister was a veterinarian. He should stop looking for reasons to call Joanie.

He brought Bubbles upstairs, and he opened the apartment and said, "Here it is, little guy. This is your home now." He could not have told you why, but he spent the next ten minutes hugging the dog and crying into his fur.

He was dreaming he was swimming in Israel, in an area up north where there were waterfalls. He dreamed that he could stand beneath the waterfall and allow it to pummel him but that it wouldn't drown him in its force. But then he woke up and realized his new dog was peeing on his head.

"No, Bubbles, no!" he shouted, and rushed him out and down the elevator and outside. Bubbles took a dump but Toby had forgotten to bring a plastic bag and a woman in her thirties on her way to work sneered, "Pig!" at Toby, who was covered in urine, and who looked around frantically for something he could use to pick up the shit. This was not what he'd imagined. He'd imagined walking the dog through the streets of the Upper East Side and it would be like he was emitting some kind of irresistible pheromone, like chemtrails, the way women would stop him to pet the dog and coo up at him.

He'd just gotten back into the apartment and turned on the shower when the phone rang. He looked at the caller ID. It was an upstate number. It was the camp. His mouth dried out immediately.

"Yes, hello?"

"Mr. Fleishman, we're very sorry to bother you this early."

He felt cold. "Is everything okay?"

"Your kids are safe. But there's been an incident. I'm going to need you to come here and pick up Hannah."

"Why? What's going on?"

"I'd rather we spoke in person."

"Jesus fucking Christ, just tell me what it is."

The director paused for a minute. "There's been some sexual misconduct. I'll tell you more when you get to camp."

Sexual misconduct. "Is Hannah okay? Did something happen to her?"

"She's fine. She's here in the office with me. She isn't hurt."

He turned on the shower and stared at Bubbles for a minute, realizing why not all people get dogs. He called up Seth.

"Yo, dude," Seth said. "It's like sunrise."

"It's eight. I need a favor."

He told him something had happened with Hannah and that there was a new dog that needed sitting. He was sorry, he didn't know who else to ask.

"It just so happens that Vanessa and I have decided to take a vacation day."

"I'll leave a key with the doorman. Thanks, man. I can't thank you enough."

"Don't worry. Children are resilient."

"They're not that resilient. Why do people always say that?"

"I mean, my parents are divorced and I'm fine."

Why did he let them go to camp? They needed him now. Instead, he was fucking all of Manhattan, really just humping a him-sized map of the place, and he was sending his own beloved children off to the lowest bidder. He felt like such a loser. What he thought as he pulled the rental car (no more of Rachel's stuff, that's it, it's over) onto the FDR Drive was this: that anyone who has ever been to just one session of couples therapy could tell you that beyond your point of view lies an abyss with a bubbling cauldron of fire, and that just beyond that abyss lies your spouse's point of view. If he were to be a real scientist about this, would he be able to find empirical evidence that Rachel had a point in rejecting him? That Rachel was right to hate him this much? Yes, right then, for the first time, he could see it. He could make his way across the abyss, and just for a minute, he could see that he was the same vile, fat, needy piece of shit he always was.

Oh my God, he hated himself. He couldn't be alone with himself for another minute. He couldn't figure out how to get the Bluetooth in the car to work, so instead of listening to his neuroscience podcast, he blasted pop music, which made way for country music as he went deeper upstate, which then made way for Christian rock, anything so long as he couldn't hear his own thoughts.

He picked up his phone and gave it an order: "Call Rachel at work." It rang five times. He hung up. What the fuck was he doing.

Two hours later, he drove through the camp gates and up the dirt hill to where the administrative building was. He hadn't been there since last year, when he and Rachel went together to see Hannah on visiting day. They'd fought the entire way up, but he couldn't remember about what, just that when they exited the car she said, "I expect you to put on a face."

The camp director, an aging Ken doll in a polo shirt, jogged out to Toby when he saw him pull up. He had his empathy-dread face on.

"What happened?"

The director solemnly took out a phone—Hannah's phone. The camp director pressed his lips together and squinted, trying to find words. Then: "A few hours ago, we discovered that a personal and confidential picture that Hannah sent to a young man was widely distributed through the camp."

"Let me see it."

"I'm not sure you want to see it."

"Let me see it."

He handed Toby the phone. Toby turned it on and saw what looked like a picture of Hannah (but it couldn't be) in just her bra, with one of her tiny breasts exposed to the nipple. She had a lascivious, come-hither look about her, like a look her mother used to give him at the beginning of their marriage. Like every picture he'd seen on a dating app in the last two months. She'd taken the picture herself. He wanted to vomit.

A few years ago, Rachel had found "sex" as a search term on her computer (these kids never pass down their wisdom to each other is the thing) and Rachel had screamed at Hannah and told her she was going to call the school psychologist since there was obviously something wrong with her. Hannah's eyes exploded with how scared she was, which Toby knew because he came home from work just then, and that night he put Hannah to bed and he soothed her by promising that it was normal to be curious and that he would never call the school psychologist. Later, in what was supposed to be a hushed conversation behind closed doors that came to shouts and slammed doors, Toby said, "What were you thinking? You're yelling at a girl for being curious about sex? You will fuck her up for life." Rachel wouldn't lower herself to answer.

"I know this is hard, Mr. Fleishman," the director was saying.

Toby looked up. "So she sent this to someone?"

"She sent it to a young man, and he sent it to a few of his friends, and they sent it around. It's camp policy that sending inappropriate materials requires immediate action. We have a zero-tolerance policy for that, and I'm afraid Hannah has to go home."

He felt weak picturing the Breck commercial–ization of his daughter's nipple. He couldn't get the image of her face out of his head, the priapic glare, the amateur lust. Did she even know what this meant? Was she imitating something? What had he missed? Wasn't she a baby? He had just checked her phone. A week in camp cannot make a person into someone new. (Can it?)

"Take me to her."

"She's in the infirmary, this way."

They passed through an antechamber that had chairs, and in it was a boy about Hannah's age who looked familiar—maybe he was from the school? No, no, something else. It hit him: It was the boy from the street that day, when Hannah was too embarrassed to look at him, then again in the Hamptons, when he dropped her off with her friends.

He stopped.

"Is this the boy?"

"Mr. Fleishman, we can't tell you which boy it is. We've called the boy's—"

"And is he going to have to go home now, too? Is he going to be humiliated in front of everyone?"

"We've called his parents."

"Does he have to go home?"

"You really should come see—"

"I want to know if he's going to have to go home."

The director looked defeated. "He's not. His parents are in Switzerland and he is not the person who sent the picture."

"But he distributed it." He crouched down and looked the kid in the eyes. "Am I right that the distribution of child pornography carries with it a heavy prison sentence no matter what age you are?" The boy looked away. Toby leaned over and put his face very close. "One day, you will have the full and certain realization of what a dipshit you are. One day you will realize you are dirt. I hope it hurts."

The director said, "Mr. Fleishman—" and Toby pulled himself back, but he knew if he looked hard, yes, there it was, it was the smirk of the entitled. What had he been thinking, raising his children among these people? He'd forgotten something essential about life, which was to make sure his children understood his values. No matter how many times you whispered your values to them, the thing that spoke louder was what you chose to do with your time and resources. You could hate the Upper East Side. You could hate the five-million-dollar apartment. You could hate the private school, which cost nearly $40,000 per kid per year in elementary school, but the kids would never know it because you consented to it. You opted in. You didn't tell them about your asterisks, how you were secretly and privately better than the world you participated in, despite all outward appearances. You thought you could be part of it just a little. You thought you could get the good out of it and leave the bad, but there's so much work involved in that, too. You take your children to a concert and expect them to hear your whisper from the background that it's not all for them. You can't expect anything of them. You can't expect them to not use the phone they've had for a week—*a week*—and take and share pornographic shots of their flat chests, covered by the bra their mother only bought them because it was getting embarrassing to be the only girl in sixth grade not wearing one.

Toby pulled himself together and walked into the nurse's office. Hannah sat in a folding chair, her arms around her stomach, her face puffy from crying.

"Can you give us a minute?" Toby asked the director. "And does she need to have him sitting right out there in the hallway?"

The director backed out and closed the door. Toby crouched beside her. Hannah wouldn't look at him.

"Hannah, Hannah." She was his mess.

Nothing.

"I told you that these phones made you make very adult decisions. I told you you didn't have to make those decisions."

Hannah wouldn't look at him. "He asked me to send it. It wasn't my idea."

Toby put his hands on her shoulders. "It doesn't matter right now."

She pulled away from him. "I want Mommy. Where is Mommy?"

Toby shrugged. "I'm the one who's here. I'm sorry."

She cried for a while, and when she began to let up, he stood and told her he'd be right back, that he had to go get Solly.

Outside the infirmary door, the director paced. "Where's my son?" Toby asked.

The director led him through the camp, which was made of new buildings designed to look old. The bunks were in the shape of log cabins, though they absolutely were not log cabins. The generation of people who thought you should send your children to camp for survival and to be slightly less comfortable than they already were all year was dead and gone.

They arrived at a bunkhouse whose door said CHIPMUNKS and walked in. Twelve nine-year-old boys were lounging on their bunkbeds, reading and talking. It smelled absolutely disgusting in there, like twelve different kinds of dirty sock smells and twelve different tween boy emissions.

"Dad!" Solly saw Toby before Toby saw Solly. He ran into his arms and knocked him backward.

Toby put his nose into Solly's hair. It smelled scalpy and felt sticky, but there was an undercurrent of something his nose read as his own biology.

"What are you doing here?"

"I'm taking your sister home. Why don't you come with me?"

Solly was confused. "Did I do something wrong?"

"No, no. I think we should all be together as a family right now."

"Dad, I'm having so much fun. It is really super here. You were right. Mom was right."

"Next summer you'll come again. I promise."

"Is Mom home?"

Toby looked around for Solly's suitcase. "Let's pack you up."

The director saw him pulling both kids' suitcases. "Solly was having a really great summer," he said. "He doesn't have to leave. In fact, Mr. Fleishman, I really do recommend—"

Toby opened the trunk and loaded the car, and only when he closed the trunk did he turn to the director again.

"Actually," he said, "it's Dr. Fleishman."

Hannah didn't want to sit in the front seat for the ride home. She wanted to sit in the back with Solly, and eventually she put her head in Solly's lap and Toby could see him shouldering the responsibility of his sister like a little adult, patting her hair and staring solemnly out the window. Fuck you, Rachel.

The heat was not nearly so bad up here as it had been in the city. The trees were so green and full. He thought that maybe for Labor Day weekend he'd take them back upstate to Lake Placid or Saratoga. There was a rest stop an hour into the drive, and they all got out to go to the bathroom, slouching and haggard like they'd just been through a war.

"Let's sit outside for a minute before we get back into the car," Toby said. There was a picnic table nearby. They took the seat. "I have to talk to you both about something."

Hannah froze. "What?"

"It's about your mother."

Solly's features dissolved into a smear and his voice reached an untenable pitch. "She's dead, right? I knew it. I knew she was dead."

"Shut up, Solly!" Hannah screamed.

"Both of you, stop," Toby said. "She's not dead. She's fine. But I'm afraid she's been having some problems with her feelings. I should have told you sooner."

Hannah's eyes went wide. "Is she in a mental hospital?"

"No," Toby said. "But I think she's realized that everything's a little too much and it's getting to her. Her work, her obligations. She's . . . I don't know how to put this. She's taking a break from things."

"Why does she need a break from us?" Hannah asked.

His head began to ring with heat and alarm. He should have consulted a therapist. He should have called the school psychologist. He should have called Carla, his therapist. Here he was, winging it, damaging his children for life even worse than they already were.

"Sometimes," he said, "people just have bigger problems than a divorce can fix. Your mother loves you more than anything." When he said the words he thought he was saying it to make them feel better, but the minute he said it he felt like it was true. It had to be true. How could it not be true? How could you not love these kids? How could you not feel lucky every day that they were yours? "It was hard for your mother to have you. She had problems in the hospital both times she gave birth. That made her a little nuts, and I don't know if she ever got over it. I don't know if she ever learned how to figure out her business and her family life together. But also, she didn't explain herself to me, so anything I tell you after this is just a guess."

Solly spoke first. "Is she ever going to come back? Where did she go?"

"I have to be honest with you. I just don't know where she is. I just know that she's safe. She's safe and healthy. I don't know what she's going to do, but I've asked and she hasn't answered me. I don't want to lie to you anymore. I know this hurts, but I had to tell you."

He remembered the day in May when he and Rachel told the kids about the divorce. This was going pretty much the same way.

"Where are we going to live?" Hannah asked, like she did then.

"With me, like you have been. Just now you'll have one house."

"It's because she hates you," Hannah said. "She can't stand being near you."

"Maybe," Toby said. Better this than the other thing. "I'm sorry we couldn't have just a regular plain divorce like other people. But we are the Fleishmans. We are not like other people."

They cried for a long time. At one point, Solly sat on Toby's lap and cried into his neck while Hannah stood up and walked around. They asked logistical questions, following their hierarchy of need: Who will come to parent-teacher conferences and concerts and the orchestra recital? He reminded them that he'd never missed one so far. What will they do on Mother's Day? That's a long way off. They asked questions that there were no answers to. He tried not to flood them with information or lies. He felt like his skin was being ripped off. He hoped that wherever she was, she was suffering. He hoped she never had another moment of peace.

"I want to tell you something, though. No matter what happens, I will never ever leave you. Not even for a day. Not even for an hour."

"So you're never going to go on one of your *playdates* again?" Hannah asked.

"I'll go on them sometimes. But I'll always come home. You'll go to school and you'll come home. We will always sleep under the same roof. How's that?"

After an hour, they all got into the car again. The minute they were belted in and Toby was on the road, they both started crying again, then stopped, then started, then Hannah asked if he was lying about Rachel and if she was actually dead and that made Solly cry more until eventually they were all cried out and just stared out the window.

An hour later they were home. It was already seven, time for dinner. They boarded the elevator, each of them leaning against a wall of it wearily.

Hannah had a thought. "Will I be able to get my stuff from the other house?"

"Yes. You tell me what you need and I'll go get it."

"Good," Hannah said. "I don't want to go."

Outside the elevator, they heard a bark. As they came closer to the door, the bark got louder. Solly and Hannah looked at each other, and for a minute, the foreboding and sadness of Hannah's face made way for something like light and happiness. How could she be these two people, he wondered? The thing he'd marveled at since becoming a father was the simplicity of the children. The simplicity faded as they got older. It was not simple to be someone who just a few hours ago had a global humiliation, then learned that her mother had abandoned her, and then, in a minute, to be down on her knees, unmoored by her new puppy. For a few years Hannah would straddle being both people, and that was just the worst. Both for her, to endure innocence and maturity in the same body, and for him, to watch the innocence vanish in drips until it was gone.

Seth and Vanessa stood back. Toby beckoned them over.

"Kids, this is my old friend Seth and my new friend Vanessa," he said. Vanessa got down on her knees to pet the dog with them.

"You are very cute, like your dad said," Vanessa told Solly. "And you—" She looked at Hannah. "You are just as pretty as your pictures. I always wanted straight hair."

Hannah was enthralled immediately. "Yours *is* straight."

"Oh no," Vanessa said. "I have to blow this dry for like an hour every morning."

"It's true," Seth said. "She wakes up looking like Medusa." Vanessa hit him playfully.

Hannah scratched behind the dog's ears. "You named him Bubbles, didn't you?" she asked Toby.

"You know me too well."

"I thought that was a good idea in like first grade."

"Well, I haven't heard better ones since, so." Bubbles licked Hannah's red face.

"Does he have one eye?" Solly asked.

"Ew," Hannah said.

Solly began to cry. "It makes me love him more."

"Let's curse the camp," Seth said. "May a pox break out at this camp that will only ever be outdone by a concurrent plague of termites, so that when the buildings there finally collapse, no one but the people inside will ever know what a blessing it was."

Toby couldn't smile.

Seth went on, "May the camp director's children die from salmonella from the eggs you accidentally left out in the sun to make their birthday cakes."

Toby's mother had told him years ago that everything bad in life was eventually a blessing. We just didn't understand God's plan. He had been crying over his height or his weight—no, it was his height. He was in fifth grade, and he found out that the three meanest girls in his class had voted him least likely to ever get a girlfriend. It was stupid, he knew that. But knowing that didn't help. His mother told him that one day they'd eat their words, when he was a rich and successful doctor, and that God doesn't give us anything we can't handle. Toby wasn't comforted. He never would be comforted by the adage "God doesn't give us anything we can't handle" after that. Because what is the metric of handling something? Not killing yourself? Toby had the sudden urge to run out of the apartment, to enter the elevator, to frantically press the lobby button, to run out the door and across the park and into Nahid's building and bury his face between her tremendous breasts and get swallowed up in the sensory-deprivation camp of her body. He looked at his children. It would be a while before he could do that.

Vanessa and Seth stayed for dinner, which was spaghetti that Vanessa made while Toby unpacked the kids and did loads of laundry and tried in vain to contact the child psychologist they'd consulted in May when they were preparing to tell the kids about the divorce. He put the kids to bed early, then took Hannah's phone out of his pocket. He went through her Facebook and Instagram. He deleted the pictures she'd taken of herself. He found an app on her phone that was a mirroring program that allowed her to have two accounts within the same interface, so that she could have one outward-facing and very chaste Instagram account, and one where she posted pictures of herself with too much makeup, or made fun of another kid at school, or asked which outfit of hers was "hotter."

He deleted texts from that boy, whose name was Zach, that were the infant cousin (and yet too alike) to the kind of texts he traded with the women on Hr. A few of them took his breath away. He didn't know how Hannah had ever figured out how to talk that way. She didn't even get her period yet.

Growing up was so fucking ugly, he thought. Growing up took prisoners and casualties and collateral damage. Yes, growing up was *disgusting:* It gave him a sense of revulsion so deep inside him that a surgeon couldn't pull it out.

"I'm not going back to the Y," Hannah announced the next morning when she came out of her bedroom. Solly was still sleeping. Her eyes were swollen nearly shut, and Toby felt like he'd run a marathon. He took another personal day, sending an email to Bartuck because he lacked the fortitude for a phone call. He hadn't finished arranging camp for Solly and now he had to figure out what he was going to do with Hannah.

"I can stay here alone," she said.

"Ha," said Toby.

"Can I go to Bubby in L.A.?"

"I'd like to keep you closer to home. And Bubbles needs you."

"How about Braverman's? I know people going there."

"You're not going away again."

"You can't send me to the Y again!"

"I think I have to."

"He should have gotten kicked out, not me."

"You have to understand that boys do stupid things to show off to each other. They don't think. But also, you have to be careful about who you pick to trust in this world. You can't give away your heart or your friendship or your body to someone who isn't going to take care of it."

"Please stop."

"Hey, I would have loved to not have this conversation with you for another three years, but here we are." He sat down at the table with them.

Toby dragged the kids to the Y, letting them take turns holding Bubbles's leash.

"I hate you," Hannah said when they were a block away from the camp.

"So hate me. You could always come with me to work."

"No, thank you. I don't even have a phone anymore."

"You could, I don't know, read a book? Remember those? Remember your bat mitzvah that you have to study for?"

"I'm not having a bat mitzvah if Mom isn't there."

"You sure are."

At the Y, Toby spoke to the camp director, a much kinder version of the guy upstate, who nodded emphatically as Toby spilled the whole story of his children's abandonment.

"This can't be easy for any of you," he said. "What a nightmare."

Toby made a brave face. It felt good to finally tell people what a fucking monster he'd been married to. He no longer had to worry about her reputation, about whether he was conveying her side of the story accurately. He no longer had to ask himself hard questions about his role in things. Just the facts: She hasn't contacted her children in almost three weeks. She's a fucking maniac. No embellishments needed.

He sat on the steps of a brownstone on Ninety-first Street. It wasn't too hot yet, and he wanted to keep the dog outside for as long as possible. He called me.

"You sound tired," he said.

"I'm just lying on my hammock."

He told me about the kids.

"I never liked Rachel," I told him. "Did I ever tell you that?"

"You've mentioned it."

He wrote another email to Bartuck saying he was sorry, the personal day was unavoidable. It was. He hadn't hired a dog-sitter yet. And he needed to deal with his window shades and his air-conditioning. He called his parents. He called his sister. He called his cousin Cherry, in Queens, who cried when she heard what was going on and told him she wanted to take the kids for the weekend.

"I don't think we're quite there yet. I think they should stay with me."

"Well, then, can we visit? Can we take you guys out to dinner in the city?"

"We would love that."

He made snow angels in their sympathy and their validation, which was also the validation of the unspoken question of every single divorce, no matter what kind of co-written Facebook announcement you read about it, which is: Whose fault was it? Well, fuckers, now you know.

His phone choo-chooed. It wasn't the hospital. It was a text from Nahid:

Would you settle for dinner here?

What do you say to that? He had been determined to let her go. He had been determined to assert his need for self-respect and say, "No, sorry, I really need a woman who would consider being seen in public with me. I've been through a lot, you see, and I'm pretty fragile."

But what if this was all for the best? Maybe this would be fine. Maybe this was all he could handle. He couldn't be a boyfriend right now. He had a missing wife and children he needed to watch closely and a fellow that he was slowly becoming sure was a romantic prospect. He needed something, and he didn't want to go back to the app. The app now seemed to him like the story of Sodom and Gomorrah. Before they all turned to salt, before they were all destroyed, they were doing exactly what he was doing. So no, no more app for right now. Don't let's go to the app tonight. A sexual, quasi-romantic relationship with a woman stuck in a tower wasn't conventional, but what had convention wrought him so far? He was fragile, but so was she. She needed a friend, too. And he could still smell parts of her on him in ghostly flashes, though it had been a few showers.

He wrote back: *Ok, dinner*

You need lunch first

I'm meeting a friend for lunch

My place tonight

————

Seth was wearing a suit. He'd been interviewing for a new job, but the job was a start-up and it was owned by women, and by the time he got to lunch, he was going on about all the PC crap he couldn't bear.

"They wanted to know how I could help make the company intersectional," he said when Toby sat down. "What does that even mean? Intersection of what? Money and money? That I can do."

"Maybe it's not the place for you."

Seth stared off into the middle distance for a second, then changed the subject. "I'm going to propose," Seth said. He said it with his eyes closed, like he was practicing lines in a play. He opened them. "I have this guy in the Yakutia who owns a diamond mine and he gets these diamonds, they're blood diamonds, but they're the best. They're not even legal to sell here." He made boom hands. "What did you think of her?"

Toby didn't know what to say. "She's lovely. She's *young*. How can you stand it?"

"That's the word for her. *Lovely*." Seth's hands were on the table now. His nails were bitten down way below the distal edge into the body of the nail. Had they always been like that? Toby couldn't remember.

"You really want to get married?" Toby could not believe that anyone who had witnessed his summer thus far would ever think getting married was a good idea—not after Rachel, not after the lectures he and I gave Seth on marriage. In fact, he thought he was maybe going to be the impetus for a couple of totally fine marriages falling apart.

"Not really. But being an unmarried man at a certain age, it's like there's no place for you in the world. The world needs you to have a family, or you're always someone's bachelor friend who he can use for a good time, but who has nothing substantial himself."

Toby was shocked, maybe unfairly but still, that Seth had such a depth of understanding of his place in the world. "My parents will die and then where will I go for Thanksgiving?"

"I'm sure Libby would invite you," Toby said. He hadn't even thought about what he was going to do for holidays. "I can cook."

"No, I have plenty of invitations. But they rely on me being wantable, you know? I'm saying that that's not the same as *belonging* somewhere. There are no unconditional invitations in my life."

Seth was right. The world knew what to do with a divorced man. Even a divorced man had a place to go and people to gather with. There were no outstanding questions about him. There were questions about men who'd never married, a suspicion about what kind of monster a healthy man in finance must be in order to not have settled down with someone by now.

Now Toby sat, trying to look happy for his friend. What a relief it had been when Toby reentered the atmosphere and Seth was, for the most part, as he'd left him: a horndog bro with much if not all of his hair left. There was something pure and everlasting about Seth's singleness: he loved parties, he loved girls, he loved sex. That had felt like a more stabilizing force than any other, as Toby contemplated divorce. But now he realized he'd been ignoring Seth. Not just recently. Maybe for the duration of their friendship. Seth was a real person. He wasn't just someone who waited, frozen in time, for Toby to be ready to hang out with again. He'd had his opportunities, sure. But the truth was, he hadn't gotten over his upbringing. His parents were so deeply worried that he wouldn't marry someone who was Orthodox; now they were deeply worried he wouldn't marry someone Jewish. He was worried that he would, that some kind of inertia would take him from his great big independent life and turn him into his miserable, God-fearing parents. All it made him was afraid.

After college, Seth's big thing was throwing theme parties in his loft in Williamsburg. He would have Super Bowl parties (where he wore eye black) and Easter egg hunts (where he dressed as a bunny) and sitcom character costume parties (Seth as Greg Brady). He had a seventies party one night where he tried to get people to agree to add a key-party element to it and curled his hair like it was a perm and wore an open shirt. He had enough charisma and magnetism and energy to almost pull it off. A full half of the women in attendance had put their keys in a bowl, though they were later shamed into removing them by the other half of the women in attendance. Toby had watched the keys' removal from the fishbowl with equal parts profound disappointment and profound relief. Seth woke up the next morning with two women, whom he never saw again.

Later his parties took on a new branding. He now called them "clubs." There was an art club and a film club and a music club and there was a science club; there was even a sex club, where he got in front of the whole key-party problem by inviting a marital psychologist ("You didn't hear this from me, but he basically saved the Clinton marriage!") to speak on the topic of bringing back free love, which made everyone horny. In the film club, "the most decorated, tenured, award-winningest" NYU film professor ("She'll probably be dean of the entire school in like five years tops") came to discuss how Reaganomics affected movies in the eighties like *RoboCop* and *Videodrome*. The music club would have the classical music critic from the *Observer* ("a Pulitzer winner") lecture on the topic "Is It Okay for Jews to Listen to Wagner?" Each club had different "memberships," which was what he called his invite lists. There was some overlap. Toby, for example, was invited to all the clubs. Mostly the invite lists were divided only slightly among Seth's male friends, but finely titrated to not include the overlap of the several women he was sleeping with concurrently, and their friends.

Toby's favorite of the clubs was Science Club, and most particularly its spinoff, Physics Club. Seth hired a Fulbright scholar ("He won during what was called the highest-stakes year that the Fulbrights ever had") to discuss string theory or the Doppler effect or the Ehrenfest theorem, and all the Ivy Leaguers would ask questions, and purse their lips and nod thoughtfully at the answers, and afterward the slow, steady stream of booze and pot that were passed around the lectures would suddenly become something quantifiable in the bloodstream of everyone there and the whole thing would descend (or transcend) into a quiet and sloppy hookup carnival.

By then, Toby was engaged to Rachel, and suddenly, Rachel kept finding conflicts with the timing of the clubs. Toby would RSVP no, but Seth kept insisting, You have to come, you have to come. Rachel continued to make excuses, saying always that they were busy with dinner with her work colleagues or dinner with their neighbor (had Toby agreed to these dinners before, or was she just making these things up?). Finally they found a night they could attend, a night so far in advance, where Rachel was taken by surprise and did not have alternative plans waiting in the wings. Finally she agreed to go, but dawdled in the apartment for so long that they were late, and by the time they got there, there was just low lighting and making out and dancing and it was clear that Rachel didn't approve. "Oof," she said. "It's like Plato's Retreat in here."

"It's a *physics* lecture," Toby answered. "Or it was before we showed up two hours late."

Seth saw them at the door and ran over. "You made it!"

"Here we are. What's new with you, man? You remember Rachel?"

"It's been forever," Rachel said.

"Of course." He kissed her on the cheek. "Listen, things are dimming here. I gotta keep up the energy." He left and put on an African mask that had been lying on the table. He called out to the room: "I am the god of copulation! Pray to me!"

"See?" Toby said. "He's always up for a good time."

She watched Seth start a small conga line of young women across the room. "Is Seth depressed chronically, or just tonight?"

He thought she was being a bitch, just hating his friends again—"I don't *hate* them, I just don't see why you like them so much! Explain it to me!"—but now he thought about that night again. He could finally see it clearly. Seth had staved it all off by being the drunkest guy in the room, and the most oversexed guy in the room. He'd pretended he was having so much fun that he allowed himself to function as other people's ids, their good times, the guy they went out with when their conventional, totally satisfying lives hit a snag. Toby had never not wanted his charisma, his height, his looks, but now he saw it: Seth didn't have anything else. He didn't have any friends. He didn't have anyone close to him. Toby had dropped off and I had dropped off and nobody had taken our place. We had probably not even been good friends to him in the first place. Why hadn't Toby understood this before? Listen to the patient, etc., etc.

Now Toby asked, "Did you talk to Vanessa about what happened?"

"I don't want to worry her. I'll have another job in no time. My old boss called me this morning that he's got a lead on a new shop and he's taking us all with him."

"Speaking as a former married person, you seem off to a terrible start," Toby said. "If you're lying now, when the stakes are absolutely nothing, I hate to see you in five years when she gets fat or has a miscarriage."

"But I love her. I really do. She's gentle and nice. And it's just time. I don't know. Are you supposed to want to get married? Or are you just supposed to marry the person you're into when you decide it's time to get married?"

"Don't ask me. I didn't do it right. Do you know she'll say yes?"

"I *think* she'll say yes," he said. He was becoming irate. "Got any more questions? I mean, we're, like, in love? She's a wonderful person? Is that a good reason? You don't seem happy for me. I was always happy for you."

The waitress finally came along to ask for their orders. Toby ordered the vegetable soup with no rice but was told that there was already rice in it, so he ordered the Cobb salad with no egg yolk or blue cheese or bacon. ("Do you have any diet ice for my friend here?" Seth asked. The waitress looked confused and Seth laughed, which made her even more confused, so she gave up and walked away.)

"I'm happy for you, man," Toby said. "I'm sorry, I'm just—I am not in what the psychiatric community would call 'a good place.' Here, let me give you a blessing: May her uterus be bountiful and yield unlimited quantities of finance babies, and may they thrive in a bull market." Seth smiled a little. "May her dowry include many different varieties of vaping marijuanas, and some Ecstasy, and may she remain too stoned to notice how easily your eyes wander to her much younger cousins."

"We need to celebrate," Seth said. "Where's Libby?"

"She's at Disney World. She sent me a picture from the Peter Pan ride."

"I cannot picture that. She would dissolve around happiness."

"I feel like people there with her should be able to demand their money back."

Before they left, Seth said to Toby, "I can't believe it was so bad for you. I always liked Rachel. I thought she was hot and nice. And you seemed happy. And then just one day you weren't?" Even with his good friends, the questions were never about him.

"Nah." He answered them anyway. "It was like the fall of Rome: slowly, then all at once."

Seth nodded in a show of sympathy and all Toby could think was: Haven't you been listening?

Toby called his therapist, Carla, whom he'd stopped seeing actively when the apps took over his attention span and his time, but it was August and she was gone to the island where mental health professionals vanished to in the summer. The useless social worker from school was even more useless than usual, camping in the Adirondacks with her family for two weeks. He called mental health services at the hospital but was told that all adolescent and pediatric psychologists were out until September. This is what happened when an entire field of medicine was as disrespected as psychologists. They made their own rules, and one of them was that nobody was allowed to have a breakdown during August, and the other was that this was fucking Europe and they got to take a whole month off from work.

Maybe couples therapists didn't go on vacation. He wondered if the counselor he and Rachel had nearly beaten to death with their vitriol was still around. Maybe he should call that guy and tell him what was going on with his patient. Dr. Joe? Was that his name? Yes, it was just about two years ago, and Toby had been begging Rachel to go see a therapist, which, naturally, she viewed as a personal assault. Then, out of nowhere, she finally agreed. That was a time when he was still sure that if Rachel could just see her anger and her nastiness through a neutral screen, she could get help and they could move beyond it. But he was also already thinking that maybe this was a last-ditch effort before realizing that this was not something that could be fixed.

It was the same bullshit. She said: "I feel like I'm being punished for earning a living." And "I feel like I have to tiptoe around my success, that he loves what the money brings and hates me for bringing it." And "I talk to him plenty nicely. He screams and throws things when he's angry and I do my best to stay neutral. I do it for the children. I wish he would, too." He was made physically weak from her accusations and her lies. *Were* they lies? Or did she actually believe all of this? As much as Toby tried, it became clear that the advantage in couples therapy accrued to the person who could hold their shit together. He wanted to cry, he wanted to hold his fists up at her and make her hear him. As they went back and forth, Toby trying to refute every half sentence, even knowing that that was the wrong thing to do, he could feel himself losing the room. Dr. Joe took his glasses off and used the heel of the same hand to wipe his eye in what appeared to be poorly veiled exhaustion.

"Look, Rachel!" he wanted to say. "We broke a couples thera-pist! That's how bad we are! Just let me go!"

Toby had married Rachel for many reasons, and one of the main ones was that she wasn't crazy. She was pretty, she was nice (at the time), she was smart (he thought), she loved him back. But mostly, she wasn't crazy. Crazy wasn't an insult the way he used it, he swore it, particularly after he called me crazy a few times. It was just a designation, a category. Yes, he admired my particular brand of ec-centricity and erraticism. Yes, it was one he didn't want to live with. He would love a dinner party full of crazy people. But he didn't want a life with a crazy person. And now look. Now look what he had to deal with.

Maybe he should have reconsidered his stance on craziness. He imagined that women who were crazy were constantly emitting their irrationality. Rachel was difficult and opinionated, but she al-ways made sense, and he was very grateful for that. Now he won-dered if she'd just been holding it all in, and so when the dam broke, it flooded. In the law of opposites, it now made sense. He was so not crazy, he was so measured and rational (according to him), that of course the person he ended up with was crazy. Why else would she disappear like this?

Once, I'd written a short story—this was back the first time when I thought I might write fiction—and it ended up in some an-thology. Three of us from the anthology were asked to read our stories at a Barnes & Noble on the Upper West Side. Toby showed up. He told me he was worried no one else was coming, which, well, no one else came.

After, Toby asked if I wanted to get a drink. I lived in the Village back then, in a dreamy studio on Bleecker Street. We began walk-ing toward the subway, but we got there and passed it. I pulled us off onto Sixty-fourth Street and ducked into the street-level door-way of a brownstone to light a joint. I'd been sleeping with—trying to be the girlfriend of—a copy editor at the magazine who kept leaving pot at my apartment, and for the first time in my life, I'd been smoking it regularly.

"Jesus, Elizabeth," Toby said.

"This is my enjoyment, Tobe." We walked quietly for another minute.

"That story was good," Toby said. "I remember always thinking that you were my funniest and smartest friend. And also that you would never live up to your potential."

"Thanks," I said.

"No, just that I'm really proud of you. I think you'll do something big someday."

I took out a cigarette. He indicated that I should give him one, too, and he took my sweater off my bag, where it was hanging, and wrapped it around his head like a Bedouin.

"Is that so she won't smell smoke on you?" I asked.

"May no man find favor in you," he said in his Beggar Woman voice.

We stopped walking.

"Because I'm so fucking crazy?" I asked.

"What?" he asked.

"I'm so fucking crazy," I said.

"Wow, you never forget anything, do you? I was drunk. That was ten years ago. I meant something else."

"What did you mean, then?"

"That I just couldn't take your ups and downs. I couldn't be responsible for them."

"You were not responsible for my ups and downs ever, or for anything about me. We were just friends."

Toby was quiet.

"I'm glad you ended up with someone so sane, Toby," I said. "I'm glad you ended up with everything you ever wanted. You got your girl on a career track, you got your great job and your big apartment. That's just fucking great. I'm happy for you. But one day you're going to understand that you were so busy being allergic to craziness that you have not realized you have drowned in something boring and predictable and unsmart and insidious."

I hailed a cab and waved goodbye. He had been so concerned that he'd end up with someone crazy that he'd accidentally ended up with someone cruel and unloving. At home, Rachel smelled the cigarette despite his best efforts, but only after realizing he was holding a woman's sweater that didn't belong to her. She didn't ask him whose sweater it was, or who he'd had the cigarette with.

The next day they learned they were expecting Hannah.

Suddenly, it was four o'clock, so he rushed back to the lobby of the Y for his kids. He stood as the lone man among the large-sunglassed mothers who talked chaotically in packs of three and four and tank tops that said RUN THE WORLD and NEVERTHELESS, SHE PERSPIRED. Soon their children came bouncing downstairs filled with requests and demands, and among them were Hannah and Solly, who looked like they had just attended a funeral. His poor kids. Toby waved to get their attention. Solly, finally seeing him, ran over and hugged him for a full twenty seconds. Hannah wouldn't even look at him.

They walked in silence for two blocks, Solly holding his father's hand tightly. Finally, Toby spoke to Hannah. "I know you don't want to be there," he said. "I don't know what else I can do."

"Everybody knows why I got kicked out of camp," Hannah said.

Bubbles had taken two separate dumps over the course of their absence: one on Toby's bed and one on the bathroom floor. "At least one is in the bathroom, Dad," Solly said. "We don't have to give him back, right?" There was something heartbreaking about Bubbles. He trembled constantly. Toby had looked up whether he might be cold, but the veterinary forum he found only said that dachshunds tend to be anxious. Welcome to the family, buddy, Toby thought.

After dinner, Toby was winning his fourth consecutive Uno game against Solly when he got a call from the hospital. It was Clay. Karen Cooper had become unresponsive—she had been talking to her children and suddenly went unconscious. She was headed into a CT scan now.

"Stroke," he said. "Minimal brain activity."

Toby rubbed his eyes. "Has Mr. Cooper been told?"

"Dr. Lintz told him."

Toby pulled on his earlobes. He shouldn't have taken another day off. He was a few days away from a promotion and he didn't want to give anyone any reason not to offer it to him. But also, he was Karen Cooper's doctor, and it was his duty to inform the family. He had problems, but he had to be responsible. He had given them hope. Now it was time to take it away.

He asked Hannah and Solly if they wouldn't mind him running to the hospital for an hour. "I have a patient who is dying. I have to talk to her family."

"Why didn't you stop her from dying?" Solly asked.

"It's not always up to me."

Toby combed his hair and left the apartment, but while he waited for the elevator—it was a building with 150 apartments and only had two elevators—Solly came out calling his name.

"What is it?" Toby asked.

"We want to go with you."

The elevator door opened. He let it close. "Okay, just get ready fast. And bring books."

When he got to the hospital, Karen's bed was still empty, but David Cooper was in her room. "What does this mean?" he asked, his hands in his hair. "I thought the surgery worked."

Toby asked Clay to get Mr. Cooper some water, but he flung his arm to the side to dismiss it and said, "How could this have happened? I thought she was fine."

Toby told him the surgery had been successful. The encephalopathy was resolved when the liver was removed. The organ had taken. But they suspected that Karen had had a hemorrhagic stroke—a bad one—and that was always a possibility after any surgery. She bled into her brain. It was random. It was one of the many things in medicine that couldn't be foreseen. She was being taken for a CT scan to confirm. But they didn't really need to. She hadn't responded to any of the reflex tests that the resident had administered.

"I'm sorry," Toby said. "We don't know a lot yet. But this isn't looking good."

"When will we know?"

"In a few hours. Why don't you go home and have dinner with your children. I'll call you as soon as we know."

David looked at the empty bed. "I can't leave her alone here."

"You're not. You're leaving her with us."

David needed some time to absorb the things he couldn't believe. Toby had heard from other doctors who worked with a poorer clientele that less fortunate people are more accepting of these things. Not the rich ones. Rich patients couldn't believe that money couldn't help, that their positions and club memberships and status couldn't help. They couldn't believe that nobody was coming to save them. But nobody was coming to save them.

David left the room, like Toby suggested, and Toby went to check with radiology. They were right; it was a hemorrhagic stroke. Surgery came in and said there was nothing they could do. The poor woman. She had just come to. She had started talking. It felt like she might have made it through this. They'd watched everything so carefully. Surviving a rare illness only to buy it with something as banal as a surgical stroke—it was like a bad joke. He headed down the hall, but when he turned the corner to the door to the stairwell, he saw David in the hallway, talking to Karen's friend Amy. He watched as David told her the news and hugged her. David left in the elevator, and Amy just stared at her phone, unsure what to do. She looked up and spotted Toby.

"Dr. Fleishman, is it true?"

"I'm sorry. This is just very bad luck."

"Is she going to die?" Amy asked.

"I don't know. She's having tests done now. It's not looking great."

Amy began to cry. Toby steered her toward the family lounge, but before they could get there, she turned to him.

"She was really unhappy," Amy said. "She had been unhappy for such a long time, but the kids, blah blah blah, you know how it is."

"I do."

"She was going to leave David."

Toby shook his head. "What?"

"He cheats on her. He doesn't give her access to the money. He gives her an allowance. Can you imagine? She gets to raise the kids and keep the house nice and entertain his asshole friends on poker night. She was a *lawyer*."

Toby sat, stunned, and realizing that his entire problem in life was that he could still be stunned by information that revealed what seemed to be true most of the time, which was that things weren't what they seemed.

Toby almost said, "But they seem fine," and then remembered that he had never known Karen Cooper to be conscious. Instead he said, "Mr. Cooper seemed very devoted."

"Of course he did. Have you ever been married?"

"I— Yes." She waited. "I'm in the middle of a divorce."

She laughed, incredulous. "Now she's going to die. I can't believe that *now* she's going to fucking die. You know, anyone who sees this will think it's a great tragedy that this happened to such a young woman. But they won't realize that the actual tragedy is that she was just about to get away from him."

It was so fucking hot. Toby opened all the windows while the super awaited some magical part for his air-conditioner that had to be ordered and couldn't be found in all of Manhattan. He lay on his bed in just his boxer shorts, on top of the blanket, and he thought about opening his app. Hannah walked in and complained that Solly had been in the bathroom for an hour. Toby went to investigate only to find Solly lying on the floor because the tiles were cold.

At nine at night, the doorbell rang. He opened it, thinking it might be the super, but it was a man wearing a bike helmet.

"Tobin Fleishman?"

The man handed him a manila envelope with the return address of a law office, which he opened to find that New York State had sent him a writ of divorce and two yellow Post-it tabs to indicate where his signature was required to end his marriage forever. He let out a laugh. How could his marriage be any more over than it was?

If Carla were around, he would have told her about his revenge fantasies. They included refusing to sign the papers at all and returning the papers back to Rachel, care of Sam Rothberg at the home of Miriam Rothberg. He couldn't think of anything else. It was so hot even his revenge fantasies had no juice. The world had become vile.

"Let's be the kind of people who have lunch after their divorce papers are signed," Rachel had said as they left the lawyer's office after presenting their list of divided assets two months before. "Let's be people who can elevate out of this."

"You taking a new yoga class?" he'd asked.

"Your hostility and your sarcasm are always so small-minded, Toby," she'd said. "You can't pull off this anger. It doesn't look good on you." He began to walk away, but she caught up with him. "One day, and I hope it's very soon for your sake, and especially for the children's sake, you'll have a revelation about how angry you are. Once you stop being so angry, your world will get better. Your problems will be solved."

"No, once I'm done with you my problems will be solved."

"See?"

"The real problem is that I'll never be done with you," Toby had said. "You will be the lesser parent to my children for as long as we're all alive. I will never get to see the day where my children had the adequate mother they deserved."

"How can you say that to me? How can you keep punishing me for doing what I had to do?"

"You didn't *have* to do any of it. You *wanted* it."

"You know, if I were a man—"

"Oh, fuck you with the 'if I were a man' stuff. Seriously. If you were a man then I'd say you were a shitty father."

He fell asleep with the papers on the pillow next to him. He dreamed he was fucking Rachel. He couldn't identify the era—if it was the miraculous early days, or the perfunctory postpartum years, or the rage-sex later ones.

"Why are we doing this?" he kept asking in the dream.

She didn't answer.

"I defended you!" he yelled at her. "I defended you!"

She just looked at him curiously until she finally closed her eyes and screamed.

He woke up feeling certain excitement, and he stayed on his back in bed, a light sweat covering his body as he stared at the ceiling beneath the weight of his big, sweaty boner. The dream felt like a memory, though he was absolutely sure that he'd never screamed at her during sex and he was just as sure she never screamed that way either. The best he could trace the surroundings in the dream was to a vacation they took in Santa Cruz, right after their wedding. It wasn't their honeymoon. Their honeymoon was in Hawaii, a year later, when Rachel could get off from work and Toby had a break in his rotation schedule. But right after their wedding, the next morning, so as not to have to spend even more time with Toby's miserable family, they drove north out of L.A. to a motel in Santa Cruz, back when she was okay staying at motels.

The place was right on the water, their patio a slab of concrete that dangled off a gigantic cliff to the beach below. Their room smelled musty and old, and the sheets smelled like they'd been in a closet that had the kind of moth repellent that was absolutely not cedar.

They walked through town each day, making fun of the hippies. They went to the Mystery Spot, Toby dazzling her with tales that could not possibly be true about the magnets in the Earth. ("They say," he whispered as he passed by one of the magnetic rocks, "that the magnet only works for people who lost their virginity before they were fourteen." She made a show of her entire body flailing over to the rock as if she couldn't stop it. They were asked to leave after ten minutes.)

At night, as the sun went down, they watched the surfers below, maybe a hundred of them every day, while the motel tried to pretend it was a hotel and served vinegary wine and shitty cheese for a twilight cocktail hour. What did the Toby Fleishmans know to be cynical? They loved it.

"It seems so clear to me," she'd said, "that the ocean would rather you didn't surf on it. If it wanted you, it would give you a more sustained wave."

"I think that's the point," he'd said. They were sitting on the bench on their balcony, she upright and he lying down, his legs crossed over her lap.

"And what do you have to show for it? Look at them. They climb onto their boards, and they fall right down. It's so sad. Even the ones that make it a few feet, where does it get them?"

"They're doing it for the pleasure of doing it."

"I can't imagine ever doing something just for the pleasure of doing it."

"Uh, last night seemed to be an exception to this rule."

"Even that. Even that, you're having sex with your husband to solidify something. Even sex isn't something you do just to do. You do it to prove something, or to build closeness."

"I don't. I do it because I love you."

She thought about this, her fingers lightly brushing his leg hair back and forth. "You have really great calves," she'd said.

"Don't objectify me," he'd said.

"They're really, I don't know, manly. They turn me on."

"Think you might find a purpose to reenter the bed chamber over there with me?"

"I'll come up with something."

For a few minutes, lying in his bed, still in the vapor of his dream, he'd forgotten what had happened to them. For a few minutes, he'd forgotten that they were a mess. He didn't like remembering the bad moments, but he didn't like remembering those moments, either. He liked to find the point in every single memory, even the good ones, where she was telling him who she really was. If he could do that, this could never happen to him again. He whacked off quickly, too quickly, then got out of bed and spent the next hour hating himself for letting his guard down so egregiously as to dream of her.

Toby's cousin Cherry, who was his favorite cousin growing up, lived in New York, unlike all his other cousins. The two or three times they visited before his father stopped speaking with her mother, Toby would tell her that when he grew up he wanted to live her life. He wanted to ride trains and eat pretzels from carts and see people kissing on the street late at night. Cherry was seven years older than him, and, by the time Toby moved to New York for college, a schoolteacher. She was the first family member he introduced Rachel to. Rachel was nice to her, or maybe he didn't notice that she wasn't. When Toby called Cherry this year to tell her about his divorce, Cherry did him the kindness of at least pretending to be sad for him.

Now Cherry called to see if he maybe needed a night off from the kids. Toby thought for a minute. My college roommate, Sonia, was having her annual party the next night, Saturday, and I'd invited him and Seth, who hadn't been to one of Sonia's parties since her twenty-third birthday. "Do you think you can come tomorrow instead? I had a party I was supposed to go to and I didn't really want to leave the kids with a babysitter. . . ."

The next night, Cherry came in to the city with her two daughters, who were teenagers, to take the kids to dinner. "We'll bring them home in one piece," Cherry said. "I promise."

"What time should I be home by?" Toby asked.

"Where are you going, Dad?" Solly looked alarmed.

"Just to a birthday party. I'll be home tonight."

"Don't worry," Cherry said. "You take the night off. We're going to go to dinner and then come back and watch TV until you get home. Have fun. Really. Promise me."

They left, and Toby adjourned to his closet to consider two nearly identical shirts. The doorbell rang. It was Seth.

"Pregame!" Seth said. He held up a six-pack of beer.

"The carbs, man. I think I have vodka in the freezer. And a bottle of sparkling rosé in the fridge."

"Sparkling rosé? Dude."

"It was from a date I had a month ago." Toby thought for a second. "Oh, wait, this is not a good story."

"Do tell."

"I met her on Hr, and we did the usual sexting thing before, and then we decided to meet. Anyway, so we go out to that bro bar on Second, we have a bunch of drinks, we have a hilarious time, then on the way back she insists on buying two bottles of sparkling rosé. And who am I to stop her?"

"Exactly."

"So we get back here, and she does this insane striptease, laughing the whole time."

"That's pretty hot."

"We get to the bedroom and I'm too drunk. I can't get it up. And I'm so stressed out about this, and she's giving me the speech about how this is okay and it happens to everyone."

"Did you have any Vitamin V?"

"Viagra? No! I'm forty-one."

"Oh, I always carry one around."

"It happens to you?"

"Nah. You carry it like Dumbo's feather. Then nothing ever happens."

"Now I know."

"You should have stuck with her," Seth said. "Only the real caretaker archetypes pull that speech out."

"Maybe it was the Beggar Woman's curse coming true."

"I don't remember that one. May you find yourself being lap-danced upon by a filthy-minded lawyer burping on sparkling rosé bubbles when your dick stops working."

Toby looked in the mirror, straightened his collar, and followed Seth out the door.

Again I'll say it: Life is a process in which you collect people and prune them when they stop working for you. The only exception to that rule is the friends you make in college.

Adam and I arrived at Sonia's party, which was at a new bar uptown, close to eleven P.M. We'd just gotten off the plane from Disney World, where we'd spent the last three days, brought the kids home to the babysitter, then driven back to the city. Our flight had been delayed for four hours. Adam was annoyed the whole car ride.

"This party is never good," he said. "I'm exhausted. Why can't we just skip this?"

But I was twenty again, and I couldn't bear that my friends were all gathered in one place and I wasn't there. The first person I saw when I arrived was Jennifer Alkon—she of Seth's Israeli yearnings and recent fifth base—in deep conversation with Danielle. The second person I saw was Seth, who was advancing on us.

"Is this the man who thawed Libby Epstein's heart?" Seth asked.

"Seth Morris." Adam showed no recognition. "It's nice to finally meet you."

Adam nodded, unsure why it was nice to finally meet him. I hadn't told Adam about Seth ever, I think. I hardly ever told him about any of these people.

Toby found us. "How was Disney?" he asked. "We took the kids a few years ago."

Adam shook his head. "I loved it. It's such a nice place. People greet you, they call the kids by name. It's clean. It's safe. Libby found it soul-crushing. Can I get you a drink?"

"Why?"

"Because she hates joy." He was still smiling, but it was his worn-out smile. He walked away.

"He really gets you," Toby said to me.

"I complain too much," I told him. I sat down on one of the couches with my legs splayed, leaning back in what would have been mock exhaustion if there were anything mock about it. The kids ate my heart out the whole time. I'd read those stupid blogs about Disney, and they all warned me that the character lunch at the Crystal Palace would fill up fast, so I should book at eleven A.M., but they did not warn me about the existential dread of being there. It was like I could finally see what I'd become, made clear through my presence among yet another entire set of women who looked just like me. I couldn't bear being this suburban mom who was alternating between screaming at her kids and being the heartfelt, privileged witness to their joy. But the people around us—the haranguing mothers and the sexless fathers—I kept trying to find ways that I was better than these people, but all I kept landing on was the fact that the common denominator was me.

Adam returned with two beers.

"It's loud in here!" Adam shouted.

"It's a bar!" I shouted back. "It's a bar in Manhattan on a Saturday night! Remember those?!"

Someone passed me a glass of champagne. I took a long glug. It was so loud I had to shout, so I shouted about Disney and how I couldn't enjoy any of it. We'd had such good accommodations. We had the club level, the concierge level. A lounge with endless food and entertainment, a hotel that was themed like the Atlantic City boardwalk, except without the criminals and prostitutes. Magicians and card players on the boardwalk. Freedom from the very thing that makes vacation interesting—which is people different from you and places that are unfamiliar—but also makes it extremely relaxing. I couldn't enjoy any of it.

"We had these FastPasses," I said. "We got into every ride within, like, six minutes. But you'd go on this empty line past the people who had been waiting in a different line, and you realized that you weren't transcending a line, you were cutting one. You had subverted the system of fairness for the people who happened to not be on the club level."

"A thing about my wife is that she can be unhappy both standing on a line *and* cutting a line," Adam said. "She's pretty amazing, isn't she?"

"You can also get a FastPass for coming to the park early in the morning, though," Toby said. "Arriving early isn't elitism."

"Sure it is. But you're missing my point. It's that even when it's not fair in my favor, I can't get over how it's not fair. I am a miserable person, and I don't know if that was always true, or if I became this way."

"I can't wait to take my kids to Disney World," Seth said. "I loved it when I was a kid."

"I hear the senior discount is sweet," Toby said.

But I couldn't stop. "No. Seth. It's not like when we were young. You go and you think of how horrible all the people are, how same-shaped the women are, how stupid everyone is. The women wear these yoga pants instead of regular pants and they yell at their children, and then you realize *you're* wearing yoga pants."

"I don't understand," Seth said. "Why couldn't you just wear regular pants?"

We drank and drank, and finally a core of us who remembered everything about particular nights in college sank into a circle on the couches and reminisced and laughed. Who knew how much time went by before Adam came over to the couches and waved to get my attention and pointed at his watch? "We've got soccer in the morning, and a babysitter who still needs to be driven home."

"Whoops! I told her she'd be home by twelve."

"We'd better get going."

"I'm pretty wired," I told him. "Do you mind if I stay?"

"Stay." He looked weary.

"Just a little while. I never get to see these people. I'm reliving the glory of my youth."

"She had a glorious youth," Sonia, who was very drunk, called into the air.

He stared at me.

"I'll get a car home," I said. "It'll be fine."

"Can we just discuss this for a minute?"

"Come on, Dad!" I laughed, then seeing he wasn't laughing, too, made an elaborate show of standing up. We talked in the corner.

"When is this going to stop?" he asked.

I looked past what he was actually asking. "It's going to be fine," I said. "I'll just take a car home." I kissed him hard on the mouth and walked back to my friends. I waited long enough so that when I finally looked up to where he'd been standing, he was gone.

Vanessa texted Seth to say things had gotten *out of hand in the best possible way* at the bachelorette party she was at and would he mind if she skipped Sonia's party. Seth texted her back, *Oh come on*. Vanessa carpeted the screen with heart emojis. I watched the exchange over his shoulder. "If I can send my husband home, you can have a night without your girlfriend."

"Have you considered that I like Vanessa more than you appear to like your husband?"

"What?" I screamed over the music, like I hadn't heard, but I'd heard.

We all talked for another hour despite the noise. We talked about Israel and college and grad school and how the real estate they had in the nineties was the best real estate we'd ever have and about wisdom teeth and tuition and Nirvana and tattoos and vitamin A. We looked up and I saw a beautiful young woman with shiny gold hair and big eyes walking toward us with a smile. Seth turned and leapt up. Vanessa glowed so bright that she seemed to take up an extra layer of attention, and suddenly the conversation shifted to her self-conscious-less twenties-ness. When she spoke, everything was a kind of self-reporting that centered on coincidence or magic. "That would only happen to me!" she ended at least two of her stories. Toby and Seth watched her like panting dogs. I watched them watching her and realized I was too drunk. I said, "We need a diner."

It was two A.M. when we finally found one. I was drunk enough to not pretend I wasn't going to eat bread and Toby was drunk enough to not feel self-conscious that he was not going to eat at all.

"Is there a bathroom here?" Vanessa asked.

Someone pointed in the back, which was literally the only place a bathroom could be.

"She seems very nice," I said to Seth.

"Elizabeth." But Toby couldn't stop this.

"Are you really going to marry her?"

Seth looked stricken. "You told her?" he asked Toby.

"Of course he told me. I'm not against marriage, Seth. I love my husband. I think you don't get that marriage isn't really about your spouse."

He stared. But I couldn't stop this.

"Have you heard of Maslow's hierarchy of needs? You have an imperative to seek out food and shelter. But once you know food is widespread and available, once you really know it, you can wonder what you like to eat and how much you want to eat. Once you have access to shelter, you can begin to ask yourself where you want to live and how you want to decorate it. What if one of the imperatives we never understood was about love and therefore marriage? Meaning, what if we search to make sure we are lovable and worthy of someone who commits to us absolutely and exclusively, and the only way we can truly confirm we are worth these things is if someone wants to marry us; someone says, 'Yes, you are the one I will love exclusively. You are worthy of this.' And then, only when you're actually married, once this need is fulfilled, you can for the first time wonder if you even wanted to be married or not. The only problem with that is that by the time you realize you have access to love, you're already married, and it is an awful lot of cruelty and paperwork to undo that just because you didn't know you wouldn't want it once you had it."

"Only drunk people talk about Maslow's hierarchy of needs," Seth said.

I ignored him. This was who Seth was going to marry. But here's what he didn't know, I told him, and what he would learn: A wife isn't like an ultra-girlfriend or a permanent girlfriend. She's an entirely new thing. She's something you made together, with you as an ingredient. She couldn't be the wife without you. So hating her or turning on her or talking to your friends about the troubles you have with her would be like hating your own finger. It's like hating your own finger even after it becomes necrotic. You don't separate yourself from it. You look at your wife and you're not really looking at someone you hate. You're looking at someone and seeing your own disabilities and your own disfigurement. You're hating your creation. You're hating yourself.

"Look at Vanessa," I said. "She's so happy to be around you, so worshipful. She likes everything you wear and your friends. I was like that, too. Rachel was like that, too, wasn't she, Toby?"

"Maybe briefly. But maybe only outwardly? I think just eventually she couldn't keep up the act."

Seth put his spoon down and sat back in the booth, never taking his eyes off me.

"Easy, Elizabeth," said Toby.

"I'm not crazy," I said. "I'm just weighed down."

"But Adam loves you," Toby said. "He doesn't weigh you down."

"He does. He doesn't mean to, but he does. It's not him in particular. The kids do, too. All of it does. It's hard to feel like this when you still remember what it felt like to be nimble and light again."

Vanessa returned to the table. "Sorry, I got a call from Tamara. She wanted to know if you guys wanted to meet up." She looked around. "Why is everyone so serious?"

I looked at her for a dangerous moment. I wanted to touch her all over her body and remember what it was like to feel like that. I would have eaten her heart or drunk her blood if I could have. But it would come for her, too.

"I have to go," Toby said quickly. "My cousin is waiting up for me to come home."

He stood up, and I stood up, too. I felt like if I let him leave right then he'd never talk to me again. It was just as hot as it was at noon. I walked him home, but at his apartment building, I continued in without a word. Inside, Cherry and her daughters were on the couch in front of a show about a sports agent on HBO. Cherry was asleep. "Wake up, Mom," the older daughter said. Cherry looked around, bewildered, then saw Toby and me.

"Libby! Is that you?"

"Cherry!" We hugged.

"You haven't changed," Cherry said. "I didn't realize you were divorced."

"Oh, I'm not. We're still in New Jersey, two kids. Husband who is still married to me."

Cherry gave me a funny look and turned to her daughters. "This is Libby, Toby's friend," she told them.

Cherry lingered for a minute, not quite understanding what it was that I was doing there, but I didn't care. She smiled something in the realm of warm and businesslike and said, "It's really nice to see you. Are you okay to get home?" like she was the lady of the house.

"I'm fine," I answered.

Cherry looked at Toby, but he was busying himself taking his wallet and phone out of his pockets. She said her goodbyes.

Twenty minutes later, I was sitting at his bedroom window, smoking a joint that Seth had given me at the party, followed by a cigarette, a pack of which I'd bought from a bodega at some point in the night, I couldn't remember. Toby was sitting up on his bed.

"It's like three A.M. Won't you be wasted tomorrow?" he asked.

"Yes," I said. "But very little is expected of me. It's so fucking hot in here, Toby. Why is it so hot in here? I swear I could see sound."

What the fuck was I doing there? I thought of a night from our year in Israel, on Purim, after I'd been dumped by a dickhead named Avi and Seth was still nursing wounds from Jennifer Alkon. We were all three drunk, just like every other student in Jerusalem. We made our way to the Beggar Woman and then made our way to the Wall, and at the Wall, Seth saw Jennifer Alkon's dowdy, flat-footed best friend Betheny, who offered to buy him a drink, and he ended up going home with her. Toby and I kept walking, unable to find our way back to the area without passing the Beggar Woman. We were drunk and making an entire thing about wanting to avoid her, but we passed her anyway. We both wanted to be told something true about ourselves. She didn't remember us—she never remembered us ever—and we passed her but we realized we were out of cash, and she called to us for charity, and Toby made the mistake of making eye contact and saying in Hebrew that he was sorry but he'd already given her his last shekel. She, of course, did not react to this reasonably. She unleashed on him a battalion of curses:

"May your children never know the depth of your love. May your children never grow." She indicated me here: "May your wife find that her love and desire for you rot like your testicles."

I screamed at the woman in Hebrew, "I'm not his wife!"

Toby took me by the arm and dragged me away. We broke into a sprint and ended up hiding behind a wall, drunk and screaming with laughter, and we crouched down until it was just like the first night we met, our faces really close to each other, and suddenly Toby seemed perfect to me. He'd been under my nose the whole time. Literally under my nose, because he only came up to there. Why did I want something hard when I could have something easy? Why shouldn't I just submit to the Tobys of the world—to Toby himself, who was right here? So far that year I'd had my heart broken by a boy who either did or didn't know he was gay but certainly was and by meatheads that I'd only gone out with because I'd lost some weight and was now finally visible to meatheads. All I'd ever wanted was to be regular, but maybe regular wasn't for me. Maybe Toby was for me. I leaned forward to kiss him. He pushed me away. "I'm not taking advantage of a drunk girl," he said. The next day he said he was sorry about the night before, but I pretended I didn't remember anything.

In his bedroom, the windows open, I extended my legs to the bed and then pulled myself over onto it. I put my head on the pillow next to his and I moved onto my side so that I was facing him. I closed my eyes to avoid his questions, and when I opened them, Toby was asleep. Look what a friendship could still be after all these years. It was a miracle, the pain that could be survived. It was a miracle what two people could move on from. It was a miracle what two people can see each other go through and still have love for each other. I looked at his face. I couldn't see signs of aging on him the way I saw them on myself. To me, he was exactly as I'd left him all those years ago, and I was the one who'd been rotting. I touched his closed eyelids with my fingers.

———

Sometime after it became light we were awoken by a sound. Solly was crying. Toby ran in and saw that he'd wet his bed again. "Don't worry, we'll just change the sheets." But Solly couldn't stop crying. "I'll be right back. Let me get a towel."

Toby ran into his room and shook me awake. "You have to go now," he said. I sat up, unsure of where I was for a minute, and put my shoes on and tiptoed out. It was eight A.M. There were joggers and dads wheeling strollers, giving mothers their weekly break. There were bagels and trays of coffee. There were shopkeepers opening up bodegas. Everyone seemed okay; everyone seemed satisfied enough or distracted enough. A man read the *Times* while he crossed the street. I shook my head at the wilderness of their complacency. Adam had texted at two in the morning, then not at all. I didn't know what to tell him. I decided to walk for a few minutes, which turned into more than a few minutes, and then three hours had passed.

Around then, Toby texted me that he was sorry, but I didn't see the text because I was with Rachel.

PART THREE

RACHEL FLEISHMAN IS IN TROUBLE

Vindication was coming. If you decided to look at Toby's life from atypical metrics that did not account for Rachel's existence or the three weeks she'd been gone or a history of their marriage or the way Solly was falling apart under a mask of fake cheer and wetting his bed at night, or how Hannah was solemn and sleeping later and later, or how the trauma was cementing into a condition, it might just be that he was doing fine. His children were healthy. He was solvent. He was getting promoted today. He was fucking a beautiful woman. Vindication was here.

This was it. This was the day it all changed. He took out a white shirt and a navy tie. He hadn't worn a tie since God knows when. He watched himself knot it up in the bathroom mirror, and he thought about ambition.

"Ambition can exist without eating your whole life, Rachel," he said to the mirror. "People who are good don't need ambition. Success comes and finds them. See? Competence and excellence are rewarded for those who are competent and excellent."

You could just be sincere and earnest and find yourself there—maybe not meteorically, but you could find yourself there. You don't have to kneecap anyone else. You don't have to eat your young. You can just quietly do good work. The system still favors good work. He felt so overwhelmed by pride and redemption that for a minute, he didn't wish that anything in his life were different. Not even anything. Not even a little.

He woke the children up, but Hannah wouldn't get out of bed. "Please don't make me go back there," she said from beneath the covers.

"I can't be late today. It's a big day for me."

"Why? Because your patient is dying?"

"Because, well, I didn't tell you this." Hannah peeked out from beneath her covers. "Today is the day that I am being made head of my subdivision."

He watched as Hannah resisted but then finally her face broke. "You're going to be the boss?"

"I'm going to be *a* boss."

At breakfast she told Solly, "Daddy's going to be the boss today. They're making him the boss."

"*A* boss. Not *the* boss. But that's good because *the* boss never gets to see patients anymore. I still get to see my patients." Toby had never felt bigger in his life.

"My stomach hurts again," Solly said.

"It's going to be a long day," Toby told Hannah. "If you don't go to the Y you have to sit in my conference room and not complain."

"Yes!" they both shouted.

At the hospital, he deposited them in what he now thought of as their conference room and made his rounds with his fellows. He saw three patients, and with each one he thought, This person is lucky that I am his doctor. Competence! Expertise! This was your Toby. This was your Dr. Fucking Fleishman.

He was updating a chart at the nurses' station computer when his phone went off. This was it. He told his fellows to take a break and headed to Bartuck's office.

"Have you checked on your patient?" Bartuck asked, and flicked his chin in indication for Toby to sit down.

"David Cooper is still hoping for a miracle."

"She's brain dead. The miracle already didn't happen."

"Yes, sir. We thought we'd give him one more day to come to terms before talking about it again."

"Hospital experience is reported worse in families whose loved ones are left to linger. Remember that." Bartuck had his hands folded on his desk. He squinted. "I'm going to just say it because there's no easy way to do it."

"No, I spoke to him. I think Marco already told him. They just need some time."

"No, not that. It's about your position." The moment stretched out while Toby blinked out of sequence. He suddenly felt cold. He heard Bartuck's words, but not in order. "Someone job for hired else we the."

Toby watched as the thing that was in front of him became real. His mouth was open.

"Sorry, Toby I'm."

"What? Who?"

"Outside hired someone from here they wanted we new blood some in."

"You're hiring someone from outside to be my boss?"

"Be the to yes subdivision head."

Toby looked out Bartuck's window. You could see the park and all the way over to the East Side from here. He had forgotten to call the super again about the ceiling stain. He shook his head. "I thought it was decided."

"Nobody doubts your skill," Bartuck was saying. "But they felt like you were unwilling to give the time."

"Time? I've been here every day and every night on the Cooper case. How much more time could I give?"

"You've taken how many personal days in the last three weeks?"

"So that's it? I'm just never going to get ahead here? I've been here for fourteen years. I've had a bad couple of weeks."

"You're an excellent doctor," Bartuck said. "Everyone agrees. But there were some concerns that you don't show any interest in research, that your grant didn't exactly work out, that you were a clock watcher. . . ." The rest didn't really matter. Phillipa had objections to Toby's appointment. Phillipa, who only watched clocks to ensure she was working as performatively long as possible! "I didn't say never. If you start putting in the face time, you never know what could happen."

"Phillipa's had this position for nine years, sir. I can't wait another nine years for a promotion."

Bartuck stood up and walked around to sit on his desk. "I'm sure you'll understand that we expect you to come to drinks tonight to celebrate Dr. Schwartz."

Toby shook his head. "Of course, sir." He had a feeling that if he were the type of guy to storm out of here, he would have been the type of guy to get the job. "Schwartz?"

"Aaron Schwartz."

Aaron fucking Schwartz. Now his boss. "We were in med school together."

"Well, that's good for him to have someone here who knows the ropes."

Toby nodded and stood up and left.

Toby stayed in a bathroom stall with his head between his legs for twenty-five long minutes and listened to a make-out session and one slurpy bout of oral sex between two residents and one very unfortunate gastrointestinal incident from an orderly.

He had fucked up his life. He had done all of it wrong. He left the stall and went to wash his hands. The electric hand dryer had instructions on it that said FEEL THE POWER with an arrow for where you were supposed to put your hands. He looked in the mirror. He was a tiny piece-of-shit motherfucker. Feel the power. *What* power? Rachel had been right. Fuck, Rachel had been right. Toby thought he would collapse from the sadness and injustice he felt—he wouldn't be able to handle one more second of it. He would be found by poor Clay, who was trying to take a nap for the first time in his twenty-four-hour shift. Clay would call in the nurses to suture his bleeding, here and there, holes in his heart and his lungs and his tear ducts.

But they wouldn't be able to save him. One day, this would be just another thing in the block universe, which already contained such a load of shit, what did one more thing matter?

He wasn't in his office for more than a minute before Joanie popped her head in. Joanie. *Joanie.* "They just sent a man to CT from the ER. They want you to consult in about twenty minutes down there."

"Got it. Come on in."

She sat down across from his desk.

"How are things going for you, Joanie?"

"You mean, like, here?"

"Yeah, in general."

"Fine. I've learned a lot. I can't believe I saw a case of Wilson's. It's sad that she's going to die."

"Yeah." He stood up and walked around the desk and sat down on it. "You know, I think you're really talented."

She smiled nervously. "Are you about to give me bad news?"

She was so kind and special. She *liked* him—just for him. She appreciated and respected him. This was what he wanted. He wanted what Seth had. He wanted what I had. No, he wanted something even better than what we had, and something more specific. Yes, he was finally able to narrow in on the exact kind of person he wanted: a plain, nonspectacular person to love him back. He wanted someone to root for him. He wanted to be the star in the relationship, just this once.

"I was wondering," he said. "Do you want to come out to have dinner with me and the kids tonight?"

She looked up at him, confused. "I . . . what? Like to babysit?"

"No, *with* us. I thought maybe, since you're not on tonight, we could all go to this Italian place we like."

How did this take him so long? He'd been so cynical about the Bartucks and about all the other guys who ended up with their subordinates. But honestly, what were you supposed to do? Just keep fucking random women forever? Turn down what is so obviously a beautiful opportunity and a delicate solution?

The kids would love Joanie. She would be a calming influence on Hannah; she could undo all the poison Rachel had injected into her veins about fitting in and aspiring. She, with her weird old-man clothes and strange vintage proclivities, could show a girl what it's like to be comfortable in her own skin. And Solly. Solly would have another person in his life who could validate his interests and let him be his own wonderful oddball self. Someone else who could talk about the universe with him—yes, someone who had also taken physics, Rachel. Someone who understood that the things that made Solly different also made him great.

It would be strange around the office, sure, but this relationship wouldn't exactly be like the rest of them. He would be taking as his partner someone who was his equal, just a little behind. Not a subordinate, not a nurse, not someone who would make his restaurant reservations—no, an equal. He would be doing the same thing Rachel was doing, really; he would be finding someone on his level, who appreciated him and didn't want him to change. Things hadn't worked out for him and Rachel. Long before she left, things weren't working out. They had been matched fine once, but not anymore. Now they were fully formed adults and that meant they knew what they wanted and what they needed. He wanted someone who found what he did to be as incredible and transcendent as it was. Joanie. Joanie! *Joanie*.

Why were the walls made out of glass? He should be able to walk over to her and put her face in his hands and say, "You are who I've been waiting for all this time."

Instead, he kept his distance and said: "Joanie. You're right that I've been going through something. I know you have, too. But maybe we shouldn't spend another day . . . What I'm trying to say is that you've been right here all along, and I don't know how I missed you." He let himself trail off because he heard his own words and they moved him and scared him equally. Yes, he thought. This was so right.

She looked at him for a second. "No, uh, thank you." She stood up. "Thank you for asking, though." She took a step back. "I'm going to check on that consult, okay?" She didn't wait for an answer.

Fuck.

He looked beyond the glass of his office and saw Gilda staring at him. He wasn't going to Aaron Schwartz's party. It was ridiculous to expect him to. He had to get his kids home. If they were going to persecute him for being a father, then he'd be a father.

He walked into the conference room. "Gather your stuff," he said to the kids. "We're going home."

"To celebrate?" Solly asked.

"Celebration's off. We're going out for pasta."

"Toby," Marco said, the next day.

"Marco," Toby said.

"Did you meet the new guy?"

"I know him from before."

"Seems nice enough. Not sure why they had to bring someone in from the outside."

Toby almost took this as a compliment, but then realized that Marco was talking about himself. Marco probably wouldn't have gotten a lashing like Toby, but he was hard to promote, too. He was cold as his scalpel and an unrivaled sexual harasser of his fellows.

He went to Karen Cooper's room. His fellows were there. He kept his eyes on his patient to avoid looking at Joanie or, more specifically, seeing how she was looking at him. He didn't know if he should apologize, or just wait for a call from HR. David Cooper was holding Karen's hand, staring at her lifeless face. He was never going to see his wife open her eyes again. Toby watched him, unable to reconcile any of this. Was he a piece of shit or did he love his wife? Was he having an affair with her friend, who helped break up the marriage? Were we all everything?

He took David outside the room. It was a good practice to not discuss the patient's imminent death in front of the unconscious patient—it read as rude, somehow.

"This is just how it goes sometimes," Toby said.

You could say that David Cooper was lucky. He got to say his goodbye. He got to be eased into the death. But he wouldn't say that. He would say that what happened wasn't fair. But what do the David Coopers of the world know about fair? As if the David Coopers of the world really wanted to be part of a system that's fair. It didn't matter. Because none of this was fair. His son was pissing his bed and his daughter was absent a maternal figure who could have maybe prevented her from getting publicly humiliated all because she was out on some wonderfuckfest with Sam Rothberg. Piece of shit Sam Rothberg, who wore nylon Adidas pants with stripes on the side on Sundays, and who had endless bets on endless brackets for March Madness. This was fair? That he would smile and take it up the ass during mediation so that they could present their children with a peaceful and amicable thing, and then the minute it was almost done, she would do the worst thing she could possibly do—a thing so bad that it wasn't even close on a list of horrible things she had done prior to this? *That* was fair? If it were fair, and you weighed Toby's sins against his punishments, you would find that he'd gotten some real kind of raw deal. What did he do so wrong but be devoted? What did he do so wrong but try? But love? But come home on time? But figure that his wife would be a partner to him the way he was to her? But maybe throw a few glasses and maybe say the wrong things?

God, he was so tired of trying to figure out how it had been wrong, what the micromaneuver that set Rachel free from him was. She had abandoned him. She'd been cruel to him. She had denied him love and respect and self-esteem. She had diminished him to become someone who nearly disintegrated into suspicion and then sorrow at the mere affectionate touch of someone. She'd been cruel to their children—their children! She'd left them! She knew what it was to be without parents and still she'd left them!

And that was when he realized it: Yes, he was angry. Holy Jesus, was he angry. All his marriage, Rachel threw around an accusation of anger that he immediately deflected, but now he couldn't see why. What was ever the merit in pretending he wasn't? What was wrong with being angry? Why was it not allowable as a standard of human emotions? Yes, he was so angry his knees might buckle. He was angry, and he could no longer see why the winning move was to pretend he wasn't. He was angry and he wanted to scream it into David Cooper's face, and then Joanie's and Clay's and Logan's, and then Bartuck's, and then mine and Seth's, and then, with all the charge this gave him, he would find Rachel and blow his anger at her until she ceased to exist so that she would only have the brief satisfaction of being right for a few seconds, and that his rage would be the last thing she ever knew before she evaporated. It sounded in his ears like a bell—no, like a siren. He could hear it. He could really hear it. His rage had a *sound* and it was a *siren*.

But no, the sound was coming from Karen Cooper's room. A nurse ran inside. Toby and David rushed in after. Karen Cooper had suffered a pulmonary embolism and was flatlining. The cart came in; Logan and Clay tried their best. Within a few minutes, he gave Clay the nod to call the time of death.

His fellows began to inch out, but he stopped them with his hand. It was important to stay for the hardest parts of this job. Toby used to wonder how he could ever be a good doctor if he couldn't understand death, if he was still so shook by it. But sometime in the last five years, as he thought more and more about things that are alive and things that are dead, he began to think that the fact that death still made him so wobbly was exactly the key to being a great doctor. We aren't meant to comprehend endings. We aren't meant to understand death. Death's whole gig is not being understood. The social worker on the floor came in and Toby followed the remaining Coopers to the bereavement room and told him how sorry he was for their loss.

The last place I lived in Manhattan before I moved to New Jersey was on the Upper East Side. Adam and I had gotten married and he owned a big place on Seventy-ninth, whereas I was renting my tiny, damp, moldy, perfect studio in the Village. On Saturday mornings, Adam would go play racquetball, and I would go to a bagel place on Seventy-seventh that had good coffee and I'd order a poppy bagel with butter and sit by myself. The Sunday morning I left Toby's apartment, I got coffee there and sat outside, eating my bagel, wearing my clothes from the night before, and smoking cigarettes. Have I ever been happier? I wondered. I wondered this despite the pit in my stomach and the tingling behind my nose that was asking me to answer the question about what the fuck I was doing in Manhattan on a Sunday morning in last night's clothing.

That was when I saw her.

She was sitting at a table on the sidewalk next to me. I hadn't seen her in years, and she looked different, but there she was, her same hair color at least, her same lithe body, eating a bagel.

I froze but it was too late. She saw me and squinted. I half waved, unsure of what my stance here should be. What do you do when you run into a ghost who had recently been the object of your summertime obsession? It's not a thing you can really plan for.

"Libby?" she asked, approaching.

"Rachel," I said. "Hi."

"It's been a really long time," she said. "I don't think I've seen you since Hannah was born?" She appeared to be trying to solve a math equation in her head.

Up close she looked different. Not just older than the last time I'd seen her, but also disheveled. She was wearing a pair of sweatpants that sagged at the crotch and a workout tank top that said NAH 'MA STAY IN BED.

She wasn't wearing makeup except for red lipstick, which only drew attention to the purple crescents beneath her eyes. Her hair was in a strange pixie cut, totally disarranged and yet, had it been brushed, matronly and unflattering. She had tried to cover the lines around her eyes and mouth with foundation, but it was caked inside them, and it hadn't been blended, so her face was a mask of several colors.

"Are you okay?" I asked.

She closed her eyes. "I'm fine." She opened them again. "How have you been? What are you doing here?"

"I . . . I stayed in the city last night. I'm about to go home." I didn't know what to say, so I said, "Rachel, what's going on?"

"With what?"

"I'm . . . in touch with Toby. He is worried about you. Your children." I couldn't finish.

She looked confused. "You've seen my kids? I didn't know you and Toby still spoke."

I thought of Solly calling to Toby from his bedroom. "Yeah. They're not doing great." She looked beyond my right shoulder. I turned around to see what she saw there. Nothing. I looked back at her. She seemed drugged. "Should I take you somewhere?"

"I was supposed to go to SoulCycle but I went on the wrong day."

"Do you need some coffee?" I looked at her bagel. It was whole; she hadn't taken a bite of it. It had nothing on it. It wasn't even cut in half. It was just a giant bagel she was holding, with apparently no intention of eating it.

Finally, I said, "Rachel. What happened to you? Are you okay? Can I call Toby?"

She looked at me and squinted. She shook her head to try to focus. "Don't call Toby. You can't call Toby."

"Why not? Someone else? A friend?"

"I don't have any friends."

"Of course you have friends." But maybe she didn't. What did I know?

Rachel stared at her bagel. Every now and again, she'd react to a small noise by jumping and looking around to see what it was, then looking at me as if for confirmation that things were out of order if so many loud noises were in play.

"Are the kids doing okay?" she asked. "I keep meaning to call them."

"You keep meaning to call them? You were supposed to pick them up three weeks ago. They think you've abandoned them."

She looked off over my shoulder again, but this time I didn't turn around. I just stared at her face. She was so gaunt. I should call someone.

"Toby knows why I'm not there. He can pretend all he wants, but he knows."

"He doesn't. I'm certain he doesn't."

She stared off at the other people in the bagel place. Every time she blinked she'd keep her eyes closed for a full two seconds.

And then she told me what happened to her.

Sam Rothberg had a nephew who wanted to be a Broadway actor, so he asked Rachel if she would go to dinner one night with them— this was when she was still with Toby, maybe two years ago. Of course, she said. She always said yes. She was in perpetual service to the Sam Rothbergs of the world and everyone at the school for whom she could do a favor. Miriam Rothberg was the closest the kids' school had to royalty. Miriam didn't even have to serve on the Parents Association. She and her money funded just about every single school initiative, which put her in this constant kind of advisor role for all the committees. She had so much power that she'd actually gotten homework eliminated completely—completely! homework!—in the lower school after "urging" the nervous, anemic principal to read through a three-hundred-page document she'd hired an education PhD from Barnard to assemble about the cost-benefit of after-school homework.

By the time Hannah was enrolled in pre-K, Rachel had achieved a lot in her life. She'd survived a literally parentsless upbringing, thrived despite the apathy of her grandmother, given birth twice (once under the diciest of conditions), married a nice man at a reasonable age so that she wouldn't encounter bad fertility odds, and gutted the oldest and largest full-service medium-sized creative agency in New York and created her own version of it, but better. She was the subject of trade paper profiles, then an actual profile in the "Go Get 'Em, Badass!" column of a women's magazine that she'd read when she was young. She was a high-level source for major journalists; she was the recipient of awards for woman-owned businesses. She'd discovered Alejandra Lopez—*Alejandra Lopez*. She'd helped usher *Presidentrix* into a *not*-one-woman musical and instead a full Broadway show not dependent on the health and stability of just one woman. She represented her after she'd dragged no less than Matt Klein himself out to the projects to see the show, and he'd called Alejandra a "no-talent windbag." She represented a carefully cultivated group of talents that you've definitely heard of. But by the end of Hannah's first year of school, Rachel would honestly say that her greatest achievement in life was getting Miriam Rothberg interested enough in Pilates to try it out with her at the studio near Rachel's office, and committing to a weekly class.

"It's such an efficient workout, too," Rachel said to her when they went to get smoothies after.

Miriam blithely agreed and then had her house manager—*her house manager*—schedule the private weekly with Rachel's assistant. Rachel attended like it was her job. All the playdates flowed through Miriam Rothberg. All the fundraisers and chances for socializing and acceptance for her children were contained in Miriam's seat of power. She and Sam Rothberg had twin boys in Hannah's grade and a boy Solly's age, Jack, who wasn't half as smart or curious as her Solly and whose eyes were too close together and would still have a better life because of who his parents were. They had a fourth child, a girl, whom they'd gotten by paying a bazillion dollars to spin Sam Rothberg's sperm down into only the girl molecules. They'd bought a girl! They controlled gender!

Miriam was small-boned and short and daffy and disorganized, and she was one of the only women Rachel had ever met who was truly free. She had no burdens. She thought she did—her wealth, her sense of social responsibility, her kids who were raised by an army of other people—but being born rich, you never really know about burden, or survival, no matter how much you think you feel it. *Becoming* rich, however, you never forget what it's like to know how close the bottom is, how easily you could be back there. Miriam didn't know about survival; she didn't know about burdens. She didn't even have the burden of supervising the many people who worked for her. Her house manager and chief of staff—*her chief of staff*—oversaw the dozens of people on her and Sam's payroll: the housekeepers and personal assistants and nannies who would travel with them, the housekeepers and groundskeepers for their supplementary four houses—I'm sorry, excuse me, three houses and a *villa*.

All this help freed Miriam up to have a life of input: what the school should be doing for the winter fundraiser (aside from asking her for a check), what the kids should be doing after school (and would Hannah like to join in on a Mandarin tutor because it would be so much more effective if they could practice with each other during lunch at school), who should be running for office in New York City. Yes, she ran actual candidates for office. Her money allowed her to have a feminist streak despite having never experienced the pitfalls of the male-dominated world the way it existed: the Matt Kleins, the low expectations, the way people either were baffled or professed to be baffled by your existence, the patronizing you-go girls, the "she's the boss" from the husband who can only say that because they both absolutely knew who the boss was and it was certainly not her. Miriam had only *heard* of gender imbalance; how could she have experienced it? She didn't work. She didn't do anything but donate and exercise, donate and exercise, donate and exercise. When she put her money toward feminist causes, she was actually just addressing *rumors* she'd heard of a patriarchy.

But she could do that. She could pick and choose her interests. Miriam Rothberg was able to think straight and read books and think about who she would vote for and be sexually available to her husband because that was what money did. It bought you an additional life that ran parallel to your regular life, and between those two lives your goals were somehow achieved and everyone around you was satisfied. Must be nice, Rachel thought.

"I don't know how you do it, Rachel," Miriam would say as they ingested a superfood after class. Roxanne and Cyndi would make mmm noises. "Running around like this. Just the kids alone!" As if Miriam were watching her own kids. Rachel was, was the thing. Not all the time; she had Mona. And she had Toby, thank God, who was actually interested in participating in his children's lives. But Rachel was involved in a way that Miriam couldn't be. Rachel and Mona were in touch ten times a day. Rachel made every decision. She knew where her kids were every minute.

One day, early on, when Solly and Jack were three, Rachel took off work when Miriam texted to see if they wanted to let the nannies have an hour off and go to the Music n Me class with the boys. Rachel canceled an interview for it—she was meeting with a potential new assistant—and said, "Okay!" like giving the nanny an hour off was a thing she had ever done. Now she needed a new assistant. But she saw that to stay in Miriam's orbit, you had to be available to her, and she felt like she was paying a large investment forward if she could be somewhat socially available and also not rely on these women for pathetic favors that would make them dread her. ("Can you pick Hannah up? My meeting's gone late.") So she went to the class and she and Miriam met on the street walking in. They entered the music place together and both Solly and Jack rushed toward them. Equally. Equally, as if their mothers were both invested exactly the same amount in motherhood. Equally, as if the depth of devotion Miriam displayed were even a reasonable percentage of what Rachel displayed. As if Rachel hadn't been up all night researching after-school programs and as if she didn't check Mona's receipts for what she was feeding the kids and what neighborhoods she was taking them to. As if Rachel didn't have to make choices, like only exercising when it forwarded her children's social agenda and never doing the actual exercise (running) that she liked. But look at them here: There was no difference, no lesser bond. It infuriated her. She clapped her hands and tapped the drums and shook the rattles according to the goofy leader's instructions and all she could wonder was what the hell was she doing this all for if Jack Rothberg was going to love Miriam Rothberg as much as Solly loved her. She didn't yet realize that children's love was like parents' love: It was understanding and enduring and destined to be a little fucked up.

Rachel had been raised on a bread-and-water diet of silence and resignation and resentment. Her grandmother didn't love her, but it was okay because her grandmother didn't love. She was cold but she was dutiful, and at least there was that. Her grandmother thought duty was the same thing as love, but it couldn't be because duty and love are two different verticals. They're two different movies. Duty couldn't be interpreted as love or as admiration or as comfort. Duty was only the lowest denominator of what you had to do, and nuns in an orphanage would have done the same. Rachel understood that it wasn't quite fair that her grandmother had raised her mother and now had to raise her mother's daughter. It wasn't fair that her own daughter was dead.

Her grandmother's chill infiltrated every aspect of their lives. The house was sparsely decorated and drafty. She fed Rachel in front of the television, lest Rachel dare talk about her day. She wore the same practical clothing for years, one "blouse" and one pair of "slacks" that were nearly identical to yesterday's. She didn't wear jewelry or laugh. To spend a lot of money was to indulge in an emotion, and her grandmother avoided emotion wherever possible. The most she ever got was angry: angry at Rachel's laziness or her questions or her giddiness or her childishness or her neediness or her humanness—her need to be fed three times a day. She was angry that Rachel wanted to play basketball or join the cheerleaders or try out for the school play. She was so angry and the anger was so scary that Rachel stopped asking for approximations of normal childhood and instead settled for what would have to pass for love, which was the absence of outward displays of animosity and rage.

Had Rachel ever complained, her grandmother wouldn't have understood what she was talking about. She was home every day when Rachel arrived. She cooked every meal. "You never went barefoot," her grandmother liked to say. She sent her to private school, a great tax on her savings and Social Security, even after the financial aid: a fancy Catholic school, even though they were Jewish, attended by the children of diplomats in D.C. and other fancy people. Her grandmother thought that she could have a good education and that would somewhat make up for all the ways Rachel had been let down so far in life. See, she wasn't totally a *monster*. More like she didn't know how to be a *person*.

But Rachel was miserable. She lived in Mount Washington, where all the middle-class Jews lived, but all her classmates were rich Gentiles and lived in Ruxton or Green Spring Valley or on no-kidding a private island near Annapolis. They were picked up in black and dark silver cars driven by chauffeurs who'd been working for them since they were babies. There were layers of wealth she overheard that unlocked for her new dimensions of possibility of privilege and access and what was possible. The girls in her class had first names like Clancy and Devon and Atterleigh and Westerleigh and Bonneleigh and Plum and Poppy and Catherine. And Catherine and Catherine and Catherine and Catherine. They went skiing in Aspen a week before Christmas break started. They went on safari to Africa. They visited a private island in Fiji or boarded a private cruise down the Nile or attended a private tour of the

Galápagos or stayed at a private hotel in Venice or a *private forest* in Brazil. They went to concerts and the opera and took French lessons outside of school and then went to actual France and they became sophisticated in a way that she wasn't—in a way she'd never be because sophistication is either your first language or you always have an accent in it.

In seventh grade, a shy girl named Catherine H. who didn't have many friends asked Rachel if she wanted to take tennis lessons. Rachel knew better than to ask her grandmother. Because it wouldn't just be tennis. It would be the outfits and the dropping off and picking up. It would be the tournaments and practices and the chaos of something new on the schedule. Rachel told Catherine she couldn't do it, but Catherine couldn't understand why.

"Don't you want to?" she asked.

"Honestly?" Rachel said. "It looks kind of boring."

Even though it didn't. It looked fun and exactly like the kind of thing that would allow her to have a group of friends she liked and could call and whose houses she could go over to and whose secrets she could know. She watched TV all the time at home so that she would one day know how to approximate normal personhood when she finally got the chance, and there was a show on cable where two best friends would sometimes talk while they brushed each other's hair, or while one was on a toilet. She used to think about that all the time, the hair brushing and the peeing. What it must feel like for someone to be touching your hair. What it must be like to feel free in front of someone. The girls who played tennis looked like they would brush each other's hair and urinate in front of one another. Catherine H. did end up taking the tennis lessons and became close with the tennis girls. Then she went to tennis camp, which was sleepaway, where they probably brushed each other's hair every night and maybe there wasn't even a door on the bathroom. One day, while she was there, she called Rachel. They weren't close, but Rachel had been too lonely that summer to be skeptical about the phone call. Catherine H.

told her she had a new boyfriend named Trey, and would Rachel like to speak to the boyfriend? Rachel said that of course she would. Rachel stayed on the phone and the boyfriend spoke to her for five minutes before he said, "We hear you like to suck cock. . . ." and then there were squeals of laughter in the background. It took Rachel a minute to realize what was happening, but by then they had hung up on her, and she was left holding the phone, looking at it.

She didn't want to be different anymore. She began shoplifting very expensive clothing in seventh grade. Her grandmother only took her to White Marsh to Woodies, which was a shitty department store her schoolmates would never walk into. On her own she went to the Nordstrom in the Columbia Mall with the sixty dollars she'd collected from a summer job as a mother's helper. Her school had a uniform: a plaid skirt issued by the school and a white button-down shirt. You could buy the shirt from the school, too, but most of the girls bought Ralph Lauren menswear shirts with little polo symbols on the breast. They kept the shirts open or one size too small so that you could see a very aggressive piece of lingerie right at the sternum. If she could only do that, she thought. If she could only look like the rest of them.

But the shirt cost ninety dollars. She went to try it on. It looked great on her. She looked like one of them. She couldn't leave without it. She knew that other girls shoplifted. They talked about it. They had plenty of money, which made it strange and pathological. But Rachel—Rachel needed to do it. She did it because it was a practical means of survival for her. That day, she just walked out of the store with the shirt. At a very fancy store, expensive shirts didn't have tags that would set off alarms because ninety dollars wasn't expensive. She ripped off a black lace push-up bra with a demicup whose tag had a picture of a woman touching her own face in the throes of ecstasy, as if just wearing the bra would do it for you. She arrived at school the next day with her shirt, the bra underneath, but it didn't help. It was too late. It was all too late.

Her sentence had been written. She just had to wait it out so that she could get to college and have a new start. And she did.

Then she met Toby. Finally, a man loved her and chose her. The way he looked at her, the way he made her feel settled and permanent in the world. She went to visit the home where he was raised and she saw the chaos and stability and she knew that this man contained all this within himself and she could, too. They married.

She started in the mailroom at Alfooz & Lichtenstein, the oldest and largest full-service medium-sized creative agency in the city, and found a place where she could channel the churning she felt into accomplishment. She was hit on by her boss, then lost a partnership because she was pregnant. This was only one of the awful parts of being pregnant. Right before you were pregnant, you were a person. The minute you became an incubator for another life, you got reduced to your parts. The insults were grand, but they were also subtle. Throughout her pregnancy, people called her *cute*. They said she was *adorable*.

Her subordinates threw her a baby shower and reduced her hard, cold glass-and-metal office to a gooey muck of pastel streamers whose evidence she still found for weeks afterward. This wasn't a party, she thought when she was there. This was a glimpse into her future. She thought of her own regard for mothers and motherhood. She thought of how every mother she knew seemed neutered to her, like they were not serious people. How had she not realized that she was joining a club she could barely tolerate? Exactly who had ever overcome the way being a mother turns you into something soft and ridiculous? She was not considered perfect before, she knew that. But now she would have to fight to just be considered regular.

And then a man literally cut her open to get at the only reason she was alive.

Toby went back to work six weeks after Hannah was born, but Rachel didn't. At six weeks, she'd wait for Mona to take Hannah on her walk and then would go into the living room, where at eleven

A.M. a ray of sunlight streamed through the window, and she would sit in the warm spot, first on her knees, and then she would bend over like a Muslim in prayer and stay there and cry. How could it be, she wondered. How could it be that the simple act of having a child did this to you? Had every birth in the world ruined every woman in the world? Was this a secret they'd been keeping, or had she just not been listening? Underneath all the vacuous, cruel wisdom the women who saw her in her late stages of pregnancy imparted to her, most of which had to do with banking sleep or measuring every precious moment because it all goes so fast, were they really telling her to mark her personhood?

The other women in her prenatal yoga class had kept up an email chain, and in their messages, she tried to discern that they, too, were terrified and violated and sad and broken, but they weren't. Trust her, they just weren't. They made jokes about how they were tired and it was a tragedy that one of them had had an epidural and it was a tragedy that one of them couldn't produce enough milk for her baby and had to supplement with formula. She wanted to write back to tell them she couldn't look in the mirror at herself. She wanted someone to understand how small she was now. She wanted to ask one of them if this was the real her—if the real her had been revealed to her suddenly that day in the hospital, or if she would somehow bounce back. Bouncing back was a language they understood: their vaginas needed to bounce back, their breasts needed to bounce back, would their abdomens ever bounce back. With a few small adjustments, these women would acclimate to life. They would recognize themselves. But would Rachel? Would *Rachel* bounce back? The entire phrase "bouncing back" seemed to her like it existed to make fun of her. There was no bouncing. There was no back.

So she sat in a fucking rape group and people told her how they were held down at gunpoint and knifepoint or how a boyfriend had turned violent and terrifying one night or how they woke up and didn't know where they were or how they'd gotten there but they

were somehow pantyless and would later find out they were pregnant or suddenly had chlamydia. She sat there with her baby, and
every time it was her turn to talk, she began to cry. She didn't cry
quietly. She howled and they just let her. They just let her do it for
five whole minutes until the other women gathered around her and
squatted down in front of her and patted her on her shoulders and
her knees until she stopped.

One day, at the hospital, she was leaving the group and she
ended up in an elevator with Romalino, who didn't recognize her.
She had four floors with him alone. She had four floors to say to
him, LOOK, LOOK WHAT YOU DID TO A PERFECTLY GOOD
PERSON. YOU RUINED ME. But she couldn't. Instead, she turned
away from him so that she was facing the wall of the elevator like a
freak, huddled over Hannah, and her heart pounded, and after it
was over she still couldn't look in the mirror because what kind of
fucking coward was she anyway. She was not what she thought she
was. She was exactly what Matt Klein thought she was. She was
what this doctor thought she was. She was nothing. She was just a
woman. This was her introduction to motherhood.

She listened to the women talk about their rapes. One of them
didn't remember her rape. She had woken up one morning, evidence everywhere, but no memory of the thing. A policeman told
her that not remembering the rape made it barely reportable. Rachel kept wondering if she'd be bothered by what Romalino did if
she'd only been informed of it and didn't experience it consciously.
She didn't know. This woman seemed just as upset as the others,
but Rachel didn't think she would be under the same circumstances.
The memories were what bothered her, how she couldn't lie on her
back without remembering all of it and so didn't sleep on her back.
She slept on her side, or upright, or not at all.

After her fourth visit to the rape group, one of the women asked
her if she wanted to get coffee afterward, and Rachel was jerked
awake to the fraud she was perpetuating. What if they found out?
What if she revealed herself and they turned on her and screamed

at her for mocking their pain? She said no, she was sorry, she couldn't, she was expected somewhere, and she never returned. She hadn't been raped. She had a healthy baby. She had had a rough delivery. Toby was right. *She hadn't been raped*. Pull it together, Fleishman.

And there was also a small tinge of this other thing, which was that she couldn't ever quite think about these women without wondering what else she had in common with them. They also didn't know if they'd been born targets, or if this just happened to them because they existed. There were so many ways of being a woman in the world, but all of them still rendered her just a woman, which is to say: a target. What had made Romalino think she was the kind of person who would stand for this? Was it the same thing that had made her not punch Matt Klein in the face when he'd put his hands on her? ("Wait, he put his hands on you? I thought it was just a verbal thing?" "I'm not talking about that now.")

She had to figure out what that thing was and eliminate it from herself, and spending more time with these women would make her more like them, not less. Because she wasn't a victim like all these women. She was the power. She was the thing that traumatized. She wouldn't ever be mistaken for the other again.

The next week, instead of going to her rape group, she went to the park with Hannah and wandered over to the playground off Seventy-second Street. She sat down. Her eyes wandered over to the other benches. There was a group of nannies tending to kids and talking to one another on one bench. On the other bench was a group of moms, three of whom had been in her prenatal yoga group. She walked over, happy to see them, and happy to be seen doing something as normal as visiting a park with her baby in a stroller. But she saw one of them spot her as she walked over and whisper something to the others out of the side of her face before smiling big and saying, "*Rachel*." She'd had no idea. They had all been in touch throughout. They continued to get together. Their kids would be friends with each other. She was excluded once again. It hit her slowly, then all at once: Having a child was signing up for enduring her entire childhood all over again. How could no one tell her?

Well, if that was true, this time she was going to do it right. Her social climbing, as Toby called it, wasn't about her and her childhood; it was about her kids. A thing about growing up the way Rachel did was that whether or not you liked being lonely, aloneness became your body's resting condition—its set point. Which is to say that she didn't want *friends*. She didn't like Miriam and Roxanne and Cyndi, or they weren't the friends she wanted. *Toby* was the friend she wanted. *Toby* was the friend she had for life. Toby was who she could be alone with. When you are someone who is rejected her entire childhood for reasons that feel impossible to discern, there is little that could happen to you in your future that doesn't feel like further rejection. Miriam likes you, but why weren't you invited to massages on Great Jones Street with her? Roxanne wants to know if you want to come for dinner before the kids have their sleepover, but then she mentions that she and Cyndi had been shopping all day and it's not that she wants to go shopping with those two, it's just that she wants to be *invited*. She wants to think she is integral to their lives. She wants them to look at her and her children like they're not *optional*. Toby didn't understand why she cared or why it mattered. How could he? He had a sister that he totally took for granted. He had parents—a mother whom he blamed for his terrible self-image, never once taking into consideration that the person he was talking to about this would have killed to have a mother to blame for anything. He had all those friends who wanted to be in his life from his youth. He had Seth. He had me. He had all the people who had ever seen him needy and pathetic and never once did that make it so that they didn't still love him.

The other problem was harder to put words to. Toby had a good job. He loved his good job. He was good at his good job. Fine. But the demands of the life that they both agreed they wanted required something that Toby's good job couldn't give them. Fine. She hadn't had these thoughts back when they were dating. When they were dating, she thought it was lucky that she had fallen in love with someone who was altruistic and smart and wanted to make sick people better. But they had shared values that they'd agreed upon. Rachel told Toby one night, whispering under the covers in her tiny dorm bed, all about her school and Catherine H. and tennis and that phone call. She said she never wanted to put children through that. He said, "I won't ever let it happen." He was talking about emotional support. She was talking about financial support. Maybe they hadn't agreed after all.

She tried for years to get him to negotiate upward, to want more, but he just didn't. More money would have been nice, he said, but what she was asking of him was to do something completely different than what he did, which was "heal the sick" (the self-righteousness was not a small thing to negotiate in these conversations). Not really, she'd said. Anything different from what I do now feels corrupt and morally repugnant, he'd say. Yes, she'd say. She would like to do kind and wonderful things in the world, too. But what about doing those things for their children first?

"We could move," he'd say.

But where else could she do what she did? Sure, they could live like kings on his salary in rural Pennsylvania, but he'd be signing her death sentence.

"I never misrepresented myself," he'd say.

That was a favorite, as if people weren't supposed to evolve and change and make requests of each other to bend and grow and expand.

At some point, she accepted it. It was up to her to make the kind of living that would allow them to participate in the life they'd signed up for. He accepted it, too. He pretended to be apathetic to the money, but you should have seen how he liked the car. You should have seen how he liked the club—the pool on the rooftop, way above the city, both metaphorically and actually. So Toby adjusted his schedule to be home a little early to relieve Mona, the babysitter. He stood back and allowed her to try for this big thing she wanted to do. She did it, not out of bravery, but out of two parts no choice and three parts because to see Matt Klein again would have been to commit a failure she couldn't have come back from.

So she did her work and Toby made the noises of someone who was stepping back, but he didn't really do it. He came home on time, sure. He made dinner when Mona didn't. But he didn't adjust his expectations of her, or leave room for how tired she could get or how harried or busy. He loved taking those long walks. No matter how late they were, he wanted to walk. Across the park, across the city. She kept trying to explain to him that time functioned in units. For all his love of physics, he never quite grasped that one: If you use this time to walk to dinner that is thirty-five blocks away instead of letting me finish this email in a cab on the way there, I will be finishing the email at the table. The email isn't optional. The email is the *entire thing*.

"Some people would say that it all could wait," he'd say.

But he didn't understand the *volume*. He didn't understand that you had to return Roxanne's stupid eye-roll emoji about something Cyndi said with an LOL, or that you had to let Cyndi know when the sleepover was or that you had to tell Miriam to STD May fifth for Solly's birthday because she plans months in advance and not having Jack at Solly's birthday would be a disaster and put both friendships on shaky ground. He could never really be aware of what he couldn't actually see. If he didn't see the exchange with Mona, it didn't happen. If he didn't see the totally degrading conversation with Miriam, he didn't understand the sacrifice. If he didn't see all the hours when he was asleep and she was up trying to figure out which preschool had the right philosophies, it didn't happen. All her contributions fell magically from the sky, or were born of something inherent in her female body. He thought her wanting to spend an extra day in Paris on a work trip was a war crime. She had to go to the Tonys and he didn't realize that his hospital gala was that night and she was a terrible person for choosing the Tonys, where she had three different clients getting nominated. He couldn't see the way the volume was crushing her.

Toby had appointments with patients. He had procedures. They were blocks of time and when they were done, they were done. He wasn't expected to be in two places at once. Everything he had to do was performed within a Vegas casino of time, walls placed around moments with no clocks or windows or easy-to-discern ways to exit. He never had to mind his phone under a table because a screenplay was at auction and an actor you represented was about to come out and needed you to help figure out a crisis publicist who could help. Sure, he had emergencies, but there were ten people behind him waiting to rush in for him if he couldn't show, groups of people he trained to be just like him for when he couldn't be there.

Fine. She worked day and night, but fine. She met deadlines and put out fires every day. She had ten, then twenty, then fifty, then a hundred people under her. She serviced more than two hundred actors and writers and producers and directors. *Presidentrix* was being optioned as a movie, and she, yes she, was no longer interested in passing it off to a film agent. She was perfectly capable herself. That was it. No more outsourcing. No more synergistic partnerships. Super Duper Creative was now full service. She grew and grew and there seemed to be no limit to her expansion. It was the opposite of parenthood, and, secretly, a necessary correction for it. It was accomplishment in a way that parenthood absolutely couldn't be. Hannah and Solly grew and she fretted over questions of whether they were too programmed or not programmed enough. Whether they should also be taking German like the Leffers. At night, she would fall asleep and in the wild hallucinogenic minefield of her pre-REM sleep her dead mother came to her and said, "Why can't Solly code yet?" This question rang in her ears for days. An actor's deal got done in a week or two and that was that. She wouldn't know if this whole Hannah and Solly thing worked out until she died and nothing bad had happened yet.

She came home each night—not at the same time, but mostly when the kids were awake—even though the work wasn't done and she finished her work in the kitchen even though it was nearly impossible. Hannah wanted to talk about why she didn't have a phone and Solly wanted to play Uno and Toby wanted her to stare at him adoringly and listen to endless, endless stories about liver diagnoses. She knew so much about that disgusting organ, she could have diagnosed at least four or five major and rare diseases. Here's how it would go every night:

HER: I'm home!

HIM: You'll never believe what happened today and how screwed/ignored/underestimated I was.

HER: Let's talk about it! Let me just say hi to the kids and answer these texts, because I have a premiere tonight. . . .

HIM: You never care about me.

HER: What? How can you say that?

HIM: Listen to you. You're barely here. You're barely a mother.

HER: Did you hear the part where I have a premiere? Did you not hear the part where I want to say hi to the kids?

HIM: I can't bear your anger anymore.

There was no way for her to voice an opinion without being accused of anger. Everywhere she turned in her own home, there was a new insult. She would wake up in the morning and walk out the door with Toby and the kids and before she headed in the direction away from school, she would hear the doorman talk about what a hero Toby was for taking his own children to school. She would bump into one of the teachers from school and the teacher would say, "It's so amazing the way your husband drops them off every morning." She wanted to say, "Isn't it amazing how I pay the fucking mortgage? Isn't it amazing how my children have schedules that are more complex than the president's and that they'll graduate from elementary school prepared for three or four careers that you need a graduate degree for? Isn't it amazing the role model I am for my children?" The teachers would call her a working mom, and somehow that was insulting even as it was true. Maybe because it was such a rarity in the school. Maybe because it applied an aster-isk to her name and seemed to be an explanation for why she was falling short.

They were invited by the Rothbergs to their home upstate for a New Year's party, and while Sam Rothberg and Toby took the boys bowling, Miriam's daughter crawled over to her and Miriam said, "I swear, it never ends." And Rachel agreed wholeheartedly—yes, sure, it appears to never end—but then Rachel said, "You're lucky to still have a baby. I'm sad I didn't have a third one." Miriam asked her why she didn't have a third one, and Rachel said, "I guess I work too much," just because she didn't really want to get into it. She didn't want to get into Toby not wanting a third child because he knew the work would fall on him and she didn't want to deal with constant blame for the way his life wasn't perfect.

But Miriam didn't do the right thing. She didn't nod and smile and try to understand, the way Rachel worked hard to nod and smile and try to understand Miriam's problems in her utterly problem-free life. Instead, she said, "Well, we all *work*."

Rachel was confused.

Miriam and Roxanne shared a look. They'd spoken about this before. "That doesn't mean you work harder than us," Miriam said.

"Right, of course," Rachel said, and then just hated herself wholesale for keeping her mouth shut. The only thing more offen-sive than Miriam not working was Miriam thinking she did work. But Miriam would never know true success. She would never know achievement. She would never know what it was like to build some-thing and hold it in your hands. She would never solve a problem or watch a show where three of her clients all sang a song together and think: These are my children, too.

The week before, she had had dinner with Sam Rothberg and his nephew and she gave advice and told him which acting coaches to talk to, to use her name, and then he should come back to her when the coach says so. After dinner, Sam thanked her and walked her to her apartment. He insisted on walking her to the door, which she thought was weird, but Sam Rothberg had always been nice to her. He told her that there was an opening at his company for a doctor, and the pay was extraordinary. He wanted to know if Toby would ever consider that kind of thing. Rachel didn't know, she said. He should ask him!

She let Sam Rothberg make the approach to Toby over the weekend, and he went crazy. They tried therapy after, but he wouldn't listen. There was nothing but his point of view—that all she did was work and neglect him and the children—that he could talk about. He couldn't even hear what she was saying, which was that she loved her work. That yes, maybe she should slow down, but she didn't quite know how. She didn't know how to trust the people she hired. If he'd listen, he could hear her. She needed help figuring this out.

If she were a man, she thought, her spouse would receive the spoils of her hard work with gratitude. He would allow her to come home from work and put her feet up for a minute before he pummeled her with the ways his life was terrible and nobody respected him and the way Aaron Schwartz was the teachers' favorite and the way Phillipa London was mean to him.

Toby liked his work so much. At least he said he did. But at some point, he forgot that what she did allowed him to do what he wanted to do. He forgot that their careers were symbiotic and he instead made their misery symbiotic: Her success was the reason for his failure. Not that he was an actual failure, but he certainly hadn't gotten as far in life as he could have. Somewhere, deep down, he had chosen her because he knew that meant he could do what he wanted with his life and not be obligated to do anything exclusively for money. And somewhere deep down, maybe she chose him because she knew that absent the hunger he clearly didn't have, she would be permitted to be the animal she always was.

And still: "You're always angry," he'd say to her. And then finally she could admit that she was, particularly after those therapy sessions where she saw just how disgusted both Toby and the therapist were by her annoyance at even having to be there. As if you had to celebrate going to couples therapy! As if you had to rejoice over the time and money you were spending not to make things better, but to get them back to bearable. It always struck her as ironic that the revelation of her anger would come not from the therapy itself but from the fact of it. Still, after all those accusations, Toby never wondered *why* she was angry. He just hated her for being so. The anger was a garden that she kept tending, and it was filled with a toxic weed whose growth she couldn't control. He didn't understand that he was a gardener to the thing, too. He didn't understand that they'd both planted seeds there.

When she turned forty, she decided to stop pretending she wasn't angry about all of this. She didn't want to make life hard for the kids, but she also saw how much energy it was sapping from her to pretend that she still liked Toby as much as she used to. She had liked him! She'd loved him. God, she had loved him. He was the first person who delighted her, who warmed her, who assured her, who adhered her to something. He was smart and his bitterness was sweet and manageable and very funny. He was honest—with her and with himself. At least she thought he was. He'd smelled so good, like soap and America. Now all he wanted was to go to therapy. But she'd been to therapy with him. He wanted to scream and throw things outside of therapy, and then he wanted to go to therapy and sit and be reasonable. She wanted to know, if you could be reasonable in the first place, why wouldn't you always be reasonable so you didn't have to go to couples therapy?

Then one day, Toby brought up divorce. This shocked her. She knew that they were different in their approach: She was just trying to survive and he was trying to have this great marriage. But divorce? Then he brought it up again. Rachel begged him to listen and to try to work things out. She asked him to consider that their problems were very much a result of the fact that it was a hard time in their lives with small children and a business that still needed attention and she knew he was sad that his grant didn't work out but they'd survive. "You don't even want to go to therapy," he'd say. "And stop bringing up my grant."

She refused to consider divorce. She'd refused it last summer, when Hannah left a table at a restaurant in Bridgehampton because she was sick of their fighting. She refused it when he got too drunk at dinner with a director she was trying to poach and they fought all the way home in the cab. And she refused it when he threw a tantrum at the Rothbergs' for being offered a job. She never once thought she deserved happiness. She never once wondered if there was something better out there. This was their marriage; this was their family. It was theirs, they owned it, they made it. If there was one thing she'd learned from her grandmother, it was an understanding that life isn't always what you want it to be, and obligations are obligations and nothing less.

"I don't want to live my life like this," he'd say.

"Toby," she'd say, rubbing her temples. "Do you understand that I don't even have time to get divorced?"

But he didn't. He only understood that she wasn't giving him what he wanted, and that once again the world had turned on him, either because he was used to her acquiescing or because he'd been sold some bullshit about how wives should be in the traditional home that he couldn't admit he wished she would replicate for him. Or because he'd gone into his field at a time when doctors could still be respected. Or because he had some sense that other people had it better. Or because he thought taller people got more laid. Or because his friends were too bohemian, and that allowed him to believe he was more responsible and upstanding and therefore more righteous than he was. Or because he was secretly heartbroken that his lab grant wasn't renewed and his research was largely deemed a waste of money and time and a disaster and he knew that to show regret instead of rage over the circumstances around the grant's nonrenewal was to have real questions about his abilities and core competencies.

Sometime in January, soon after the kids were back in school and everyone was back at work, Sam Rothberg showed up at her office with flowers. She hadn't been expecting him. He wanted to thank her for her help with his nephew and apologize for causing tension between her and Toby that weekend in Saratoga. When he gave her the flowers, she broke down crying. Sam Rothberg asked if he could take her out for dinner, that it looked like she could use a friend. She could. Rachel told him all the things Miriam had never seen her closely enough to ask about—that Toby hated her for her drive and success, that every night was a new fight that was also the same fight.

"Come on," Sam Rothberg said, coy. "You're lying to me."

"What? What would I be lying about?"

"Drive is sexy," he said. "If I had one complaint . . ." He looked off. "I shouldn't." He looked back at her. "Well, I would not mind if Miriam had a little more going on."

"What do you mean?" Rachel was loving this. "She's so busy!"

"Being busy spending money is not the same as really creating something in the world, you know?" He leaned forward and raised his eyebrows like his face was asking a question. "I'd be lying if I said that I didn't find all that you've accomplished a real turn-on."

Sam Rothberg told her that Rachel's drive and success made him want her more. He was married to a lazy heiress. He loved Rachel's ingenuity and her forward motion. Before she knew it, they were eating at a small, candlelit place in Brooklyn, where no one they knew would find them.

Well, Rachel was flabbergasted. The part of her stomach that registered wins felt a deep convulsion of triumph. Not that she ever wanted to cheat on Toby; not that she ever wanted to betray poor Miriam. But not wanting to win doesn't make the win any less real.

Over dinner, he gave her that look—too close, too melty, too intimate—the one that meant a man wanted you. She was rusty, but she wasn't blind. It took her breath away.

But she was married. What was she doing here? Then again, she had a husband who was asking her for a divorce. Suddenly, she could see herself from outside her body. She looked down and she saw herself at dinner with Sam. She was still young. She was in good shape. She was still pretty. She saw that she, this pretty, young woman in good shape, was being desired, and the desire he had for her turned her on. It made her every move poignant, like she was being watched, which she was. When was the last time?

One of the many reasons she didn't want to get divorced was that she felt like the world was a vast chasm of nothing for a woman who was over forty and single. Toby would be desired and get laid and she would be this matron who maybe once in a while got set up with a divorced cousin with no hair and fungal toenails. It wasn't even age. It was how dating was now. Her assistant, Simone, was twenty-nine, and she dated on apps and through computers and phones. The expectation now was for a woman to show up, panting with horniness, on all fours, just begging for it. Then, once it was over, wink and giggle and recede into some background and pretend that this was all okay, that the intimacy was a physical need she had and feel free to never call her again. Rachel would not have been able to bear that.

But here Sam Rothberg was, and she felt the heat of his stare, and the power of his aggression—like he had decided on her and now there was nothing she could do about it. Her toes curled in her shoes. Her breath was shallow and her swallows were audible. It had been so long since she wanted to fuck someone this badly. It had been so long since she had wanted to fuck someone at all.

His car brought them back to her building. She pushed him through the door of her office, past Simone's desk, against her own desk. Super Duper Creative was on the thirty-third floor, and her office had floor-to-ceiling windows, and she turned to the window and couldn't believe the unfathomable sexiness of the city and all the lights—the reflections and . . . look at her! Look at him! Him, on his knees, kneeling in front of her. Him, pushing her up against the window. Him, pulling her on top of him. Them, as they came together, the sound of Ah: revelation! Ah! This is what I should have been doing this whole time! This is *who* I should have been doing this whole time!

Afterward, they lay on the leather couch, her on top of him.

"So this is your office," he said.

"It sure is," she answered him into his chest hair.

"No one's going to come in?"

She laughed. "Are you expecting someone?"

She put her skirt back on but not her stockings or her underwear. She threw those away outside in a trash can. Sam Rothberg wanted his driver to drop her off. She said no, she'd rather walk.

They saw each other weeknights at hotels. They ordered food and fucked on the floor and on the bed and in the shower. They fell into a relationship that was supposed to be temporary, until finally one day, Sam said that he wished Rachel could be with him forever.

"I'm only happy when I'm with you," he said, naked, over sushi. "I wish we could figure that part out."

Rachel thought about this for a long time. Here was a guy who really wanted her. Here was someone who was strong and smart and driven and successful and wouldn't see her similar traits as a referendum on him. The more time they spent together, the more she realized that Toby's criticism of her had slowly seeped into her pores and become her own criticism of herself. What if she didn't have to live like that anymore?

"How would it work?" she'd ask, pretending it was just a fantasy when really she was incapable of anything that wasn't planning.

"We would just do it," he'd say. "We'd say fuck 'em all, this is how life goes sometimes."

She kept trying to picture it. It would be a scandal at the school. They'd have to take their kids out and put them in different schools for high school. Or maybe they wouldn't have to and the kids would survive. This happened! Right? She didn't know anyone it had actually happened to, but it happened. It had to have happened. She pictured walking into school, seeing Miriam and Roxanne and Cyndi all in a huddle, staring venom at her, and she shuddered.

Just at that moment, Alejandra's movie, which had been through eight scripts and three directors, got the green light and began filming, and she was suddenly the happy recipient of another load of cash. She thought she would use it to take over another floor of the building, but she stopped. She'd been going out to Los Angeles once a week these days. A year ago, it was once a month. Her clients were more interested in Hollywood, and it seemed like every single writer and actor was up for hire because the new streaming market was endless. She loved L.A. She never slept as well as she did when she was there. There was so much health available there: anything you liked made into a juice, yoga classes around the clock. There was so little *rushing*. Time seemed to expand there. What if she opened an L.A. office? What if she opened an L.A. office and became someone who believed in her staff and didn't rush?

"What if I opened an L.A. office?" she'd ask Sam either at the Waldorf or at his company's corporate apartments or even once at his upstate house in Miriam's bed just one floor away from where she'd once pretended that Miriam saying that all mothers worked was a good point.

"What if *I* did?" Sam would ask back. His pharma company was in New Jersey and the commute was depressing. The labs where they formulated the cancer drugs were in Manhattan Beach and there was talk of a need for supervision.

Rachel thought about completely extracting herself from the world she occupied. Fuck Cyndi Leffer. Fuck Roxanne Hertz. Fuck Miriam Rothberg extra hard. Toby could move, too, if he wanted to. He hated New York, anyway, and he was from L.A. and he always said it would be nice for the kids to have more interaction with his family.

She could picture it all. She could see herself boarding a plane with her children. She could see herself taking yoga and having a meditation coach who would teach her how to trust the people who worked for her. She would come home on time. She would pay attention to her children. She would run a victory lap for the life she'd built and she'd let it support her. She'd pass her smaller clients on to some of the agents beneath her. She'd keep her big ones. She'd create time.

One winter night, at their home in East Hampton, she finally turned to Toby and granted him his divorce. They told the kids just before Toby moved out. Once he did, she was alone in her apartment. She stayed home with the kids for the first two weeks to help them transition. Solly slept with her every night that week. She took Hannah to yoga with her after camp.

And at night, once the kids were asleep, she was free. She no longer answered to anyone. She wore just underwear and a bra and watched reality shows and put pore strips across her chin and picked her nose and didn't finish the dishes, which could no longer be seen as de facto asking someone else to finish the dishes. You're supposed to be depressed and miserable after a divorce. Not Rachel. Rachel put the entire failure of it aside. She'd done her time. She had someone in her life who loved her for who she was, not who he had hoped she was. She had someone who understood her. She felt so bad for anyone who remained allegiant to a life they'd built just because they'd built it. She had two children—warm, witty, spunky Hannah and sincere, smart, curious Solly. She could finally give attention to them without worrying about her husband's ego.

Then, after she heard from Todd Leffer that he'd seen Toby out at night with a woman, she realized it was time to tell him. She was at the office, but everyone had gone home. She called Toby and said she wanted to talk about something.

"What is it now?" he'd asked.

She told him she wanted to open an office in Los Angeles.

"Are you fucking kidding me?" he'd said.

He went silent as she tried to tell him all the ways this was good news without having to humiliate herself and tell him that she could no longer withstand the pressure of the school and its demands on her. She couldn't tell him she was finally ready to live on her own terms and teach her children confidence and wasn't that good news? He could finally stop being on the treadmill at work. He could live near his family and the kids would get to know—

"Don't agent me," he'd said. She realized for the first time that he might have been drunk. There were noises in the background. He was out. Shit.

"If this isn't a good time," she'd said.

"Do you have to ruin every fucking part of my life, even now?" he'd asked her.

She apologized. She said she didn't realize that he was out. She felt sad to think of him with someone else. Part of her still couldn't bear that her marriage hadn't worked out. Part of her still couldn't bear that she no longer had Toby. Yes, she liked her freedom. Yes, divorce was the right move. She always thought divorce would come from hate, but her anger was never based in hate. It was based in disappointment that someone she loved misunderstood her so deeply. They were so different, but they had grown up together. He was her first great love.

"You're always apologizing," he said. "It was too much to ask of me to raise the kids and teach you how to be a person. Go to California. But you're not taking the kids. Go. Seriously. They wouldn't even notice if you were gone."

He hung up on her.

That night, Sam texted her that he'd gotten two last-minute spots at Kripalu and they could go for the weekend if they left early the next day. She couldn't shake off how cruel Toby had become. She couldn't sleep at all. There was too much going on, and she'd been getting very little sleep lately with all her excitement. First it was her enjoyment of staying up and watching bad TV without anyone to impugn her. But then, slowly, she realized she didn't want to go to sleep. Or rather she couldn't. She couldn't remember how to fall asleep. It seemed right there, but just out of reach, like the mechanical rabbit they use for dog races.

She packed for Kripalu. She waited until it felt like a decent enough hour to bring the kids over to Toby's, but early enough that he would still be asleep because she didn't want to see him. Sam picked her up an hour later. They drove to Massachusetts in silence. She tried not to cry, but she was so tired, and she cried when she was tired. Sam told her, "You're being a drag." She looked over at him. He'd said it in good humor, right? She was too tired to know.

When they got there, they had sex, but she barely registered it. Then they did it twice more, all in the same twenty minutes. Toby was still like a little boy in this department, but even he needed some recovery time. They signed up for massages and classes and Rachel signed up for a one-on-one meditation breathing class. A man with long red hair and no eyebrows coached her through her breathing, saying that when her breath caught in her lungs or in her trachea, she should monitor where it was and scream through it.

"Scream?" she asked.

"Trust me," the man said.

She breathed up and down her body, and her breath caught practically everywhere. At first, she just yelped, but then she screamed. And then she screamed more. At first her screams were high-pitched and thin, but then, as the guy moved his hands around to indicate that her screams should originate beyond her throat in her sternum and solar plexus, she reached deeper and began making big, disgusting, guttural sounds. One of the screams was for Toby. One of them was for Hannah, who had caught her disease of desire for love and acceptance. One for Solly, who thought he was allowed to be himself in the world. One, the biggest one, was for herself, for all that she had been made to endure in her life—how she'd never stood a chance, how she'd never even really been loved. Yes, that was it. She'd never really been loved. Not by her parents, not by her grandmother, not by Toby, not really.

The session was only halfway done. She was hiccuping from her sobs now. When it was over, she booked the screaming therapist's remaining slots for the next day.

She found Sam for dinner. She couldn't wait to tell him about her weird afternoon, but he was annoyed with her and stayed on his phone.

"What's the problem?" she asked.

"My problem is that I thought you were going to be a little more fun," he said. "I thought you'd be more available. I didn't realize you'd opt for a three-hour screaming session over, I don't know, hanging out?"

She tried to tell him what the sessions were like, how cathartic it all was, how different she felt afterward. "I've never been loved," she said. "I realized everything that's wrong with me is because I've never been loved."

He didn't look up from his phone; he couldn't be less interested. When she talked about business, he would say it turned him on. But now she saw in his eyes something like contempt. It scared her. She got up from the table and went back to the room.

Sam came in and put his hands around her waist. He started humping on her, then bent her over the bed and pulled down her leggings. She was tired from the screaming but too worried about letting him down. Afterward, he lay splayed out on the bed asleep and she sat at its edge. She couldn't sleep. She looked back at him and something about his snore seemed very foreboding to her. She tried to shake him awake, but she couldn't, and that was when she remembered that he took sleeping pills.

She stood up and tiptoed through the room to his Dopp kit. She found a bottle of Viagra (oh) and a bottle of Ambien. She took it to the bathroom and sat on the toilet staring at it. It felt so serious in her hands. A prescription. She felt like if she took it, it would drown her. What if she was one of the people who killed someone while she was on Ambien? She put it down on the sink and went to go lie down.

At some point, she might have fallen asleep, though she would have sworn that she hadn't. But Sam woke up at six, like he always did, his dick already hard and his hands already poking around her thighs. She told him she couldn't sleep. He said, "You know, I don't get a lot of vacations." (But it wasn't true. He and Miriam had been to Madrid, Lisbon, and Africa in the last eighteen months alone. He meant he just didn't get a lot of vacations from Miriam.)

If there was one thing she was always good at, it was inference. It was self-awareness. It was taking other people's behavior and allowing herself to consider that it all added up to something. She learned this from watching the world not interact with her for so many years. She thought of what Toby had said the night before. She thought about Sam now.

And she thought of her kids.

Not Solly, because Solly loved her. He traced her face and burrowed into her neck and held on to her pants while she walked. He asked her if she liked his outfit and what it was like to be a grown-up. He had no judgment against her yet, but he was young. No, it was Hannah she saw as she considered a full-scale evaluation of her life. Hannah used to beg her to be a class mom or a lunchtime volunteer server, and how could she do things like that? Even for a day? She couldn't chaperone the overnight trip to Washington. Even for a night? She couldn't even pack a lunch for trip days. "I don't do it," she would tell Hannah. "But I make sure it gets done." "I wish you did it," Hannah would say. Rachel didn't ask what the difference was because she knew what it was. You have to remember that Rachel didn't have a mother.

She thought of something Toby said to her once, as a way of trying to comfort her. She'd said it was sad to her that she was considered this oddity at the school for being a woman who worked.

And Toby, meaning well (maybe), had said: "They would if they could. They just can't rationalize it because they have so much money." She glared at him but he didn't realize what he'd said, that yes, for sure, working was the unkind thing to do to your children.

Her crystal understanding of all of this came in layers. Yes, for sure, Sam was hoping she'd stay some kind of alpha fantasy for him—a fun power fuck with not an emotion in sight. Yes, for sure, he was never going to stay with her because where does a woman this ambitious leave a man? And yes, for sure, her marriage couldn't have survived because what kind of woman is like this? And yes, for sure, the people were treating her in these ways to let her know who she was in the world: just a woman. And women—they are vile. Those men's varying degrees of politeness shielded the world from their real feelings, but politeness is ultimately unsustainable. And so that doctor abused her. And those men raped those women. And Sam here couldn't bear for her to do anything except bend over and take it.

Maybe she was worthless. That was what they were telling her. Maybe that was the whole point. Like I said, she was good at inference.

She found Sam, who had done a reflexology session, pounding away at his phone under a tree. He looked up to see her and was annoyed at the interruption, but then more annoyed when he saw that she was crying.

"What is it this time?" he said.

She couldn't answer because she was crying too hard and ashamed of her tears.

They went back to the room and he started to pack. He said, "This was a mistake. You get that, right?"

Of course she did. What had she ever been thinking? She couldn't take Miriam Rothberg's place. She couldn't fade into that kind of existence. She was herself. And the kind of woman she was was unacceptable: Unacceptable to a man like Toby, who couldn't forgive her for her success. Unacceptable to Sam, because he might pretend he liked her bigness, but he couldn't actually accommodate it into his life—he couldn't bear what it took to be around someone whose obligations were as important and as nonnegotiable as his.

It was official. She was unacceptable; an illegitimate kind of person. Her success made her poison. Her weakness made her poison. There was no one for her. Her husband had rejected her. Now her boyfriend had, too. Maybe Toby was right. They would never notice if she was gone. But now she had nowhere to go.

And so she stayed at Kripalu. She found that she still couldn't sleep, but thought that this—these feelings, this insomnia—must be part of the process unleashed by her new breathwork. She lay in bed, her body humming every night, and at one point she decided to stop caring that she couldn't sleep. She went back to the screaming coach. She screamed more. She did yoga. She called Simone and said she was staying a few more days, but please don't contact her and please defer client emergencies for a few days to Ben or Hal or Rhonda, and she was not to answer any of Toby's questions. Simone called with a question, and she screamed at her that no—NO!—she really didn't want to hear from her.

"Toby said it's your turn with the kids."

"Say one more word and you will not have a job," Rachel said. Then, more softly, "I'm having a little bit of a time, Simone. I haven't had a vacation in years. Not a real one. Do you think you can cover for me and I will come back just as soon as I can, good as new?"

"Okay, but Rhonda was a little worried because one of the producers—"

"I think you're not really hearing me, Simone. You've been on my desk how long?"

"Four years."

"This is where we learn if you're someone who will go beyond my desk."

But the emails still came in. The texts still came in. Where was she? Could she ask a client to chair this event? Could she take a look at this script? This contract? This email? Could she circle back? Circle back circle back circle back. Time was a flat circle back. The entire world wanted to circle back until it ate itself.

She saw a flyer for a silent retreat program and she signed up for it. In the silence, she allowed all her fights with Toby to play out in her head. She lay in bed more nights, not sleeping, sometimes making a hum in the back of her throat to make sure her voice was still available for when she went back to using it. Sam's Ambien stayed on the bathroom counter, but she didn't dare touch it.

She was so tired, though. She lay in bed, staring at the ceiling. She was alternatively panicked that the time was going by and angry it didn't go by faster. At least in the morning it would be normal to be up. She sat up in the middle of the night and realized something: that it was her phone that made it so that she couldn't sleep. She had turned it off. It had been off for a couple of days, but perhaps she had adapted to the phone so much that she could feel the phone when it wanted her. The phone filled and filled and didn't get full. It was like the burning bush, on fire but not consumed but still on fire.

She had to kill the phone. That was the only way she'd ever get to sleep again. And so in the middle of the night she walked a mile down a trail and buried her phone alive. She walked back to her room knowing for sure that she would sleep but of course couldn't.

Then the silent retreat was over, but still she didn't leave. She went back to screaming classes again, and she screamed out the remaining fights with Toby. She screamed out the ways she felt diminished. She was empty. She was a rag. She was ready to go home. She was a few days late, but she'd explain everything to Toby. She would apologize. She understood now that she was destined to be alone. She would tell him that she understood now that she was unacceptable.

She went out into the woods and looked for her phone, but she couldn't find it. It had been night when she buried it, and there was no marking; only dirt. Had it been a mile? A half mile? A hundred yards? She didn't know. It was gone.

She used the phone at the front desk to call Simone and ask her to call a driver.

"Toby is trying to get—"

"I don't want my messages!" Rachel screamed. "I don't want to hear about him, and I don't want to hear that you told him anything about me."

A car came and brought her the several hours home. She sat in the backseat, staring out the window. How long had she been gone? A day? A week? She arrived at her apartment and stood in the middle of it and didn't know how to proceed. She had only eaten vegetarian bullshit for the last few days. She needed something with meat. She called the Chinese place. She was about to order her usual, her shrimp in lobster sauce, when she was struck by the memory of her roommate from when she was at Hunter with the eating disorder who could find a reason to eat pasta at any hour. When they ordered Chinese, the roommate would try her hardest to order steamed chicken and vegetables, but sometimes she would say, "I give up," and she'd order beef lo mein. Rachel never would. She hadn't given up. She would never give up. But the lo mein always smelled so good, and it seemed to fill the roommate with this extraordinary sense of well-being. "Ahhhh," she would say as whatever seratonic hormone it was that made pasta a miracle food flooded her system.

So Rachel ordered lo mein because fuck it. Fuck everything. Fuck her body and fuck her soul. She gave up! She was going to eat beef lo mein. Then she could get to sleep. She looked around the apartment. It felt like a green screen, like she was a motion-capture object inside her one special-effects movie. She turned her head and she heard a whooshing sound. She took steps and she heard an echo. She sat down and she heard a crash. It was all happening near her. Nothing was happening to her.

The doorbell rang and she was still trying to figure out how to be in this apartment. She gave the deliveryman a tip and began to eat, sitting on the floor under a beige painting that the art consultant had picked out for her. Why did she like this painting? What was this painting? Did it just move?

She spat the lo mein back into the carton. It was disgusting. Why would you eat spaghetti from a Chinese place? Maybe she was just tired. She put it in the fridge and decided to lie down. But when she got to her bed the stakes felt too high. She knew if she couldn't sleep there right then, she would never be able to sleep again.

She felt like she should call the kids, but she was worried. How could she call the kids when she hadn't slept? It seemed dangerous somehow. She left the apartment. She went out to the health food store on Third, and an old hippie told her about all the teas that would help her sleep. There were six different kinds, so she bought all of them. She brought them back to the apartment and drank all of them, but all she could do then was go to the bathroom.

This wouldn't do. She began to panic. The apartment walls seemed to be breathing, in and out, in and out. She had to get out of there. She had to actively change her emotions. Nobody had ever done anything for Rachel Fleishman. She had to do it all herself. So she walked over to Bergdorf's and shoplifted a pair of chandelier earrings made from gold and jade—tried them on and walked right out, but even the adrenaline didn't make a dent. When she returned, the doorman said, "Ms. Fleishman! It's been a minute!" She froze like she was a criminal. But she wasn't the criminal. This was her house.

She tried to watch TV in the den. There was a *thirtysomething* marathon on Lifetime. She sat trying to figure out how these marriages were all doing fine, how everyone was so bland and earnest and good. Where had she gone wrong? What was so bad about her?

Then it was somehow morning again, without her ever realizing it had been night. She stood up fast and hard from the couch, an involuntary impulse that her own nervous system had somehow orchestrated. She had to get out of here. Good God, she had to get out of here.

She called Simone from the home line and asked her to order a car to Baltimore. She had to go somewhere where she knew she could sleep. She never once had a sleepless night in Baltimore. She would just go check on her grandmother, whom she hadn't seen in more than six months. It would be fine. It was totally normal to do this.

Five hours later, she pulled up to her old house. Her grandmother was old now, but time hadn't made her sentimental. Nothing made that bitch sentimental. She opened the door and looked beyond Rachel to see who had brought her here.

"It's just a car service," Rachel said. The skin beneath her eyes was purple, she was so tired.

"I wasn't expecting you," she said.

"Surprise!" Rachel said, and brushed past her.

She told her grandmother she was in town on business and didn't want to stay at a hotel. She wanted to get some sleep, would that be okay?

Her grandmother looked toward the door, as if getting Rachel to also look at the door would help lead her to the other side of it. "I didn't prepare anything. I don't have food for you."

"That's okay, I just want to sleep. It's been a long day. Tons of meetings."

She went upstairs, past the chintz sofa and the old wooden country furniture, and lay on her old bed, but it was worse this time. The house was so fucking flimsy. Her grandmother's life was so small. But there was her bed, the one that had given her nights of delighted sleep. She could taste it. She took off her clothes and got under the covers.

At one point, she found herself in the quiet of a dream. In the dream, she was trying to figure out what day it was. She wasn't really asleep, she realized. You can't plan your days in your sleep. She sat up and looked at her old mirror, which had a mirror behind it and therefore looked like a hundred mirrors. Her grandmother had removed any remnant of her that there was—the Bon Jovi poster, the class pictures. Her grandmother didn't love her, either. This was a bad place. Her grandmother was bad. This bed was a piece of shit when you were used to sleeping on a mattress that was sourced from Sri Lankan unicorn feathers.

She called Simone from the Princess phone in her old bedroom and asked her to order her another car, this time to the airport, and a ticket to Los Angeles. On the plane, every time she blinked, she accessed a level of nauseous almost-sleep that was not quite sleep. The man next to her fell asleep immediately and was snoring, making it so she couldn't sleep at all, which was probably for the best since she wanted to be extra tired when she got there.

The hotel building itself was nestled in a wooded area right off Sunset. "Ms. Fleishman," said the special VIP concierge at the hotel. "No luggage today?" She was taken to her villa. Ah, she thought. Here is the place. There were a thousand pillows. The smell was having a Pavlovian effect. When she came to L.A. for a work trip, she was not supposed to enjoy it because she was supposed to miss her children too much. She did, she did. But this place, man. Outside her villa was a pool. In the morning she would go swimming when she felt normal again.

But now she worried. What if she fell asleep and then was so delirious that she walked outside and drowned? How could she sleep when doom was so nearby? This was so dangerous. She kept nodding off but then jumping back up to alert until she was a raw nerve ending, her eyes bugging out and her breath short and terrified.

She lay in the hotel bed, surrounded by every form of luxury. She went out onto Sunset Boulevard and found a marijuana dispensary. She bought two lozenges that the drug dealer there told her would mellow her out, and she spent the next three hours pacing in her room.

Finally, at close to midnight, she ate both of the lozenges, and sat by the pool until someone asked if she'd like a drink and she was too smart to mix alcohol and pot so instead she ordered a cheeseburger and a Cobb salad and three smoothies and a French onion soup. She ate the food methodically—it had been years since she was stoned—and when it was done she registered that her stomach felt close to bursting but her mouth needed more, but she felt overwhelmed by shame and so she went back to her room and lay on her back on the couch.

What was she doing here? By five that morning, she'd left for the airport.

"Leaving us already?" the concierge asked as she walked out the door. From the back of the car, Los Angeles looked foreboding and awful. The buildings seemed to breathe. The palm trees were there to trick her. She couldn't live here. She could never even return to visit. She found a pen and paper in her purse and wrote herself a note: "DON'T MOVE TO LOS ANGELES."

She couldn't remember how she got on the plane, but there was a fucking baby in business class, which was crazy because business class is for businesswomen and businessmen, and babies don't do business. She gave the mother a dirty look as she went to the bathroom, and then saw herself in the reflection and realized she looked like a witch. Into her reflection she made a lion face and growled.

She arrived back at home, back at the Golden. Her apartment was so big and empty and she felt like a ghost in it. She needed something to eat. She called the Chinese place. She was about to order her usual, her shrimp in lobster sauce, when she was struck by the memory of her roommate from when she was at Hunter with the eating disorder who could find a reason to eat pasta at any hour. When they ordered Chinese, the roommate would try her hardest to order steamed chicken and vegetables, but sometimes she would say, "I give up," and she'd order beef lo mein. Rachel never would. She hadn't given up. She would never give up. But the lo mein always smelled so good, and it seemed to fill the roommate with this extraordinary sense of well-being. "Ahhhh," she would say as whatever seratonic hormone it was that made pasta a miracle food flooded her system.

So Rachel ordered lo mein because fuck it. Fuck everything. Fuck her body and fuck her soul. She was going to eat beef lo mein. Then she could get to sleep. The doorbell rang and she gave the deliveryman a tip and began to eat, sitting on a rug she'd bought recently, though its fibers poked through her underwear and she didn't know why she'd bought it.

She spat the lo mein back into the carton. It was disgusting. Why would you eat spaghetti from a Chinese place? Maybe she was just tired. She put it in the fridge.

She felt like she should call the kids, but she was worried. How could she call the kids when she hadn't slept? It seemed dangerous somehow. It had been a week. Or two weeks. Or maybe just four days, she didn't know. She just knew she missed her kids and she couldn't see them again until she had a few hours of sleep. She tied a pair of tights around her face. Maybe it was the darkness. There was never enough darkness. She'd bought the apartment because it had such good light and now all she wanted was darkness.

Fuck, she realized. It was Friday. It was Friday at three P.M. She had to get to SoulCycle in an hour. Things hadn't worked out with Sam. She obviously couldn't move to Los Angeles because check out this note in her purse that someone had written to her. She had to maintain her stature in the community. She had to be normal for an hour so that she could go back to losing her shit slowly and steadily, so that her friends would still be there when she returned.

She took out her exercise clothing and put it on and left, but she got to the SoulCycle and found that her bike wasn't reserved and also it wasn't four P.M. and somehow it was not Friday but Wednesday.

"Are you okay?" asked the front desk woman. Rachel looked at the other women, with their flatironed hair and their Botox and their fake tans. Why did they have to look this way? It was too much. There was too much being asked of all these women.

She walked out the door and went one avenue over where she found a Supercuts. She waited in line behind a family. Her problem, she realized, was her maintenance routine. It was eating her alive. She got into the chair and a Puerto Rican woman said, "You want a trim?" and Rachel said, "No, no. Something bigger. I want to look like Tilda Swinton."

"Who is he?"

"It's not a he. Do you have a phone? Search it." She stared into the mirror in front of her at the woman sitting in the chair whose hair was touched every time Rachel's stylist touched Rachel's hair. Uncanny, she thought.

She walked out, feeling like she could finally breathe. A new haircut! Why had she been holding on to that haircut like it was her religion? Like it was important that she never change? She felt so light that she might float away. She stood on Second, trying to figure out what to do next. She saw a woman with a beach chair strapped to her back walking west. The park. She remembered suddenly the people in the park who slept in their sweatpants, the ones she and Toby used to make fun of. What if they knew something she didn't? She went home and foraged through her belongings for a pair of sweatpants that she knew she didn't own.

She left again and went to the Gap and when no one was looking, she stole a pair for old times' sake. She didn't even do it in the dressing room. She just took her leggings off in a corner and put them into her purse and then put the sweatpants on.

Sweatpants! Now these were something. She had always been so dismissive of sweatpants, but had she ever really allowed herself to try them? The way they formed warm hugs around your legs while you walked. The way their friction slowed you. All the leggings ever did was enable movement. Had anyone considered that this feeling—of moving through clay—was much preferred?

She moved to the park, luxuriating in her leg hugs. It was so hot, though. How long had it been this hot? Was it ever going to not be this hot again?

In the park, at least the heat had context. She lay down, right there on the grass. She put her arm across her eyes. What had been so crazy about this? This was wonderful. It was sunny and hot. This might work. She began to drift, down, down. She swore she almost got there. She was so close. . . .

"Rachel. Fleishman."

She removed her arm from her eyes to find Cyndi and Miriam, standing over her and laughing.

"We thought that was you," Cyndi said.

"Someone missed Pilates," Miriam said. She was holding a smoothie. Then, looking closely at her, "What happened to your hair?"

Cyndi laughed. "Did Roberto do that?"

Rachel propped herself up on her elbows. "I'm just." She touched her hair. She didn't know how to finish.

"You want to come to Soul? It's Beyoncé vs. Rihanna."

"Oh yeah, I'll be there. Soon."

Miriam and Cyndi looked at each other. "You okay, Rachel?" Miriam asked.

"Ha, yes, of course. I'm taking some me-time."

Me-time they understood. They made some noise about being late and headed out of the park.

Rachel went home. She realized she needed something to eat. She called the Chinese place. She was about to order her usual, her shrimp in lobster sauce, when she was struck by the memory of her roommate from when she was at Hunter with the eating disorder who could find a reason to eat pasta at any hour. When they ordered Chinese, the roommate would try her hardest to order steamed chicken and vegetables, but sometimes she would say, "I give up," and she'd order beef lo mein. Rachel never would. She hadn't given up. She would never give up. But the lo mein always smelled so good, and it seemed to fill the roommate with this extraordinary sense of well-being. "Ahhhh," she would say as whatever seratonic hormone it was that made pasta a miracle food flooded her system.

So Rachel ordered lo mein because fuck it. Fuck everything.

Fuck her body and fuck her soul. She was going to eat beef lo mein. Then she could get to sleep. The doorbell rang and she gave the deliveryman a tip and began to eat, sitting at her big Swedish dining table whose wood stained when moisture went near it.

She spat the lo mein back into the carton. It was disgusting. Why would you eat spaghetti from a Chinese place? Maybe she was just tired. She put it in the fridge and decided to lie down. But when she got to her bed the stakes felt too high. She knew if she couldn't sleep there right then, she would never be able to sleep again.

Ten more days passed. She couldn't account for them. She didn't not remember them, exactly. It was more that they felt all like one day. If you stop to watch a *Boy Meets World* marathon in the middle of the afternoon when it's light, and the next time you look outside, it's still light, does that mean you missed the night? It had been twelve hours, but did you really just miss the night? Like that.

The morning I saw her, she stopped trying to sleep at four A.M. and took a walk. Before she knew it, she found herself way downtown, near Alejandra Lopez's apartment. She looked up and there it was and she thought, Maybe I should visit. I've been out of pocket for a few days. Nothing like a personal touch.

Yes. Maybe that was the problem. She wasn't accustomed to not working. Maybe if she worked a little, she could sleep. She approached the lobby but then realized she shouldn't be stopping by casually without bringing something. She went to a bodega nearby and looked around. Nothing really spoke to the moment, so she got a turkey sandwich and a plastic gallon of water. Alejandra had once ordered a turkey sandwich over lunch, she remembered. A good agent remembered things like that. She went back to the apartment building. The doorman was busy so she walked by with a wave. She went up to the apartment and rang the bell.

Alejandra's wife, Sofia, answered the door. Sofia was a WASP from the Upper West Side who had stopped working to take care of their three daughters. She took one look at Rachel.

"Alex," she shouted to the next room. Then, to Rachel, "Are you okay?"

"Sure," she said. Big smile. "I had a meeting here and it's been a minute. And I haven't seen the kids in forever."

"It's six in the morning."

She hadn't realized it. Alejandra came to the door in her pajamas. She was built like a coil, with a thick neck and thick ankles and a wide waist and the dreamiest eyes. She didn't wear any makeup but it always looked like she had liquid liner on her upper lids. "I was in the neighborhood."

"Rachel. Wow, you cut your hair."

Rachel held up the turkey sandwich. This didn't seem so bad. What was the big deal? Reentry was going fine.

"I didn't expect you," Alejandra said.

"Is it ever a bad time to visit my favorite client?" She had never once visited a client at home, unannounced, before.

"I haven't heard from you in weeks," she said.

"Well, I try not to hover."

"I think this is very aggressive of you."

She was confused. "What do you mean? I know I should have called but I've been out of town and I lost my phone. I can come back later. Or never? We can just have lunch."

Alejandra and Sofia looked at each other. Sofia shooed the children to the next room and Alejandra took Rachel to the couch and asked if she was okay.

"Of course I'm okay."

"We've had a pretty bad week here," Alejandra said.

"I'm sorry to hear that."

Alejandra searched her face. "Do you not know anything I'm talking about?"

Rachel searched her brain. She shouldn't be here. She wasn't prepared. She smiled.

"I've been out," Rachel said. "I had a family emergency."

Alejandra leaned back without taking her eyes off Rachel.

"I lost my movie. Do you not know this?" Alejandra's screen-writing deal had fallen through that week, which of course Rachel had to know since she'd told Simone that Hal should handle it. Simone had punted her to Rhonda, but Rhonda had gotten into a pissing match with the production company and Alejandra had woken up to the news that her play was no longer being adapted to film. Again.

Rachel closed her eyes. "I can fix this."

"You don't have to."

She opened her eyes. "Why?"

"Because you can't."

"Trust me, I've fixed worse."

"No, you *can't*. You're not my agent anymore."

Rachel blinked, but the blink felt once again like she was falling. "What? Alejandra." The next question came out even as she knew the answer and couldn't bear to hear it. "Who?"

But she didn't need Alejandra to tell her.

"I went with Matt Klein. I just think Matt's better equipped to help me. I'm grateful for everything you did. I would be nothing without you."

"This doesn't feel like gratitude, Alex."

Alejandra looked at her with concern. "Can I call Simone?"

"Matt Klein is a snake."

But there was nothing more to say. Rachel was better than this. She had to handle this like a professional. So that was that. She left.

Now it was official. There was no one for her. After twelve years she took a week off. Okay, it was two weeks, or three, but she *unplugged*. Isn't that what Roxanne was always doing? "We're going to [insert private island here] and we're really going to *unplug*." And she didn't, of course. Instead she posted Instagram pictures of herself in her stupid fedora and her bikini with the abs that tried too hard. Rachel really did unplug. She'd murdered her phone in cold blood! And now look at her. She had finally let it all out. She'd screamed. She'd taken her foot off the gas for a minute. But it was not permitted. It was unacceptable. She was unacceptable.

She got in a cab. She looked at the time. It was eight A.M. on what she now surmised was a Sunday. She had an idea.

The rape survivor support group at Toby's hospital had moved to the ground floor, which was just as well, because it allowed her to get in and out quickly, without having to wander around for Toby's colleagues to gawk at. She was fifteen minutes late when she entered. The group stopped and welcomed her.

Someone had just finished talking. The leader of the group looked at Rachel.

"It seems like we have a new visitor," she said.

"I'm Rachel," she told the group.

"I'm Glynnis," said the woman. "I'm a trainee. Our regular leader is on vacation." That's right, Rachel remembered. August. In August, you can't get crazy because all there are in August are trainees. "Would you like to share?"

A Pavlovian instinct overtook her as she sat and she began to cry. It felt good. She hadn't cried in forever, since she'd watched Sam leave at Kripalu, which was either five days ago or twelve weeks, she wasn't sure.

Rachel had never spoken in the group way back when she attended after Hannah was born. Maybe that was the problem. Maybe she never left room for healing because she didn't participate enough. Maybe what Toby had said about her vis-à-vis parenting was true that whole time, that just showing up wasn't enough. Participating was the only way to have real meaning. Yes. *Yes.*

This time, she was really going to do it, she decided. She began to talk. She told them about Hannah's birth, and how she used to come to this group all the time. She told them about her marriage. She told them about her business and about Sam Rothberg, and the screaming. She told them about Alejandra, though she didn't use her name. She told them about Toby and her children. She told them about having nowhere to go and no one to love her—how she was fundamentally unacceptable. She talked and talked. She didn't think anyone had ever let her talk that much before in her life.

When she finished, she was out of breath. She took a long inhale through her nose and no longer felt what her scream therapist had called hiccups. She was in trouble. She hadn't seen her children in was it weeks? Days? She had lost her biggest client. But she was going to be fine.

Finally, Glynnis spoke. "This is a rape survivor group," she said slowly.

"Yes," Rachel said.

"Have you been raped?" Glynnis said.

This confounded Rachel. "Well, not technically, not the way—"

"This is a rape survivor group," she said. "I'm afraid you have to leave."

See? Unacceptable.

She hailed a cab and went to the Upper East Side. She arrived at Toby's apartment; she pulled out her key but couldn't bring herself to use it. She walked back to her building. She couldn't even enter. She thought she might have a bagel and go to the Met and see what was going on there. Maybe the Impressionists would bore her to sleep. She was also thinking now that maybe she could bring herself to take a Tylenol PM, but it was early in the day and she should wait for night.

"I think you need some help," I told her. "I think you should let me call Toby."

"Toby doesn't want to hear from me."

"He does, I promise."

"He can't see me like this. He will take them away from me. That's what he does: He takes away."

I asked her if I could walk her home. She didn't say yes and she didn't say no. We got to her building and went upstairs and I walked her to her bedroom. She lay down on her bed, on her side, and I patted her hair for a while. I got up to go get water, but she pulled me down. "I need you to stand guard for me," she said. I sat on the edge of her bed until she finally, finally fell asleep.

Toby had taken them to the Museum of Natural History after I left his apartment Sunday morning. He wanted to see the Vantablack again. He was getting hooked on disorientation.

"I don't see what's so crazy," Hannah said. But Solly was lost in it, crying.

Afterward, they took the crosstown bus home so they could walk Bubbles. Hannah didn't object to the bus like she usually did. It was either because she didn't see anyone around whom she was embarrassed in front of, or because she knew her father couldn't take anything more. The kids watched *Ferris Bueller* again. He hadn't thought about dinner. This was what life was going to be like for him for the next ten years. Work, dinner, *Ferris Bueller*. Okay.

"Can we watch *Horse Feathers*?" Solly asked, and the bottom of Toby's stomach dropped out because the Marx Brothers made him think of Joanie with a pang of longing and HR-based fear.

He told Solly to read until he came to tuck him in. He was hoping Solly would fall asleep on his own, but he didn't, and so Toby went in and began reading him *The Hobbit,* which they'd started before Solly left for camp. He read by rote, not absorbing anything, no inflection in his speech so that he had to start sentences over again, not understanding any of Solly's questions.

"You know, I'm a little bit tired," Toby said. "Can we read this tomorrow?"

He sent Hannah to bed to read, too. She immediately made her body into her posture of resistance, but he wasn't having it. "I've had a really hard day." She acquiesced in what appeared to be signs of empathy. Maybe it was a good thing that Hannah was his now, and only his. He could make her into a good person.

He lay down on his bed and stared up at the shitty stained ceiling. At the museum, they'd gone to the planetarium show. It was about everything that scientists don't yet understand in the universe beyond Earth. A voice boomed out and talked about dark matter, which is a substance they know nothing about but that seems to bind objects in space into some kind of rhythm with each other. You can see the objects, but you can't see the dark matter. The dark matter is the mystery, and yet everything depends on it— you can't see it, but it drives everything into motion.

"What was your favorite part, Dad?" Solly asked as they left.

"I liked how he said that wherever you were in space, it felt like you were the center. I really related to that."

"Like as a planet?"

Toby laughed.

"I liked the fact that you can't even see the thing that's most important," Solly said. "That's just crazy."

"What did you like, Hannah?"

"I liked that it was over."

"Come on," Toby said.

"I didn't like the dark matter part. I feel like you can't just decide something must exist because everything's reacting to it. You can't just give it a name and hope it's true."

"But maybe the objects are just behaving in a way we don't understand. Maybe nothing is making them act that way but themselves."

That Sunday, I called Toby after I walked Rachel home, but his phone went to voicemail because he was at the museum. By the time he called me back, I was lying on my hammock, stoned.

He sat and listened to the entire story, silent. I wished I hadn't been stoned.

"That's it?" he asked, when I finished.

"She's had like a full nervous breakdown."

He was quiet again.

"You have to do something for her, Toby."

Still nothing. Finally, he said, "I don't have to do anything for her."

Toby went to visit Nahid in her apartment, but when he arrived, something was different.

"Toby," she said. She kissed him hard on the lips. Did she change her hair?

"I have an idea," she said. "Let's have lunch."

"Should I order?" he asked. Maybe she was wearing more makeup than she usually did?

"No, I mean outside. Downstairs. I'm tired of this. I want to live my life." She smiled, searching his eyes for acknowledgment of what a gift this was.

Ah. That was what was different. She was dressed in clothing—full-on outdoor street clothing. Jeans and high-heeled boots and a sleeveless denim shirt and chunky gold jewelry.

"Are you sure?" he asked.

Outside, it was the first time they'd walked anywhere together. She was an inch taller than he was. He hadn't realized that. She walked slowly. When they cleared her building she took his hand gently in her fingers. They went to the Thai place that they'd ordered from once. It was one, and the inside was fully booked. They ate outside, right there in the open.

"Did you decide to go into medicine when you were young?"

He answered her, but all the while he was thinking, Now, what kind of dumb question was that. It was like a date from 1992. Small talk. Politeness. It was like they were strangers now.

He watched her looking at the menu. He almost wanted to explain it to her, but he stopped himself. He had to keep reminding himself that this wasn't actually her first time out in the world. Her forehead had three horizontal creases that he'd never noticed before. Maybe the lighting in her bedroom wasn't the best. Or maybe it was, when it came to this kind of thing. If you looked closely, she had about two centimeters of gray hair at her temples. She had said she was forty-five. She might actually be forty-eight. That's almost fifty.

He asked her if she'd ever worked. She said she hadn't, which was fine, because she never wanted to. Her degree was in accounting, which was boring. She loved costume design, but it seemed hard to break in. He didn't know what to do with that.

"Do you have any interests? Like, hobbies?"

She laughed. "Of course I have interests. I read a lot. I have hobbies. I took a drawing class last year at the Met. It was interesting; it was all about shadows. I was thinking of taking a painting class, too."

He couldn't think of a follow-up question that didn't sound completely patronizing, because honestly, that was how he felt. He felt patronizing.

"Well, this is something," she said.

"How does it feel?" he asked.

"It feels scary. And right."

She reached across the table to take his hand. He squeezed hers back. He never realized her arms were so hairy. It was a dark, thick hair that grew somewhat wiry toward the wrist, like a man's.

He tried to look back at her in the eye, but he suddenly couldn't bear her. What was he doing here? What had he thought he liked about her so much? She talked, a vapid prattle of superficial nonsense: Paris, the dance lessons she was thinking of taking. He nodded and ate, but he was quiet for the rest of the meal, and so was she. She was newly shy, and newly confused, sensing an annoyance from him. He felt bad about it, but that's what sunlight does sometimes. It shows you what you couldn't quite see in the dark.

At least that was what he told himself as they said goodbye. They stood on the sidewalk and he shook her hand and touched his phone and pretended he had an emergency at the hospital. He walked in the direction opposite her building quickly, and he didn't stop till after he turned a corner.

———

"So what happened?" I asked Toby on the phone. I'd loved the Nahid story—this prisoner trying to gain freedom for herself through the random secret fucking of men in her apartment. It was like a dirty fairy tale.

"She just wasn't who I thought she was," he said.

"What was she?"

"She was just regular."

I was heading into the city. My train was about to go into the tunnel. "I have to go," I told him.

"Okay, talk later."

"Have you ever considered that you're kind of an asshole?"

But he didn't hear me. The day after I saw Rachel, I had come into the city again to bring her to a doctor. He said she was okay, but she was dehydrated and exhausted. He gave her an IV, then sent her home with antidepressants and a sleeping pill.

"That's it?" I asked him.

"Well, she should see a good therapist, it looks like," the doctor said. "But she's otherwise healthy."

I brought her back to her apartment, and sat on her bed again. There were real estate listings for Los Angeles on her computer.

The doorbell rang. A weary young woman—it was her assistant, Simone—came into the apartment with an armload of manila folders.

"You have to sign all of these," Simone said. "And we have to schedule your week."

Rachel got up to find her lucky signing pen.

"How's it been going without her?" I asked.

"It's been a disaster. I mostly convinced everyone she had a family emergency and couldn't be bothered."

"But she didn't."

"Yeah, but that's the only thing that's forgivable."

"I hope she knows how loyal you are," I said.

"I don't know if she really thinks about people's values like that," she said. "I think she only thinks about what is in front of her face at any given moment."

Simone left with the signed papers. Rachel asked if I could stay a little longer. She was going to go back to work, she told me. She had been on vacation long enough. She had to check in with all her clients, but mostly, she had to get a week's worth of sleep so that she could reenter her world and do some damage control. She'd read the article in *Variety* about Alejandra going back to Alfooz. She couldn't let that happen again. "I'm going to get my shit together, and then I'll call the kids." She didn't want to hear anything about them. She didn't want to hear where they were, or what they were doing. "Not till I'm okay." She asked if I could stay while she took a nap. "I can sleep if you're standing guard over me," she said. I put my hand on her foot. As she fell asleep, she whispered, "I always liked you."

I spent the rest of the week coming into the city and going to the movies. There was a Diane Keaton retrospective at Film Forum. The ticket taker told me he'd never seen a more dedicated Diane Keaton fan. Then I'd leave and check on Rachel, who was now at home, with a nurse/minder she and I had hired to sit with her while she slept. She kept saying that she would call the kids if she could just get a few more hours of sleep.

I was watching *Baby Boom* when I got a text from Seth. He wanted Toby and me to come to his apartment Saturday night. It was important, he said.

That Saturday, Adam said he wanted to stay home with the kids. "They've been with the babysitter a lot this week." This was the closest he would get to registering a complaint with me. Toby asked if I wanted to go together, so I picked him up in a cab. We hadn't spoken in days.

"You're very quiet," Toby said.

"I'm just tired."

He was annoyed. "Why are you so unhappy?"

I shrugged. "I'm really just tired."

Seth was still in Williamsburg, the same loft, now worth a kajillion times what he bought it for in 1999. His home looked like if *Wired* had a home and garden issue. The furniture was now all slick, 1980s leather, and the tables had been imported from Denmark and Sweden. There were nap pods in the corner and velvet bean bag chairs. There were beams on the ceiling now that hadn't been there the last time I'd seen the place. Seth's art was gallery-purchased—a painting of Winged Victory, but made out of garbage; a Coney Island mermaid photograph, made into a funhouse mirror painting. Construction had created two more bedrooms and a second bathroom. There were motorized window shades that adjusted themselves for climate control.

It was a strange crowd—not just Seth's friends from the bank but also his parents and sisters. Everyone was more dressed up than they should be, maybe just by twenty percent. It was like being at a bar mitzvah.

"The TV used to be over there, right?" I said. "I can still picture it."

Seth found us. He was wearing a suit. "Heeeeeeeeeeeeeyyy," he said. He seemed nervous.

"Oh God," Toby said.

"What?" Seth asked.

"You're going to propose tonight, aren't you? In front of all these people? You're such a dick."

I looked around. He was right. Suits. Seth's parents. It was true. We were at a surprise engagement party.

I saw Vanessa in the corner, greeting people. "Does she know yet?"

"Not yet. Any advice?"

"We've already given you our advice," Toby said. "We are happy you ignored it."

Seth squeezed our arms and said, "Here goes." Then there was the sound of spoons hitting glasses.

"Can I have your attention?" Seth asked. He waited till everyone was quiet. "I've had a lot of parties through the years," he began. "This place has seen everything from toga parties to math lectures. When I was thinking about what I wanted the theme of this one to be, I realized that I wanted it to just be about this incredible woman I've been seeing. All the lectures we used to have here for Art Club and Physics Club, for those of you who remember, they all were to celebrate something that we didn't understand. Today, we are here to celebrate something I still don't understand, which is love."

"Are you crying?" Toby asked me.

I watched Vanessa watching him, her face a lovely pillar of confusion, her piano teeth proliferating when she finally understood what was going on. Seth—beautiful Seth, whose hands had been on just about every woman in this room at some point—got on his knee, like a fucking idiot. "Vanessa, please spend your life helping me learn the other things I don't understand." She put her hands over her mouth and he took one of them. She nodded as he put a ring on her finger. The place exploded in applause as they kissed.

Seth came over after their parents and friends hugged them and squealed and opened champagne. "Do you think I'm being stupid?" Seth asked.

"Marriage always reminds me of that old saying about democracy," I told him. "It's the worst form of government, other than all the other forms of government."

"Shall we curse you for good luck?" Toby asked.

"You know," Seth said. "Everything the Beggar Woman said was true. She said you were good, Toby. She said Libby would never be happy." Out of simple decorum and this being his engagement party, nobody reminded Seth what she'd told him, which was that he'd never truly have love.

"She said you would make the world better," I said to Toby.

"But that was only when I had money to give her."

———

Later, the grown-ups left the party and it was just Toby and me. We were sitting on the floor the way we did all those years ago in Israel, but we kept adjusting our positions because nothing felt right or good in our joints anymore. We could feel every day of all the time that had passed.

"I'm just lost," I said. "I'm sorry. I think I have to figure out what to do with my life."

"There's someone at home who loves you," Toby said. "Don't you know how I would have killed for somebody to love me? *You're loved*, Elizabeth. Do you understand how special that is?" Then, "And you're talented. You should write that book."

"Maybe I will," I said. "Maybe I'll write a book about us."

"What about us?"

"About all this. What you've been going through. Our summer."

"Maybe. But how would you end it? Rachel is still gone. There's no ending yet."

"Maybe this is the ending," I said.

"God," he said. "Imagine that. Don't end it here. It's a bad ending. Engagements are bad endings."

"Or maybe I can wait for Rachel to figure shit out and come back to the kids, but I don't know. What will her coming home do? You can't unleave."

"That's good. I like a nebulous ending." He hadn't wanted to hear about Rachel or the time I was spending with her.

"Or maybe it'll end with her returning," I said. "I think I like that better."

"So she just comes back?" he asked.

"Maybe."

"What does she do when she comes back? What does she say? What happens?"

"I don't know. She'll just appear. It will be raining outside and you'll hear a key in the door and the creak of the hinge and you'll turn around and suddenly she'll appear in the doorway."

"And then?"

"And then the book is over."

"But what happens after?"

"I don't know," I said. I was crying again. "I don't have an imagination for that. But I can't wait for her anymore."

Toby leaned in like he was going to tell me something, but then suddenly his lips were on my lips and our mouths were open and hot and dry. We sat with our mouths open against each other, not moving, not kissing either, just kind of resuscitating each other, our eyes closed and our noses touching. When finally Toby pulled his face back, my mouth was still open and my eyes were still closed.

"You are still you," he said. "You are still crazy and dark and good. I can see it. You haven't changed as much as you think you have." I closed my mouth, and I felt tears down my cheeks. After a long moment, he said, "May God grant them happiness."

I opened my eyes. "May God condemn the children of their enemies to digestive nuisances and larger-than-average pores."

"Yes," he said. "May God fill the hearts of those who have blessed them with amounts of cash in denominations of $18 but that do not exceed $360 with pus and bile."

He stood up and he extended his hands and I took them. He hoisted me up, and I continued rising long after I surpassed him, just like all those years ago.

I asked him, "Do you think you'll ever get married again?"

He looked at Seth and Vanessa dancing. "I hope so." He said this quickly, without thinking. He blinked in surprise at himself.

Toby told me that he'd meet me outside; he wanted to use the bathroom. We'd walk across the bridge and uptown together, like old times. I went outside to wait and I found the last of a pack of Camels at the bottom of my purse and I leaned against the façade of Seth's building and lit one.

I watched a couple go by, burrowing into each other so that they were nearly facing each other but still walking forward, like on the cover of that Bob Dylan album. I pitied them. I saw the girl in the couple, who couldn't have been more than twenty-four, and I knew now that in a few years, that girl would be just some guy's wife. She would be someone her husband referred to as angry—as angry and dour and a nag. He would wonder where her worship went; he would wonder where her smiles were. He would wonder why she never broke out in laughter; why she never wore lingerie; why her underwear, once lacy and dangerous, was now cotton and white; why she didn't like it from behind anymore; why she never got on top. The sacred organism of the marriage—the thing that prevented him from opening up to his friends about his marital woes— would be the last thing to go. The fortress where they kept their secrets would begin to crack, and he would push water through those cracks when he would begin to confide in his friends. He would get enough empathy and nods of understanding so that he would begin to wonder exactly what he had to gain from remaining with someone so bitter, someone who no longer appreciated him for who he was, and life's too short, man, life's too short. He would divorce her and what these divorces were all about was a lack of forgiveness: She would not forgive him for not being more impressed by her achievements than inhibited by his own sensitivities; he would not forgive her for being a star that shone so brightly that he couldn't see his own reflection in the mirror anymore. But also, divorce is about forgetfulness—a decision to stop remembering the moment before all the chaos—the moment they fell in love, the moment they knew they were more special together than apart. Marriages live in service to the memory of those moments. Their marriage would not forgive them for getting older, and they would not forgive their marriage for witnessing it. This guy would sit with his friends and he would not be able to figure out how all this went so wrong. But she would know; I would know.

When Rachel and I were little girls, we had been promised by a liberated society that had almost ratified the Equal Rights Amendment that we could do anything we wanted. We were told that we could be successful, that there was something particular and unique about us and that we could achieve anything—the last vestiges of girls being taught they were special mingled with the first ripples of second-wave feminism. All that time, even as a sixth-grader, I remembered thinking that it seemed weird that teachers and parents were just allowed to say that, and that they'd say it in front of the boys and the boys didn't seem to mind. Even back then I knew that the boys tolerated it because it was so clear that it wasn't true. It was like those T-shirts all my daughter's friends were wearing to school now, the ones that said THE FUTURE IS FEMALE in big block letters. How they march around in broad daylight in shirts like that. But the only reason it's tolerated is that everyone knows it's just a lie we tell to girls to make their marginalization bearable. They know that eventually the girls will be punished for their futures, so they let them wear their dumb message shirts now.

Rachel and I, we'd been raised to do what we wanted to do, and we had; we'd been successful, and we'd shown everyone. We didn't need to wear apocryphal T-shirts because we already knew the secret, which was this: that when you did succeed, when you did outearn and outpace, when you did exceed all expectations, nothing around you really shifted. You still had to tiptoe around the fragility of a man, which was okay for the women who got to shop and drink martinis all day—this was their compensation; they had done their own negotiations—but was absolutely intolerable for anyone who was out there working and getting respect and becoming the person that *others* had to tiptoe around. That these men could be so delicate, that they could lack any inkling of self-examination when it came time to try to figure out why their women didn't seem to be batshit enthusiastic over another night of bolstering and patting and fellating every insecurity out of them—this was the thing we'd find intolerable.

I got something else—I got to live in a constant fog of regret and ambivalence. The fog made me directionless, until one day, I found myself scrolling through stupid Facebook, whose passive stream gave me room to wonder, and I thought: How could I find my way back to a moment where my life wasn't a flood of obligations but an endless series of choices, each one designed to teach me something about existence and the world as opposed to marring me for life? At some point, I didn't remember when, I had taken all my freedom and independence, and pushed them across the poker table at Adam and said, "Here, take my jackpot. Take it all. I don't need it anymore. I won't miss it ever."

I was about to sign off. It was too depressing to no longer be able to fantasize about what became of people and instead know they ended up just like you—fat and typical and suburban and boring. I was about to delete my whole fucking account, when suddenly a notification popped up over my friend request icon, and I saw it was from Larry Feldman, my first boyfriend (my first a lot of things) from eighth grade.

He was my first obsession, too: spin the bottle, seven minutes in heaven, then the lights just went out permanently and he fumbled for me everywhere. I was driven crazy by lust that day and for the weeks that followed. During the week I saw him pass outside my classroom on the way to the bathroom and I'd get a pass and track him like a wolf, but I could never find him. On weekends, he'd show up at the same party or same movie theater and my eyelids would lower halfway and my breathing would become shallow. It all happened so fast. Larry FastPassed me to adulthood in a way that made me ashamed and afraid. Before I got used to the kissing, his hand was on my shirt. Before I got used to that, it went underneath it onto my bra. Then under my bra. Then outside my pants. Then he tried to put his hands down my pants, but it was that year that girls wore loose pants and leggings underneath them. He couldn't navigate through. He couldn't figure out in the tiny spurts of time we had before a parent came in what was pant and what was underwear, and so I went home and drowned in my own hormones.

Sitting at my computer, the new friend request icon alive on my navigation bar, I felt something alive in me that hadn't been there moments ago—unsettledness, itchiness. Anything was better than this fucking suburb, with its ample space and a bathroom for every member of the family. I clicked Accept, and almost immediately there was a new private message for me. There was excitement in my tissue. I thought of my high school friend who'd recently left her husband—completely blindsided him, to hear him tell it—for her college boyfriend, whom she'd reconnected with on Facebook. "I feel like I'm me again," she told me. I thought about what it might feel like to feel like me again.

I clicked on the message.

LARRY: *I don't know if you remember me, but we were in school together? Like 8th grade?*

So it was going to be like this. You touched my virgin body until you owned it and you don't know if I remember.

ME: *Of course I remember you.*
LARRY: *I think about you a lot.*

Whoa. I had been hoping for some subtext, a polite conversation with the stinky air of teenage shenanigans about it. He was going right for it.

ME: *You do? That's weird.*
LARRY: *I think about how warm your vajayjay was.*

I slammed down my laptop and tried to swallow a dry heave.

Later that afternoon, before the kids came home, I opened my laptop up again with a finger, like it had a disease. I poked around Larry Feldman's page. He had a daughter, it looked like. He still lived in the same Long Island suburb that my father had lived in. It didn't appear that he'd ever been married, but it was hard to tell. Most of his pictures were car selfies, taken with him slack-mouthed and dazed like he was figuring out the technology on his phone and had somehow programmed it to immediately post to Facebook without any human quality control measures. I unfriended him, and I felt immediately repulsed by all of it—by men, by aging, by humanity, by my disgusting needs.

And that was how I felt when my kids came home and then Adam came home, and that was how I felt when the phone rang later that night, and I saw Toby Fleishman's name on the screen, and I picked up the phone and listened. He told me he was sorry it had been so long. He told me he was divorcing Rachel. He told me he missed me. Yes, I thought. Yes, *this* is my youth, not that dipshit Larry. I wasn't who I am in eighth grade. I was who I am later, in college.

I went to see Toby. Then again. Then again. Then Seth was there. And it was so nice to never have to explain who I was; it was so nice being a better-than-average manifestation of who they'd expected me to become. I spent more and more time with them, and every time, I would come home a little more unmoored, a little more adrift. Those nights, Adam, always so passive and compliant, would watch me undress and try to gauge who exactly was getting into bed with him—his wife, or the creature I'd been for the last few months.

That summer, I treated poor Adam like a roommate. I came home late. I ordered Chinese food for dinner again and again. He mentioned once that I was ordering Chinese a lot and so I ordered Thai. I dared him in the mornings to ask me questions so that I could tell him about how I didn't know how to live anymore. God, I wanted to say, how are you supposed to live like this, knowing you used to answer to no one? How is this the arc we set for ourselves as a successful life? But he'd never understand that. He had the life he wanted. So did I. And yet. And yet and yet and yet and yet and yet.

What were you going to do? Were you not going to get married when your husband was the person who understood you and loved you and rooted for you forever, no matter what? Were you not going to have your children, whom you loved and who made all the collateral damage (your time, your body, your lightness, your darkness) worth it? Time was going to march on anyway. You were not ever going to be young again. You were only at risk for not remembering that this was as good as it would get, in every single moment—that you are right now as young as you'll ever be again. And now. And now. And now and now and now.

How could we not impugn marriage, then? It becomes so intertwined with your quality of life, as one of the only institutions operating constantly throughout every other moment of your existence, that the person you are married to doesn't stand a chance. You hold hands while you're walking down the street when you're happy, you turn away icily to stare out the window as the car goes over the bridge when you're not, and exactly none of this has anything to do with that person's behavior. It has to do with how you feel about yourself, and the person closest to you gets mistaken for the circumstance and you think, Maybe if I excised this thing, I'd be me again. But you're not you anymore. That hasn't been you in a long time. It's not his fault. It just happened. It was always going to just happen.

But Toby was right. I was loved. I was loved by a man who had no questions about me. I saw that even if passivity was Adam's first response, it was kindness that was his second. We were different that way. All Adam ever wanted was his independence taken away. All he wanted was to love me back. And what did I want instead? What was so much better than stability and the love of a good person who rooted for you? We fall in love and we decide to marry in this one incredible moment, and what if everything that happens after that is about trying to remember that moment? We watch ourselves and our spouses change, and the work is to constantly recall the reasons you did this in the first place. Why is that honorable, to live in service of a moment you have to constantly work so hard to remember?

I *did* want it. Or I wanted it mostly. Or I wanted it in the background. Or I was bored. Or my personal hierarchy of need had advanced to the point where once you question the necessity of the stable marriage, the only way to go is down. Or I was just destined to be a miserable person, no matter what marital state I was in. Or New Jersey is a place that people choose very often over New York and I should just get over it. Or I just wanted some independence and some time alone to watch whatever I wanted on television without being judged. Or I wanted my abdomen to look less like a topographical map of Sarajevo. Or I wanted to understand how to live a life that I was not the star of, to learn to recede into the background and be what my children needed from me and every time I came close I felt a vast abyss and ran in the opposite direction. Or I wanted to feel relevant again, like I mattered. Or everyone else could hear a U2 song from her youth and smoke a cigarette and not lose her life to nostalgia for a time that probably sucked just as badly as now did. Or all I had was a brief midlife crisis, maybe not so different from Rachel, and even our midlife crises had to be confined—hers in search of one good night's sleep and a man who wasn't threatened by her existence, and mine having to outsource my own unhappiness in service of something that looked like helpfulness to an old friend but was actually neglect of the family I'd opted into voluntarily.

You can't fix this, I realized. Even our crises had to be small and polite. What I did was forgivable; what Rachel did was unacceptable. But ultimately it was the same for us both: The world diminished a woman from the moment she stopped being sexually available to it, and there was nothing to do but accept that and grow older.

The problem with Toby, I thought now, as I smoked my cigarette, was that he'd ended up with Rachel because all he wanted was someone not crazy. That was his mission statement. He said it all the time. All this time he was allergic to the girls he thought were crazy. Even me. Even me! I watched Toby in his young twenties reject everyone who seemed like anything outside of totally conventional, and that was how he'd ended up with Rachel, who he thought was normal. And yes, if you believe his version, she was a vile kind of ex-wife (all ex-wives are vile, to hear it), but she was also someone who had been driven crazy. Maybe it was the insult of childbirth. Maybe it was the overwhelming unfairness of what happens to a woman's status and body and position in the culture once she's a mother. All those things can drive you crazy if you're a smart person. If you are a smart woman, you cannot stand by and remain sane once you fully understand, as a smart person does, the constraints of this world on a woman. I couldn't bear it. I saw it too clearly and so I retreated from it. Rachel, she endured. She tried. And she got the punishment.

But it didn't matter. It wasn't my problem. I realized that in one big exhale of delicious nicotine, leaning against Seth's building. None of this was my problem. My family was my problem. My roiling—it would have to wait so that my family could feel safe and loved. They were loved. They were safe with me. What was I doing here? Leaning against the outside of the building, smoking, waiting for my friend? It was time to go home.

I thought of Adam. His face. His hands. How he could spend hours down a rabbit hole of information about something dumb, like a certain kind of garden weed or a certain kind of aircraft. Adam who was the best-case scenario in an incredibly flawed system. Suddenly, my face warmed. I felt jealous for Adam's summer. I wanted every minute with him. It wasn't too late, was it? I'd chosen this. I'd stood under a chuppah and asked for this, I had! I was loved, just like Toby had said I was. *I was loved*. I would *still* choose this. The crack that I had opened up in our fortress could be repaired before too much else got in.

So I would go home and would wedge myself back into my life. I would wonder, globally, how you could be so desperately unhappy when you were so essentially happy. I would start to try again. I would sit next to my children while they watched inane television shows and I would smell their heads and allow the hormones inherent to motherhood to wash through me. I would try to find peace with my regular life. Or maybe I would one day see that the regularness was actually quite extraordinary. I would try. I would wonder what exactly it would take to make me something more like content. I would admit to finding small joys with the other women in my neighborhood who were in their forties and all felt like exiles of relevance, too. I would try to be a good wife to Adam, and I would try not to put too much weight on the moments that are the worst in marriage: when one of you is in a good mood and the other can't recognize it or rise to its occasion and so leaves the other dangling in the loneliness of it; when one of you pretends to not really understand what the other person is saying and instead holds that person to a technicality they don't deserve.

I would maybe learn to cook. Or take a cake decorating class. I would allow myself to become a little more neutered. I would stop fighting it all so much. What would be so wrong with finally mellowing out? What was I clinging to? I would go to the exercise studio down the block, and I would take that dance class the other moms from school took, where we danced to songs that had once, many years ago, broken our hearts and set us on fire. The songs reminded us that we were once young—that once, we didn't have to pay a twenty-dollar fee to dance—we didn't even need to be led in it. Once upon a time, we just knew how to do it. Now we channel all the sex and all the hope and all that was left undone into a cha-cha-cha, or a figure eight of the hips that once didn't have to be told to swivel. The teacher would play a jacked-up version of the cheez-whiz top 40 songs from high school and college and we would all laugh. But those songs would dig at a pathway to our youth, and so at the end, during the cooldown, when the teacher played the Eagle-Eye Cherry song or the Sade song, now our bodies were moving more slowly, lumpen, leaden, and we would see just exactly what they had become: people trying to remember something but not quite able to.

And Adam—he'd be at home waiting for me. Even after all of this, he would be waiting for me. He would watch carefully to see if I was still in upheaval, and I would watch him watching me and a boulder of guilt and sadness would overtake me for what I'd put him through—what I always put him through. He would examine me at night while I slept and pray that I was no longer in chaos. And I would make this up to him in small ways: an excess of sexual availability, kindness toward his bitch sister, acquiescence to a sci- ence fiction show he'd been wanting to watch. But tonight, I would crawl into my dark bed with my husband, and I would make my- self into his shape like I was a new layer of skin for him. I would whisper to his back, "I'm sorry I'm late." And he, either awake or awoken, would whisper, "You always come back." I would love him so much right then that I would cry for hours while he patted me, mystified as ever.

I didn't belong anywhere, either, Rachel. I had tried to beat the odds. I had worked at a men's magazine, trying to do work I could be proud of, only to learn that a woman at a men's magazine is like a woman in the world—unwelcome, auxiliary at best, there to fill in the rough spots that men don't want to. I would never be Archer Sylvan, but I would write my book, and it would have something in it that Archer was incapable of, which is all the sides of the story, even the ones that hurt to look at directly—even the ones that made us too angry to want to hear them.

I stamped out my cigarette before I was done with it. It was making me nauseous. I shouldn't be smoking anymore. I shouldn't be smoking and I shouldn't be here. This was no longer my enjoy- ment. I hailed a cab and told the driver to take me back to New Jersey, which was where I lived.

Sitting on the floor with me, Toby had listened to my plans and waited for the panic to rise in him again, the same panic that washed him in sweat every time these last few weeks that he contemplated the future. But this time it didn't. Was he getting used to his new situation? Was he healing?

What if he was? What if he could think of Rachel in a new way? What if he could figure out a way to extract himself from the idea that he lived in contrast to her? What if he met someone nice and he got married again? What if Rachel was one day just his first wife? One day, the gloaming of this marriage would be over and the fumes of their sadness would dissipate. Maybe they already had.

After he left the bathroom, Toby got sidetracked looking for Seth, who was standing in a hidden corner of the apartment, getting eviscerated by Vanessa for smoking pot at their engagement party. He watched them, Vanessa trying to save face with her frozen smile and hushed whispers, Seth just totally baffled. By the time Toby got outside, I was gone, and so he walked home through the heat of the night. By the time he got to Union Square, though, it was raining and so he got on the train.

He paid the babysitter, and once she was gone, he stood in his living room, where he pet Bubbles for a minute. He took off his wet clothes to take a shower so that he wouldn't smell like weed when the kids woke up. How could you be this far along in life and still so unsettled? How could you know so much and still be this baffled by it all? Was this what enlightenment felt like, an understanding that life is a cancer that metastasizes so slowly you only have a vague and intermittent sense of your dying? That the dying is happening slowly enough that you get used to it? Or maybe that wasn't life. Maybe that was just middle age.

And also in that moment he thought about the fact that things crept along incrementally, which was why change was hard to see. His divorce was going to be final. In fact, he would sign his divorce papers tonight. He was born without Rachel and he'd lived. He'd married Rachel and he'd survived. And now Rachel was gone— maybe she was gone forever. If he could imagine that, that she'd just sort of ascended into the heavens and would remain a ghost that some people sometimes saw, he could proceed. He would move on. Not everybody follows rules. Not everything was fair. Hadn't he learned that yet? His children would understand one day; his children would have grown up with that lesson, and the losses they endured in their lives after this would never hurt quite so much again. That was not nothing. He would be a good father. He would protect them forever. This was spanda, he realized. This was what that dumb yoga teacher was talking about. The universe did contract in both ways. See? He didn't know everything. He breathed in, and he breathed out. It was happy, and it was sad. It was good, and it was bad.

The heat wave in Manhattan was finally broken. The rain came down hard for ten good minutes. Toby would start looking for a new apartment tomorrow, one where everything worked. He deserved an apartment where everything worked. He looked out his window. He saw his reflection, and beyond that, through his reflection, he saw the lit-up windows of the next building, a see-through version of himself filled with the lights of the city, the windows, the people inside the windows. In those windows was everything—hope, sadness, loss, triumph, sex, betrayal. Everywhere was hurt and everywhere was sex. Everywhere was love and everywhere was death. You could die of the loneliness, but you could die of the optimism, too; the optimism was just as crushing in the end. Time would move forward, but he had logged some optimism into his block universe. It would stay there forever. He watched the people move around in his ghost body and he felt that he had room for them all, that they could all stay and he could accommodate them and be their host. He stood staring with this thought for he didn't know how long until he heard a key in the lock and a hinge creak open and he turned to see Rachel standing in the doorway.

ABOUT THE AUTHOR

Taffy Brodesser-Akner is a staff writer for *The New York Times Magazine*. She has also written for *GQ*, *ESPN the Magazine*, and many other publications. *Fleishman Is in Trouble* is her first novel.

taffyakner.com
Twitter: @taffyakner